STAR SPARK

DAY LEITAO

SPARKLY WAVE
MONTREAL, 2020

Paperback ISBN: 978-1-9992427-3-2

Hardcover ISBN: 978-1-9992427-5-6

Cover illustration by Natalya Sorokina (J Witless)

CONTENTS

1

STUBBORN FLAMES

The flickering flames of eleven lamps illuminated Saytera's face. Legs crossed, sitting on the floor, she was focused on the tiny fire in front of her. Or at least she should be. Her task was to quench only one flame and leave the others alone. Control like that was still challenging, but the real problem was her mind. Wandering mind, fast-beating heart, with the anticipation of what the night would bring.

Instead of fire, a face occupied her mind; Cayo's. He'd left her island over six months before. Lately, her letters to him went unanswered. Her insides twisted with the possibility that he'd forgotten her, but her mind told her that perhaps he was just too busy. Too busy for her. Yes, she knew what it meant, and still… She had to see him, and in three days she would, at the great summer celebration. For good or bad, Saytera would have her answer.

She sighed, then almost regretted it, as some flames moved. She wasn't supposed to use wind or any physical means to quench the fire—or to think about a friend in that way either, especially a friend who'd been away for so long and hadn't answered her. Perhaps he was an ex-friend. The idea hurt.

Focus, Saytera. On the flame, the flame. Doing poorly in her lessons would gain her no favors. Her lousy performance was the very reason she hadn't seen Cayo and his sister Kilmara, as they had moved to Blaze Island to study and advance their matterweaving. They all knew how to make fire. Saytera was still only quenching it, and not that well. And still on Ken island—left behind. Thinking about her yearning to move wouldn't help her. Doing well in her lesson would.

Matterweaving was weird. There wasn't one technique that worked at all times. But then, perhaps it was Saytera who still hadn't mastered the right way to do it and was getting her results by accident. She stared at the flame and imagined the black in the middle getting bigger, swallowing the orange and yellow.

It got bigger—and so did the rest of the flame. No good.

Her body tense from hours of sitting on the floor of that dark cabin, she lay on the ground. The flames cast dancing forms on the ceiling. She relaxed and appreciated the beauty of them, ignoring her exercise. Struggling never accomplished any result. She knew it. Sure. And yet. All of this because of her stupid obsession with a guy who couldn't take five minutes to write her a note. Wonderful. If only her heart were that logical, if only she could quench its flame like she quenched real flames. Haha, as if she had an easy time quenching flames. Pathetic.

Lying on her back, she closed her eyes. There was no cabin, no task, no matterweaving, no upcoming celebration. She took a deep breath and enjoyed the darkness of her closed eyelids, her breath in and out, the soothing comfort of the soft earth on her back. Stars in the Universe, stars within; one body, one soul.

And then she was walking under the stars, heading to the Blue Beach, where there was a fire. Yansin, Kerely, and some other people were performing a passing ritual, celebrating a loved one's release from the physical body. Kilmara was there. Yansin's eyes were swollen from crying. Crying? What would make Saytera's powerful, wise master so sad?

"Death was part of life and shouldn't be mourned," she always said. Her eyes and her expression told a different story, though. Kerely held Yansin's arm and patted her back as if consoling her. This was so strange. Saytera got close to the scene when they were about to burn a cloth with the person's name on it. Whoever had passed had lost their body, perhaps in the belly of a sea serpent or in the bottom of the sea. The cloth was a replacement.

There was an S in the beginning of the name. Saytera ran the names of masters and apprentices in her mind. A few started with S, but none of them important or close enough to Yansin. Her insides were starting to cool with a dreadful feeling. Then the cloth turned, allowing her to get a better look. Her breath got caught in her throat. The name was Saytera.

She gasped and sat up. What had that been? A vision? Everything was dark and she didn't know where she was. Hang on. She remembered. And she had screwed up. All the lamps had been put out.

The heavy old-fashioned iron gate and fences did little to keep Dess out of the Staralloy mansion's grounds. He knew that place better than anyone, having run through these trees for so many years, chasing dreams that had been as real to him as the artificial atmosphere he breathed. He also knew its security system, having once imagined that there were monsters chasing him. Good times. Now the monsters rarely left him—they were in his mind.

He found the point where the fence could be bent, allowing a gap between it and the floor, through which he slid inside. If caught, he'd be arrested, taken for a thief or even an assassin. If caught—which was unlikely.

That garden with those trees and that grass calmed him, grounding him in the memory of who he was, even if the splendor of its flowers was long gone. What once had been a house now headquartered the mining company on his moon.

Dess clutched the doll in his hand—a reminder. Like the sight of the mansion, so that he wouldn't forget the reason he had to focus, study, and become the best initiate he could.

The test tomorrow would seal his destiny. He was by far the best in his class, but that didn't put him at ease, as the appointments were rigged. Deemed a nobody, he would need to do three times as well as the others—which he already did. Still, grounding himself wouldn't hurt. His classmates were partying. Who in their right mind partied before such an important test? Oh, silly question. Those who knew they had a secure place, and the dumb ones who didn't realize they didn't.

Dess stared at the lit windows from the mansion, remembering nights reading stories, a happy time that had been stolen from him. An entire life. Coming here was not only for grounding. Anger was his fuel. If the Starfire had chosen to keep him alive, it had been for a reason. Find and crush each and every one of his enemies—that was what kept him going.

~

Saytera didn't remain long in darkness. The door opened, bringing so much brightness that she could barely see who was coming in except for a flicker of light on silver hair. Of course it was Yansin.

The old woman's voice confirmed it. "Well done."

Really? After she'd botched her task and quenched all lamps instead of just one? Perhaps she'd forgotten what the assignment was. Well, Saytera wasn't going to be the one to remind her. Still squinting and somewhat dizzy, she got up, her mind trying to understand what had just happened, what that vision had been.

Yansin then added, "Go, or there won't be any lunch left. I'm not coming, I have a meeting."

For the first time in her life, Saytera heard a hint of apprehension in Yansin's voice. "What's wrong?"

"Wrong?" Yansin seemed startled. "Nothing's wrong, just a visitor."

They always had visitors, people who came from all the other islands to learn with Yansin. They usually stayed for a few months, some stayed for a year or two. There were also other island leaders who often came by. Yansin had never sounded like that.

"Who is it?" Saytera asked.

"Not an apprentice. Not an island leader." She had a faint smile. "But you knew that already. It's just someone from the continent. Nothing for you to worry about. Go. I'd better get going as well."

The old woman turned around and took the path to the meeting house. Saytera kept looking at her master, wondering what the wrong "nothing" was. It had something to do with this mysterious visitor. Perhaps it was nothing indeed, just more meetings, apprentices, other islands. Or not. It was something different. It had to be. She stood there for a moment, trying to think, until her stomach reminded her to get moving.

When the walls of the dining house were within view, a person came out of the trees surrounding the path and stood before Saytera. It was a strange woman, unlike anyone she had ever seen. Her hair was dark brown and quite short, cut above her shoulders, and her skirt was wrapped around both legs. That had to be the mysterious visitor. Everyone in the islands had long hair; the men sometimes just below their shoulders, while women had them longer. Saytera's was light brown and down to her waist.

The woman's eyes locked on Saytera. She was used to people staring at her due to her mismatched eyes; one green and one brown. But this newcomer's stare was different, as if she were looking at something inside Saytera, not just checking if her eyes had different colors.

She said, "Hello Saytera. I must look funny to you, right?"

Definitely. And how did she know her name?

The woman didn't seem to expect any answer and continued, "I'm Vivian. You were a baby when I last saw you, more than fifteen years years ago. I'm really happy to see you again."

Saytera wondered if the woman meant universal years or Mainland years, not that the difference was that great.

The woman likely noticed her puzzled look, and said, "You must have so many questions."

She didn't seem to imply the difference between universal standard and Mainland years, but something much deeper, more important. Why was the woman saying that? Before Saytera said anything, asked anything, another woman's voice came from behind her.

"Vivian!" Kerely ran towards them. "There you are. We

were wondering…" Kerely noticed Saytera and seemed uneasy, but continued to address the weird woman. "Were you…lost?"

"Yes," Vivian replied. "I'm so sorry. The paths are different but they all look the same. Strange how I could have forgotten. I'm glad you found me."

Kerely looked at Saytera as if to confirm if the woman was saying the truth. Saytera shook her head slightly, because the woman didn't seem lost at all. It was more as if she'd been wanting to talk to Saytera. Kerely noticed it, but didn't say anything. All Vivian did was wink at Saytera before following the other woman to the meeting house.

If only Saytera could follow them, but she wasn't allowed, and she was hungry anyway. She had indeed spent too long doing her exercise.

There were only leftovers at the main table. Some apprentices were already putting the food away, while others sat and drank tea. Saytera made a plate and ate quickly, not paying much attention to the food, rather wondering who that woman was and what she wanted with her. She seemed to know something about Saytera, or at least wanted to tell her something. And now she was talking to Yansin. About what? Perhaps she should push her curiosity away. But then, what if it was something important?

After finishing quickly, she ran outside, meaning to find her friend Nowla. She first tried the Deep Lake, then she went to the Yellow Beach, where her friend was sitting on a rock surrounded by yellow petals from the tree above it.

"Hey." Saytera greeted her friend then sat at her side, breathless from running, wondering how to mention the strange woman and what she wanted them to do.

"Where were you?" Nowla asked. "You didn't eat."

"I just did. I was training this morning."

"The whole morning? Were you trying to levitate something?"

Saytera wasn't sure if the question was serious or a joke. "No. I had put out a lamp."

She then wished she could pull her words back in her mouth, because Yansin had forbidden her to tell anyone about her exercises.

Nowla laughed. "You spent the whole morning trying to put out a lamp?"

"I had to do it with my mind."

The girl shrugged as if that did not make any sense.

Saytera knew she should stop talking, but she couldn't. "I mean no blowing, no touching, no fanning."

Nowla had a puzzled face. "But if you blow it, aren't you still using your mind to do it?"

Saytera crossed her arms. "Uh, I'm not supposed to talk about the exercises."

"You're the one who started."

Indeed. Saytera looked down at her footprints on the rough brown sand. She shouldn't have said anything. Nowla was an outsider. Her family's shuttle had crashed in the ocean just a couple years before. Nowla had been the only survivor, and she quickly became Saytera's friend, telling her about the world outside the islands, how life was on the continent, and the war against the planet's moon. But she would never understand, she wasn't even supposed to understand. Still, now that Kilmara and Cayo were gone, Nowla was her only friend left, and Saytera sometimes forgot how different she was. Oh, no, Saytera had been doing so well. She'd spent the last fifteen minutes without thinking about him.

Nowla got up and smiled, as if to end the subject. "Anyway, I have good news. There's this woman, her name's Vivian, she's from the Continent and… you have to meet her, she'll tell you all about the real world."

That was exactly what Saytera wanted to talk about. Not the real world, but the woman. "I saw her. Don't you think she's weird?"

Nowla frowned. "No. Not at all. Why?"

"She was wearing a weird skirt. Like, around her legs."

"Weird skirt?" Nowla paused, trying to understand something, then she cracked up. "You're so funny. Those are pants, that's what normal people usually wear. You really need to meet someone normal, other than me."

Right. Yeah. She'd seen pictures. Saytera ignored the teasing. "When did you meet her?"

"This morning. She said…" Nowla hesitated. "She could take me home. And also bring you. For a visit. Or…"

"She mentioned me?"

"No, she just… she lives there and can take me home. I'm the one who mentioned you. I think. I'm actually waiting for her, she's coming to talk to me."

Saytera shook her head. "She's with the island leaders. Or at least with Yansin and Kerely. Leader meetings. Or something. And…" Saytera was getting to the important part. Her heartbeats reverberated through her body. "Do you want to come with me and help me listen?"

"I thought you were afraid of getting caught."

More than afraid. The prospect of eavesdropping on Yansin in plain daylight gave Saytera chills. But she had to know.

"I thought about it. One of us watches, the other listens."

Nowla got up and shrugged. "I don't mind. Let's go."

Her friend actually seemed excited. Saytera was surprised. She thought she'd need more convincing. In fact, perhaps she had almost hoped Nowla would dissuade her from listening.

But no, her friend was already several steps into the path. It was too late to change her mind.

The meeting house was built differently than the others. It was underground, accessible from three separate small entrances. Saytera had been there before because it was the only house with electricity and communication devices, and she had learned a little about them. In theory, the house—or hole—should block all sound, but Cayo had found a rock on the floor from where it was possible to hear a little, or at least he said so, because Saytera had never tried it herself. Let alone trying it in daylight.

At least Nowla offered to go first. Saytera watched as her friend knelt and put her ear on the right spot, half expecting the girl to get up and say there was nobody inside. Instead, the girl waved for Saytera to come closer.

Saytera's ears touched the rock before she had time to consider if it was appropriate or not.

Yansin's voice was soft and muffled. "Do you want everyone to know about her secret?"

"Of course not. You know I care about her safety. But it's a bigger issue." At first Saytera didn't recognize who was speaking, but then she realized it was the woman, Vivian, who continued, "It could affect the entire Human Universe. Why don't you tell her about her destiny?"

"There's nothing to tell. She'll make her own."

Saytera wondered if they were talking about her, but then all this talk about destiny seemed to be about someone more important.

"But if you don't tell her the truth, you are robbing her of her decision." Vivian replied.

"She knows what she needs to know. For now. Everything

in its own time."Yansin's voice was firm, the tone she usually had when lecturing people.

"You love her like a daughter, don't you?" Vivian asked.

For some reason this question made Saytera think they were talking about her. Her heart beat louder trying to anticipate the answer she did not know. But if there had been an answer, it was in silence, the kind of answer Yansin gave with her eyes only.

Vivian continued, "Consider then what's best for her. Her future is not here, she was never meant to stay, and you know that."

"Nobody ever said she wasn't meant to stay."

"Why wasn't she adopted like a daughter then? Why? Why doesn't she go to Blaze Island like the other children? Why? You want her to stay? For what? While war rages on, she has to play around her little island some more, surrounded by people learning arts she's not even supposed to know exist. Think, Yansin. She's no longer a child. And she could help our cause immensely."

"Your cause? You still want to get involved in someone else's war? Since when do we meddle in little squabbles?"

"As opposed to what? Hiding? How useful is that? As to the girl, you knew who she was—and what it meant—when you took her. Why are you ignoring this now?"

No answer came, only silence. If this was one of Yansin's typical eye-only answers, that was a very long one, more like a monologue.

Another voice was heard, "Saytera?"

It was Kerely. And her voice was not muffled, but clear, as if she were standing right beside… Saytera's stomach sank as she looked behind her. Nowla was nowhere to be seen. And Saytera had been caught.

2

BEFORE THE STORM

Kerely had a calm, gentle expression, with her big brown eyes and dark hair flowing with the wind. Saytera almost asked about Nowla, then realized that it would be better not to get her friend in trouble. She probably hadn't had time to warn Saytera. Probably.

The woman smiled and asked, "Do you want to come to Little Lizard Island with me?"

That was not the reaction she'd expected. Stunned, Saytera nodded and followed her, wondering if she hadn't realized what Saytera was doing or if she was just playing coy.

Kerely walked towards the inner beach then pushed a row bow to the water, and they jumped in. The soft sound of water and the movement of the boat felt soothing, as well as Kerely's loving eyes and her poised manner, except that it was unnerving that she wasn't saying anything about what she'd probably seen. The boat kept going farther and farther from the shore, away from the little bay and into the open sea.

They were now in a very dangerous place for anyone who didn't know those waters, for not only it was full of scattered rocks, storms were frequent. But a master like Kerely or Yansin had no problem going from island to island. They led their boats with ease. Saytera had started to learn a little about it, something about feeling the water, but she was still far from capable of taking a boat anywhere outside the inner bays. Her solace was that most apprentices, even though they were older and experienced, couldn't lead a boat through the rocks either.

As Little Lizard Island got closer and closer, even Kerely had to concentrate because it had such a rocky shoreline. The boat entered an inner bay and Kerely docked on a natural protruding rock formation, which had a wooden post for tying boats. She jumped out and reached out her hand to help Saytera.

"Stay and watch the shore," Kerely said. She then looked at Saytera and frowned. "Where's your bow?"

Saytera pointed back to Ken Island. "I… I was training."

Kerely removed her back pouch with the bow and arrows and tossed it. "Here. Take mine. If anything comes, they'll come from the water. Keep watch. I'll just get some herbs and be back in a moment."

"No problem."

Saytera was still wondering how come Kerely hadn't mentioned anything about the overheard conversation. Perhaps she wanted to torture Saytera with anticipation until she confessed it. Maybe.

She placed the pouch on her back. It fit. Nothing should disturb them here, though. Canteens, the lizards populating and naming the island, were harmless. At this time of the year, there were no sea serpents. Gigantic insects were rare. Saytera sat on a rock, trying to collect her thoughts and plan her next steps.

So there was something Yansin was hiding from her. How

could Saytera ask about it or try to learn about it without letting her know she'd heard her?

She'd need to think about it later, as something was coming out of the water, a few meters to her right. Saytera got up and moved away from the shore. It was a crab-king, and a huge one. Each of its pincers was almost Saytera's size. Perhaps it would ignore her. Saytera pulled the bow and an arrow, just in case. It would be sad to kill such a majestic animal. Indeed, it would be sad to kill, period, as she'd never done it before.

But now it was grabbing onto the rocks and going in Saytera's direction. It had definitely seen her, and she wouldn't be able to outrun it. Aiming for the soft spot in the middle of its face, she let the arrow fly—and missed it. The arrow rebounded from its shell and the creature gained speed. A sound beside her startled her. Not her lucky day. Another crab-king was coming from the other side. She couldn't shoot both at the same time, so she turned back again to face the first one, but this time she waited for a good shot. It also meant that if she missed it she'd be dead, but on the other hand, if she missed it when it was far away and she had no time to get another arrow, she'd be dead too. And she had only four more arrows anyway. As it got close enough, she shot—and hit the right point. The creature didn't fall dead, but kept moving forward while jerking its body. This wasn't good. Saytera turned and shot crab-king number two—and missed.

It didn't help that she had Kerely's bow, not her own. It wasn't that different, but it wasn't the same either. It also didn't help that Saytera was far from a good shot. Meanwhile, crab number two was near. Focus. Thinking about her odds of dying wouldn't help her. She had to imagine it was just a target. A moving target, but still, she'd practiced with those. The trick was to predict where it was going. She observed the movement of the creature, aimed, and released the arrow. She turned as she felt something behind her. Crab number one was trying to hit her, but its movements were clumsy, slow, and she stepped away, watching the creatures: the first one on its way to death, the second one already still. She must have botched the first shot. After a few seconds, both creatures were immobile and she exhaled in relief.

Another sound startled her. She turned and saw Kerely.

"You need more practice with the bow, Saytera." She sounded angry. "And never go anywhere without yours. You could have died today."

That wasn't fair. "I didn't know I was coming here. And I don't have any consistent practice like they get in Blaze Island. My archery training is haphazard at best."

Kerely sighed. "I'm just saying you need to practice more, that's all."

"Sure. If I went to Blaze Island, I'd practice."

Kerely stared at her as if searching for something, then said, "Training with Yansin is a great honor. You know that, don't you?"

"Yeah, I do." Saytera looked down.

She'd heard that many times, but she didn't really agree. It might have been an honor for someone who completed their training and came to Ken Island to advance their matterweaving. It was a sign of accomplishment. Saytera, for her part, had always been trained by Yansin. There was no honor in that, especially when she failed at basic tasks and was the lousiest shot in the Storm Islands.

Kerely smiled and patted Saytera's back. "Anyway, you got us dinner, so maybe I should tell you good job."

"We can't carry those."

Kerely shook her head. "I'll send someone. Come. We'd better get going."

As they went back to Ken Island, heavy clouds could be seen far on the horizon. Rain would come soon, as with every afternoon at that time of the year. Sea and sky blended in dark grey. But the sea was still mirror-calm, and the air was stuffy. Such stillness in expectation of the disruption soon to come.

When they got back, Saytera rushed to her sleeping house, wanting to find Nowla, ask her how she'd gotten away, why she hadn't said anything.

On the way, someone stepped out of a tree. Vivian.

Saytera was startled, but decided to ask her the things that were bothering her. "Why do you say I have a destiny? As if it's something that's already set? Is it, uh, is it some kind of prophecy?"

Vivian took a moment to think, then said, "Hum, a prophecy could be one way of putting it, yes."

"But prophecies are not true, they are silly superstitions. "

"Is that what Yansin told you?" Vivian chucked. "Look at the sky. What do you see?"

Saytera looked up, but she didn't see anything special. "It's cloudy. I can't see anything."

"Your answer makes no sense. Either you can't see anything, or you see the clouds. You see them, don't you?"

"Well, yes, but I thought…"

"Well, first you see, then you think. Not the other way around. Anyway, you see dark grey clouds. What do they mean?"

Saytera shrugged, not sure what the question was about, then said, "It's about to rain?"

Vivian smiled. "Congratulations, you've just made a prophecy. Is that a silly superstition?"

"That's a *prediction*, not a prophecy."

"Call it what you will. It is a potential for something. You can't change what you are."

"And what am I?"

"You'll learn it. When the time is right."

Saytera rolled her eyes. "Great. Well, I guess I'll see you around."

The woman smiled. "For sure."

Dess's alarm clock rang. It was still dark. They were turned away from the Mainland Star, but the city used lights to mark day and night. Humans needed that constant light and dark ritual. Sapphirelune provided it on its streets. Still, those lights had not yet been turned on.

Even on an exam day, and after having spent hours and hours at the simulator the previous night, Dess still had to work. Perhaps it also helped him focus. He got dressed quickly, not forgetting his beloved rings adorning his right hand. Circles, reminding him of infinity and power. He also lined his eyes, to remember to be open to see the truth. Well, that, and it also looked good. Black eyes, black hair. Black and straight like his mother's, hair he'd never touch again.

Dess closed his eyes, wishing the memories away, focusing instead on his dreams, his goals, his future. He glanced once at his universal reader, his most prized possession. That reader had the greatest collection of rare books in this system, perhaps in this galaxy. It beat the Sapphirelune library. From here he kept his dreams going, and not only dreams, but real hope about a universe where magic reigned unleashed.

He put on the kitchen uniform and stuffed his academy one

in his bag. He checked it; no parts needed stitching. Yet. Soon he'd need a new one, but at least he'd been extending its useful life by sewing the parts that were ripping apart and washing it by hand. Well, if it all went well today, he'd get a new uniform.

He stared at the couch. It looked empty without Azael, the old man everyone thought was his grandfather. He'd passed away a year before, but his presence somehow lingered.

Dess still recalled Azael's hands pulling him back from the fire, back from the "accident", back from his family and everything he'd held dear until then. Their old gardener became Dess's surrogate father, even if he lost his job soon after that. The confusion at the time, with the war and deaths, allowed him to register Dess. And that was how Dess had become a nobody, an old retired gardener's grandson.

But Azael had also given him life, a second chance, a chance to fight for justice. Somehow he'd found a new home.

Dess was good at chopping vegetables, but hadn't done so in a long time. His early morning job was to supervise the early cricket delivery and feed it into the compounding machine, together with the other ingredients. It made some kind of fake meat patties, some days meatballs, sometimes some chicken imitation. He used to think that his colleagues would stop eating if they saw how their food was made, but that was nonsense; eventually they'd be hungry and get rid of their fussiness. Hunger was a real threat in an artificial human colony on a satellite without fertile lands. The luxury of a garden with trees hit him, but that garden had been from a time when commerce with the Mainland Planet and other systems was still strong. Would his family still keep a garden in the current situation? He'd never know.

Dess also supervised the kitchen droids. He adjusted the grabber unit, which somehow never positioned itself properly, then removed some of the thickener from one of the machines. The mixer always put too much. Once everything was running smoothly, he changed into the white academy uniform. Dess was the first one in the waiting room. Another chance to focus. He ran his fingers over his rings, closed his eyes, remembered all that he studied, all the time in simulators, training stations, all his readings. Everything came to his mind fresh as if he'd just learned it, and yet solid and deep, as if it was something he'd always known.

From this test the students going to command training would be chosen. Command meant getting near the power in Sapphirelune. Power meant he could do more against the planet who'd turned their back on their own, and now kept the Sapphirians semi-starved. The planet who had sent someone to kill Dess's family. He'd also have better access to an investigation to get proper justice to whoever helped the Mainlanders kill his family.

"Hey." Marcus's voice startled Dess at first, but he was glad to see his friend's brown face and long braids.

Dess smiled. "A little early for you, isn't it?"

His friend leaned back and stretched. "I knew you'd be here. It's a nice job you have. You're never working."

Easy for Marcus to say that. But it wasn't his fault if he had no idea what it was like to be the only one working and studying and still have to outperform everyone.

Dess shrugged. "Never partying either, I guess. How was last night?"

Marcus had a glimmer in his eye and a smile. "It was good."

Good had just gotten a whole new meaning in his friend's voice; something magical and wonderful and special.

Although surprised, Dess smiled. "See? It wasn't boring without me."

Marcus looked down and shook his head. "Far from boring."

There was something Dess wanted to ask, and he wasn't sure how to approach it. Sylvia. He'd almost skipped his time focusing and studying to go there and see her. Perhaps he should tell Marcus what was going on, but then, he wasn't sure if there was something really going on, considering technically there wasn't. What were a few looks and smiles?

He approached the topic carefully. "And... who else was there? Layla, Sylvia..."

Marcus leaned back and laughed. "I'm thinking your eyeliner thing is working, Dess. You're getting the eye."

"The eye?" He'd explained it many times and still his friend never got it right. "This is not to see the future—or present—just a reminder to see with the eyes, not with my mind's preconceived notions."

"Well, it's working." He ran his hand on his braids. Like Dess, Marcus didn't crop his hair short, but it had to be tied in tiny braids, since it was so curly. "Sylvia was there."

There was something odd about the way her name rolled out of his mouth, and it wasn't him teasing Dess. It was... He looked at his friend. "And there's something you want to tell me?"

He showed the palms of his hands and shrugged as if defeated. "You shouldn't be ripping the truth out of me like that. It was supposed to be a secret."

Dess had a queasy feeling in his stomach. "Then keep it a secret."

"Sure, so you shoot me with your eyes. Well, Sylvia and I, we... you know."

No, he didn't. Were they together? Had they kissed? And all this time, Dess had been thinking…

Marcus rolled his eyes. "Great. You're going to tell me she's ugly. Yeah, maybe she's not the Academy's greatest beauty, but she's cool."

"I didn't say anything."

"You're saying it with your face, Dess. You're staring at me as if I told you I decided to desert and become a fisherman on Mainland."

Dess was startled, thankful his friend hadn't caught half of what his face might have said. "I was surprised, that's all. I mean, I never saw you two flirting, and you never told me anything, what am I supposed to think?"

"Well, we didn't. It all happened last night. We started talking, and it was fun, and we got into big ideas, like life, death, especially death. You know, it looms over us, watching and waiting."

Dess shrugged. "Yeah, people fall in love over shared ideas, I guess. I'm happy for you."

Marcus had a confused frown. "No. We didn't… It's not love. I mean, I don't think it was. We just decided we didn't want to die without doing it."

It. It? Like that? But he teased his friend instead. "I don't know if you're aware, Marcus, the exam is hard but it's not deadly."

His friend took a deep breath. "Well, the truce is ending in six months. We'll have a real, raging war. It was a spur of the moment thing. She's cool, she's fun, and it was good. You say partying before an exam is a bad idea; I disagree. I think I'm a lot less stressed now. Then maybe it was that, the stress of the exams. I'm telling it so you know, not to brag."

"It's not like I wouldn't notice you're seeing someone."

Marcus ran his hands over his braids again, but more as if he were confused. "It's not like that. It was just last night."

Right. Just… a night. Like that? Was that why she had been giving Dess attention? Had she been looking for someone for a night?

Marcus waved his hands. "Stop with that look. I told you, she's cool. I'm not you, who can snap your fingers and girls will come running to you."

Dess frowned. "You think I have girl-magnet-finger-snapping magic?"

Marcus shrugged. "You know what I mean."

Dess stared at his friend and snapped his fingers. The sound reverberated on the walls, accentuating the silence around them. He wanted to joke to forget the nauseous feeling he had. The silence didn't last, though. Sylvia and Layla walked in.

Dess looked away, unsure whether they looked in their direction or nodded "Hi". It didn't matter. What mattered was ahead of him, a single moment in time condensing years of training, his future about to be decided. At least it was in his hands. He touched his rings: infinity and power.

3

CHEERS FOR THE BROKENHEARTED

Nowla wasn't at their sleeping house. Saytera was about to look for her friend somewhere else when she noticed the room looked different. Her friend's shells were not on her table. Saytera opened a chest, and found it empty. Nowla's clothes were not there. Had her friend finally left the island, like she wanted? Perhaps. But why so soon? Had she been punished for hearing the conversation? If so, why only her? Rain poured outside, and the wind shook the trees. Still, Saytera was determined to find Yansin and ask some questions. Before she left, she heard a soft knock on the door and opened it. Yansin was there, looking dry and unaffected by the rain. The woman entered the room, looked at Saytera, and seemed to understand her every thought, which was comforting and scary at the same time.

"I'm sorry Nowla did not have time to say goodbye. Vivian left, and took your friend with her. You know how much she wanted to leave."

That was true. And still… "They couldn't have waited? Just a couple hours?"

"Unfortunately not."

That was a very dry answer – even for Yansin. It seemed to relate to the argument Saytera had heard earlier. Saytera had to ask, and by the way Yansin stared she could tell she obviously knew how much Saytera had heard.

There wasn't much point in pretending. "What did Vivian want with me?"

Yansin shrugged. "She believes your future is in the place you were born, because you're not from here."

That was a simple answer. Perhaps too simple.

Yansin continued, "Now, I don't necessarily disagree with her. But I believe your future depends on how well prepared you are for it. It's no use to rush."

Saytera still had more to ask but somehow all her questions did not quite fit into words.

Yansin seemed to notice her questioning eyes and said, "Patience. Trust time."

Yansin tapped Saytera's head then left. The remaining question was "for what?", not that Saytera thought there was no point in what she was doing, only that she did not know or understand where she was going or where she was supposed to go. Time was an endless line. Everything seemed to fit together, but into what shape?

The next day an apprentice, Myomi, was assigned to oversee Saytera's training. As if it would make up for all her friends who were gone. The girl was clearly upset at missing her training with Yansin, perhaps thinking she was babysitting Saytera. All she did was share her glorious knowledge of the Trinity Systems. Saytera knew about them, okay, perhaps not too much, but she didn't understand why they were talking about these distant systems. Myomi talked especially about the planets she called the big three: Ringon, New Glory, and Spacitude, with some strange obsession on Ringon and its revolution gone wrong, bringing a totalitarian government that controlled a big chunk of the Human Universe, calling themselves the Peace Alliance.

All this talk about war only made Saytera wonder about the Mainland Planet, where they lived, and its war with Sapphirlune, its moon. She couldn't help thinking whether she did have a destiny and all this talk about the distant universe was just a way of distracting her from her nearer reality.

Those distant planets were in Viarena, where most human systems were located. Mainland was in Spiraly, as far from Ringon and their deposed evil monarchy and new evil government as one could be. Fine, the Peace Alliance in theory ruled over the Mainland system, too, but it wasn't as if they bothered to come and help them get rid of those stupid Lunars. Reading or hearing about Ringon was like learning about the Blues or the Lost Galaxies. Interesting, but then, how useful was it, when there was a moon staring at them and sharpening its weapons at that very moment?

At least Myomi left her alone on the day of the Summer Celebration. As Saytera got ready for the party, she felt as if a cold storm raged inside her. Eagerness and fear. So much fear, and it was strange that she should be afraid of something she'd been anticipating for so many months. Just the thought of Cayo stirred something inside her perhaps more terrifying than facing crab kings. Well, that was ridiculous. Maybe not. She'd shot the crabs. She'd never be able to shoot him—or her feelings. And then those unanswered letters. How could eagerness and dread occupy the same spot? Well, they did, and they seemed to be quite close together, like some sort of cousins.

Then there was all that talk, the woman, Nowla being sent away… The answers were not coming tonight, so she'd better not dwell on that. Later, with time, perhaps she'd get Yansin or Kerely to reveal bits and pieces of whatever truth they were hiding, and then Saytera would put them together. Tonight was a time for fun—if she could quiet down her inner storm.

Saytera made her way through the sandy path towards the ceremonial fire, when someone called her, "Teh!"

Soft, warm, familiar. Only one person had that voice, only one person called her that. Saytera turned around slowly, almost afraid that it had been an illusion, but it wasn't; it was real. Cayo was there, with a friend. He looked taller. Same deep eyes, hair tied back. Saytera had to catch her breath.

Thankfully he didn't wait for her to speak. "Hey." he looked down, as if embarrassed or if something wasn't right. "I wanted to see you."

He didn't sound as if he meant it, which was odd. But he'd said it. Something must have happened in the time he'd been away.

"I'm here," she replied.

"I know." He looked at the ground as if he'd dropped his words and was trying to find them. He faced up, smiled, then said quickly, "I… I want you to meet my girlfriend." He pointed to the tall girl standing next to him.

Girlfriend? Time stopped, as Saytera tried to understand what he'd just said. Girlfriend. She knew the word, she had seen apprentices kissing and holding hands, and yet, and yet, she had no idea it could happen. Not to Cayo. Not already. Saytera tried to look at the girl, but somehow her vision became blurry. All she saw was a tall shape.

Cayo continued, "Saytera, this is Neoma, Neoma, this is Saytera. She's practically a sister to me."

What a bizarre thing to say about a girlfriend. No, wait, he meant Saytera. Sister. Had she been upgraded from friend? Or downgraded from something that had never really existed? The walls of her throat decided to stick together, so talking was almost impossible.

The girl approached her. "I'm happy to see you. Cayo talks so much about you! So, do you plan on ever coming to Blaze Island? To study?"

Saytera shrugged.

"Or visit?" The girl insisted, apparently waiting for a response.

"Don't know," Saytera managed to mumble.

"Cause then we could spend more time together. But I know you are here with Yansin, and I understand you wouldn't want to trade it for… just being one of us…" She laughed.

One of whom? Saytera had no idea what the girl was even saying.

"Come," Cayo pulled Neoma, seeming also eager to end that awkward conversation. "There are more people we need to meet."

Before turning away, his eyes met Saytera's for a second. A brief second, then he immediately looked away, almost as if he was afraid to look. What if he'd caught a glimpse of her silly pain? On top of her dizziness, she now felt embarrassed. But then, perhaps he had no idea. At least now she understood the reason he'd stopped visiting or writing. A silly reason. If they were friends, they shouldn't stop being friends, should they? And yet, there was this something, this distance between them.

Saytera found herself sitting on a bench and staring at the huge ceremonial fire without any idea how she'd gotten there. On a corner, they were roasting the crabs. Perhaps she should feel a tinge of pride. The drums, the shees, and the forlum stood at one end, waiting for their owners to weave power and beauty from them. Would the music still sound the same?

"Hey, how is it going?" A voice snapped her out of her thoughts, and she turned to see Kilmara sitting by her.

Saytera was happy to see her friend, but had to muster some effort to speak without crying. Crying, now this was really going too far. "Good."

Kilmara frowned. "Really? You don't look too well."

"Uh, tired."

"Going on boat adventures with Kerely?"

Saytera nodded.

Kilmara laughed. "Right, right. Same little Saytera. I missed you. I was just looking at this fire… and thinking. It seems like yesterday we were kids running around it. Yesterday. And now…" There was a tone of sadness in her voice.

"Now what?"

Kimara shrugged. "I don't know. I like Blaze Island and everything, but sometimes I wish I were still the little girl who would get up and run whenever she felt like it."

Saytera looked at the fire and her friend. In reality, there was nothing stopping them. "Let's go," she teased.

Her friend laughed.

Saytera felt lighter. "It's good to see you." Her voice was returning. "And your brother… I'm happy he's happy and, uh, I'm super happy."

"Yeah…" Kilmara sounded uncertain. "I'm glad you feel that way."

Saytera smiled. "Delighted." Ouch, that sounded super fake. She didn't want her friend to notice her feelings. "Cause he's like, almost like a brother to me, so it's good to see him. And you too." The last part was true.

The girl kissed her cheek. "It's good to see you too. Wanna get up and run around the fire?"

Of course the girl was kidding. Saytera scrunched her nose. "Nah."

"Oh, you liar!" More laughs. "Do you want to come sit with us?" Kilmara pointed to a group of teenagers.

Cayo was there, sitting near his girl. He didn't seem the same playful, relaxed Cayo. Instead he stood still as if afraid of something. Or was it that Saytera saw him differently now? She didn't want to go over there; she wanted some time alone. Just some time alone.

"Later," Saytera replied, as her throat started to close again.

"No problem."

Her friend walked away. Saytera looked down at her feet on the sand, as she felt the fullness of the bitter taste in her mouth and sick feeling and her stomach. The music started and she closed her eyes, feeling the drums reverberating through her heart, the melody taking her mind away from her thoughts.

A few familiar chords were strummed, and with them, some cheers and yells from some apprentices. Saytera liked that song, but she hadn't understood why it seemed to be everyone's favorite—until now. How appropriate. "Cheers for the Brokenhearted".

Before the melody started, the singer said, "Today I bring a song. It's not any song, it's a special song. Because you deserve some cheers!" The singer was the one who got a loud cheer. Perhaps the cheers were for her too. Actually, they probably were.

The melody was sad but beautiful, as if it transmuted pain into something else. And then came the words, not sad, not angry, not even meek, but strong and powerful, and yes, cheerful, of course.

Then the shees and forlum quieted down, leaving only the drums. As if they refused to stop beating. The instruments came back, and the song went to the other part, softer and more melodic.

The words faded away from Saytera's notice as she looked at his direction again. He was not hugging or holding the girl's hands. If he hadn't said anything, Saytera would never have known.

As she looked, he looked in her direction and their eyes met before Saytera looked away. What had he seen in her eyes? At that distance, she wasn't sure what was in his. One thing she knew was that he still looked in her direction. What was he looking at?

Everyone else was busy. Nobody would notice her absence, except perhaps Cayo, but at this point, why should she worry? Soon some apprentices would change the color of the fire or do other demonstrations—nothing she hadn't seen dozens of times. She got up and made her way back to her sleeping house.

Halfway through the path, someone called her. "Something wrong?" Yansin was right behind her.

Saytera looked down, afraid that her master would look into her eyes and find out the reason for her sadness. "Tired."

"Go. Rest." Yansin kissed her forehead. "Tomorrow the sun rises again. And so will you."

Saytera nodded and continued on her way. Did Yansin know what she'd been feeling? No way to know. The one thing Saytera knew was that the Sun did not rise. The planet was the one that circled it.

She lay down, hearing the drums in the distance insisting on beating. Nowla called her in a soft whisper. A dream? But then someone shook her shoulder: her friend, standing right in front of her. The surprise was such that Saytera gasped.

Nowla took a step back and whispered, "I thought you'd be happy to see me."

"No, it's just… such a surprise!" Once the surprise sank in, Saytera became happy and excited. "Did you come back? How come nobody…"

"Shh." Nowla put a finger over her mouth. "Don't speak so loud. I'm not supposed to be here." She leaned in. "Can you come for a walk?"

"Now?"

"Yes, I have some things to tell you." She looked around. "But I don't want anyone to hear us."

Saytera looked around, searching for the imaginary listener they had to avoid, and found nobody. Still, she was curious, so she nodded instead of protesting. Nowla got up, peeped outside, then gestured for Saytera to follow her. The girl stepped on the side of the patch, over moss and plants.

She turned to Saytera. "Make sure you don't leave footprints."

Nowla was being a little paranoid. Who would look for footprints? And even if someone found their footprints, so what if they went for a walk? Still, Saytera did as her friend said, walking over plants and trying to ignore the prickling on her feet. Nowla led them to the inner beach, walking without difficulty in the dark, much like Saytera, who knew the paths on the island well. The tide was low and the boats seemed very far from the water they were supposed to reach. Sapphirlune shone brightly over the sea, and it would have looked beautiful to anyone who didn't know about its attacks on the planet. Nowla walked over the grass by the beach until its far edge, then climbed the rocks that led to an even smaller beach, only accessible at low tides. As Saytera climbed the sharp and slippery rocks, she started to think that this walk was literally going too far.

Nowla finally stopped and sighed. "We're safe here."

Saytera agreed they were safe, although she thought they would be just as safe in the sleeping house—if not even safer. But the fresh evening air and the soft sound of small night waves were pleasant, as well as seeing her friend. Walking on the sand instead of on the prickling grass was good, too.

Nowla looked around, then found a branch on the sand and sat on it. So did Saytera. Her heartbeat faster than usual, maybe because of the walk, maybe in anticipation of something, something… she had no idea what.

Nowla then asked, "Did you catch anything from the conversation we heard?"

Saytera nodded. The mere mention of that talk gave her goosebumps.

Nowla also nodded. "I spoke to Vivian about it. She explained to me what she could, cause I think Yansin put a curse on her or something."

In another situation, Saytera would protest that curses didn't exist, but she was too curious to interrupt Nowla.

Her friend continued, "She said we could be important in ending this war, that both of us have missions, but she can't give us details—yet. "

In a lighter situation, Saytera would laugh at trying to picture herself as having anything to do with any war. In fact, what she feared most about leaving the islands was facing a war and who knows what else that would come with it.

Nowla didn't seem to notice Saytera's disbelief and added, "You see? We're both important, that's why we're here. Why do you think Yansin herself took care of raising you? And taking me? No other children were raised in Ken Island, except for Cayo and Kilmara, but their parents are here."

Saytera sighed. "But then, if Yansin took us, maybe we should trust—"

"Yansin is too scared to be trusted. Why do you think her people hide in these islands, live without comfort, electricity?"

Saytera opened her mouth to answer, but felt at a loss for words.

Nowla got up. "For all her good intentions—and I'm giving her the benefit of the doubt by assuming she has good intentions—Yansin is paralyzed with fear. You can't be guided by someone else's fear. You won't fulfill your destiny if you stay here."

That word again… Saytera looked at her feet in the sand. They both looked grey in the night light. She didn't believe in destiny, but then, that was what Yansin had taught her. What if Yansin had taught her not to believe in destiny on purpose? And still, there was one more possibility. "What if Vivian is wrong?"

Nowla raised an eyebrow. "Then both Vivian and Yansin are wrong. Remember that in the little we heard from the conversation in the meeting house, Yansin never contradicted Vivian. They seemed to have the same opinion, only different takes on how to go about it. So what Vivian said cannot be wrong, unless they are both wrong. "

Her friend had a point. A good point Saytera hadn't yet considered. Yansin did indeed seem to agree with Vivian.

Nowla continued, "Ignore all this destiny talk if you want to. Now, I know you like to learn. Have you ever thought there is so much more for you to learn? So many places, so many things you don't know. Wouldn't you like to see the rest of the world?"

"Well, of course."

The girl smiled. "You know, you could come for a visit. You don't need to stay long. Just come, see how it is, then later you can decide. At least you'll know what the rest of the world is like, what a city is like."

A gust of wind from the ocean made Saytera cold. Or perhaps it had been her friend's words, for some reason. "Well, if Yansin agrees, of course I could come. For a short visit."

Nowla stroked her chin. "Right. Of course. You'd ask Yansin. But what if… what if you didn't have time to ask her? What if you had to make a decision?"

Saytera froze. This question didn't sound like a random hypothesis. "What do you mean?" She felt her heart accelerating.

Her friend took a long, deep breath, then looked at her. "Saytera, Vivian is coming now, to this beach. If you want to leave with us, this is your last chance."

Saytera's heart pounded. She got up. "But I can't. I haven't told anyone, I didn't bring anything. And Yansin will be worried."

Nowla got up and put a hand on Saytera's elbow. "Don't worry, it's just a visit; one last adventure. One last time. It's my opportunity to show you the continent. It's an opportunity for Vivian to tell you about you."

Answers… That's what Saytera most wanted. But leaving like that didn't sound right.

Saytera pulled her arm and stepped away from her friend. "I'm not saying no, Nowla. Maybe I can visit you some other time. Maybe we can plan this better. Just not like this, no."

There was resignation rather than disappointment on Nowla's face. "I wouldn't count on that. Vivian said she won't come back. We'll never see each other again. But it's all right. I'm sure you'll be happy."

Saytera was hit with an unexpected pang of sadness.

A very small rowboat approached, and Vivian pulled it on the beach. It looked like one of the boats Kerely used for her day trips. Vivian looked like a normal person. Indeed, perhaps she could tell Saytera about who she was, and what her destiny was.

She ran to Vivian. "Can you tell me anything? About my destiny, who I am?"

The woman smiled. "Calm down. You'll have plenty of time."

Nowla caught up with them. "She's not coming."

Vivian didn't seem upset, just surprised. "Oh. Really?"

Saytera shrugged, feeling uncomfortable. "I can't. I didn't tell anyone. I don't think Yansin…"

"She'll understand," said Vivian. "She might not like the idea now, but, once she knows you're well, she'll understand. Kerely told me you like to travel, but you travel so little here, you don't even know all the Storm Islands!"

Saytera shook her head. "I'm sorry. I can't come. But could you at least tell me a little of what you know about me?"

Vivian shook her head. "I can't. I gave my word and I don't mean to break it." She turned to Nowla. "Let's go, or we won't reach the gap before sunrise." Then to Saytera. "It was a pleasure meeting you. Good luck."

That was easier than Saytera had expected. Somehow, she thought the woman would be more insistent.

Nowla entered the boat, Vivian pushed it into the water and jumped in. Saytera watched as her friend was about to disappear among the calm night waves, dreading walking back to the houses alone. Ugh, plus there was Cayo and his girlfriend and all the nauseous feelings the idea gave her. For a second she wished she were in that boat with them, going to the unknown. But then she remembered Yansin, and how worried she'd been when mentioning Vivian. That woman couldn't mean anything good, if she could discompose wise, serene Yansin.

The boat was disappearing in the distance, but still fairly close. Perhaps Saytera could still run or swim to them. What was she thinking? Of course she wouldn't go. She wanted to stay and learn with Yansin, and then make the most of her potential. But could a short trip hurt her? Just a short trip? Well, Yansin would be mad. With that thought, Saytera tried to muffle the crazy idea that was growing inside her and stop looking at the boat, but then she looked at the sky and all the stars reminded Saytera of the vast Universe that she knew nothing about. Would she spend her entire life in the same place?

The boat was getting smaller and smaller. Couldn't Vivian have insisted more? A dry "no, she couldn't" from Yansin seemed to be the answer. "Yansin is too scared," she heard Nowla in her own mind. Was Saytera scared too? What was she scared of? Didn't she want to learn about herself? Suddenly, she was overcome with the greatest fear she had ever felt, and it wasn't fear of disappointing Yansin, or facing an unknown war: it was the fear of never knowing what else life could offer her.

The boat had already disappeared in the darkness of the ocean, amidst the rocks surrounding the bay, but it couldn't be too far. Would she go with Vivian and see whatever the woman wanted to show her, or would she stay and never know? Not knowing: that was a risk not worth taking. A little voice inside her head whispered, "Saytera, don't, Saytera, don't go". It was Yansin's voice, and Saytera understood it as her voice of fear, which kept repeating, "Don't go". Saytera muffled that voice. It was not too late, and it could be her last chance.

She ran into the water, waved her arms, and shouted as loud as she could. "Come back! Vivian! Nowla! Come back, please! I want to come with you!"

Stopping only to yell, she swam in the direction of the boat. Her yells muffled the "don't go" in her head, but she feared Vivian and Nowla were too far and couldn't hear her, or maybe it was too late for them to turn back. She kept yelling, but heard no reply other than the ocean rumbling like it always did. Feeling empty inside, she let her body float in the water. Perhaps it had been for the best. One day she would travel outside the islands. One day. When? With whom? At that moment her island became such an insignificant thing, a little prison. How could she want to stay there? For learning? She didn't even learn the basic stuff all the other teens were learning at Blaze Island.

A shout interrupted her thoughts. Nowla was calling her name. They were coming back. Of course they'd come back for her. Saytera watched the boat as it approached her.

Vivian pulled her up. "We almost left without you."

"I know."

The night breeze was cooler than Saytera had supposed at first, and with her clothes wet, she shivered.

Vivian seemed to notice. "I'll get you some dry clothes on the boat."

"Aren't we already on the boat?"

Vivian laughed. "This? No, it won't take us to the continent. Look, over there."

4

NEW PATHS

Dess looked at the panel announcing the names chosen to move on to command training. The names. Not including his. He felt disconnected from his body, from reality, from everything, because nothing made sense anymore. There was no ground below him, no sky above, just a strange nothingness. Logic brought him back to the moon. A mistake, perhaps? Probably.

His memory took him back three days. There hadn't been a single part of the exam he didn't know inside out. Everything had opened up for him and he focused as he'd always done. Whatever problems from before were gone, just him and the simulator, or him and the questions, no past, no future, just that moment. The only thing bugging him was how easy it had been, as if most of what they'd studied didn't matter. The result had come a few minutes before. He'd gotten 99%. The highest grade in his class—as expected. And yet, he hadn't been selected.

Displaying publicly the winners just made everything twice as awkward, but then, everyone would soon know who'd been chosen. But he wasn't prepared to see that, he wasn't prepared for this result. For all his life planning and preparing, this was something he had never expected.

"It might be a mistake." Marcus's voice.

Strange to hear a familiar voice in this strange reality. Oh, he was standing by Dess.

"Yeah…" Dess said.

His friend tapped him on the shoulder. "For real. It doesn't make sense, right?"

"I don't know." He didn't know anything anymore. "Yours is not there either."

Marcus sighed. "Not sure I was counting on it."

Unlike Dess. For the first time, he looked around, to see how other people were reacting. Many were glancing at him. They knew. They all knew he'd been counting on it. There were only six names there, including Sam and Amil, those idiots. They were all decent students, but most of them were not better than Marcus, and they were definitely not better than Dess.

Focusing on his friend was good. "Why not?" Dess asked. "You're better than some of them."

"Maybe."

Strange. With Marcus's influential parents, Dess had been sure he'd be picked. Perhaps at the end of the day it didn't matter much for him, or it was just something he didn't care about. Strange.

"Look," Marcus pointed. "There's commander Serra. Why don't you ask her?"

Indeed. The old woman walked by them, dark hair tightly tied in a braided bun, very un-military high heels clacking on the floor. Dess felt somewhat uneasy to approach her like that, but he had to know.

. . .

Serra's office had an imposing dark wooden desk. Very fancy, considering how rare wood was on Saphirlune.

Her hands were steepled on the table. "What is your question, Mr. Starspark?"

That last name usually got an inner scoff from Dess, but today nothing was funny. He'd gone through it in his head and decided to go straight to the point. "Is there a problem in the announcement panel, or was I not chosen for command training?"

The commander leaned back and smiled as if she'd been expecting that question. "There's no problem with the panel. Is that all?"

"No. I would like to know the reason why my name is not there. I've always had the best performances among my colleagues."

"Oh." She feigned surprise. "Is that so? Well, Mr. Starspark, as you should be aware by now, the choice for command is based on a myriad of factors, performance in class and exam results being just two of them."

Myriad of factors. Right. Some damn excuse to put whoever had the most powerful parents. Dess had to control his temper. He decided to play the woman's game. "Can I understand which factor, amongst this myriad, explains why my results didn't count?"

"First of all, your results are not that superior. Our chosen applicants got 89% to 95% on their exams. The difference is small and not significant."

"Because the exam was ridiculously easy!" Dess slammed his fist on the table.

She smiled. "There. That's one factor."

He wished he could punch her face, not the table, but he swallowed his anger and pride. "I apologize. This is a delicate moment for me. I've never disrespected a superior before." He looked at her in the eye. " I dedicated the last seven years of my life for command."

Serra took a deep breath. "Well, Mr. Starspark, don't think we haven't noticed you, or that we don't appreciate all that you bring to our forces. But try to look at it from a rational angle. Instead of continuing training, you could go straight to the army. It means you can earn a wage. This is good for you. It doesn't mean you can't progress. In fact, if you prove to be remarkable, you might find yourself eventually in command. No huge change."

Everything changed. As much as in theory they said that command was open to every initiate, there was no precedent for it.

"I don't need a wage. I work. I've worked throughout all my training!"

"Well, there. I'm sure you'll agree we can't have a commander working in the kitchen, can we?"

All the anger he'd kept bottled down burst out.

Saytera woke with the movement of her bed rocking gently, reddish-blue sky outside a window. This was neither dream or nightmare, just a strange reality she could not quite grasp. Had it really been her, the previous night, who had decided to come? Or just a strange part of herself? What difference? For good or bad, there she was.

She sat up, got out of bed—and almost fell, as the floor was tilted sideways. Boat. Right. She also noticed she was wearing those weird skirts—pants, tying both of her legs. Nowla was sleeping in another bed. Saytera went upstairs and outside, where a heavy wind hit her face. They were moving faster than any boat she had ever seen or been on. It had poles with some kind of dark grey fabric—sails. She had heard about them, but had never seen one.

Vivian was on the back, behind a huge steering wheel. She smiled but her expression was focused. Saytera wanted to talk to her, but the wind was too noisy.

There was no sign of land or even rocks behind them, just a trail of foam heading into the purple-orange sky. In front of them, the sun emerged from the water, a trail of light meeting them. They were encircled in horizon, which meant they were outside the Dotted Sea, far from the Storm Islands.

Saytera's legs trembled. She sat on a bench on the low side of the boat, her hand touching the fast-moving water, feeling half excited, half terrified, as if these feelings were not different sides of the same something she could not quite explain.

A dark shape appeared beyond the clouds, like a rock. Probably an island. The boat slowed down and straightened. Was that "the gap" they had to reach before sunrise? All Saytera could see was a solid rock wall. They were headed in that direction, which made little sense, as there would be no place to dock. As they got closer, Saytera noticed a vertical opening, like a crack in the cliff, so perhaps that was indeed the "gap". Still, where were they going to stop? The boat kept moving towards the cliff, and it wasn't as slow as Saytera first thought. Vivian looked calm, perhaps only a little more concentrated than before, and it would be stupid to interrupt her to say they were about to crash, even if that was what it looked like.

When Saytera saw that the rock wall was about to embrace them, she prepared for the impact, but, instead of crashing, the boat glided smoothly into the opening, almost touching the walls on both sides. The gap was not as narrow as she had first thought, although barely wide enough for the boat. The passage got wider and wider as they entered. It was a large cave, illuminated by some rays of light coming from a small, far opening on the opposite side. Vivian docked near a small inner beach and tossed an anchor. The cave was beautiful, with small crystals here and there reflecting the little light in it.

Vivian smiled. "We travel at night. It's safer."

Safer only meant there was some danger. The cave's beauty vanished: it was just a strange place Saytera should never be at. Her stomach clenched wondering what would happen to her when she returned. When she returned. Saytera felt chills that were not exactly due to excitement.

Saytera glanced at Vivian. "You're going to take me back, right?"

Vivian crossed her arms. "Of course. Unless you want to stay longer. Or visit other places… or planets. But I'm giving you my word that I'll take you back if you ask. You know Terens don't break their word."

Saytera had never heard that word. "What's a Teren?"

"Sorry, Saytera, I'm… just, using… old names. *Islanders* don't break their word."

"But you're not an islander."

Vivian rolled her eyes. "Indeed. We're much more than that. Still, I don't break my word."

She sounded sincere. Perhaps this wasn't so bad. And there was no point worrying about something she couldn't control. For now, all she could do was enjoy her trip. The cave had tiny crystals shining here and there, like a night sky from where one could glance at the distant universe. But these stars, they were close enough. If Saytera wanted, she could get out of the boat and touch them.

"Is this the gap?"

"Yes," Vivian replied. "It's beautiful, huh? But don't go outside. There are things in the water."

The crystals on the walls still reflected light in all directions. So close, and yet unreachable, and Saytera was not sure if that made them more beautiful or less.

"C'mon!" Marcus pleaded. "We have to go."

All Dess wanted to do was remain home, researching texts in his universal reader, finding maybe that lost bit of magic he missed, the key to moving forward, finding strength when all was lost. He felt as if the floor had opened below him and he was falling, falling, falling.

But then, his friend had no idea what had happened. Dess decided not to make it a secret, and took a deep breath. "I quit. I'm no longer in the academy, or the military. I'm not even sure I'm welcome there."

Marcus sucked in a breath and widened his eyes, but then he just acted as if nothing happened. "I'm sure you can change your mind. And it's a graduation ceremony. Even if you never step foot there again, you have to go."

Dess wasn't sure Serra would allow him to change his mind. He'd thrown his insignia in her trash bin. And broken her fancy wooden desk. At the time, he thought he was being the master of reason for not punching her. Now, he realized perhaps it'd been foolish. But he didn't want to talk about it. He just asked, "For what?"

"You never know. They watch us. Do you think they have the party after the names are announced for no reason?"

He touched his rings, trying to find something there, some courage, some power, something. "They had one before the exams too."

"Of course! And you know what it was? A trap. For those gullible enough to forget their commitments."

"You were there."

Marcus tilted his head. "True, but I didn't remain long. I mean, fine, maybe I didn't sleep as much as I should, but still. Anyway, you know what they want? They want to see who's bitter and jealous, that's what they want. And that's why you're supposed to go and pretend you're not bothered in the least."

Dess took a deep breath. "I *am* bothered. Their process is unfair, stupid, and they feed us lies for years. Why should I pretend everything is fine? If all they wanted was to get people with powerful parents, why make us go through all that? The people they chose are all a bunch of dimwits."

Marcus looked down. "Sylvia was accepted."

Dess shrugged. Strange that he had barely registered it. "I guess if they don't pick at least one initiate with brains it'll be too obvious."

His friend looked him in the eye. "I know you're upset, but look at the bright side. Nobody will notice it. You're always gloomy and quiet. Come with me, please. I don't want to go alone. This one time."

"Can't you go with her?"

Marcus looked away and back. "It's not like that. We aren't together or anything. And… I'm not you. I can't just quit the army. My father would never let me do that. I need to go and make a good impression, but I need my friend with me."

It was odd how sometimes Marcus spoke as if his life was worse than Dess's. Still, he got up. "I'll get ready."

It felt good to dress in something other than the uniform and get in his old clothes. His pants and shirt weren't exactly appropriate for the occasion, but he covered it all with a long coat. The temperature was never too cold in Saphirlune, powerful heaters in the city dome keeping it just comfortable enough not to require thick clothing. He lined his eyes, aware of the irony in the fact that he'd never seen his failure coming. Not his failure, though, the academy's. Still.

That reminded him to stop and see—really see. There was always more to be known. Perhaps there was something hidden behind his cloud of anger. Perhaps this had some meaning. He didn't even want to start to think about how he'd make a living tomorrow. Either way, on to the party. Perhaps he had to forget he had no plans, no job, no prospect for tomorrow and enjoy today while it lasted.

The mood was gloomy at the grand salon at the academy headquarters. Or perhaps it was just Dess. Sam and Amil, who'd been accepted, were boisterous and noisy. Some of the failed initiates were also having the time of their lives. The truth is that, for most of them, not getting in command training meant things were about to get real. If armed conflict resumed, they'd be in the thick of it. Not Dess, though. He had no idea where he would be, since he'd just thrown away an entire life. Not entire. There had been a life before that, a life with stories, magic, and great hopes for a future that never came. He ran his hands on his rings. Infinity and power.

"What are you thinking?" Marcus asked.

They were both leaning against a wall, and he didn't want

to consider if it looked casual or as if they were just moping. "The war. It might restart. You're going to be there."

Marcus hit Dess's shoulder. "So will you. You think they'll let a talented initiate like you get away?"

"Maybe a talented initiate like me wants no more of this bullshit."

"Maybe."

Dess couldn't convince his friend that he wasn't going to change his mind or that they wouldn't accept him back. Denial. He'd get over it. Dess would get over it. The other unspoken issue was that they would be pulled apart. He hadn't considered it when he'd thrown his insignia in the trash, but, to be fair, in his state of mind, he hadn't considered anything.

Sylvia and Layla walked in. Another two friends who would be split. Sylvia had her dark hair tied in a tight braid, and didn't act as though she'd been one of the few picked for command. Neither of them greeted Dess and Marcus or even looked in their direction.

"You think she's angry?" Marcus asked.

"How can I know? Did you do anything to make her upset?"

His friend fiddled with one of his braids. "I don't think so…"

"Then no worries."

Dess wondered if Sylvia would have done the same thing to him. He'd better stop wondering anything related to him and her, though, as that path no longer existed. Still, he kept thinking about how sometimes people treated each other as if they were disposable. In this case, he wasn't sure who was treating who like that, and didn't care. Fine, maybe he did. His friend was the one worried, so it was her.

Marcus still stared at Sylvia, looking dejected. It was sad how their group of friends was crumbling. He closed his eyes.

No wonder Saphirlune had no access to Mainland, and it probably never would, if its future soldiers were more interested in hooking up with each other than in fighting. Youth. Perhaps if a large part of the adult population hadn't died in the Battle of Stars, five years before, they wouldn't need to depend on teens like him to defeat that stupid planet.

He opened his eyes and saw his friend still looking at Sylvia.

Dess turned to him. "You can congratulate her."

Marcus had a puzzled look.

He added, "It's polite, and doesn't mean anything."

"I guess," Marcus said, still leaning on the wall looking almost as if he'd been asked to volunteer on a dangerous mission.

Dess stared at him. "Just go."

His friend took a deep breath. "You're right." He stepped away from where they stood.

Dess closed his eyes again. He needed to be alone with his mind, just for a moment. When he opened his eyes, Marcus was gone. For fun, he snapped his fingers.

"What are you doing?" Nadia was standing beside him. She was Leader Aziz's daughter, obviously chosen to go on to command. The fact that her father owned Staralloy didn't make things any better.

"Snapping." He didn't bother to look at her, since she was there just to humiliate him.

"Listen, I… I feel really bad. This was a horrible mistake. I could speak to my mother. If anyone should be in command training, that should be you."

"Save your effort." Like he predicted, she wanted to humiliate him.

"You're going to tell me you don't care?"

Dess finally looked at her. Her blond braids were neatly tied, unlike most people in the party who had adopted a more casual look. He said, "I shouldn't have to depend on anyone's favors."

She tilted her head. "But it's not a favor, it's setting things right. Justice's not a favor."

"Justice is relative."

"I'm serious, Dess. Is there something I can do for you?" She looked at him expectantly.

"There is. Leave me alone."

She sighed then walked away. Perhaps offending the leader's daughter wasn't the best idea. But then, it wasn't as if it could make any difference, and at that moment he hated her family and everyone in the military leadership.

Neither Marcus nor Sylvia were anywhere near Dess. Layla was with another group of people. Having accompanied his friend, his mission there was completed, and Dess walked outside. That was a tiny garden, with some bushes, but still, he'd spent more hours there than he could remember, between lessons and training.

Not real nature, though. The only resemblance of nature in that moon was in the Staralloy mansion, in the garden that had once been his. Real nature was hundreds of kilometers away, on the planet he'd never set foot on. All his readings on the Terens spoke about nature and power, and how the two were connected. But from here, all he had was the magnificent view of the Mainland Planet, with its great oceans and gigantic storm clouds. He looked at the rings in his fingers, then, for fun again, snapped them.

This time nobody approached. For once he could prove his friend wrong, except that his friend was probably too busy to know. He decided to head back home to try to find answers in the quietness of his bedroom. Maybe he had to know what questions to ask.

"Excuse me?" a woman's voice called from behind him.

Dess wasn't sure if she was talking to him, but turned. She was looking at his direction, so he asked, "Yes?"

She wore a fake leather attire, and didn't look like someone in the military, a mine worker, or any of that. "Are you Dess Starspark?"

He frowned. There was something odd about her. "Why do you want to know?"

"It came to my knowledge that you might be looking for work. Come to the civil port tomorrow at noon our time."

"The civil docks are abandoned."

They had been for a long time, since trade and flight out of the system had been banned.

"I never said they weren't." She looked around, then leaned on him and whispered, "Tomorrow," and walked away.

Weird. At least that was one person who knew he had to make some big decisions soon. Soon. What kind of decisions required going to an abandoned port was the question hanging in the air.

5

MAINLAND

The night sky was clear as they continued their journey. Saytera contemplated the surrounding universe before Saphirlune rose again, menacing and terrible, and yet beautiful.

Rocks appeared among the moonbeams on the water. Vivian still guided the boat at a great speed even in darkness. She knew. It was not about seeing the rocks, but feeling them. One Great Ocean. Everything connected. Still, Saytera had always thought that guiding a boat through the Dotted Sea was about knowing it. But Vivian couldn't possibly know the entire ocean, could she?

Saytera again stared at the darkness outside, when she saw a light on the horizon.

Vivian approached the girls. "That's a monitor ship. Make sure you don't use the kitchen downstairs. If they catch us, they'll ask too many questions."

She seemed a little apprehensive. Saytera asked, "Won't they see us?"

"Their sensors look for artificial electricity. Fire can sometimes set them off." She smiled. "But they don't know there are other ways to travel."

As they got closer, that thing looked scary. It was gigantic, with its lights illuminating the water by them. They spent many minutes passing by the ship. It was hard to believe that Vivian's boat was invisible for that massive structure, but since nobody approached then, it must have been.

They reached the continent a few hours later. Vivian's boat docked in an underground cave connected to a large house through tunnels. Eating house, sleeping house and more were all in the same building, which was illuminated with lamps powered by artificial electricity, with switches on walls. Saytera turned the light on and off in one of the rooms. That was an easy way to control it with her mind… She could even understand why Nowla thought her exercises were useless. That thought reminded her of Yansin, but this wasn't the time to think about her master.

The bed Saytera lay on was by a window, but the air was stuffy that night, and she couldn't feel the ocean breeze the same way she felt in Ken Island. Ken Island… For a moment she feared never seeing it again. Nonsense. Vivian had given her word, and she meant it. Still, Saytera had a tight feeling on her chest. Her sleep was accompanied by troubled dreams with gigantic ships and dark corridors that led nowhere.

A soft whisper woke her up, "Saytera, run".

Kerely's voice. Saytera sat up, startled, but apart from Nowla, still sleeping, there was nobody in the room. A dream, most likely.

The sun shone outside, so she got up and went to another division in the same house. Vivian ate at a table. Maybe it was Vivian that Saytera had heard. Maybe. She sat down, thoughtful.

"Saytera, Saytera", the woman said. "It's not time to worry. Enjoy now for what it's worth."

Indeed. There was a reason she had come. "Can you show it to me now?"

"The village? You should perhaps wake up your friend so you two can go."

Saytera looked down. "No. I mean, the things you said about my, uh, destiny."

Vivian smiled. "You're curious, aren't you? Don't worry. I know why you came, and you should know that's why I brought you. You will learn the truth about you."

"And you can't tell me now?"

She sighed. "I gave my word that I would never tell you, and you'll never, ever get anything from my mouth or my writing. Now, if by any chance you happen to meet someone who can tell you… that's different, isn't it?"

So Saytera would meet someone else. "Who is going to tell me?"

"Don't spoil the surprise. You'd better eat now, and I'd better wake up your sleepy friend."

Saytera sat back. Vivian sounded certain. That was promising and exciting. Strange how only now she realized she had doubted Vivian. And still she had come.

Vivian had to go out and do some things, but told the girls that they could go for a walk. Saytera definitely wanted to get to know the village.

Outside, there was a dock with several boats, bigger than rowboats, but smaller than Vivian's boat. None of them had sails, and none of them looked like the boats in the islands.

This was just the rest of a former merchant village, now ruined because of the war.

According to Vivian, there was a fishing station and a military base a few kilometers from there, but the village had nothing to do with any of it. Villagers fished or farmed for subsistence or did small work. Some hunted squid. Monetary exchange was rarely used over there; the inhabitants traded food, goods, or services. Still, even if the village was small, Saytera enjoyed getting to know somewhere different from the islands where she'd grown up.

The people had clothes similar to the ugly ones she was wearing, and most men had very, very short hair, cropped near the scalp. Saytera made an effort to avoid staring after one of the men looked at her and smiled in a way that made her uncomfortable. The ocean looked calmer than it was around the islands, almost like a lake, instead of the wild and furious sea she knew. Even the bays in the islands were not as calm.

The girls then walked away from the sea. There were a few buildings here and there, surrounding a very wide path.

Nowla whispered in Saytera's ear, "If you want to learn about your future, there's a place I can take you."

Saytera's heart beat faster. "So you know who can tell me the truth about me?"

"Uh, I don't mean whoever Vivian wants you to meet. I don't know who that is. But… while we wait, we can talk to a stargazer."

The word was mildly familiar. Oh, she recalled it. "They predict the future, don't they?"

"That's part of what they do."

"Yansin told me it's forbidden."

Nowla snorted. "What's not forbidden for Yansin? But you

don't need to talk to her, just come with me because I want to ask some questions."

Saytera had a small curiosity about that. "You think this person would know about my secret? About whatever Vivian wants to tell me?"

"I don't think they can tell you very specific stuff. But perhaps they can tell you other things. It's fun." She looked down, then smiled. "You shouldn't take it too seriously."

Nowla took Saytera to an old wooden house with a door painted golden. "That's it."

They entered. Two women were sitting on the only two chairs in a small room. The other door in the room was closed. It had an eye painted on it, in a colorful background, very beautiful.

"I guess we'll have to wait," Nowla said.

The two other women were probably waiting as well. The girls stood on a corner. She had a question for her friend, and whispered in her ear. "Do you think Vivian will mind that we're here?"

"She told us to walk around the village. That's what we're doing, isn't it?"

Nowla laughed her mischievous laughter Saytera liked so much. Perhaps that was what she would miss the most. One of the women who were sitting down stared at the girls, as if noticing something. Perhaps she didn't like the fact they were laughing? She got up and left.

Nowla rolled her eyes. "Oh, no. Now it's going to go faster for us. How terrible."

Saytera felt a little uneasy, as if they were perhaps disrespecting the place.

Her friend seemed to notice and got serious again. "It's a small village. What are we supposed to do around here? At least there doesn't seem to be much war going on. Too small even for that. Oh, but you have to stay for a few days. I want you to see a big city, perhaps Citarella."

That was the capital of the planet. Quite far from where they were, based on Saytera's calculations and her memory of the Mainland map.

Nowla continued, "Maybe you'll like it, maybe…" The girl stopped and bit her lip.

Saytera didn't want to give her friend any false hopes. "Nowla, I have to go back. You said it was just a visit."

"It is. I know. That's why I want you to see as much as you can."

Guilt still gnawed on Saytera when she considered how she'd come without telling anyone. All she wanted to do now was learn whatever she had to learn then go back home. Still, it was good to be with her friend, and it was good to be in a different place.

Saytera smiled. "Maybe one day I'll come and visit you."

Nowla tilted her head, as if unsure. "Maybe."

A woman opened the door. She wore the same kind of clothes everyone wore, seemed to be about Vivian's age, and had brown hair slightly below her shoulders. Saytera felt a little disappointed. Somehow, she'd expected the stargazer to look more, more, she didn't even know what she expected. The masters on the islands had something about them; their appearance commanded reverence. This woman was just a woman. Maybe it was her clothes. But then, thinking about it, Vivian also had some of that commanding presence the masters had, even in ugly clothes. Maybe Saytera just expected something different.

The woman recognized Nowla and took a second to smile.

"Oh, if it isn't the doctor's guest. Now with a friend. Well, come in."

They walked in and the woman closed the door behind them. Doctor. So that's how Vivian made a living in the village. In fact, she was surprised she hadn't questioned it before.

The room looked plain, with a rectangular table in the middle that didn't look much different from Vivian's table in her eating room. Nothing in the place gave any hint that it was where one saw the future—or tried to, not that Saytera had any idea of how such a place should look like. The girls sat at the table.

The woman looked at Saytera, "So what's your name?"

"Saytera."

"And what do you want to know?"

Saytera blinked. Was she supposed to answer that truthfully? "Everything."

Iona stared at her, then burst out laughing. "You do realize there are ten thousand known galaxies, two of them with systems inhabited by humans, that we know of, of course. Do you want to know the secrets behind the interspace tunnels, what exactly the Blues are, and what other intelligent species roam our universe? Or do you want to know about the plants on this planet, and which ones can be used for what? What about the strange animals seen on the islands, or what exists on the other side, in the great Tormented Sea? Or would you like to know about the stars beyond human reach? Girl, your will is commendable, but you have to define 'everything.'"

"I know." Saytera had no idea why she'd said "everything". At least now she saw something special about Iona. It wasn't the same captivating presence that the islander masters had, but there was something commanding about the way she spoke. But this wasn't the time to notice how exactly the woman was different from the islanders. Saytera tried to think about why she was there. There, not only at Iona's place, but in the continent. She wanted to ask about her destiny, but she feared sounding silly. "I… I don't really know how this works. What about you tell me?"

"Ooooooh, you want to hear answers for questions you didn't ask? Not everyone is ready for that, you know?"

Saytera at first thought that was a hint for her to try to ask a correct question, but apparently, no. The woman got up and used a switch on the wall to turn off the light. A cubic grey box on the corner of the room was now the only source of illumination. The woman picked it up and put it on the table. She held Saytera's hands and closed her eyes. Saytera should perhaps close her eyes as well, but she kept looking at the strange box. The woman then opened her eyes and put hers and Saytera's hands on it. The top of the box, where the hands were, started turning black, while the bottom became lighter, like sand in cloudy water.

Iona then pulled a bolt from one side of the box and spun it. The luminous bottom came up in little dots. They illuminated the ceiling and walls of the room, like a night sky, except that in this case the "stars" were too spread out, unlike in the real sky when they were close together. Still, it was beautiful.

"What's this supposed to mean?" Saytera asked.

"It's your universe. As it stands, now."

"Now?" Saytera thought that was interesting, and it led her to a conclusion. "So you don't see the future."

"Give me two dots and I'll see where the line is going. It doesn't mean I see the rest of the line. But you'll get me out of my concentration, dear. This is about you."

True, that wasn't the best moment to ask about how her "seeing" worked. The woman remained in silence, and Saytera wondered if she was supposed to say anything, but she didn't know what.

After a while, the woman started, "You are not from here."

Iona got points for catching the obvious.

"And there's something you want to know?" The woman looked at her, expecting an answer.

"Well, yes." Saytera decided to give it a shot. "I heard something about my destiny, about me being important for the war, I want to understand what it is."

If Iona thought the question was silly or Saytera was delusional, she didn't show it. She nodded, then looked at the "sky" in her room and squinted.

"You know that each person makes their own destiny. Your importance is up to you to decide. But I'll see what I find here."

She was sounding like Yansin. Saytera wondered if all she would hear were some obvious generalities. Well, why should she even be disappointed or surprised? At least the projecting box was beautiful and the experience was interesting. And the woman seemed harmless and unlikely to try to predict any future and influence anyone.

The woman finally started speaking again, "I don't see anything here about some predetermined destiny, no. I'm afraid there isn't such a thing. What I can tell you is what's immediately around you. That's more useful. Now..." The woman's face hardened. Even in the dim light from the projecting cube, Saytera noticed it had turned pale.

The woman got up and turned on the light. "You have to go. Now." She opened a back door. "Leave. You're in danger. Run. And get away from here."

Nowla crossed her arms. "Fine. I'll never come back, then."

"I'm sure you won't. Sorry, it's for your own good. Follow me."

They entered an eating room, then the woman opened a door leading outside, and gestured for the girls to get out. "Don't walk on the main road. Don't go back to the doctor's house. Go away, and try not to be followed."

"What are we supposed to run from?" Nowla asked.

The woman stared at the girl, then said with the most solemn voice, "Imminent danger."

6

IMMINENT DANGER

Saytera's heart was beating fast. The woman's behavior had been a little weird, but she did seem truly scared.

She turned to Nowla. "What was that?"

"That? You know what it was?" Nowla shook her hands beside her face and said with a deep voice, "Imminent danger!" She then started laughing.

Saytera laughed a little, too. Her friend's impersonation of the stargazer made her realize how ridiculous the "imminent danger" had been. But still… "Maybe we should be careful."

Nowla waved a hand. "Nonsense. Where did she even get that from? It makes no sense. She was probably getting embarrassed that she had no answers. Your fault, with your big questions. You know, people usually ask about boyfriends and stuff."

Saytera had never thought people would ask about that. "Really?"

Nowla rolled her eyes. "Of course, you want to live in that island where there isn't anybody for you, you obviously don't care about that stuff."

She thought about Cayo and felt a pang in her chest. She then looked at Nowla. "Was that what you wanted to ask about? A boy?"

She fiddled with her hair. "No. Maybe about the future, where I'm going and stuff."

"I thought you were going to stay."

"In this village?" Nowla had a grimace. "Are you crazy? I'm going to a military academy. Vivian told me she'd set it up for me."

"But then you might have to face a war."

"Well, if I am going to be important, I have to start some-where, right?"

That made sense. "It's scary, though."

"Like everything that matters. Well, I'm not just going to watch my planet crumble and do nothing. I can't. You... you should maybe consider coming as well."

Saytera sighed, unsure what to say.

Nowla seemed to notice and said, "I know. I know you want to go back. But it was just a thought. Anyway, I'm going to make a difference."

Unlike you, her friend's look implied. Saytera could reply that she was the important one, but then, how exactly was she planning to make any difference? Not a thought worth follow-ing, at least not before learning whatever Vivian had to show her.

Saytera noticed they were approaching the wide path. "I still think we should avoid the main road."

"That's stupid. If anything, we're safer where there are more people."

That made sense, regardless of whether the "imminent danger" was a real threat or not. Perhaps Saytera was jumpy for no reason.

The main road had a few men with their freaky short hair walking ahead of them, but other than that it was empty. And normal. And safe. Saytera almost laughed at her silliness. It was just a wide path—or road. At least the false "imminent danger" would help Saytera understand how dangerous these things could be and how they could influence a person.

When Saytera was about to turn to her friend and comment on that, she felt a strong hand over her mouth, so that the scream that formed in her throat came out as a whimper. Another arm was around her waist pulling her away from the path. She tried to jerk free or elbow her captor but it was like trying to fight a wall. There were rings in the fingers of the hand covering her mouth, scratching her lips and cheeks.

On a path of grass behind a house, he let her go, and she found herself beside Nowla, surrounded by four people, three men, and one woman. They had long grey cloaks closed in the front, covering their clothes.

Now that nobody was silencing her, Saytera screamed, "Help!"

The woman had brown eyes and hair, and shook her head with a smile. "It won't work, darling. We sealed the sound here."

Saytera glared at her and screamed again, but this time louder, "Heeeelp!"

The woman sighed and rolled her eyes. It was probably true that screaming would be useless, since she didn't seem the least worried. Saytera considered trying to run, but she was surrounded, and plus she didn't want to leave Nowla.

The woman shook her head. "Don't be afraid."

If anything, she looked like an islander, except that she wore rings in one hand and had her brown eyes heavily lined.

"Who are you?" Saytera asked, realizing that her voice was hoarse from her screaming.

"None of your concern," the woman replied. "We mean no harm. Which one of you is the girl Vivian wanted to introduce to us?"

So *these* were the people who were going to tell Saytera her secrets? They didn't seem friendly or trustworthy. Saytera stared at them in silence.

"Which one of you?" the woman repeated.

"We don't know what you're talking about," Nowla shouted.

The woman turned to the men. "What now? Kill both?"

"They could lie anyway," a man with a deep voice replied. "It's better to be safe."

"And spill innocent blood?" The woman sounded uncertain.

"Let's just get it over with," the other men said.

This sounded horrible. Saytera dashed between the two men, but one of them soon grabbed her. This time her arms were held back and the tip of a knife was pointing to her neck.

"If you want, this can be painful," the man who held her said.

Why hadn't Saytera listened to the stargazer? Insisted more on running? But regretting was useless.

The other man was holding Nowla. Saytera felt guilty that maybe they would hurt her friend because of her. Perhaps even kill her.

Saytera looked at her captors. "It's me. It's me you're looking for."

"It's me!" Nowla yelled.

Saytera wasn't sure if her friend just wanted to cause confusion or if she thought that it would somehow help them. The man now covered Saytera's mouth again, and she couldn't even consider saying something else, pleading, threatening, maybe again trying to at least save Nowla.

The woman shook her head. "Don't worry, this is going to be fast and painless, and then your fire will be free of this physical prison."

Death was part of life, sure, but not so early, before accomplishing anything, achieving anything. Saytera shivered. What a steep price to pay for a stupid mistake, a stupid decision. The question that got stuck in her throat was "Why?" Why would anyone want to kill her without even knowing her? Was it fear, hatred, what? And Saytera would never know the answer.

The woman extended a hand towards Saytera, its rings shining in the sunlight. Saytera closed her eyes, at this point hoping that it was true that her death would really be painless.

Then, there was a scream. At the same time, the man holding Saytera let her go. Saytera opened her eyes and saw the woman stepping back as if hurt.

"Let them go!" Vivian was running towards them, out of breath. "This is not what we agreed on. Since when do we kill children?"

So indeed this had been Vivian's fault, even though it was clear she didn't want Saytera killed. Yansin's worry hadn't been for nothing.

"Better than *pretending* to kill them, Vivian." The woman replied. "Aren't you ashamed? Now don't get in our way or you might regret it."

Vivian shook her head. "I have enough regrets as it is."

She stretched her arms and launched a stream of fire on the woman, but it wasn't real fire, as the woman just fell backward, unburned. The man let go of Saytera, then Vivian sent her fire towards them and then yelled, "Run!"

Saytera wanted to help Vivan, though, so she hesitated. But then, the two men fell forward, as if hit by something.

"Run!" Vivian repeated, desperation in her voice.

Saytera turned and started to dash away as fast as she could, until she bumped into something—no, someone—solid. Someone who seemed to have materialized in front of her, someone who held her and twisted her arms behind her in a way that was very painful and didn't let her move.

Nowla was also being held, and two women and two men all dressed in black surrounded them. The people who had threatened at first lied motionless on the ground. Vivian stood, fists clenched.

A man with a black hood and silver embroidery approached Vivian. "Murdering innocents… And then they dare say *we* are the problem. So, are you going to help us or would you rather die?"

Vivian's eyes were blazing with hatred. "Don't you dare touch them."

"Oh, you are mistaking us." he waved a hand. "The murderers are your lovely Teren friends. Aren't you glad we were here to save you? You can show your gratitude by letting us take the girls. We can figure out which one we need later."

"You'll kill one and enslave the other," Vivian gritted through her teeth.

"No." He shook his head. "We'll just take her home."

Vivian had her eyes closed. "Run, don't look back, don't trust Terens."

Saytera realized that Vivian was talking to her and Nowla, but how could she get rid of that grip? Then there was a column of fire around Vivian, Saytera felt the man loosen his grip and took the chance to run away as fast as she could, hoping Nowla was running as well. A loud bang made her turn back to look. There was smoke where Vivian and those people had stood a moment before, and the grass was black, as if it had been under a huge bonfire. On the ground, their bodies, and she couldn't look any more or she would vomit. Nowla was alive, though, near Saytera.

No, those people weren't all dead. The man with the silver embroidery appeared in front of them, as if materializing out of thin air, and stretched his hands towards her and Nowla. The rings in his hand shone.

7

TRYING TO ESCAPE

Since the war had taken over their system, no private ships left Sapphirlune. Technically, no military ships either, stuck in place by a cease-fire. It meant exportation had stalled, and nothing reached the moon. Travelers trying to go to other systems found their way out blocked by "peace" forces from the neighboring system Sumeria. Ships trying to reach the Mainland planet were obviously shot before getting a chance to get there. That was why the civil port had been abandoned and hadn't been operational for a long time.

Dess wondered why there would be a meeting there. Perhaps it was something illegal, and the place had been chosen carefully to avoid prying eyes and ears. He wasn't sure he wanted to break any law, but at the same time wasn't sure in which direction his life could go. He'd given it a lot of thought in the last couple of days, and in a way regretted all effort lost into the academy, into doing what he thought was expected of him. He sighed. Maybe if he'd just swallowed his pride he'd be in the army now, with a job. Now—he had no idea what to do.

The large engraved metal doors were closed. At some point, this had been a busy port, but he remembered very little of it. He hadn't asked how he'd get in, but decided to go around the building. He found a regular-sized door with a bell and rang it. He still felt that he was wasting his time, not that his time had any use now. Running his hand over his rings, he thought about Marcus's idea of apologizing and becoming an initiate soldier. Apologizing. He dreaded the prospect. That said, nobody was coming to this door and he was even doubting he'd gotten the right instructions. After a few minutes, he walked to the other side. This time, he found another door, which was open, and walked in.

There was an office with dome desks and terminals with screens. Behind a glass wall, he could see a multitude of ships.

A middle-aged man with a gruff beard stared at him. "Are you the new pilot?"

The question had been directed to Dess. Pilot? "I... I don't know."

The man had a huge laugh. "That's a good sign. Peeps come in all confident, thinking they got the hang of this, when they don't."

Dess frowned. He had no idea what the man was talking about, maybe he was even mistaking Dess for another person, and decided to be direct. "I'm sorry. I wasn't properly briefed on why I was called here. Could you clarify, please?"

"Hehe," the men still laughed, then pointed to the glass. "Is that a mystery? Look at those ships. They won't move by themselves."

That wasn't correct. He spotted a C-3 model. Its autopilot was quite advanced. "Some of them can."

The man raised an eyebrow. "Not where you're going. If you don't quit first, of course."

He decided to be even more direct, "My name's Dess. I trained in the Star Academy. A woman, I'm sorry, I didn't get her name, told me to come here for a job."

"Got to the right place, boy! We always take pilots. It's the pilots who don't want the job."

Job was a magic word. That caught his attention immediately. "What is it?"

"Where do you think we get our water from?"

That was easy. "There's a desalinator right beside this building."

"Indeed. You don't think it produces water, do you?"

It hit Dess. The desalinator was right beside the civil port. He looked at the man and frowned. "We bring it from the planet?"

"Well, that's obvious, isn't it?"

It was. And Dess had never thought about it. "But how can one get down there if they're shooting every ship that comes close to the continent? Do they go to the other side of the planet?"

The man shook his head. "Too many storms. You need to get near the continent and be good enough not to get shot, that's all." He looked at Dess and frowned. "But you don't have experience, do you? That might not be for you."

"I know how to pilot. My stats at the simulator are the best in the academy."

The man leaned back laughing. "That's a toy, kid. But I guess there aren't any more real pilots left but toy players. Alicia said you would be interested. Are you interested in risking your life?"

Alicia was probably the woman who had told him to come.

"What are the terms?"

"You're a private operator. Technically, nobody knows

about you. You buy a spaceship, and then when you bring the cargo we pay you. You should start with water, since it's easier."

"I have to *pay* to risk my life?"

The man waved a hand. "Not a lot. But we can't risk losing ships or you taking a ship, not coming back, you know…" He pointed to the glass. "They're not expensive. They vary from a thousand to about fifty thousand shells each. You'll get ten thousand shells for a single cargo of water."

Dess didn't even have a hundred shells. Most of his wages went into his tuition, and it wasn't as if he earned a lot. But if he would make the money back… "Can't I borrow the money?"

The man grimaced and shook his head. "I doubt anyone will be willing to lend to someone who's risking going to Mainland."

Dess's stomach sank. For a moment, he'd felt a flicker of hope, even excitement, to fly out of that city, get to know the planet, nature. Plus, do something useful, put his knowledge into something practical. But he decided not to show his disappointment. He doubted a lot of pilots were eager to take that job, and it seemed that there were a lot of work-related casualties. *They* should be desperate to get a pilot.

He shrugged. "Well, then, when you run out of people and wave this payment, come and contact me."

He took his personal token and tapped on a screen, so as to give the man his coordinates. Dess turned around and walked outside. He was sure the man would run after him. Instead, he went home followed only by silence.

Saytera felt as if her muscles had been paralyzed, and that was a relief, since that was better than dying.

Then she felt someone putting a hood over her head, so that she couldn't see anything anymore. Saytera and Nowla were pushed while still hooded. A strong hand over her mouth prevented Saytera from yelling. Still, she held hope that someone would see the scene and help them because it must have been obvious that they were being captured. Nobody did, though. They stepped on something with a metal floor. Hollow metal floor, echoing their steps. Probably a boat. Then someone removed their hoods, pushed them into a room, and closed its door. Nowla was there, pale, eyes wide. It was a tiny room, less than two meters long and wide, with no bench, chair, anything. The walls were made of metal sheets. No windows. The unsteady ground confirmed that they were on a boat.

Nowla looked somber, then sighed and sat on the floor, on a corner. "At least they won't kill us."

"Yet." Saytera wasn't sure what they'd do once they figured out which of the girls was the one they wanted.

Nowla stared. "You're so cheerful, Saytera."

"But it's true. We need to escape."

Nowla gestured around her. "Well, if you find a way, be my guest. But don't forget that some of the boats we saw in the village were squid hunters."

"Why should I care about the marine life in the area?"

"If you jump in the water they might kill you." Nowla shrugged. "Not that there is any way to jump out of this box."

Saytera didn't want to give up the hope of escaping. No windows. She checked the door. It didn't have a mechanical lock, but some kind of electrical system keeping it locked. If only she could turn it off as if it were a lamp...

She sat down by Nowla. "Vivian gave her life so that we wouldn't be taken by them."

"It was a good try. She failed, though. Sometimes we fail, it happens."

"True. But don't give up." She decided to go to the door again and see if maybe there was a way to force it open. She pushed it. To her surprise, it moved. It led to an empty hallway. Saytera turned to her friend. "Let's go."

Nowla was still sitting and shook her head in fast movements. "Don't. I'm not jumping in that water."

Saytera crouched in front of her friend, dreading the precious seconds she was losing. "Let's try."

Nowla grabbed Saytera's hand. "Please. These people don't mean to kill us, or we would have been dead already."

At that moment, it was clear that Nowla would never try to escape. And it was a foolish, risky idea anyway. But she had to try. She had told herself she would listen to her gut, and she had a horrible feeling that she had to leave that boat right away.

She looked at her friend's eyes, trying to see if she changed her friend's mind. "Please. We have to try."

Nowla held tighter. "There are things in the water. You won't survive. Don't leave me."

A hard place to be. Saytera didn't want to leave her friend, but she didn't want to remain there either. There were so many things worse than death. Then she figured that if she escaped, she could help for Nowla. If she stayed, they'd both be doomed. "I need to try. I'll find someone to help us."

"Don't go." Nowla's eyes were misty.

Saytera pulled her hand and walked out the door, heaviness in her chest, feeling like the worst friend in the world. She understood that Nowla was frozen with fear, but she wasn't, and she could at least try, so why not? The hallway was empty, but she looked for a side door from where there could be a window, a door leading outside, something… She didn't dare look back at her friend. The friend she was leaving—if she managed to escape.

There was a ray of light coming from one of the doors and she swung it slowly—to see a man reading a datapad. But there was a window. Saytera ran as fast as she could towards the window. It led to the sea below! The man pulled her leg but she kicked his hand with the other leg and jumped. Her body was then submerged in cold water, and she heard yells coming from the surface. As much as she wanted to breathe, she kept under the water, moving away from the boat. When she felt her lungs couldn't take it anymore, she allowed her face to go up. A projectile hit the water beside her, and she dove, this time determined to make the longest distance she could before getting more air. Her life, her freedom depended on it.

It was then that she felt it; something wrapped around her leg and pulled her to the bottom. Squid. Right. She cursed for not having any cutting object, any weapon. She tried to kick it with the other leg, but it got entangled as well. Perhaps Nowla had been right that trying to escape was stupid.

Saytera was pulled away from the boat and the projectiles. One good side. The bad side was that her lungs were about to betray her and try to suck oxygen from water. If only her matterweaving had been better, she could perhaps do something to that squid. Now she was about to be taken to some deep, dark depths, and become food for the food people ate. No. That was incorrect. Squid didn't eat people. They only ate small fish. What was it doing, then? Self-defense.

Struggling and trying to attack it wouldn't help her. Saytera tried to close her eyes. One big ocean. Stars in the universe, stars within. At which point did her life end and the squid's start? Weren't they both part of something bigger? Gears in the machinery of life. Saytera tried to relax her muscles, while at the same time focusing so as not to try to breathe water. She felt a tentacle lose hold of her leg and immediately went up to the surface. As she caught her much needed air, another tentacle pulled her down before she even knew in which direction the boat or the coast was. Of course, her sudden movement must have startled the creature.

Now she was again being pulled. This time it was easier to relax, as she focused on letting the air in her lungs leave her body slowly, sparkly bubbles against the sunlight coming from above. One ocean. One starfire. Saytera wasn't going to try to fight the animal. Poor thing, more scared than she was, so often hunted. Time passed, like an eternity in a few seconds. Her lungs were out of air and tempted to try to breathe water. Saytera decided to be the water, let go, and hope for the best.

To her surprise, the squid let her go. She emerged and saw that she'd traveled a lot more than she'd guessed. She was far from the beach, but far from the boat where she'd been. There was a rocky shore up ahead, with waves crashing against it, and she'd need to avoid it. But this wasn't the time to try to swim anywhere. Instead, she dove again and remained there, for as long as she could, coming up only for some air.

The boat was a spec in the distance—and then it wasn't. A bright flame consumed it and a loud bang reached Saytera's ears. No, no. This couldn't be real. But there was no boat, just bits and pieces scattered around it. Bits and pieces. No more boat. Some strange reality, strange nightmare.

Her friend was gone. Why, why hadn't Saytera insisted? But then, how would Nowla have survived the squid? Regretting wouldn't help, wouldn't change anything, except that if Saytera had stayed on her island, none of this would have happened.

Saytera's body was cold and she wouldn't be able to stand much longer in that temperature, but she felt cold inside, and numb. But dying in that water wouldn't bring anyone back, wouldn't change anything.

There was a sandy beach in the distance. As weak as she was, she forced her legs to propel her forward, cloudy water and waves above her. After a long time, the bottom of the sea was close enough that she could get up and walk, and so she did, until she collapsed on the shore. No, she shouldn't stay there. Somehow, she still feared someone could find her. She walked to the woods surrounding the beach, so that at least nobody would spot her from above. If there was anyone. Perhaps she was paranoid.

So far, she'd escaped. She had a squid to thank. Saytera took a deep breath. She was free—probably. On the other hand, she had no money, no contacts, no food, no means to hunt or defend herself, and no way to go back to the islands. Plus she'd left her friend behind—and now she was dead. Saytera took a long, deep breath. She couldn't change the past, just try to fix what she could for the future. Alone and helpless, with no idea where to go, she'd have to figure out a way to survive.

Marcus's eyes were gleaming. "So you could go to Mainland?"

Dess shrugged. "If I manage not to get shot, sure." He still hadn't mentioned the money issue, and even so, his friend seemed a lot more fascinated with the job than Dess would have predicted.

"But if people go there, there's a way. I mean, there's a way to go there and back. Do you know what this means?"

"A lot. But tell me what you're thinking."

"Freedom. And the power to actually do something that matters. Isn't it what you always wanted?"

Dess shifted in his seat. They were in his small kitchen, drinking artificial juice, one of his last food supplies. Dess had never told him who he was and what had happened in his past, so his friend had no way to know that he also wanted justice. But yes, he wanted to do something that mattered too, except he wasn't sure if getting water was the solution.

He sighed. "It's not like I'll be fighting or collecting information."

"Why not? Once you figure out how to get to the planet, the rest is just a matter of planning."

"Yes…" He decided to change the subject. "And how's life as an army initiate?"

"Boring. Normal. We don't do anything different other than training and stuff. There are more people there."

"You don't like it?"

"I don't know. I feel I'm just… just a number. You got lucky, Dess, you can do something unique."

"I haven't said yes."

"Are you insane? If I could, I'd be right away setting a course to Mainland. Imagine, you'll finally be able to see the ocean from up close. Mountains. Real nature."

Dess laughed. "You talk as if I was going on a tourist expedition or something. It's not a vacation."

"But you're going, right?"

"Uh, yeah, once I figure out certain things." He didn't want to tell Marcus that he couldn't take the job because he couldn't buy a ship.

"And what if you don't take it? What are you going to do? I still think they'd take you back, you know?"

"I'm considering a few options." The options were pretty much starving or trying to find work in the mines or some other kitchen, but he didn't want to say it.

Marcus laughed. "Something funny. They say the food in the academy sucks now that you're gone."

"See? I have at least *some* value. I won't say I'm upset that Serra and the teachers have to starve a little. They deserve it."

Ideally, Dess should have talked to whoever had replaced him, explained some of the droid's particularities, but it wasn't his fault they didn't value his work.

Marcus said, "They should give you a medal for the wonderful work in the kitchen." He then looked at Dess seriously. "So you truly aren't coming back?"

"You know the answer."

Marcus nodded, thoughtful. "I do. I really do. I know the answer."

The cool breeze from the ocean didn't help Saytera, whose fingertips were purple. If only she could make fire. Why think about that now? What she had to do was figure out a way to go back home, but her mind gave her no answers. No boats would take her there—especially when she had no means to pay them. Plus, nobody knew how to get there—not even her.

Perhaps she shouldn't worry so much about her future because if she didn't do something soon, she might not have any. What she had to do was find shelter and maybe some food. Surely someone would be kind enough to give those to her.

Saytera was unsure of direction, but she spotted some hills and walked in their direction, figuring she was distancing herself from the village. That place still gave her the creeps and she would rather not bet her life on all of those people being dead. She still felt a heavy weight in her chest thinking about Nowla.

A sound of leaves cracking caught her attention. Somehow, she knew it wasn't an animal. A person. Perhaps she could deal with just one person, if they didn't shoot weird fire or who knows what from their hands. Saytera grabbed a rock and a twig but then decided it wouldn't do much if they decided to use matterweaving. It was better to play along with whatever they were going to do.

A woman approached. She had clothes similar to the villagers, but wore a skirt.

"Saytera?"

"Who are you?"

The woman raised her hands. She had no rings. "My name is Carla. I was sent by Yansin."

Saytera took a step back. "Can you prove it?"

"The last thing she told you was that the sun would rise again."

Saytera exhaled in relief, as she remembered those words. There had been nobody else around them at the time. She could hardly believe this was true. "You're taking me home?"

"I'm getting you to a safe place. You'll need to hide for a while. Yansin's location has been compromised. They'll have to hide as well."

"Where are we going to hide?"

Carla took a deep breath. "I'm sorry, Saytera. You can't rejoin them right away."

The same feeling of cold numbness she had in her fingers

was now taking hold of her whole body. It wasn't just the woman's words, but her apologetic expression.

Saytera asked, "Can you help me, though?"

"Yes. Yes."

"I need warm clothes."

The woman looked at Saytera up and down. "We could perhaps swap clothes. There's no time."

It was then that Saytera noticed that the woman was pregnant. No way she'd give cold, wet clothes to a pregnant woman. She shrugged. "I can keep my clothes."

Carla nodded. "There's a truck going to Kamia, and you'll have to get in it. In that city, look for the military academy. Your entry in it has been arranged. Tell them your name is Selma." She gave Saytera a metal stick. "Give them this."

Saytera took it. The woman wasn't making sense. "But aren't they dead? The people who wanted to take us? Why do I have to hide?"

Carla again had that sad, apologetic look, and shook her head. "I'm doing what Yansin asked. She probably had her reasons."

Saytera sighed but kept walking with the woman, trying to understand why she was being sent away. "Are you sure I can't hide with Yansin? I can apologize—"

"It's none of that. It's just that she thinks it's best if everyone believes you're dead. At least for now."

"Why?"

Carla showed her palms, as if to show she had nothing in her hands. "Hey, I left the islands years ago. I don't know anything about their secrets or yours. All I know is that nobody from the islands can know you're alive, so you need to stay away from them."

Saytera was shivering. *Stay away from them.* It sounded

harsh, bitter, and sudden. Was Saytera just going to be thrown in the world like that? On her own, without direction? Well, the academy was a direction. And still, she was being ripped from everything she'd always know, everything she'd always held dear.

Carla looked at her. "You'll be fine. They'll give you food and a place to live. You could even get a job. It's a way to make a living. Plus, the truce has been holding for years now. It's probably going to be renewed. The risk of you going into war is tiny."

Tiny. Tiny risk of being sent to die. As if it didn't matter.

8

NEW LIVES

Dess entered the old civil port with confident strides. It had taken them two days, but they'd contacted him. Whatever they had to tell him was obviously different from what they'd told him before, and he was eager to listen.

The woman who'd spoken to him was there, as well as the middle-aged man. Dess really should rethink his manners and start asking people's names. Or start remembering them. He hadn't been thinking much in the last few days.

The woman smiled. "There you are. Zizo here was saying you had chickened out. I was sure you'd come."

Dess stepped closer to them. "It's my pleasure. Can I have your name?"

"Alicia. Just Alicia, in case you're wondering. We have no titles here."

That meant nobody would call him Mr. Starspark. One more thing to like about this place. "Nice to meet you."

"So," Alicia continued, "I was told that you couldn't afford a ship. Is that right?"

"I said I didn't want to pay for it in advance, I never said—"

She waved a hand. "Sure. Doesn't matter. Something changed. You could go as a co-pilot. Would you do that?"

"What's the payment?"

She raised an eyebrow. "Half. You'd get 5 thousand shells for a cargo of water."

"And when I come back I could buy my own ship?"

She shrugged. "If you want, of course."

"I guess it is a good idea for me to go with someone more experienced."

"He's new, too. We aren't going to split an older team that has been working well."

A noob. Dess wasn't sure if he'd want to obey a noob. "I'd need to talk to the pilot."

"First you accept our terms, then you get to know who your partner is."

Dess sighed. It wasn't as if he had any other choice. He should stand his ground and negotiate, but that was hard to do when he was close to starving. "Sure. What are the terms?"

When Dess signed the last contract, he realized that he hadn't done a tiny bit of negotiating. Basically, he was risking his life and would get no help from Sapphirlune. In fact, if he were captured or questioned by the Mainland government, they had the right to deny any connection with him. Technically he would be a rogue ship disobeying his government. Other than that, he wasn't supposed to quit and start living on the planet.

Zizo injected a chip on his neck. The pain was deeper than physical, it was the pain of knowing he was going to be taken advantage of without much in return. No, there was something in return. He'd be able to make a comfortable living and have the freedom to fly away from that rock. He sighed.

"Easy there," Zizo said.

Right. Dess wasn't supposed to move.

"There. You're ready to fly."

Dess touched his neck. "So basically… if I die or if I'm captured, you won't do a thing to help me, but if I decide to live on Mainland, somebody will come pick me up? Interesting."

Alicia looked at him. "It might sound strange, but once you see the ocean, the forests, and the blue sky, you'll understand why it could be so tempting to forget everything and hide. We can't risk that."

"What if I paid for the ship, though? You'd have nothing to lose. I'm not saying I'm planning on doing that. The idea is ludicrous, but—"

"Just imagine what would happen if a bunch of our people, military-trained people, changed sides. Our secrets would no longer be secret and that would make us even more vulnerable than we already are."

Vulnerable. Dess had never thought of his moon that way. Safe high above in the sky, against a planet that had almost no functioning spaceships left, he thought the moon was pretty safe. Different opinions. "Right. I won't quit and become a fisherman, you can be sure of that."

Zizo pointed to Dess's neck. "Oh, we are."

Saytera shivered under the jacket given to her. Her idea of seeking shelter had been mainly to find some place warm. Instead, she was in a refrigerated truck, staring at dead squids.

Guess who was whose food now? Her fingers were still purple and her only consolation was that it wouldn't be more than two hours. Two hours. Almost freezing to death.

Her heart tightened thinking of Nowla. Oh, so much guilt. If only she could tell her past self never to get in that boat with Vivian. Now she was away from her home, from everything, and couldn't say she didn't deserve it.

And yet she still knew nothing about herself and the mysterious reason she'd been sought by those people.

Carla's words came back to her. "Do you think Yansin would have trusted me if I knew whatever secret you have?"

But Saytera didn't have secrets. Other people held secrets about her, and she, the most concerned person in all this, was kept in the dark. In the dark. Almost. A tiny red light allowed her to stare at some dead squid.

At least the woman had given her some information about who those people were. Terens were groups of people who studied ways to bend reality and affect matter. Matterweaving. She knew that. Yansin's group was one of them, but it was rather isolated. The other difference was that Yansin and her followers didn't believe in using objects for channeling and concentrating their power, thus the lack of rings, swords, or other metallic objects. Most Terens used those.

And why two groups? Well, again Carla's words were vague. According to her, Maxterens were said to believe in their superiority and the right to dominate the universe. Terens fought for peace. Hard to swallow, when Terens were the ones who had wanted to kill her. But Saytera had said none of that, afraid of implicating the woman in secrets she shouldn't know.

She remembered when she asked, "But how come they all live on this planet?"

"They don't."

"But the Mainland System gate is blocked."

"We know things that most people don't." Interesting her use of *we*, as if she were still part of that group. Saytera remembered how Vivian had passed right through the monitor ship.

And that explained why Yansin was going to leave Mainland. Leave Saytera. Leave her islands. Probably because of what Saytera had done, how she'd gone away in the middle of the night without telling anyone, knowing well that there could be some danger. At least if she died of cold, it would be deserved.

The trip didn't feel like two hours, but an eternity. The jacket helped a little, but not a lot, when her clothes were still damp and when the truck was cold. If only she could make fire. Well, that was a stupid thought. She'd spoil the squid and risk the truck catching fire. Brilliant, brilliant, Saytera. The only thing she could do for now was focus on the infinite star fire burning within her, in every cell, every atom, and try to make it burn bright and hot, countering the cold outside.

After a long time, the truck stopped. One of the drivers opened the back door. "Here, girl. The academy is that dark building over there. Don't tell them how you got here."

"Tha-thanks." She was shivering.

"Good luck." With that, he closed the door of the cargo area, went to the front, and the truck left. There was a city nearby, she could see buildings at a distance, but where she was there was only one building, large and ominous, with dark glass walls. It looked small to be an academy, but maybe they were smaller than she'd imagined.

Saytera walked towards it and knocked on a metal door. No idea what awaited her behind it.

~

The ship assigned to Dess was a Zeta-33. It was a civil model, without weapons or shields, but quite fast. It wouldn't have been his choice. It had a shiny silver polish and sharp angles. Made for civilians to show off. His stomach was growling, as he'd made the best dinner he could out of some leftover dry cookies. Today he'd come prepared in civil clothes. He missed his pistols, which had remained in his locker in the academy, to which he no longer had access. That said, if they were only going to the sea, he wouldn't need any weapon.

He stepped in carefully and a bit wary. His trip would be a nightmare if he had to listen to a noob. One trip. He could get his own ship once he returned. If he succeeded. If he survived. The door was open and he climbed in. To his surprise, the pilot seat was empty. Someone was sitting in the co-pilot seat: Marcus.

It couldn't be. "Are you… my partner?"

Marcus leaned back and laughed. "Haven't I always been?"

"Are you sure? You have a good family. You don't have to do this."

Marcus shook his head. "And be another number among the initiates? Nah. I'm good. Plus, we never know, we could all die in six months. At least I'll have seen the ocean. From up close."

"Does your father know about it?"

Marcus bit his lip. "He does."

Something was odd. "And he accepted it. Like that?"

Dess's friend was silent for a moment, then said, "He kicked me out of the house."

"Oh. Where are you living?"

He tapped the dashboard. "Here. For now."

Dess wanted to tell his friend that this was not for him, that he had better options, that he didn't need it, but Marcus's resolute expression prevented him from doing so. One trip wouldn't change much—unless they got killed—but Dess wouldn't let that happen. Maybe his friend would quit after that.

Dess sat down and sighed. "I see. Listen, there's something I need to say. Once we come back, I want to get my own ship. It's not that I can't take orders, it's just—"

"That you're an insanely good pilot and you know it. Why do you think I left the seat for you? Hey, we can be a team."

"Your father's going to skin me alive and think it's my fault."

Marcus chuckled. "Sure. You definitely need to please my father and everyone in Sapphirlune's government circle. They've been so good to you, recognized all your effort and all, promoted you—"

"Yeah." His words were poking his wound. "I get it. What if he hates me, right?"

"Exactly. You owe him nothing. I owe him nothing. And being free is the most wonderful feeling in the world. You know what it is? Freedom. We do whatever we want."

"There are certain procedures."

His friend still had a glimmer in his eye. "Sure. I've read it all. That said, as long as we come back with the water, nobody will say anything."

Water. Dess got up. "Do you know how we'll get it?"

"Container on the back with a suction tube. We just have to fly over the sea for a few minutes. I can tell you all about it on the way. It's a while, you know?" Marcus threw some packages to Dess. "And I brought snacks."

"Cookies? We'll have crumbs flying all over when we go to zero G."

"We can keep the artificial gravity on. You can also put the whole thing in your mouth and chew it. No crumbles."

"I guess." Dess noticed the dashboard. Everything had a label explaining what it was for. Definitely a ship for amateurs. "We didn't have a lot of practice with those civil models."

Marcus looked down. "It's what I could get. My father—"

"It's fine. This is fast. Plus, I think all this metallic finish will camouflage us."

"We'll get a better one once we're back."

Dess nodded. "Yeah. I'll get it. And I'll pay you back."

"As you wish, Mr. Pride." Marcus laughed.

"You're kidding, right? Is everything ready?"

"I was waiting for you."

"Let's get going, then."

In a way, Dess was happy to have his friend by his side, but it was a selfish kind of happiness, as Marcus was defying his family and this wasn't good for him. Then again, he'd talk to him once they got back. He hit the communicator. "Permission to leave?"

"In thirty seconds", a man's voice replied. Zizo, probably.

Seconds? Dess was thinking he'd need to wait a few minutes. He took a deep breath while the lights went from yellow to blue. The massive metal doors opened. He hit the antigravity switch then flew into the airlock. As it finally opened, the infinite universe was in front of him. Dess was part of it. On his way to finally set foot on land. Mainland.

The woman who opened the door to Saytera had brown hair

cropped short and wore pants and shirt stuck together in a one-piece suit. A jumpsuit. That looked horribly uncomfortable. "Yes?"

Saytera hesitated, then passed the stick.

"What's this?" the woman frowned.

"For me. To enter the academy."

The woman looked at Saytera up and down, a disgusted expression on her face, then closed the door. If she took too long to show up Saytera would need to walk to the city and beg.

Instead, the door reopened in just a couple minutes. "Follow me," The woman said. Then she frowned. "Goodness, dear. Where were you? In a refrigerated truck?"

"Sort of."

"Hum. You'll need a warm shower and new clothes. What's your name?"

"Saytera," she said without thinking, then immediately regretted it. Carla had told her to give a different name, but she'd forgotten what it was, and for a moment even forgot she had to keep her identity a secret. It was hard to have coherent thoughts while almost freezing.

"Right. I'm Kia and I'll be responsible for you from now on. Follow me. You'll join the others tomorrow."

The woman descended some stairs and led Saytera to an underground passage and then a hallway. She crossed some young people wearing white and blue jumpsuits in a material that looked hard and uncomfortable. They looked at her with surprise and curiosity. Some of them laughed and sniggered. Saytera looked back and noticed that more people had come out of the doors to look at her. What were they looking at?

Kia pulled Saytera's arms. "Ignore them. After a shower,

that smell will go away and tomorrow they'll forget how you got here."

That smell. So Saytera stank of squid. What a glorified entrance. Wet, shivering, and stinky. Her hair was mostly hidden under the jacket, and she noticed that nobody had hair long like hers. She'd probably have to tie it from now on. One more thing she didn't like.

The bath place had many stalls with metal doors and no bathtubs. Kia left her there and got out, promising to bring dry clothes. Saytera looked at the mechanism. There was a pipe with a thing from where water probably came. So that was a shower. On the wall, a set of switches she had never seen. Saytera was a stranger in a strange land of which she knew very little.

Based on her best guess she pushed the silver button in the middle—and screamed, as cold water reached her body. As if she weren't cold already. There were two other buttons, numbered 1 and 2. She'd need to figure it out. And find a way to belong in this place—at least for now. Yansin would find her, she had to believe it. Meanwhile, she had to learn how to use a shower.

The uncountable hours in the simulator were nothing compared to the feeling of actually flying. Not that it was harder or different, just that it was real. As they approached the planet, Dess was careful to find the right area to enter the atmosphere. It couldn't be far away from the continent, where storms could make flying very difficult, and it couldn't be too close, where they'd be shot from one of the many anti-flight bases on the shore. He'd seen a map of where they were, at least in theory, or at least according to information from years before.

They descended quite fast. His heart was warmed at the sight of the blue sky and grey ocean. Pictures, videos, and simulations didn't compare to the reality of being there, seeing the land in the distance, and the powerful ocean below them. As much as the universe was overwhelming with its vastness, sky and ocean were powerful and humbling, and Dess felt tiny in his ship.

Marcus was quiet, staring at the window, then turned to Dess. "I thought I'd never see it."

"We're here." Dess patted his friend's shoulder. "Can you set up the water collector?"

Marcus nodded and got up. "On it."

Dess realized that this was a job to be done by two people. Had Marcus not volunteered, would they have partnered Dess with somebody else? He wasn't sure if he liked the idea. Then again, he knew he'd have to talk some sense into his friend once they got back. At least he'd seen the ocean. It was huge, wild, almost looked like a sentient being with its waves, its energy. They'd take a little bit of that home. Dess wished he could land, walk outside, smell and feel that air. Maybe later, once he got a better hang of where to go and where not to go.

As he contemplated a future with delightful trips to the planet, his ship was shaken and jerked. There was nothing around them but wind. Just wind, although quite strong. A storm he hadn't seen coming.

He turned back and yelled, "Stop the procedure. Find a place to hang on tight."

Piloting in the atmosphere and facing storms were things for which Dess had trained a lot. Perhaps he'd always wanted to come to the planet. He still had the anti-gravity on, although it affected just the weight of the ship. The attraction of the planet still affected Dess and his friend. Like he'd simulated so many times, he turned against the wind and turned on the thrusters to counter it. Or maybe he tried. The wind wasn't coming in one direction, but circling them, like some kind of mini twister. He'd been trained to fly in wind like that. The secret was to power up and get out of its circle. But it wasn't working.

Dess was about to lose control of the spaceship, and that meant it could be thrown against a rock, taken too close to the shore, anything. All the procedures he thought he knew weren't working. Then he had one more idea. The ship was being tossed around because, without gravity, it was light like a feather. He'd never heard about it or done it in the simulator, but he turned off the anti-gravity.

The ship fell on the water.

"What's happening?" Marcus yelled from the back.

"It's all under control." Kind of. But worrying his friend wouldn't help.

The ship was submerged and once it got below the turbulent surface, it found calmer water. There was still some risk of hitting rocks, but this wasn't a rocky area. He hoped at least all the maps he'd studied were correct, unlike the simulator.

Marcus ran to the front. "We're under water!"

Dess leaned back and put his feet on the dashboard. "We're fine. Let's get some water."

Marcus had a grimace. "You do know that the thrusters won't work under water, right?"

"We'll get out of the water first. This is good. Nobody will shoot us here."

His friend shook his head. "I hope you know what you're doing."

"You hurt my feelings by doubting me."

"Whatever, Dess. I'll get the water."

In fact, of course Dess had no clue what he was doing. It was nothing more than a guess. Educated guess, maybe. Then, maybe, uneducated, because he had to throw everything he'd learned away. Now he had to figure a way to face the storm when they emerged. No. That made no sense. No storm lasted forever.

9

NEW REALITY

A horrific strident noise awoke Saytera. It was as if a dolphin were dying in terrible pain. She'd never heard that, and had no idea if dolphins screamed, but that was what it sounded like. Without daylight, she hadn't noticed it was already morning. She got out of her bed and turned the light using that switch on the wall, but it hurt her eyes. So sudden, so strong, so artificial.

The bedroom had white walls and two beds, one on top of the other. She'd slept in the bottom one. There were two wardrobes. One was locked. Everything was cold, impersonal, as if it weren't meant for a human being. Saytera had slept in dark grey pants and a shirt, but knew she'd have to put on that horrid jumpsuit for the day. The material was artificial, impermeable, and not something her skin would be able to breathe in. Whoever had chosen these things didn't consider the extra time required to take it all off to pee. White and blue, shiny. The people she'd seen the day before were wearing them. She still remembered the comments and sniggers and wasn't looking forward to meeting them.

No. That was stupid. They had probably just been surprised by her appearance and smell. Today it would be different. She had to believe they'd be nice and friendly, otherwise she'd be rude to them unwittingly end up justifying their impression. At least Yansin used to tell her stuff like that, about her perceptions and expectations affecting the way the world responded to her. Saytera tried to expect the best.

As she was zipping up the dreadful thing, the door opened. A girl with short blond hair, already dressed in a jumpsuit, got in.

"Hey," she said without looking at Saytera. "I'm your roommate. But don't worry, I never come here, I usually sleep with my friends. I just came to pick up something."

The girl opened the wardrobe that had been locked. It had a few objects in the bottom and no clothes. The girl closed it and walked to the door. "Sorry for disturbing you."

"It's no problem."

The door then closed. Saytera wondered if she should have said something else, realizing that she'd never had to introduce herself or try to make friends. Whenever someone new arrived at Ken Island, Yansin usually introduced them to Saytera. Now she was clueless about what to do. Had she been rude to the girl? No way to know.

Saytera wished she had someone to help her, someone to guide her. She tied her hair in a bun, got out of her room, and recognized the hallway from the previous night. Some other apprentices were walking all in the same direction and she followed them. They reached a large room with natural light from windows by the ceiling. It had about fifteen tables for six people each, and a counter. The place didn't look like an eating room. It lacked warmth, life. The walls, floor, and tables were white, and the counter was silver. The fact that everyone wore similar clothes didn't help to make the environment any more hospitable. Apprentices were coming in and lining up before the counter. She wasn't sure if they were called apprentices, but didn't know what else to call them—and herself.

Lining up, Saytera was aware of every muscle in her body, not in a good way, as in being grounded, but rather as if she were trying to prevent a wrong movement. She looked at the others to see what they did, got food on a tray, and sat by herself on a table far from the counter. Older people, in entirely blue uniforms, sat together at another table. She figured they were the teachers. There were fewer people than she would have expected, as some tables were half empty and others were empty, so that there were only about fifty students.

The woman, Kia, approached her. "Feeling better today?"

Saytera smiled. "For sure."

"You'll just get in the classes with everybody. If you're not sure where to go, just ask any other cadet around you. This morning it's shooting." She tapped Saytera's back. "Good luck."

"Thanks."

Follow the crowd. Cadets. Fine. It shouldn't be too hard.

The shooting arena was a giant room with booths from where one could shoot round targets far away. There were only five booths, though, and several seats, in a semicircular area around a podium. Since everyone else was sitting, Saytera did the same.

A bearded man in a blue uniform walked to the podium.

"Saytera," he said in a thick voice, as if he were annoyed.

The word startled her, as it sounded as if she'd done something wrong, when she'd just gotten there.

"Yes?" her voice came out thinner and higher than she'd expected, and a few sniggers didn't help her feel any more comfortable.

"Come, come," he said. Saytera got up and walked to the middle. The man continued, "This is the most important class you'll have. Can you tell me why?"

Some of the words she'd heard on the islands came back to her. "If you're going to shoot, shoot right, or else you'll alert your enemy."

The man pointed to her and turned to the class. "See? Now that's a good answer." He turned to her. "Alert your enemy. That's interesting. So how do you avoid it?"

A lot of her stress was gone now that she'd gotten an answer right. "By only shooting when you have good aim."

The teacher seemed satisfied, then asked, "What if you can't get a good aim?"

She tried to remember a little of her haphazard lessons. "You do the best you can and take cover."

"Impressive. Where do you come from?"

Saytera's stomach sank. What was she supposed to say? "My… village." Her voice had never been so thin and high.

"All right. Somehow you got a good basis in *your… village.*" He made a high voice.

The class burst out laughing.

Saytera took a deep breath, trying to calm down. The man walked to the first booth. "Come. Let's see what you can do."

"I've never used a pistol before." This time Saytera's voice had been firm. She wasn't going to be afraid of rude people.

The man put a pistol in her hand. "That's what you're here for: to learn." He pointed to the circle far away, "Point there," then he touched the weapon, which had a little button close to the handle. "Then press here. Hold it with one hand only."

Saytera took the pistol. Focus. The secret was to focus. She made sure to hold the pistol at a comfortable enough distance not to strain her arm and to make sure its angle was towards the target. Hopefully she wouldn't make too much of a fool of herself. Saytera held her breath and pressed the button. Nothing happened. She pressed again, this time harder. Something was amiss. She felt all eyes on her and it was as if the air were compressing her body. But she was doing it correctly. She looked at the pistol again. She had seen pictures of pistols, she knew what they could do. This one felt as if it were dead, though. She angled the pistol toward her to figure out why it wasn't working, when a strong hand took the pistol from her.

"Wow, wow, wow," the man said. "No need for drastic measures. Not being able to shoot is no reason for suicide."

The students burst out laughing again.

Saytera stared at him. "I wasn't going to shoot my face, and this thing's clearly defective."

"Nonsense." The man pointed to the target and pressed the button. Nothing.

He put the pistol aside, took a new one, and aimed at the target. A burst of energy came out of it and hit the outer rim of the circle. It was some kind of sensitive surface. The outer circle lit up for a few seconds, until the man pressed a button on the booth and the light faded. Seeing that his aim sucked gave Saytera some satisfaction.

He passed the new pistol to Saytera. "There. This one works."

Saytera focused, calm with the knowledge that getting a better shot than the man wouldn't be hard. She held her breath and pressed the button. Nothing happened again. The teacher tore the pistol from her hand and tried to shoot. Nothing happened.

He glared at her. "Twice now. If you keep ruining our pistols there won't be any left."

This was unfair. She hadn't done anything.

"I won't," she said, then turned around and left the room, under the looks and laughs of her so-called colleagues. All she wanted was to leave all of that behind, that stupid teacher, those stupid cadets, that stupid place. She was better than that. She just needed some time alone, some time to collect her thoughts, quiet down her anger. Halfway to her bedroom, the lights in the hallway went out.

Dess had never been to *The Blue Aquarium*, or to any restaurant for that matter, since… It hurt to think about it. There he was, with his best friend, ready to eat a decent meal after a long time. Still shaken by his experience on the planet, he needed to relax, celebrate. He'd spent so long in his simulator, and yet, he had to forgo most of his training, he had to fight acquired instincts, as beating the winds on the planet proved to be quite different from what a machine could mimic.

So long he'd spent in that silly simulation, only now to discover that most of it meant nothing. He'd considered telling someone that the simulator was faulty, but then, perhaps winds were just unpredictable, and then, perhaps some things were only ever understood with experience. He was glad he'd come back alive, a lot more relieved than he'd expected, when he thought the job was going to be an easy-peasy in-and-out flight. A lot of what he'd learned was plain wrong, and somehow that idea shook him to the core. And that was why he wanted to celebrate with Marcus.

A quick look at the menu told him that most of the dishes

were made with cricket base. Most of them, not all.

Marcus pointed to something. "Hey, check it out. We could have *real squid,* no idea what the difference is from regular squid, for two thousand shells. Want to splurge?"

Dess laughed. Should he tell him what the difference was? Then something else hit him. "I guess it's not just water we'll be bringing."

Marcus cocked his head. "What do you mean?"

"Where do you think the squid comes from?"

His friend frowned. "You think?"

Dess was pretty sure. His thoughts were interrupted by a man in the elegant council suit walking in the restaurant, scanning the tables with a murderous glare.

"Marcus," Dess whispered. "Your father's here."

His friend's body tensed right away. Counsellor Okonjo was a tall and large man, skin just a bit darker than his son's, hair cropped so short one couldn't see his curls.

He addressed Dess. "What do you think you're doing with my son?" He didn't yell but that was probably just so as not to cause a scene in public.

Dess ran his right hand through his hair, displaying all his rings. "We were about to order dinner. Want to join us?"

Marcus got up. "Dad, can we talk outside?"

Counsellor Okonjo followed his son, but not before shooting some death glares at Dess.

Marcus would probably go back to the army. It would be sad to lose his friend as a partner, but despite Okonjo's influence, Dess wasn't worried. He knew two things: One; Sapphirlune depended on the work of independent traders for survival—and for fancy items on a restaurant menu. Two; very few people were capable of flying in and out of Mainland's atmosphere, collecting water or whatever they wanted, and coming back alive. It meant Marcus's father couldn't make Dess lose his job. Yes, Dess had been lulled by a false sense of security before, thinking that being the best in the academy was some kind of security. Still, this, this was different. He even wondered whether they'd failed him on purpose.

Marcus walked back in and sat. "Don't worry, everything is fine."

"What does that mean?"

"We continue doing what we were doing, and my father continues to be angry and not accept me at home."

"You need to talk to him."

Marcus shook his head. "He'll understand. There's honor in being a cog in a big machine, of course. But there can be much more when you can operate on your own. I'm sure eventually I'll make him proud."

Yeah. Maybe they'd bring a giant squid or something. But that was not what he said. He tapped Marcus's shoulder. "You will."

There was no way Saytera would find her room in that dark hallway. She considered going back to the dining hall, which had natural light, but she heard voices from that direction.

Someone—it sounded like the shooting teacher—was telling the students to stay calm and together, or something. So they feared an attack. Could Lunars get here, though? Her heart then tugged, thinking about Terens, which was much more likely. Could someone have found her?

All she could do was listen. If anyone was after her, she'd better not join large groups, even if she hated every single one of them. That wasn't a good thought. She couldn't give a crowd a hateful sniggering face. It was just some of them. Her mental talk didn't soothe the rage bubbling up inside her. Islanders had techniques to channel anger, but she didn't want to call even more attention to herself by yelling alone or kicking piles of sand. Not to mention that there wasn't any sand there. Was she just going to leave that anger there, eating her body, sticking to her energy? Perhaps later, when the light came back, she could punch her mattress. One advantage of having a room for herself.

A faint light at the end of the hall called her attention. So there was another room with windows. The structure was underground, for good reasons, of course, but they probably had small buildings from where they carved windows. She didn't know why they didn't have any kind of natural light in the bedrooms, though. It felt so weird.

As she approached the light, she saw that it was coming from large glass doors. Saytera pushed them open, and was faced with a gigantic hangar with some thirty ships. It smelled —or felt—old, stagnated, lifeless. Still, the place had windows and didn't have anyone, and that was what she needed to get her thoughts together.

That until a yell startled her, "What are you doing here?"

There was an old man, wearing grey clothes, hair unkempt, bulging eyes, staring at her.

Saytera wasn't sure if yelling was a normal way to ask a question. Either way, she decided to tell the truth. "I was taking a break. Electricity's down and there was light here."

He gestured frantically for Saytera to come behind a ship, away from the door. "Hide. Hide. They are coming."

"Who's coming?"

He widened his eyes. "The Lunars. They want the planet, they want the planet!"

10

___

FRIENDS

As far as Saytera knew, the danger was mostly on the shore, where she'd been attacked—not by Lunars, but by Terens. The man's attitude was so excessive that it brought a smile on her face, but he had a point. "Let's hide, then."

Saytera spent the next few hours inside a broken ship listening to incongruent rambling about the war and the Battle of Stars. The old man had been in it and survived. She'd always heard that the entire Mainland fleet had perished. And indeed almost everybody had died, as he recounted the loss of friends. His narrative wasn't easy to follow, jumping up and down in time, but she listened.

The man's name was Nick. After a while, he got up and told her the names of some of the spaceship models. Saytera understood that his job was to fix the ships, except that since there had been no importation for years, the solution had been to take functioning parts from one ship to the other, to the point that what had been left there were just empty carcasses that would never fly again. As he explained for the third time how the war had impacted importation, that dreadful wailing sounded again. How could anyone live with that?

"What's this?"

Nick put his hands on his ears "They want to kill us, kill us. Heart attack. It's lunch, girl!"

The heart attack thing was a good point. It also meant electricity had returned, unless it worked on a separate system than the lights. Saytera was hungry, but wasn't looking forward to seeing her lovely colleagues. Nick's nonsensical rambling had calmed her down, though. Here, in this horrible place, she had security, food, and shelter. All she had to do was hang on tight enough for Yansin to get her back. And hanging tight enough meant doing what they'd told her to do, which meant following the crowd—at least for now.

Saytera ate alone again, but this time she wasn't feeling guilty for not being friendly and she didn't think she was missing anything by not sitting with those people. The food was dreadful, but it was food.

The afternoon was history class. Saytera actually enjoyed that they were talking about the war against the Lunars. This lesson focused on the moon of Tarahi and its discovery. That was the reason Mainland and Shapphirlune were fighting. Tarahi had an incredible reserve of gravity stones, or Ilanium. It was the main compound in the anti-gravity systems allowing spaceships to take off easily.

The Lunars, from Sapphirlune, thought that it should be all theirs, because, according to their deranged minds, Tahari was a moon, therefore it was their territory. But their territory was just their own moon. Why they thought it gave them ownership of the whole universe around them was anyone's guess. And from there they'd been fighting.

The teacher explained well why Lunars had acted unfairly

against the planet, in right grabs that had no limits. They even wanted to be allowed to come to the planet to collect food and water. And that was what the planet was counting on; cutting off their supplies and pressuring them to concede defeat. In six months the terms were going to be renegotiated, and they expected the Lunars to cave.

Either way, it was better than the lessons about distant planets like the deposed Ringon monarchy and other stuff that had no relation to her own life. One good thing—as long as she ignored the fact that people still shot her glares, laughed, and whispered behind her back. She'd gotten a new nickname: Giant Bun.

Whatever. It didn't matter. At least they weren't making fun of her eyes. Well, the bitter taste in her mouth and the tightness in her stomach told a different story. She'd just work really hard at punching her mattress and get those feelings out of her system.

It was still strange to think about day and night, with the excessive lights and lack of windows. Alone in her room, Saytera was about to start her mattress-punching session when soft knocks on her door caught her attention. Saytera was expecting her should-be roommate, but it was another student instead, a petite girl with dark hair to the chin—who had probably mistaken the door.

"Yes?" Saytera asked.

"Can I come in?" the girl whispered, almost as if afraid.

Saytera nodded and stepped away from the door, wondering what her visitor wanted.

The girl walked in. "I'm Christina, but they call me Kiki."

"Saytera."

"I know." Everyone knew, of course. The girl looked away, then looked back and locked her eyes on Saytera. "Listen, don't let them get to you. It's normal. Most new recruits go through it. It will pass."

"I didn't do anything."

"You walked away. Some even suggested you sabotaged the electricity panel."

That was absurd. "There wouldn't have been time for that, and I don't even know where it is."

"Exactly, it couldn't have been you. I know." She then changed to a cheerful tone. "Do you want to practice? I'm sure you'll do better when nobody's looking."

"If the pistols aren't defective, I guess."

"They aren't. And it's fun."

Fun was a nice word to hear after everything she'd been through. "Sure."

Kiki smiled. "I'll go in. Then you go. I'll leave the door open. It's the door just beside where we had our class this morning."

Saytera didn't understand why they couldn't just go together, but she'd figure it out later. "Fine."

After the girl got out, she changed quickly and went to the door Kiki had told her. Yes, it looked fun. Instead of the ranges and booths, this place had some rocks, some small weird platforms with stairs, small walls, big walls, and rectangular targets in movable panels suspended by wires.

Kiki stood by her. "Much more like the real thing, isn't it?"

Shivers went down her spine as she remembered her only real encounter with enemies. They weren't just one or two, moving slowly in the distance.

The girl then added, "We'll probably never see any of that.

Still, it's good to practice." She handed Saytera a pistol. "We call this a zapper. It's an energy pistol. Crackers are the projectile pistols, but we don't have them here."

The *zapper* was similar to the ones she tried to use before, with the teacher. It felt heavy and uncomfortable in her hand, not that it was really heavy. "What do I do?"

"It's set up like a circuit. You have to go through it and shoot the targets."

"Won't we get in trouble for being here?"

Kiki shook her head. "I got special authorization from Kia."

Saytera stared at the circuit, trying to figure out how to do it.

Kiki held one pistol in each hand. "I'll go first, then you do what I did. It's fine if you go more slowly, and you'll obviously use only one pistol."

"Why two?"

She looked down and shrugged. "I want to train to use both hands. Commander Faetee says it's stupid, that I only have one pair of eyes." She shrugged. "I got two hands, though. And who knows, I could maybe use a zapper and a cracker at the same time." She smiled again. "Watch."

Kiki ran through rocks, got up and down stairs, sometimes squatted by walls, all the while using both hands to shoot the targets. She got most of them on her first shot, with the exception of one or two that she had to shoot twice.

As Kiki got back, Saytera said, "That was amazing!"

The girl was almost out of breath. "I wasn't showing off, I just wanted you to know how the circuit works."

"Still. That was pretty good. Had it been a real situation, you'd probably survived up to the fourth target, when you missed."

Kiki nodded. "I know. I botched it. That's why I come every night. To get better. I need to tell you a secret: I was terrible at

the beginning. Terrible. Like, couldn't even hold the pistol properly. As you noticed, commandeer Faetee doesn't bother teaching you how to do it. I got teased. Well, their laughter and their silly words became my fuel. I decided I'd become the best in the academy."

"Are you?"

She cocked her head. "I think so. Commander Faetee prefers Jonas, though, but he's much slower than I am."

That commander was a nitwit and his opinion only meant that Kiki was likely a lot better than this Jonas dude. "How come nobody else practices in the evening?"

"They do sometimes, not always. Your turn now."

Saytera walked to the place where her new friend had first stood. As she tried to shoot the first target, the pistol didn't respond. Unwilling to go through the whole "it's defective, it isn't" ordeal, she just got back to where Kiki was. "I'd rather watch you do it a couple more times. I think I could learn a lot."

"It's fine if you do it slowly and miss. You should have seen me a year ago."

"I know, but it's been a stressful day."

Kiki nodded. "All right."

Saytera sat down. She didn't understand whether there was something she was doing wrong or if her energy was messing with the pistols. They kept electronics away from the islanders because they said they messed with the training. What if it was the other way around? That didn't make sense, though, as it meant Saytera had any kind of strong matterweaving abilities, and she didn't. She could be crap at more than one thing, though.

At least one student was being nice to her. When all her insides were being turned to ice, with the horrid memories of that boat exploding with Nowla inside it, Vivian dead, and the thought that perhaps she'd never return home, a little bit of kindness was like a small flame warming her heart.

~

Dess had accepted three things: Marcus wasn't going to quit being his partner, they were going to split expenses and profit, and his friend had moved permanently to his house.

The next morning, they'd have their second incursion to the planet. Excitement sizzled through him as he realized he enjoyed this private trader thing more than he'd ever expected.

Someone knocked on the door and Dess opened it. Sylvia was there. Sure, technically he and Marcus were sharing the house, but his friend could at least have told him he'd invited her. A quick look at Marcus told him that it wasn't the case.

"Hey," she said. "I came to see how you two were doing."

Them two? Right. More like Marcus, and they'd probably do the whole we're-just-friends thing. And yet, the visit felt strange. A good thing he was no longer interested in her, or he'd rather be caught dead than let her see his humble two-piece house. It was still strange because she likely lived in one of the luxurious high rises in the center of the city. Marcus didn't show any signs of being embarrassed, though. Good for him.

"Can I come in?" she asked.

He'd been so lost in thought he'd been just standing there. "Sure."

"I brought some firewater." She held a bottle.

There had been a lot of illegal drinking in the academy and Dess usually stayed away from it, but he assumed it was her own way to show niceness, so he decided not to say anything. Dess put three glasses on the table and they sat down.

"I know what you're doing," she said. "I hope you're careful."

"I thought it was supposed to be secret," Marcus said.

As if nobody would notice ships coming in and out of the moon.

His friend then added, "Except for the high echelons, of course. Does that mean you're there already?"

"Yes and no. I did some digging." She opened the bottle.

It was Dess who was curious now. "So you do get access to some private information."

She sighed. "A little. Nobody can know I'm here, by the way."

Marcus shrugged. "Makes sense."

Dess wanted to smack the bottle on her head. How dare she be ashamed of his friend? He frowned. "No, it doesn't."

Marcus glared at him. "Dess. Her family is like mine. You wouldn't understand."

Right. He was the non-family person there. It wasn't his fault that some wacko had decided to explode the ship carrying his family seven years before. But he'd never told anyone that. Marcus knew he'd lived in the mansion, but thought he'd been raised by Azael, the gardener. It didn't matter.

He got up. "Right. I'm tired. If you don't mind, I'll relax a little, uh, here on the couch." He turned to Sylvia. "If you by any chance get tired and want to, uh, rest, there's a mat under the bed."

She rested her glass on the table. "I wasn't going to stay long."

"Sure. Just in case."

Marcus shook his head. "You won't rest with us talking here."

Dess shrugged. "Talk in the bedroom then and close the door. Or here. Don't worry about me."

Knowing well he was going to have trouble sleeping completely dressed, he lay down on the couch trying to recall the sound of the ocean in his ears, wondering when he'd be able to walk on real sand and feel the waves hitting his feet. He ran his hands over his rings, thinking about all the power that was still unknown to him, and if he'd ever really come close to it. Reading about it was one thing. Maybe one day he'd see it, experience it. His thoughts almost lulled him to sleep, but then the sound of Marcus and Sylvia "talking" in the bedroom distracted him.

Dess understood how chance sometimes made things right in ways that weren't clear at first. Had he made a move on Sylvia, his friend wouldn't be happy right now. Plus, Dess would never accept someone who wanted to "talk to him" but only in secret. His body was made of stardust, carrying the energy of the stars, and deserved a lot more than that. Fine, so was Marcus's, but if he thought this was good enough for him, then it was. Dess wanted something better than that. For now, he wanted to dream about beaches, the ocean, and some insanely good piloting.

~

Saytera's troubled dreams were interrupted by a strident sound of dolphins wailing in terrible pain. It was the middle of the night. She took a look at the display by her bed. No. It was morning. Ugh, getting up in darkness was horrible. Plus, how was anyone to have a decent mood being awoken by that dreadful sound? Perhaps that explained people's crankiness and bad attitude. She even wondered if she'd been cranky. Well, probably. Plus, she'd forgotten to do the mattress punching the previous night. She headed to the eating hall trusting that things were going to get better. Well, at least she had a friend.

Tray in hand, she was glad to see Kiki's face in the crowd. The girl didn't seem to see Saytera, though. Even as Saytera approached, Kiki was focused on her plate.

Saytera sat by her and said, "Hey." The girl didn't reply. "Are you all right?"

Silence. Someone else sat at the table.

Saytera insisted, "Kiki?"

The girl turned, face blank. "I'm sorry. Do I know you?"

It hit Saytera. And it hurt. The girl was ignoring her on purpose.

Saytera smiled. "Of course not. I got confused." She got up and went to the corner table, now her table, a nauseous, dark feeling in her stomach.

The panels on the wall and the lights in the hall went down. At least now it was clear that it wasn't Saytera's fault, and at least she was in a place with natural light. There was no panic this time. Probably just a faulty system. One faulty thing among so many. At least she could find refuge in the hangar. Stomach closed, she threw the food in a trash bin and left that hall.

On her way, she bumped into Kia. The woman said, "Your schedule changed. You'll take mechanics in the morning. Commander Santi is taking you in an apprenticeship."

Commander Santi? Mechanics?

"In the hangar," Kia added.

"Nick? " She was surprised that the old crazy man was some kind of teacher.

Kia nodded. "It'll be good for you. You're lucky. He doesn't usually take apprentices."

Lucky indeed. Incoherent rambling was better than a mocking class and an egocentric teacher. At least one little light. And she followed that light at the end of the hallway.

As she got there, Nick yelled, "What are you doing here?"

Perhaps he'd forgotten. "I'm your apprentice."

"So you want to learn? See that one there?" He pointed to a black ship. "Tell me what's wrong with it. I'll come and check on you before lunch."

Impressive teaching method. Plus, it was likely that he'd forget what he'd asked her to do by lunchtime. Still, she got on the ship and tried to imagine what it would be to fly it above the atmosphere, to see the stars from amongst them. Not something this thing would do.

Her thoughts turned to Kiki. Now that she considered it, her behavior wasn't strange at all. Yesterday she'd made sure they weren't seen together. Not only did Saytera not fit in there, she was some sort of undesirable company.

Saytera took a deep breath. This place didn't matter. She was a lot more important than any of those nitwits would ever be. She just had to find out how. If only her thoughts would clear in this immense loneliness.

Away from her island, her rituals, anything resembling nature, under artificial light, Saytera thought that punching a mattress was ridiculous. As she got ready to do it, alone in her room at night, she was disturbed by soft knocks on the door. Saytera opened. Kiki was there.

Saytera glared. "You're kidding, right?"

The girl walked past Saytera and closed the door.

Saytera protested, "Hey, I didn't invite you and I don't care if anyone sees you talking to me in the hallway."

"You're upset?"

"No. I'm delighted. What do you think?"

Kiki shrugged. "I told you. It'll take some time for people to get used to you. They used to mock me too. If they see me hanging out with you…"

Saytera opened the door. "Nothing to fear, then."

"I thought you wanted to train."

"I don't." And it was true. Something weird happened when she touched the pistols, but that obviously wasn't the main reason she didn't want to train.

Kiki shrugged. "Well, then, you won't improve. And if you keep that attitude, you won't have any friends."

"Who? The lovely people you're afraid will turn around and mock you? How's that working for you?"

Kiki walked to the door. "Pretty well. It's human nature, Saytera, we all crave belonging."

"You can pretend, Kiki. It doesn't mean you can belong where you don't belong."

"If you change your mind and decide to train, come to the training grounds in the evening."

"Why can't *your friends* train with you?"

She looked down. "They're lazy. I don't care. Less competition."

With that, she left. Saytera needed something soft and natural to punch and the perfect idea came to her mind: Kiki's face! Yansin's voice came to her mind. "Never release your anger on other people." She wondered if Yansin knew that people could be mean just for the fun of it and wondered how controlled her master would be in a place like that stupid academy. Thinking about Yansin calmed her down. This was temporary. Her heart always knotted when she remembered Nowla, though.

CHANGES

The second time should make things easier, except it didn't. Flying into Mainland's atmosphere while trying to stay away from its monitoring towers perhaps would never get easy. Still, Dess and Marcus were back with their cargo of water.

For the first time, he saw a ship belonging to other independent traders. A girl with pink pigtails was checking something outside a yellow T-45. That was a pretty good model. Dess walked towards her, Marcus by his side, and tapped softly on the hull.

The girl was startled, looked at him, and blushed.

"So you also go down to the planet?" Dess asked.

"Yes." Her voice was almost a whisper.

"I'm Dess." He extended his hand.

The girl shook his hand but was visibly nervous. "Sophie."

His friend also extended his hand. "Marcus."

The girl was an example of why you shouldn't judge people by their appearances, since she looked to be about fifteen, and seemed far too scared for someone who did something as dangerous as piloting among storms and potential enemy fire.

And perhaps Dess should have talked to other people doing this *before* venturing there blindly. In fact, Zizo should have introduced them or given some kind of training.

"How long have you been doing this?" Dess asked.

"Just a moment." The girl ran inside the ship.

He exchanged looks with Marcus. His friend was also puzzled by the girl.

After a while, a woman came out of the ship with Sophie. Plump and muscular, she was a stark contrast to the younger girl.

She stared at Dess, then turned to Sophie. "You weren't kidding. He *is* beautiful."

Dess controlled himself not to roll his eyes and had a half-smile. "Ain't I?"

The woman laughed. "Pure stardust in human form."

"Aren't we all?"

"Maybe. But we don't all look like you." She then changed her tone. "I'm Tara."

They introduced themselves again. Sophie was flushed and looked panicked.

"So," Dess started. "I see you've never been in the military academy. Where did you train?"

"There's a simulator in the orphanage."

"Oh." The orphanage. The place Dess could have gone. And it was just weird that his life had turned out different. If he hadn't worked hard in the military academy, perhaps he'd be at the same spot right now. "And did you find the simulator helpful?"

Tara snorted. "What do you think? It's a piece of crap. I think they want us killed."

"Maybe."

"Not maybe. Sure. The fewer good pilots the better for the competent ones. What about you? Looking all fancy and all. Don't tell me you're academy rejects?"

The way she said it was as if they belonged in some sewer.

Thankfully, Marcus was the one who replied, "We volunteered here."

Tara nodded. "Interesting. Your type usually stays in your little circle. But I guess there are exceptions."

"Listen," Dess wanted to get to the part that mattered. "You're obviously highly skilled and experienced." Stroking their egos couldn't hurt. "We're just starting out." Pretending humbleness didn't hurt either. "Do you have any advice for us?"

She sighed. "Get a strong shield. And pray to the star fire that you don't get shot more than you can stand."

Like a lot of people, she got the whole star fire thing completely wrong, but what she said was interesting. "So you do get shot?"

"Well, yeah. It happens."

"Any other tip?"

"Yes. The west part of Mainland is easier to fly. Start there. Don't always go to the same place, though, or you'll eventually be spotted."

Dess nodded. "Got it. Thanks so much."

They walked away from the woman. When they were out of their earshot, Marcus laughed. "Really, Dess? Ain't I?" He mocked Dess's voice.

Dess was surprised. "What? When did I say that?"

"The woman was saying you were beautiful."

He shrugged. "Wasn't it you who told me to accept compliments gracefully?"

Marcus laughed. "That was quite—" He paused and rolled his eyes. "—graceful."

"Yeah, while you're worried about my grace or lack of, remember that they probably wouldn't mind seeing us killed."

"Why do you say that?"

"They told us to go to the west part of the continent, and yet they go to the east."

Marcus smiled and shook his head. "To be fair, they told us to *start* there. Maybe they consider it advice for noobs, you know, and since they aren't noobs… And how do you know where they fly?"

He hadn't told Marcus that. "I got the reports from Zizo's station."

"Why?"

"Curiosity. Do you know how many teams are presently doing this other than us?"

"No idea."

"Just two. And maybe they don't want competition."

Marcus made a gesture with his hand as if dismissing Dess's idea. "You got that competitive mentality from the academy. This is different. You think a single ship could supply Saphirlune with water?"

"The way we save and reuse? Maybe." Another idea hit him. "We could do more than that, though."

"I bet we will, soon. I think you're right about the fish."

He stared at Marcus. "Wasn't it you who wanted to make a difference? Let's go after bigger fish."

Saytera's mornings varied between being left alone and listening to Nick's incoherent ramblings. There was something there, though, loss, blood, the insanity of war. It was as if he feared that his life would go to waste unless someone heard about it, unless someone learned its lessons. Saytera listened. It was much better than facing the other kids in the academy. In time, she learned to pick up her meals early and go back to the hangar, so that she could eat alone. She also got a data reader and instead of going to the history and theory classes, she read the material on her own. Kia was very accommodating and Saytera was thankful for that. She tried to find information on Terens but found nothing, as if they didn't exist.

Sitting by herself in her bedroom or in that black ship from the first day, all the events in her life revolved in her mind without reaching a spot where there was any meaning, any truth. That disconnection from the surrounding nature caused numbness. Then, sometimes, when she was alone, she moved a small object or tried to turn off the artificial light in her bedroom. It was very different from fire, she knew it, and yet she wanted to keep a piece of herself intact. The light sometimes flickered, but it was hard to know if it was something she'd done or just imagined. Another problem were the frequent electricity outages. How could she know she'd turned her own lamp off when all the complex suddenly became enveloped in darkness?

It felt like a lifetime since Dess had walked in Serra's office. Very ironic that they had assigned her to receive his request. Maybe it had been on purpose to piss him off. At least he'd convinced Marcus not to come, and if Dess by any chance did something stupid, at least his friend would be out of it.

Dess sat, leaned back, and put his feet on her table. Serra's eyes moved to his boots but she didn't say anything. Power. He was starting to understand that it had little to do with an insignia someone wore or a position someone had, but the fact that he could offer something nobody else could. Power was how much one could put on a negotiation table—not counting the boots, of course.

Perhaps he'd understood some of it when he'd spent hours and hours training and studying to be the best. The issue was that anyone could hold a high position in the high echelons of the government. No special skills were required. That made everyone replaceable.

Flying in and out of Mainland, though, that wasn't for everybody. The third team had already died and nobody had yet volunteered for their place. Meanwhile, Dess and Marcus had been successfully bringing water and fish for three months. But he knew he could do a lot more than that, and he knew he could make a difference. He wasn't going to waste a lifetime preparing to defend Sapphirlune.

Serra's voice was dry. "How can I help you, Mr. Starspark?"

Dess hated that name and one of the reasons was that it was a stupid name he'd invented when he was ten. Then, maybe, there was something neat about seeing these so-called important people saying that name with a straight face.

"The other way around, Commander Serra. I have a proposal for you."

"Really?" She had a smile that didn't reach her eyes. "Is that so?"

"The truce is going to be renegotiated in six months. I could help us get some leverage."

"Mr. Starspark, without access to confidential information you're in no position to know whether we have leverage or not. And I'm going to ask you not to put your feet on my desk."

Dess didn't move. "Right. What if I told you I can get you precise information of where all the Mainland shore bases are and how they operate?"

Serra rolled her eyes. "We know where they are. We do use information from private contractors like you to know where they're shooting from. Is that all?"

"No. I'm tired of bringing fish. I can bring intel. People who can be questioned, who can give us better information than just average locations without any clear data on weaponry and equipment. And who can be hostages, if we ever need the leverage."

She narrowed her eyes. "That would violate the truce."

"I violate the truce every three days, commander. Or rather, I don't, right? Since I have no connection to any governmental organization whatsoever, even if all the information about what we do goes to you. Anyway, if I were to bring people, it would be in the same capacity.

She raised her eyebrows. "Except for the part where they say we broke the truce."

"Indeed. And what are they going to do? Send their half dozen ships after us? Continue shooting us if we approach their planet?"

She twirled a pen in her hand. "Well, Mr. Starspark, if you do happen to bring some people and get some information, we won't mind. Is that it?"

"Of course not. My offer has a condition."

She leaned back and had a mocking smile, as if what he was saying were absurd. "A condition."

"The A-11 prototype, and I want Marcus to be reinstated in the army. At least in theory. He'd be operating undercover with me."

That was the other reason he'd insisted for his friend not to come.

Serra scoffed. "And you seem to think this is quite reasonable."

"Quite a humble request, indeed. Plus the usual payment, of course."

Serra leaned forward. "Perhaps I could tell you that we are going to think about your proposal and then get back to you, but I don't want to lie. Go back to your glorified fishing, Dess."

"I will."

Dess left the room feeling satisfied. He knew that Sapphirlune needed to act quickly if they were to negotiate better truce terms. Nothing like threatening Mainland in their own land to make them more malleable. Serra perhaps wouldn't even pass along his proposal, but it was fine. He could try to go through Sylvia's parents and even Marcus's father. Dess knew that his idea was good, that it would work, and that it would change the tide for his people. They'd obviously accept it. The matter was just when.

He headed back home. Dess now rented a new two-bedroom with Marcus. It wasn't the most luxurious thing, as Dess was saving. He wasn't sure for what, but he wanted to save. At least it had two bedrooms, which made Sylvia's visits a lot less awkward. Other than the fact that she and Marcus still only met in private and called each other friends, their relationship was going well. He was almost home when his personal key buzzed. The council leader wanted to see them. That was faster than even Dess had predicted.

Stealth and speed. And trust in the inner fire. Those were Dess's weapons. They had to bring three Mainland soldiers, and only then they'd gain full trust from the council. Dess had gotten the ship he wanted, though. Small, fast, and agile, it would make the task easier. Not only that. The A-11 had never been produced en masse because they couldn't see its value. His mother had designed it, almost as if she'd guessed that one day Lunars would need to hide on the planet. He named the ship Vera, and perhaps it wasn't that subtle, since his mother's name was Veronica, but nobody would know what he called his ship.

His mother. She'd survived the explosion. Long enough to give him her last words.

"Hide, Dess. Don't let them know who you are."

And so he'd been hiding, while replaying the events of that morning a thousand times in his head. His little sister had been crying, asking for her doll. Dess told them he'd just run in and out, and he did, but Anelise never got it, as she was blown up with the ship, in front of Dess's eyes. All these years he'd been wondering if his short trip inside was what killed his family. If it had all been his fault. Over and over he went back to these memories and didn't go back for the doll. His family flew away, alive.

"Are you all right?" Marcus's voice startled him.

This wasn't a time to be distracted, to dwell in the past, to try to find a way to change it. They were flying towards the Mainland Planet. He had to focus. Dess shook his head. "Lost in thought. Sorry."

The first time for everything was nerve wracking, and this was no different.

As they approached the planet, Marcus crossed his arms. "I don't know… when we were discussing it in our kitchen, it sounded so much easier."

"We haven't even landed."

"We could get killed or captured."

Dess shrugged. "Obviously. Do you want to quit?"

Marcus waved his hands. "Hey, can't we just talk about the difficulties without coming to conclusions?"

"It's not that. We could get killed, for sure. It's a fact."

"We could also get killed bringing squid or fish and water. This is just… a bit harder." Marcus took a deep breath. "That was what I was talking about."

"And you have a family and a girlfriend. You might not want to do that."

"Yeah, but if we get this right… at least maybe my father will stop giving me dirty looks."

A miracle that he hadn't argued the girlfriend point. But his comment about his father was odd. "I thought you hadn't seen each other for a while."

"Manner of speaking."

As usual, they approached the planet near enough the shore that they were far from storms and far enough from it that they were not in the line of fire. This ship moved underwater, and that was another reason he'd wanted it. Dess's plan was to wait for a light rain cloud strong enough to disguise them but not strong enough to smash them to pieces. Hidden by a storm he could fly inland and find sand dunes where they could hide.

The ship also had a camouflaging system, which should keep it hidden enough. From there, it was all about observing, finding a base, and waiting for an opportunity to get someone unaware. It would likely be easy in the beginning, when the bases were set up just to counter air attacks. On the other hand, he had no experience capturing people and was sure that it would be quite different from any training he had.

Maybe what he really wanted was to breathe the ocean breeze and this was an excuse. No. What he wanted was for his moon to win this stupid war, and he also wanted influence and power over the council. This was a way to achieve both.

Ship on the sand, Dess stepped out for the first time on real land. He took a deep breath. The air had the smell of the ocean, of trees, of life and so much more.

Marcus stood by the door. "Maybe we should take a vacation here."

"Well, we do have to find where the nearest base is."

Marcus smiled. "Are you sure?"

Dess turned and saw a red building with an observation tower and a clear anti-aerial cannon. "They aren't the most discreet, are they? It's as if they're saying 'bomb me'."

Marcus shrugged. "They probably don't think anyone could get close enough."

"We did." Dess sighed, wondering if he could perhaps change his strategy. No, that would be open war and quite stupid. He looked around him at that natural vastness and breathed the ocean air. "It's not right, you know. That they try to keep this for themselves only."

"It's selfishness. It's not just about the Tahari Moon."

That name always tugged Dess's heart. He wanted to change the subject. "I'll go there to check. Stay here."

Marcus was stepping out of the ship. "I'm coming with you."

Dess took a deep breath. He didn't like leaving Vera alone even if he knew it would be partly hidden. "I'll just check things, I'm not going to be at any risk. It's not like I'm carrying a sign saying I'm from Sapphirlune."

"You think you look like a fisherman?"

"Well, isn't that one of my jobs? Anyway, they probably get visitors from Citarella or something."

Marcus was already closing the door and activating the camouflage. The result wasn't perfect. In fact it was far from perfect and pretty obvious that it was there. Perhaps it was just because they knew there was a ship there and not just sand. Still, night was falling and should help hide it. As they walked towards the nearest bushes, Marcus diligently used the compressed air pistol to erase their footprints. Dess had the sleeping gas bombs, gas mask, zapper, cracker, and a chill in his stomach.

They walked through trees at the base of a hill. The air was cool and windy and Dess wished his jacket were a bit warmer. They climbed the hill and used their infrared binoculars to check the movement in the base. They were all inside, as Dess had predicted. One way to do this could be to throw a sleep gas bomb through the window, then enter the complex and get a person, but he didn't want to call attention to himself and what he was doing. The fewer people suspecting that Lunars were landing on the planet, the better. After many hours, he saw a sight that made him smile. Two people were patrolling. Dess descended and gestured for Marcus to follow him.

"I can take both," Marcus whispered.

Tasers didn't work at a long range, but they had a tranquilizer pistol. Marcus was a good shot.

"We'll do it at the same time," Dess said. "Take the tall one, and I'll take the shorter guy. Three, two, one."

Two darts wheezed through the night. Marcus got the tall guy's back. Dess's target moved and he got his arm.

The short guy yelled, "Hey." He then fell with another dart.

Dess turned to Marcus. "Thanks."

This wasn't exactly how Dess had predicted it to go. Ideally, they should have gotten just one person, but two wasn't the end of the world. "We'll pick up just one."

As they approached the fallen soldiers, Dess noticed that the shorter soldier was a girl.

Marcus pointed to the guy. "Let's take him."

"She's lighter."

"She reminds me of Sylvia."

Right. She had nothing to do with their friend except maybe the hair color and length.

"I'm brokenhearted, you know?" Dess whispered.

Marcus frowned. "Why?"

"Doesn't the guy remind you of me?"

"No eyeliner."

Dess rolled his eyes. They picked up the darts quickly and proceeded to carry the guy. Damn Marcus. Why did they have to carry such a heavy person? They were each carrying one side, and it was clumsy and slow, not to mention that he didn't know how they would erase their footprints once they reached the dunes if they had to use their hands to carry the guy.

When they were almost there, a siren blasted from the base. Of course. That was the reason it had to be one person only. If they found the girl unconscious, they'd know they had been attacked. So stupid. So much work for nothing. And to make matters worse, day was breaking.

Marcus turned to him. "Let's leave him and run."

That would be the appropriate solution, but Dess didn't want to waste all their effort. "Go first and get the ship ready."

Dess slung the soldier over his soldier and almost collapsed. He had physical training in the academy, but not any kind of weight lifting.

Marcus frowned. "You can't…"

"Go."

Marcus set off on a dash. Dess tried to run. Was he being stupid? He then had a better idea. He lay the unconscious soldier on the floor, ran back, and threw a smoke bomb in the opposite direction from where they were. It would have little to no effect out in the open, but maybe it could distract the Mainland soldiers. He got back to his charge. This time he seemed even heavier. Dess moved as fast as he could to his ship, hoping Marcus had gotten it ready, but all he saw was his friend moving back and forth. Dess reached him. "What's wrong?"

"I can't find it."

"Press your control. It will light up."

"Indeed." Marcus pressed the button. "Where?"

The sand disguise ended up being too good, and the sun was coming up, so they couldn't see a faint light. Dess looked around and saw no sign of Vera anywhere.

GOODBYE

Dess tried to think. One solution would be to hide, then wait for when things were calmer to find Vera. But lots of things could go wrong. Dess put the soldier on the sand and tried to recall the moment when he stepped out of the ship and looked around, and recall the angle everything was. "That way."

It looked wrong, as it was too flat, and the ship had been on a little hill when they'd left. This time Dess dragged the soldier over the sand, carrying him by his arms. It required a lot less effort. Marcus erased their footprints as fast as he could, or at least the footprints from a certain point. Vera was indeed in that flat area, and Dess finally saw through its imperfect disguise.

When they got in, Dess's arms were shaking from the effort. All he did was fly low then hide underwater. They had to wait for some heavy clouds to disguise their escape and give the soldiers in the base time to get tired and not so much on alert. He put the soldier on the back, on a chair specially made for prisoners. Next time they'd better have two chairs, just in case, and they had to prepare a lot better. Still, despite all the mistakes, they had their prisoner.

~

Even isolated in her room and the hangar, Saytera noticed that there was something different in the energy of the other students that morning. She got her breakfast and ran to ask Nick.

She rarely approached him, but this time she found him sitting by an old TT. "Is there anything special today?"

He was startled and yelled, "What are you doing here?"

Funny. Saytera thought he'd changed his "good morning" routine. Apparently not. "What's happening in the academy?" she insisted.

He waved a hand. "Same. Different. Same. Nothing. You stay here and they won't find you. And they postpone. I think they'll postpone. Still, you're safe. These kids, though, they think it's funny to fight a war, they want to go to Citarella, fancy places, they think it's fancy, until it starts for real."

"What do you mean Citarella?"

"Or someplace else. Today some of the cadets leave. They leave happy, proud, smiles on their faces. Let's see how long they last."

Leave. That was promising. Saytera thanked him and ran to the eating hall, where a man she'd never seen before was talking.

"...this gives a chance to strengthen our defenses and pressure Sapphirlune some more. They are blocked, and they can't come down. They'll have to declare defeat."

The truce. The truce would be renewed, or canceled, in three months. There was something unpleasant about what the man said, almost as if they were expecting something to happen. Mainland had been extending this truce for five years now, and yet nothing had changed. There was the fear that this war would never stop. But then there was the fear that war would start—for real. The man changed the topic then, talking about the students.

"Your value, your skills, and your dedication will determine your future."

Future. Right. Nobody would remain here forever. This was just preparation for the real thing, or almost real, if the truce kept being renewed. This man was showing them a way out of this academy.

The man then was going on and on about honor and dedication. "The elite guard takes very few from isolated ground troop academies, like this, but it doesn't mean you don't have a chance. There are also the shore bases. Being a sentinel is honorable, too."

There would be a test in the training room, the place Kiki went in the evening. At least one person there had good chances.

Saytera walked back to the hangar. It didn't matter that she had no chance of going anywhere. Perhaps she should just sit tight and wait for Yansin. But then, waiting and learning very little wasn't taking her anywhere. She wished she could leave, go somewhere else. Instead, she would probably be stuck in that place for a long time. That was a dark thought. The lights in the hallway went down. The electricity outages were a rather common occurrence now and nobody panicked anymore. It probably looked bad for the academy when they had the recruiting team inspecting its cadets. Their fault for not fixing it.

Reading didn't help Saytera quiet her mind. She wanted to

go back and watch the tests, see what they were like, who had been chosen, but then she remembered how she didn't belong in any of that. At dinner time, she went to the line when the bell rang instead of passing by earlier and getting her food from the back. The mood was different, as if a cloud had settled there.

Kiki sat by a table and looked down, disappointed. Saytera felt vindicated. No, not really. She knew how hard the girl had worked and hoped she'd get the deserved recognition. In a way, she'd been the only one who'd at least tried to be nice to Saytera. Could have tried a little harder.

When Saytera went to her room, she was surprised to find someone there. The blond girl—her roommate, who had never set foot in that room other than on the first night. She was sitting on the floor and crying, then raised her eyes when Saytera saw her. "Oh. You."

It was Saytera's room, but she felt bad for the girl. "I can leave you alone if you want."

The girl got up. "It's fine. It's your bedroom. I shouldn't even be here. I just came to..." Her sobbing was loud now. "I won't bother you anymore. Again. Ever."

Saytera stood in front of her and took her hands. "Do you want to talk?"

The girl collapsed on Saytera's shoulder, which quickly got wet with her tears. That was awkward. Here was a girl whose name Saytera didn't even know—despite having lived in the same complex for months—resting her face on her shoulder. But crying was good. Saytera knew it. It washed away the pain. It was just something that she didn't particularly like.

The girl seemed to realize how odd that was, then stepped back and dried her eyes with the back of her hand. "Sorry."

"It's fine."

"I didn't want them to see me crying."

"I understand. Do you want to tell me what's happening?"

The girl snorted. "I was selected. Remote shore base. Middle of nowhere. I know that they just ditch recruits there, don't even give them any support, nothing. It's going to be the end of my life, the end of everything. No chance of ever getting a promotion, plus the risk of being killed for nothing."

A word kept ringing in Saytera's mind. A hope. A glimmer of her long lost home. "Shore. You mean by the ocean?"

She gestured frantically. "Exactly. The ocean. Where they'll attack us from."

"Is there any way someone else could go there?"

"I placed fourth-to-last among the qualified cadets." The girl shook her head. "A stupid mistake. I'm not that bad."

An idea was reaching Saytera's mind. "Could someone…" She paused and took a breath. "Volunteer to take your place?"

She shrugged. "I guess. "

Saytera perked. "Is there any criteria? Let's say, if the worst qualified cadet wanted to take your place, could they go?"

"As long as they're over sixteen, yes. Do you happen to know any wacko who would be willing to go nowhere?"

It was like a wave washing away all her troubles. "I do. Very well."

This was Dess and Marcus' fourth kidnapping mission. It never got any easier. They'd spent days trying to locate a base. Then they had to find a safe place to land. The worst part was immobilizing and bringing the Mainland soldiers. Yes, they were enemies and wouldn't hesitate to blow them to pieces, and still… They were so young. It was just by fate that they had been born on the planet. They could well have been their colleagues in the academy had life been different. And yet, it wasn't. If Dess wanted to end this war, end the need to send teens to blow up ships with other teens, he had to do something. Perhaps it was a lot to take on his own, but then, it was something that few people could do.

As they submerged in the water, Marcus let out a sigh.

"What?" Dess asked.

"I don't know, I thought we'd get shot or something." Marcus was edgier than usual.

Dess felt odd too, but perhaps it was just his friend influencing him. "We have a shield. There's something I haven't told you yet, do you know what Sophie and Tara do?"

"No idea."

"Check it out: when they get shot they turn off the anti-gravity."

Marcus paused for a moment. "So they fall."

"They turn it on again when they are low, near the water, but whoever shot them thinks they fell."

"Quite risky. I mean, depending on the velocity they reach in the fall, they won't be able to avoid impact." He frowned. "How did you find that out?"

Dess smiled. "I checked their flight reports."

"Why?"

Dess shrugged. "I wanted to know what they do."

"Yeah, still sounds weird to me, though. Just turning the anti-gravity again is not going to slow the descent enough."

To be fair, Dess also thought it was weird. "It's been working for them. Maybe they have amazing thrusters, and they probably turn them on, too."

They were underwater now, waiting for an opportunity to come out. There were no dunes near this base, and this was the first time Dess would try to leave the ship by a forest. Perhaps this was what was bothering him. Perhaps it had been the latest mission, when the soldier had awoken on the back and kept banging and screaming to them. Dess had quickly tazed him, but the memory still left a bitter taste in his mouth.

They left the ship by a lake. The sun was just about to rise. They'd found that the early morning was the best time to slip in and out of the planet. In theory, Mainlanders should keep watch twenty-four hours, but in practice, they were likely late sleepers. Dess didn't know until how long, though. The communication on Mainland was encrypted and hard to reach, and it didn't seem like they were on alert against intruders. But once that happened, Dess's luck would probably change. So far it had been fairly good, though.

His apprehension proved to be pointless when, from the forest, he saw a young man walking on the beach alone, wearing the unmistakable red Mainland uniform. Alone, unarmed, unaware. Everything they needed.

Marcus and Dess shared a look, then Dess's friend made his way to the beach and shot the young man. Thankfully it was a guy, or else his friend would start with the "reminds me of Sylvia" nonsense. They now had a type of stretcher with small wheels to drag their victims. Victims. What a thought. It almost made Dess feel like a criminal. But then, nobody was getting hurt, and the people in Sapphirlune were starving and could potentially have even bigger problems if Mainland strengthened its defenses against private contractors like Dess and Marcus or Tara and Sophie.

A loud bang interrupted his thoughts. It was coming from the forest, from the opposite side of the beach. In less than one second, Dess saw blood on Marcus's arm, took his own zapper, and shot back in the direction where the sound had come from, where he saw a red shape moving. He ran in that direction and found a Mainland soldier lying on the ground. Dess's vision went blurry and he almost fell when he noticed the black mark and a whole in the young man's chest, then his unfocused, glassy eyes. Dead. It was as if time stopped, slowed down, and an abyss opened beneath him. Dead. He'd been trained to kill, and yet, it was as if a bit of his own fire had dimmed together with the one he'd quenched. But this was no time to mourn. He looked up, searching for other enemies. Nobody yet, but the sound would attract attention. The dead young man had a cracker pistol. Made to kill. This was a reminder that they weren't joking. Dess ran back towards Marcus.

He was holding his wound and asked, "What happened?"

"Let's leave this one. I… *injured* the other." The true word wouldn't come out of his mouth. "Are you hurt?"

"Just a scratch. Let's take both. Or they'll have evidence."

Dess sighed. "True."

There was a dark hole where Dess's heart should be. He dragged the fallen soldier's body and put him on top of the unconscious one.

Marcus stared at him. "He's—"

"I know!" He yelled. That was stupid. "We need to take him."

The journey back to Vera took forever as Dess dragged the stretcher on his own. He didn't feel the extra effort, taken by a feeling of numbness.

Vera. What would Dess's mother think about him? Think about this? But then with the memory of his mother came the memory of running back to the shuttle, Anise's doll in hand, to be greeted with a loud boom and an explosion.

"Dess, Dess!"

Marcus was calling him. He'd been frozen, staring at the ship.

"Hey," his friend continued. "He could have killed me. They would have shot our ship without even blinking. It happens."

Dess nodded. He knew all that. And yet, the feeling…

It was a sad flight away from that base, then up above the storm clouds, from where they threw the body. That felt wrong, too. So many wrong things. He was trying to fix them. At that moment, though, it just felt that he was making everything worse.

Kia shook her head. "It's a no, Saytera."

She closed her eyes and decided to be honest. "I can't stand it here. Everyone hates me—"

"They don't hate you. You just have to give these kids a chance. Plus, you might be assigned a better place next year, once you learn more about mechanics."

Saytera almost replied that she wasn't learning that much, having to figure out everything by herself, but she didn't want to out Nick.

The woman added, "And it's dangerous for you. I know you're not good with pistols. How do you intend to survive out there? Things are not as calm as they seem. I need you to be safe."

Safe. Kept safe. She looked right into the woman's eyes. "Who do you answer to?"

"My superiors." Kia narrowed her eyes. "What kind of question is that?"

"I mean about me." How silly that only now Saytera considered that. "What was in that information stick I gave you?"

"I thought you knew." Kia sighed.

"I don't. I was separated from my family, from everything. I need to know if someone will come back for me. I need to know what's happening."

The woman nodded. "I understand. I understand you want to know more, but I can't help you. I received an anonymous communication, together with a large deposit. I was to receive you, a girl with mismatched eyes. If you were safe at the end of one year, I'd receive another deposit again."

Saytera wondered if it had been Yansin or even Carla, the woman who'd helped her. She never thought Yansin could have access to money, but perhaps she had been wrong.

She had to try to convince Kia. "Fine. They said I had to be safe, they didn't say I had to be here. If it's a remote base, I'll be even more hidden, even safer."

The woman shook her head. "If the Lunars attack, the shore bases are our first line of defense. It means they'll be the first to fall."

"Except that there's a truce. And those bases have powerful anti-aerial cannons, don't they?"

The woman sighed. "Some people have disappeared from these bases, Saytera. Some of it might be desertion, then some of it… Many things. There are sea creatures, too."

"I grew up by the beach. I know how to deal with them."

The woman had a smirk, as if Saytera's words were funny.

Saytera had an idea to convince Kia. If she could make the woman understand how she was different, how she faced unique threats… "I have a secret to tell you. Watch."

The woman's desk had many objects; a datapad, a pointer, an old pen. This had to work. Saytera closed her eyes and focused on the pen. She imagined it floating slowly. Saytera's levitating skills were terrible, and without much practice, without time to focus, she wasn't sure she would achieve it. A loud crashing sound startled her. Saytera opened her eyes to see the glasses in the office cracked. The light was down, too, illumination coming from a tiny window by the ceiling.

Saytera's heart sank. "I'm sorry. I—"

What she'd wanted was to tell her that she had Terens after her, that they could put Kia and all the academy in danger, but the furious look on the woman's face prevented her from doing so.

"What are you?" the woman asked, her voice trembling.

Saytera looked down. "In my... village... we practiced this stuff."

"How, how did you do that?" The woman looked incredulous and maybe scared.

"It wasn't on purpose!" Saytera pleaded. "And I didn't mean to—"

"I'll set everything up for you to take Tamara's place. Now go."

Saytera got up. She should be happy that she got what she wanted, but she felt empty instead. Somehow, having Kia look at her that way reminded her of the disappointment Yansin must have felt.

It all felt so strange and lonely. In her current life, the only person who liked her was half crazy. Maybe that said something about herself. But then, starting tomorrow, she'd have a second chance.

The sun had barely risen when Saytera got on the back of a truck. Few familiar faces. Kiki noticed Saytera but then looked away. Tamara held another girl's hand and grinned at Saytera, who smiled back. Both were happy. Tamara didn't seem bad.

Why hadn't Saytera ever taken the time to get to know the other cadets? She glanced at Kiki. Perhaps that was the answer. The girl's rejection had been such a blow. Saytera wasn't sure if she'd handled the situation well. Were isolation and loneliness better than tolerating rude people? Once, she'd have said yes. Now, she wasn't so sure. It didn't matter anymore except as a lesson learned. They could all be idiots in this base she was going. And this time, she'd have to stay there for a long time, perhaps forever. She sighed.

The truck stopped at a small port, from where she embarked on a shuttle. At least now she'd be by the ocean. It wouldn't be Storm Islands, but at least she'd be connected with nature again, maybe she could be herself again.

Dess's hollow chest didn't prevent him from feeling the odd energy in the port. He'd told Marcus to leave while he checked Vera and remained in the port. But he had an odd feeling.

Zizo was on his desk and he walked there. "Something happening?"

The old man shrugged while tapping on his screen. "Not much, not much. Nothing unusual."

"What kind of not-unusual thing?"

"We just..." He closed his eyes. "Haven't heard any news from Sophie and Tara."

Dess was taken aback. "Are they alive?"

The man's eyes were back on his screen. "It seems so, but they are far away from the continent, maybe trapped in a storm or something."

Dess didn't really like those girls, but still... "We have to rescue them."

Zizo shook his head. "We'd risk losing another team. It's too dangerous. If the storms stop, you can try, otherwise we have to hope they make it."

"Hope they make it? Hope they make it? Is that all you do? Why haven't we had any training, any guidance, nothing? You're sending us there to die!"

"I'm following orders, boy. You have a problem, take it to the council."

"Yeah, that's what I'll do."

13

—————

FIREWATER

Saytera's heart was pounding as she walked to the isolated red building. Was it excitement that she could see the ocean? Or was she nervous to be—again—getting to a new place on her own? She carried no luggage, no bag. She'd come to Academy 7 with nothing, and had left with nothing but the dreadful grey clothes she'd worn on arriving there. Nobody had come to greet her. The shuttle pilots were a young man and a woman. They had waited a bit, but eventually had to leave.

Saytera almost asked to go back with the pilots, fearing maybe the base was abandoned or had been attacked. If that were the case, how long would it take until anyone realized it? She knocked on the door a few more times and had no answer, then decided to walk around the building.

Emotion swelled up in her chest. The ocean here looked green rather than grey, and she stood on top of a gigantic cliff, watching waves crashing on the bottom on rocks and a long, sandy beach. So much beauty and power, and at that moment she had no doubt she'd made the right decision. The place was brimming with energy, and she could feel it flowing through her, the same fire in her and in the nature around her. She sat down, feeling the softness of the grass, hearing the lovely sound of the ocean.

"Hey!" a voice called her.

Saytera turned. A young man in a red jumpsuit was walking in her direction. He had messy brown hair and hazel eyes.

She extended her hand. "I'm Saytera, the new recruit."

His eyes widened. "Oh. Right." He smiled. "I'm Kay. Welcome to the end of the world." He stared in her eyes.

"Yeah, they're mismatched."

Kay cocked his head and had a cute dimpled smile. "I think they match you."

Saytera didn't know what to say, so she pointed to the ocean. "This place is beautiful."

"It's amazing. We're on the tip of a peninsula. Quite isolated, as you see. Come."

He walked back to the building and opened the door she had knocked on earlier just by turning its handle.

"You don't lock it?"

"There are people inside. And nobody comes here anyway."

Saytera nodded. "I see."

He led her to a winding staircase in the middle of the building and they climbed it. They came to a top room with controls and a window facing the ocean. A guy and a girl were kissing on a couch.

"Hey," Kay yelled.

The two teenagers turned.

"Manners," Kay said. "This is our new teammate. Saytera."

The two waved. Saytera waved back. Kay pointed to the girl. "That's Nara. She's our fierce crab catcher."

The girl was a petite blonde with green eyes. "He's kidding."

"That," Kay pointed, "Is Saulo, our charmer. He's also our best cook."

He had brown hair and blue eyes. Saulo laughed and said, "Welcome to paradise!"

Kay got out and closed the door, then said softly. "These two will spend the whole day like that if we let them." He descended one floor. "You'll share a room with Larissa. She's grumpy and doesn't like me." He pointed to a door. "It's here."

The room had a window overlooking the ocean, and two beds, but nothing in it was clinical, cold, like in the academy. The beds were made of wood and they had colored quilts over them. There were two wooden chests and small bedside tables. It all looked lovely and warmed her heart.

Kay looked at her hands. "Where are your things?"

"I… didn't bring anything."

"Wow, that's freedom!"

Saytera shrugged. "Maybe."

"Well, Larissa will give you your uniform. I'll show you our weapons. There are always vultures and crabs, sometimes spiders. Some sea serpents sometimes come to the beach. You can never leave unarmed."

Saytera's insides got cold, but she nodded. "Sure." She noticed he wore a belt with two pistols, but had another question. "And do we have to wear the uniforms?"

"Yeah, the eternal debate. I know, right? Red. It's like saying 'shoot me'. The idea is that if something happens our forces can identify us more easily. It also helps the villagers see that they're protected."

"Is there a village nearby?"

Kay laughed. "One hour from here. I know. Nobody will see. Still, Commander Stone said he'd leave us without supplies if he saw even one of us without uniforms. Not that they give us much, mind you. Still, we get used to them. Plus, not sure you noticed it, but there are no clothing stores around here."

"True." Especially in Saytera's case, who hadn't brought anything. She was also trying to understand the hierarchy of the place. "So this Commander Stone is the one in charge."

"In theory. He supervises four bases. Rarely comes here. We're on our own. We had a supervisor, but she left."

"I thought nobody could leave."

Kay waved a hand. "Nonsense. You can be transferred if you know who to ask and how to ask."

"They said at the academy—"

"That this was a life sentence? I know. I wonder if they spread those rumors to avoid everyone coming here. You know, nothing to do, no supervision. We call it paradise."

Saytera smiled. "Looks like it."

"The tricky thing is just getting our food. Other than that, we're free."

"We also need to supervise the anti-aerial-cannon, right?"

"Yeah... sort of. It's kind of automatic. Larissa will explain it all to you." He smiled and held her hands. "I'm glad you're here."

His smile was really nice with his cute dimples. Saytera felt relieved to be in the same base as someone friendly—not to mention good looking. Not that she was thinking anything. Maybe. Probably. Hopefully.

A girl's voice interrupted them. "Kay, calm down, will you? She just got here." A tall girl with thick curly black hair approached them. "I'm Larissa. Come. I'll show you the bedroom."

She pulled Saytera by the hand and closed the door.

"Okay, so there's only one rule here: stay away from Kay."

Weird. "Oh. That. I... He was just showing me the place."

Larissa shook her head. "He's a flirt and a heartbreaker. We lost two sentinels. Two. They left. And I don't want to lose you too."

"Well…" Saytera didn't know what to say. The guy was cute and all, but she hadn't thought of any of that. Finally, she smiled and said, "Thanks."

Larissa shrugged. "Well, yeah. I try. The last one got angry. She thought I was jealous or something. Frankly, he's not even my type. Anyway. Watch out for Kay." She then looked at Saytera up and down. "You need your uniforms, right?"

They came to the hallway and Larissa pulled a package from a drawer. "It's here. Two jumpsuits, one set for sleeping, one coat, a raincoat, some underwear, black boots. If anything happens to them, there are sewing supplies in the armor room, downstairs. You'll only get new ones in a year, so be careful with them."

Saytera opened the package. The jumpsuit had no sleeves and was made of an ever thicker material than the jumpsuit in the academy. Saytera had promised herself she'd be different this time, but the prospect of wearing that thing forever made her stomach churn.

Larissa thankfully didn't notice Saytera's hesitation and said, "Let's go downstairs."

They went to the ground floor, where the girl opened a sliding door. Behind it, there were some twenty different pistols. "Whenever you leave, take these with you." She handed Saytera a belt, then one pistol. "This is a zapper." She handed her another pistol. "This is a cracker. Use it wisely because our supplies are limited. But the other ones don't work well against crabs."

Saytera nodded. She wasn't going to tell her that she and

pistols didn't get along very well. Hopefully she'd never need to use one.

"Go get in your uniform, then you can rest or walk around today. We don't have a lot of stuff to do here, but we share the duties. I'll set up your personal comm. Any questions?"

"No. I'm fine. I'll ask them as they come."

Saytera went to the bedroom and got out of her old clothes. In a way, it was good to get rid of them, as they brought her painful memories of Nowla, Vivian, and the life she'd left behind. Better not to dwell on that.

At least the uniform wasn't dull and grey, and she was happy to get in bright colors again. The main issue was having her legs constrained, tied. Perhaps she should have gotten used to it.

Saytera looked out the window at the magnificent view. She had no clue what her destiny was, no idea if Yansin or any islander would ever come back to her, and no idea why some people wanted her dead and others wanted her alive. Maybe she would never know. Maybe she should stop trying to know. And she had to stop blaming herself for Nowla. She sighed.

Here she was safe and isolated, and here she could start a new life. No more waiting, wondering, letting her life pass by. She was going to find a way to be happy and start over. Her life was here now. Here now. Maybe forever. She'd better find a way to get comfortable.

Saytera ran downstairs and found Larissa walking out the door. "Wait."

"Yes?" the girl asked.

"Can you show me the sewing supplies?"

Adjusting the jumpsuit had been quicker than Saytera had

predicted. She put it on, glad to have some freedom on her legs. She left the bedroom and went downstairs to ask Larissa more questions.

Larissa nodded when she saw her, then stopped. "What happened to the pants?"

"I just turned the bottom into a skirt. Pants suffocate my… uh, yeah, they're suffocating and bothersome."

The girl was still staring.

Saytera shrugged. "The rules state we need to wear these things. They also state we can adjust them. There. And I'm happy now."

Larissa shook her head. "The worst that can happen is we won't have ammunition for a week if Commander Stone sees you and doesn't like it, but I guess we'll survive."

"Well, I hate pants and I'm not gonna spend the rest of my life wearing them. We're in the middle of nowhere anyway."

Larissa snorted. "I guess." Then she lowered her voice. "I hope you're not doing this to impress Kay."

Saytera exhaled. "Right. I base my life decisions on what guys think of me." Perhaps Larissa was jealous. "Plus, I'm not going to fight for a guy. You can have him."

"Not my type!" she protested. "I'm just watching out for you."

Five Days. That was how long Dess would need to wait to speak with Leader Aziz. Meanwhile, people were dying and they were the only team left going to Mainland. It probably meant they'd need to go back to collecting water and fish again.

Dess looked outside his window at Sapphirlune city, now illuminated by their system star, days and days without night.

Marcus put his hand on his shoulder. "Hey, it happens. It happens. It's a war. They're soldiers."

"Sophie and Tara weren't soldiers."

Marcus sighed. "They knew they were doing something dangerous. It had been their choice."

"Choice? Against what? Working in the mines?"

"Dess, you can't change the world. I mean, maybe a little. If we want to change things we have to win this war, and we're helping, aren't we? Who knows, it might make a difference a month from now, when they renegotiate the truce."

Dess closed his eyes. "I know."

Their bell rang. Marcus went to the door. Dess was about to go to his room when he noticed that it wasn't only Sylvia, but Sylvia and Nadia, leader Aziz's daughter. She was also the daughter of Mr. Tarell, the current head of Staralloy—the company that used to belong to Dess's parents. It was annoying to have her in his home. The girls sat at a table in the kitchen and Dess ignored them.

He walked to Marcus. "Can I have a word?"

They entered Dess's bedroom.

"What's she doing here?" Dess asked.

"She's Sylvia's friend."

"Great. Now we're going to host parties. I mean, it's my apartment as well. I could at least have been warned."

Marcus shook his head. "I didn't know she was coming. What am I going to do? Kick her out?"

Dess shrugged. "You three can go somewhere else, perhaps."

"You know Sylvia and I can't—"

"Be seen in public. Yeah, I get it. You have no problem with that, good for you. I have a problem with that. I don't want visitors who'll pretend they don't know me."

"She's the leader's daughter, Dess. Seriously, you should just relax. Maybe she can help us."

"You don't get it, do you? What if she's interested? I say no; I'm screwed. I say yes; I'm screwed."

Marcus rolled his eyes. "In what world is the second possibility something bad?"

"Her mother."

"Chill. Maybe she was just bored and wanted to go somewhere with her friend. The world doesn't revolve around you. And maybe this is your chance to get an audience with leader Aziz"

Dess didn't like it. The timing was too convenient. Sill, he decided to go to the kitchen. Sylvia had brought a bottle of firewater.

Dess sat down. "Celebrating? Two of our colleagues died today. Fun, right?"

Marcus glared at him.

Nadia said, "I'm so sorry, Dess, so sorry for your colleagues."

"Sorry for me, right? Our moon didn't lose shit. They'll just replace them."

The two girls looked at each other.

Sylvia said, "It was something we wanted to talk to you about. We don't like the way things are done either."

Dess nodded. "Indeed. And it's super sad, right? Cause it's not like you two have access to anyone in command, or can even talk to the council leader."

Nadia stared at him. "I want to talk to my mother, but I need to know what to say. That's one reason I'm here."

"Well, ask her to give me an audience earlier. It's not like we can wait forever. We need to train people to go there. Decently."

Nadia nodded. "Yes, and you could do it, right?"

He hadn't been thinking of taking charge of the training in person, but it wasn't a terrible idea. "I guess."

"It could be a way to restore your position. We could give you the leadership of that branch."

Dess glanced at Marcus. "You mean us both."

Nadia had a half-smile. "Sure."

Dess got up. "Great, then. I'll be waiting."

"Hey," Marcus said. "Have a drink at least."

"Let's go out, then, or else I think I'll fall asleep." It was his way to hint at Sylvia's ridiculous shame of his friend. They were silent.

He turned to go back to his bedroom but someone pulled his hand. Nadia.

"Where do you want to go?" She leaned in and whispered, "We can have drinks in public, if you want."

Dess glanced at his friend, then whispered back, "They are the ones who should be doing that."

"That's their problem. Don't you want me to talk to my mother? We could discuss it."

That was true. "All right."

They left their apartment and walked toward the residential high rises.

Nadia turned to him. "So that's all you want? Train people who go down to the planet?"

He felt uneasy talking to her as if she were her friend, but he had to remember who her parents were. "Well, we could also maybe try to get into some of those bases and find out how to crack their code, their signals. We could disable their defenses. I've seen their security. It's almost nonexistent. I can get information from their terminals."

She sighed. "I'm not sure we have the resources to attack them and win yet. The shore isn't that hard, if we find a way to disable their cannons, but getting into the continent and to Citarella would be very difficult. "

"I think the more information we have, the better. We could even establish a permanent base on the planet."

She shook her head. "That would so break the truce."

Dess shrugged. "Maybe. Either way, at least we need to train people who go down there. And get more information."

"That I agree with. But it needs to be well coordinated. That's why you need to be in a position where you'll sit at the council table, you know?"

Dess laughed. "I don't think even your mother has the power to pluck me from where I am and make me a counselor or even assistant counselor, without going to command training."

She looked in his eyes. "It's all a matter of planning, Dess. And command is not out of the question, either. You know I think you deserve it."

Alarm bells were ringing in his mind. "Why?"

Nadia rolled her eyes. "I want the best for Sapphirlune, too. And I believe in you."

"That's flattering." Dess wasn't sure if he was taking the compliment graciously. He asked, "So you'll get me an audience?"

"Sure. And I'll talk to her, too."

Something was still odd in all this. Too easy, too… He decided to ask the question that had been bothering him. "Why do you believe in me?"

"We trained together, Dess."

They stopped in front of a high rise.

He looked at her. "Where are we going?"

"Didn't you want to be seen in public with me? Well, it's a party."

He followed her to the elevator. He wasn't sure if he should tell her to turn around and go somewhere else, but then, he had been the one complaining about being seen in public. But that was mostly about Sylvia and Marcus.

Dess said, "You could have told me it was a party."

"I thought that was what you wanted."

He shrugged. The elevator doors opened, and Dess froze at the sight of so many ex-colleagues from the academy. A world that he hadn't been a part of for months.

Nadia had a big smile as they walked in and greeted people.

Someone asked Dess, "So, what have you been doing these months? You disappeared."

Nadia answered before he could reply, "It's classified, sorry."

Dess wasn't supposed to tell anyone what he did, but he thought that the way she'd said it was too on the nose. Whatever, she probably knew what she was doing.

All those people still made him uncomfortable when he remembered the day he'd learned he hadn't been chosen for command. Most of them were now just initiate soldiers, but it didn't look like much had changed. His discomfort in parties hadn't changed either. To make matters worse, she held his hand. Dess didn't want to push her, especially when all eyes were on them.

He whispered to her, "Do you want to stay here long?"

A guy bumped into him. Dess hated that. "I... don't like crowds." He took the chance to pull his hand.

· · ·

They were silent in the elevator. Awkward silence. He didn't like being alone with her either.

When they were outside, she asked, "Is that why you were always grumpy in our parties?"

"I didn't know I was grumpy."

She shrugged. "Now you know."

"Thanks for the information."

She shook her head. "But you're not like that, right? It's not that you don't like people, it's just that you're quiet."

"I am quiet."

"I like it."

Dess wasn't sure what she meant. "Can I walk you home?"

"It's early."

"I leave for Mainland tomorrow, Nadia."

"Aren't you going to stay here and train people?"

Dess laughed. "Is your mother that fast?"

"I am fast. You'll get what you want, Dess." She touched his hair.

He wanted to push her hand away but he didn't want to offend her. "Nice. Listen, I'm tired. I'll walk you home."

"Not without Sylvia. We were going to go back together."

"She knows the way, you know?"

Nadia laughed. "Oh, yeah. Memorized by heart. We still said we'd go home together."

Dess sighed. What annoyed him was that she knew she could get him to do whatever he wanted, so he didn't have a choice. He was just confused as to what exactly she wanted.

When they got to his place Sylvia was still in the bedroom with Marcus, which was not surprising.

Nadia sat at the kitchen table. "Can I have some firewater while we wait?"

Dess poured two glasses. He still felt uneasy with her. One wrong step and who knows what her mother would do to him.

"They might take a while. Are you sure you want to wait?"

Nadia stared at him. "Dess, are you kicking me out of your house?"

"Of course not."

She stared straight into his eyes, as if daring him. "You can say so if that's the case."

Dess took a long sip. "It's not the case."

She looked around. "So what happens now?"

He sighed. Maybe he was imagining things, maybe he wasn't, maybe she'd be angry, but he had to say it, "I think you're really nice, Nadia. I don't want to hurt you."

She scoffed. "Wow. Nice. And tell me, how do you think you're going to hurt me?"

Dess took another sip. Unlike her, he didn't think what he had said was funny. She was making things difficult. "I don't think that's the case, but in case that's the case, I mean…"

"Spit it out."

How could he even say it? He leaned back and took a deep breath. "I'm not… in a stage in my life where I can be, uh, romantically involved. Not that I think—"

"I want to marry you?" She rolled her eyes. "Please. Why the drama, Dess?"

"I'm just saying."

Nadia got up and sat on his lap. "I'm not a delicate flower."

Was it her smell, her touch, her feel? Dess wasn't sure. Maybe it was the firewater numbing his reason. He was kissing her. And it felt good. Soft lips and the feel of her tongue against his. It was wrong. It wasn't romantic, it wasn't deep. At first he wanted it to stop, and then he didn't want to stop.

Yes, his body was stardust. But wasn't everyone else's as well? Including Nadia's? Born from the same fire. Stars in the universe, stars within. And what if they mingled their stars? Was there anything wrong with that? Meaningless. Did everything have to have a meaning, a reason?

14

CLIFFBOUND

The storms in Cliffbound were no joke. Sometimes Saytera thought the base was going to be ripped from the earth and thrown on the hills, but it was just an impression. After two months, she still had the same impression. A little silly that her home had been called Storm Islands, when the storms had no comparison to the ones here.

When the weather was calm, it was usually very warm, and it was when they collected food. Other than that, there was a lot of freedom in Cliffbound. Larissa was great with technology, so their cannon and radar could be operated remotely and sounded an alarm if something appeared on its screen. So much of their safety depended on trusting those cannons, trusting that nobody would ever get close, and yet Saytera knew that some people could bypass the planet's defenses. They hadn't been Lunars, though. At this point, she was sure that the Terens who wanted to find her had lost her trail. She had to, otherwise she would go paranoid.

Since their sole role was making sure that the cannon

worked, there wasn't much to do. In a way, life in Cliffbound was a little like life in the Storm Islands, except that Saytera had never really collaborated much with cooking and fishing back home, unless killing a crab or two counted.

And that was how she was walking with Nara on the southern beach, the calmest one, with the sea sometimes calm as a mirror—when the weather was good enough that allowed them to walk there. They were going to catch some shrimp for dinner. Larissa liked to schedule them together so as to keep Saytera away from Kay.

She'd been thinking about it, though, and started to wonder if her friend wasn't exaggerating. Kay had been nothing but nice, and she was starting to think he liked her. But then she remembered Larissa's warnings. Did the girl just want to slander him for no reason? It was confusing.

Their sun rays reflected in the small waves, making it sparkly. Saytera wanted to go in the water, but they had no swimming gear, which was a little weird, considering where they lived. In theory the uniform would dry quickly, but it was clunky.

Saytera looked back at their base and cannon on top of the cliff, an odd chill coming to her spine, with a slight fear that their trust in that thing could be misplaced.

A sound startled her and she turned. A crab, but not a crab-king, more like half its size, was coming out of the water. Perhaps it wouldn't see them.

Just then, Nara let out a deafening scream. The crab then obviously advanced in their direction. Saytera instinctively reached for her back to pull an arrow—which didn't exist. Stupid. She had to reach for her belt—and hope the pistols would work. Nara was shooting it with a cracker that made a sound like thunder, but she might as well have been doing it with her eyes closed, as none of her shots were reaching the target. Perhaps the girl *was* shooting with her eyes closed.

"It's just a crab." Saytera tried to calm down her colleague.

It didn't work. Nara tried to climb rocks, since the creature stood between them and the rest of the beach. Saytera aimed with her pistol—and nothing happened. So she did have an issue with pistols. She had been thinking that maybe it had been a fluke at the academy or something, but apparently, no. What a wonderful time to confirm that. Her zapper was dead, too. Her heart raced. No, that was stupid. The crab wasn't much taller than her. It shouldn't pose any danger—if she had her arrows. Kerely's voice telling her to always be prepared came to her mind, then interrupted by Lara, screaming, "Shoot it."

"My pistols don't work."

Saytera would need to find another solution. Going into the water wasn't going to help. Climbing would be too slow. The crab got close and Saytera jumped at it and punched its soft spot, then hit it with her pistol. She heard a thunderous sound. Kay was at the stairs leading to the beach and shot the creature some five times. What a waste of ammunition, to be doing it from that direction. But that slowed it down enough that Nara came close and shot it. The creature died.

Nara ran away and climbed the stairs back to the base, as if scared the creature would return to life.

Kay approached Saytera. "What happened?"

She showed her pistol. "Not working."

He took it, aimed elsewhere, and nothing happened. "You'll need to test them next time. This is serious. You could have died today."

Saytera nodded. She agreed with the need to test the pistol, except that she had a feeling none of them would work—but she couldn't tell anyone this. As to almost dying, that was a bit exaggerated. It wasn't that big of a crab, and only one, but maybe he underestimated her.

He pulled her hand. "Please, be careful. If something were to happen to you…"

She had to catch a breath. "I will. don't worry."

His hand felt warm against hers. It felt good. Their eyes met, her heart raced, but then Larissa's voice was in her mind. Saytera didn't want to disappoint her friend. But was it worth it to trust someone else's fear? Was it worth it to step away and remain wondering about what could have been? Before she could find the answer to any of these questions, his lips were on hers. And then there was nothing to regret, lost in his warmth, feeling his body close to hers, being wrapped in his arms. She didn't need to feel left out anymore, she didn't need to feel that nobody would ever want her. This was it. She was kissing and it was wonderful—hoping she wasn't doing anything wrong.

He stepped away after a while, breathless. "That was good."

Saytera smiled. "They'll be wondering where we are."

"Where we should always have been."

He kissed her again, then moved his mouth and licked the tip of her ear, giving her shivers down the spine. He whispered, breathless. "Wanna continue? Tonight?"

They had just kissed. Was he already suggesting what she was thinking? "I…" She wasn't even sure what to say.

He bit his lip, then said, "Can't wait to get this uniform off you."

Ewwww. So it wasn't an impression. Saytera was so shocked she couldn't even come up with a reply.

He didn't seem to notice anything and winked. "Just knock the door to my room. Now I'll go get help to bring this food to the base."

Then he disappeared up the stairs. Saytera touched her lips, unsure how she felt about the kiss, but positively certain that she wouldn't come knocking on his door. Perhaps she should be glad that he was straightforward about what she wanted. Maybe all guys in the continent acted like that. She would never know, since he was the only guy around. In fact, she would never know a lot of things. Saytera shouldn't complain, though, she was alive, and her heart felt cold thinking about the people who were now dead.

The others soon came down the stairs to cut the crab and bring it up for cooking. Kay was acting normal, with his dimpled smile that she was thinking was obnoxious.

Saytera helped them, then went to her bedroom to collect her thoughts. That kiss had been stupid. And she should have noticed the way he looked at her. It wasn't romantic, it was… Just gross.

Then something else, a lot more serious, bothered her. Today she hadn't been in danger but if there had been more crabs it could have been a close call. It was quite reckless to walk around unarmed, or with weapons she couldn't use, which was about the same.

If only she had her bow and arrows. But why didn't she? Not only did she know how to build one, there was a lot of wood around the base.

Her memories took her back to the Storm Islands, she and Kilmara making their own bows, imagining one day getting lost in the wilderness. Making a bow wasn't the issue. What was the issue then? This was about life and death, perhaps even other people's lives. She'd find an excuse. For now, she went outside in search of wood.

~

Dess waited for Marcus in the docks. He wanted to go away from that moon, escape everything. He'd woken up to find Nadia sleeping on the couch and fled like a coward. He had no idea what to say to her, what to think. He wasn't even sure what had happened.

Marcus showed up after about an hour. "What's wrong with you?"

"Me? You knew we were flying today."

Marcus rolled his eyes. "I mean Nadia. You freaking just left her there?"

Dess shrugged. "She was sleeping. I didn't want to bother her. I had to come check the ship."

Marcus shook his head. "How dedicated. And rude."

"Is she upset?"

Marcus sat down. "You ask her."

"Did she say anything?"

"She asked about you and left."

Dess sighed. "She knew we were going to Mainland. Speaking of which, are you ready?"

"I guess."

"Let's go, then."

Soon he'd be hiding in a storm cloud, nature and his mind in syntony. Messy, confused, wild.

~

Kay didn't even look in Saytera's direction all day. She

wondered if he'd actually waited for her to knock on his door the previous night and thought that it was hilarious.

In the late afternoon, the shuttle pilots, Zack and Cynthia, came with supplies and information. Since they were going to spend the night, Kay decided to have a party by the base and Larissa and Saytera had no option but to agree. Nara and Saulo agreed, too, but they were nowhere to be seen yet.

The fire on cliff rocks usually warmed Saytera's heart, reminding her of home. Even if she knew that nobody would change its color to blue or green, just watching it while hearing the ocean was calming, healing, and brought back that peace of heart she'd been looking for.

The evening was warm and pleasant, and the only annoying thing was that Kay had been flirting with Cynthia, and they now sat holding hands. So he could do that before wanting to take off someone's clothes. It wasn't that Saytera was jealous, just that sitting by the fire, watching a guy she once thought she was interested in with another girl brought back memories: the summer celebration in Ken Island, seeing Cayo, running away, and then all the tragedy that followed. Perhaps her heart had already died a little. What she'd been trying to do was distract herself.

Zack was in his twenties, and had sandy hair and tan skin. He sat by Saytera and asked, "So, what's the deal with the bow and arrows?"

Cynthia also turned. "Yeah, I'd never seen that."

Saytera sighed, realizing all eyes were on her. This was it, the moment where she'd find out whether they would all laugh at her or think she was a weirdo. Then, maybe she was, in a way. Larissa hadn't said much other than being curious about it. Perhaps curiosity was all that it was. "It can save ammunition."

Zack smiled. "Sounds nice."

"Is the arrow sharp enough, though?" Cynthia asked.

"It is." Saytera took one of the arrows and passed it to her.

The girl examined it. "Yeah. People in the bases all scramble and improvise sometimes. It's usually for food, but that works, too."

Saytera smiled, even if Kay was holding the girl's hand. She felt so much herself with her arrows and her hair loose, and it was great to see that nobody had any issue with that. Perhaps it was because she was starting to feel good and confident in her own skin.

Zack was then serious. "Regardless of what you use, make sure you're armed at all times when surveying the area."

Kay stretched his arms, then put one behind Cynthia and pulled her close. "Yeah, we get our fair share of giant crabs here. Sometimes sea serpents, too. I killed one the other day."

Zack nodded. "Yes, that's one reason. But there's something else going on. We had a few sentinels disappearing from the bases in the last months."

Larissa shrugged. "Isn't it desertion?"

He cocked his head. "Some of it, sure. Not all of it, though. Quite a few seem to have simply vanished, and their colleagues say they were not planning on running away or anything."

"Would people tell their plans?" Larissa asked.

Zack thought for a moment. "You usually know who's dissatisfied, who has family to go back to, who has the means to find a new identity and try a living in Citarella, for example. It's not everyone. Kay here, if he disappeared, would you think he deserted?"

Larissa laughed. "I'd think a siren lured him to the depths of the sea and he got what he deserved."

Saytera and Cynthia also laughed. Zack was serious. "True.

There are dangerous sea creatures. Not sirens, though, fortunately—or unfortunately. A sea serpent could kill you and drag your body. Nobody would ever find you. So sure, that's one thing. But… there's something odd happening. Command doesn't really talk about it, but some suspect Lunar kidnapping."

Saytera's heart raced, a cool chill inside her like she'd felt the previous day. "But they can't reach us, can they? At least not after we blow them to pieces. Isn't this the whole point of these bases? Making sure the anti-aerial cannons are working?"

Zack shrugged. "I don't know. It could be somebody inside the planet. Maybe the Lunars have infiltrated us. Maybe it's somebody—or an organization—who's being paid to weaken us. The fact is that there have been mysterious disappearances. And again, sure, some might be desertions, some might be sea creatures, but it can't be all of them."

That didn't make sense. "What would they want with people in the shore bases? We don't even get any central information. What are they going to find out? That we shoot incoming ships? No kidding, genius."

It was Cynthia that spoke now. "There's a theory that Lunars still come for food and water. It's been too long and they haven't conceded defeat yet."

"Another planet could be helping them," Larissa said.

Saytera thought it was unlikely. "Interstellar travel just for water?"

Cynthia shrugged. "All we know is that there have been some disappearances from the shore bases. Command doesn't want rumors about it, so they consider them all desertions."

Zack's face got somber. "And then there's Somersault. It's a base way North."

Saytera was almost afraid to ask. "What happened?"

"They were all killed. Every one of them. The bodies were found a couple days later."

Saytera felt nauseated.

Larissa voiced her concern. "Shouldn't they tell us? So that we're on high alert?"

Zack shrugged. "We *are* telling you. It's just not something we want in our records."

It didn't make sense. "Why?"

"Who knows the reason?" Zack asked.

Kay got up. "After all this cheerful talk, I think I want to take a walk." He turned to Cynthia. "Want to come with me?"

She got up. "Sure."

Saytera laughed. "Yay, that makes sense. There's unknown danger around the bases. Let's go be vulnerable somewhere."

Kay shrugged. "We're both armed."

"We won't go far," Cynthia added.

Perhaps Saytera shouldn't have said any of that. It sounded as if she was jealous. It was just that it was illogical and reckless.

Zack waved a hand. "We can't know if we're more vulnerable far from the bases or near them. Or around a fire, telling people far away that we're here."

That was true. "Well, The base is freaking red on top of a cliff. It's not like it's hard to find us."

He nodded. "Exactly. Now let my co-pilot have her share of fun."

Saytera stared at Larissa, wondering if she'd protest or say anything. "You also think it's fine."

The girl shrugged. "They're sometimes like that." She then gave Saytera a pointed look. "She knows what she's doing."

Zack picked a flute from his pocket. "Would you want me to play a song?"

It wouldn't be anything even close to the bands in the Storm Islands, but still… Saytera smiled.

When he was about to start, their comms beeped red. Larissa took hers and opened the channel.

"Help!" It was Nara's voice. "We think someone has entered the base."

15

INTRUDERS

"Are they still there?" Larissa asked.

"We didn't find anyone," Nara's voice was shaky over the comm. "But someone tried to break into our terminal."

"We're coming up." Larissa turned off the comm, an incredulous look on her face. "How did they even get here?"

Saytera was about to dash towards the base, but then stopped to think. They had to have come by ship or boat. And they were probably going to leave the same way, maybe even with information from their terminals.

"What are you looking at?" Larissa was beside her.

Saytera decided to run to the inner beach. "I'll go check. I'll be right back."

Larissa yelled something but the wind was getting strong again and she didn't quite catch it as she dashed down the hill towards the calmer beach. Calmer not counting crabs and other creatures. She just wanted to check. It was a hunch, it could be stupid, but she had to know.

A few drops of rain started falling on the sand as she looked at the sea, searching for a sign of a boat. What was she thinking? Well, this place was too far for someone to have come on foot. They must have taken a boat. Or something. And since the other beach had strong waves, this is where they would be —unless—could someone have flown in?

An image came to her mind; the small outer beach. It was just a strip of sand among rocks. Still. A rogue spaceship could land there. Saytera turned around—and bumped into Kay. He probably had gotten the same communication as them.

He asked, "Where are you going?"

"The outer beach. I can go alone. There are no crabs or other sea creatures there."

He stared at her.

Saytera added, "If there's a person around here, it could be a place to hide. I'll just check."

"Be careful."

She turned and ran, and was relieved that nobody ran after her or yelled anything. The waves were crashing on the shore like thunder. Wild, unpredictable, untamed. She loved the ocean.

Stars shone in the night sky. So many millions of unknown worlds, unknown to humans, who lived in just a couple dozen systems. Unknown to Saytera, stranded on a planet from where nobody flew in or out. She sighed. Unless people flew in. They took it for granted that nobody could reach them because their radar said so. Kind of stupid to lean so much on what a machine measured. Terens had landed on Mainland Planet, Yansin had left it. There were other ways to travel, and maybe other ways to travel undetected. Perhaps that was what she was facing here.

Saytera reached the small strip of sand and shivered, thinking for the first time that perhaps if there were intruders, they weren't from Mainland or Sapphirlune. If that were the case, she should better go back to the base and stay as hidden as possible. But there was nothing on the beach. False hunch. Except… she felt as if there was something at the other end. Having come so far, she'd have to know. Saytera walked by the woods, as quietly as possible. A cool breeze came from the ocean and she shivered.

At the opposite end of the small strip of sand, she found it. It looked as if there was mist or something, but then she walked to it and touched something solid; a hull. Why did it look invisible? Saytera took a better look. Far from invisible, but somehow it was camouflaged against the background. Now that she'd seen it, she could perhaps even spot it from far away. That had to be an intruder ship, which had come from water or space.

The best solution would be to blow it up right away. Saytera walked back to the woods and touched her comm to Larissa.

"Where are you?" the girl asked.

Saytera was about to reply, when a strong hand covered her mouth.

She tried to bite or kick it back but the grip on her was too strong.

Her comm was still open. "Saytera?"

Then the hand holding her ripped the comm from her. It was the chance she needed. Saytera stepped away, turned, and had her bow pointed to a guy in front of her. And stared at the barrel of a cracker pistol aimed at her. In the dark, she saw just the black hair of the guy pointing the gun at her.

"Stalemate," he said. "Except mine's faster."

Saytera's comm was crushed under his foot. And then she looked at his right hand and saw them; rings. The guy was wearing a coat, but it was long so he could well be wearing robes under it. In the faint glimmer of the moon, she saw that his eyes were lined. Teren. But why was he using a pistol?

Another voice startled her. "Drop it."

A young man pointed a gun at her. He wore pants and a jacket, had shorter, braided hair, dark skin, and didn't give her that Teren vibe.

Saytera lowered her bow.

The black-haired, Teren-looking guy took a zapper, pointed at her, and pressed the trigger. Nothing happened. A shadow moved behind him. Kay had a cracker pointed towards the intruder.

"Watch out," Saytera yelled.

It must have been by reflex, because it didn't make sense for her to defend a Teren. The black-haired guy turned and stunned Kay, who fell on the ground. Saytera turned to run. She had to get help, save Kay.

"Stop right where you are," the black-haired Teren guy said.

Saytera turned and noticed that he had a cracker aimed at Kay's head. He continued, "If you run, I'll kill him."

"You gain nothing from killing him." Her voice wasn't as strong as she wished.

"And I lose a lot if I let you go. I'll have to shoot you, too. Now come back, and everyone lives."

Saytera hesitated. If she ran, she had a chance. They could try to shoot her, but they could miss. Kay on the other hand was fallen, unconscious. No way he'd be able to defend himself. Shooting him was just a matter of pressing a trigger. As upset as she was at him, she didn't want him to die. And it was her fault for having alerted the black-haired guy. And the idea of leaving someone to get help brought her horrible memories that she didn't want to repeat.

There wasn't much she could do, but she could at least try to negotiate. "Let him go, then."

The Teren guy shook his head. "We're two against one. You have no grounds for demands."

"I saved your life!"

He raised his eyebrows. "Oh. Did you?"

What a jerk. "Let him go and I'll come with you. If you don't, maybe I might think you're going to kill us both. In this case, I have nothing to lose by running."

The guy with the black hair and long coat was walking towards her, and she realized it would be hard to run once she reached the rocks. Saytera stepped back. "Let him go."

"Fine. We'll leave him here. But you come with us."

"Promise."

He pointed his zapper at her. "Just shush it, will you?" He pressed the trigger, but nothing happened.

Could it be that she was affecting other people's pistols? She couldn't know. Her heart was beating fast, but she didn't want them to notice how afraid she was and laughed. "Is your equipment always that faulty?"

He pulled the other pistol. "Want to test? You're trying my patience and my colleague is going to start hurting your friend."

She took a small step back. "I just want you to promise to leave him."

"That will be a nope."

The other guy hit Kay's head with the back of his pistol.

Saytera was almost shaking. "I should have let him blow your brains out."

The black-haired guy just rolled his eyes. "Yeah. Keep looking back on what could have been. Are you coming or do you want to add regrets to your list?"

Eerily insightful. Saytera sighed. "Coming."

She walked forward to the misty weird thing that now she thought was a spaceship. Maybe Larissa or the others would find her. They had to. As they approached the other guy, he pulled an energy pistol. Somehow Saytera wasn't that surprised when it didn't work. So perhaps she could affect other pistols. The black-haired guy held her, and the other guy then took a syringe and stuck it on her neck. Saytera wasn't sure what was happening, who those people were, and in how much danger she was. As the liquid took effect, though, her fears—and everything else—disappeared.

Marcus was lifting the unconscious guy from the floor.

"What are you doing?" Dess asked.

"We can't leave him here. He'll alert other people about us."

Dess shook his head. "It's not like he knows how we got here. I doubt he even knows what we look like. Too much trouble to take both."

Marcus stared at him. "Is it because you promised?"

"I didn't promise anything." He was still holding the collapsed girl in his arms. Part of him wanted to leave her. There was something unusual about her, dangerous maybe. No. That had to be an impression. Either way, she'd be sedated until Sapphirlune. No difference. "We'll take her. *She* saw a lot."

He dragged her to the ship, eager to stop having to look at her, then strapped her on the back chair in the inner cabin.

Marcus looked at him. "Why not put her in the back?"

Weird hunch. "Not sure. I think she's dangerous."

Marcus just stared. Dess then went back outside, knelt and picked up her bow, wondering how she'd gotten it and why she used it. He shouldn't be taking anything from a hostage, but he wanted to compare it to the bows he'd read about. It almost looked like a Teren bow. No, perhaps that was imagination. Maybe other people in the shore bases used those. It was information.

Marcus's voice interrupted his thoughts. "We'd better get out of here soon."

Dess nodded. "I know."

He got into the ship and they flew right above the waves then down underwater, where hopefully they wouldn't be found. They just had to wait for a light enough storm to escape that place without being shot. He held the stick in his hand. At least he'd taken information from the terminal. What idiots, all sitting by the fire and leaving the base practically unattended.

Saytera was jolted awake. More like shaken. Glass, and something dark grey beyond it. Pilot and co-pilot chairs in front of her. Her hands and body in metal enclosures. The ship shook again, and the black hair in the main pilot seat reminded her of her unpleasant encounter. She was being kidnapped, but that was far from the worst; they were flying in the middle of a storm cloud, being shaken like a twig over crashing waves.

"You're gonna kill us. Are you insane?"

The guy on the co-pilot seat turned, startled. He had brown eyes, dark skin, and braided hair.

The guy on the front didn't move, but said, "Sedate the hostage."

The ship was tossed sideways now. Saytera would have been thrown against the window hadn't she been so tightly bound.

The co-pilot must have had the same idea. "Once we leave this storm."

Saytera was wondering if they were suicidal or something, when she remembered how storm clouds would show up on the radar. They were using it as camouflage. *That* was how they reached the planet. Sneaky—if they survived.

If that shaking continued Saytera would puke—but it didn't. They left the cloud behind and now had the light of their star illuminating the ship. But then Saytera's insides turned to ice. Who were those guys? If the black-haired guy was indeed a Teren, it would mean that Vivian's sacrifice had been in vain. So many deaths for nothing. If he wasn't, and if she was going to be imprisoned and maybe killed, again that sacrifice had been for nothing. Her life had been so short. Whatever destiny she had would be forgotten, unfulfilled.

She stared at the light bathing them as she contemplated the future loss of her freedom, her life. All of that because she hadn't been cautious enough to bring more people with her. All of that because, by some stupid reflex, she'd warned the dark-haired guy, preventing Kay from killing him. He was expressing his gratitude by taking her away, to who knows where. Not fair. Anger was rising inside her at the unfairness of the situation, at the lack of honor from her captors. They shouldn't get away with it. And Saytera didn't want to be taken away from Cliffbound, the one place where she was finding some sort of happiness after so long.

Talking wouldn't make a difference, but she had to vent, and said, "You'll regret this."

The dark-haired guy turned to the co-pilot. "The storm is gone. It's safe to sedate her now."

"Yeah, sedate me. It won't erase your guilt or the blood in your hands."

The co-pilot was approaching her, syringe in his hand. She wished she could poke it in his eye. No, in that other guy's eye. Those were dark thoughts.

The syringe never reached her neck, as the guy was pushed backward. The ship was being jolted again. So they hadn't left the storm. Saytera felt a chill in her stomach, as the ship slowed down, then started accelerating again in the other direction; back to the planet.

The black-haired guy turned to her. "Stop what you're doing. We're going to crash!"

Indeed they were falling, but his words made no sense.

"She's tied, Dess," the co-pilot said.

The black-haired guy, Dess, didn't seem to hear it. "Stop it."

Saytera couldn't believe him. "Are you insane?"

Dess turned around, trying switches. Everything was off, and hadn't it been for the sun coming through the windows, they'd be immersed in darkness. If they were falling like that, it probably meant that the anti-gravity had failed, and since they hadn't gained enough momentum to counteract the planet's pull, they were being pulled back. Great. The one time her mechanics study had any use was just to tell her how screwed she was.

No idea why the guy had blamed her. None of this was her fault. The thought of being a hostage was way better than dying.

Their plummeting was slowed down in the storm cloud, where they were tossed like a leaf.

"What's happening?" the co-pilot asked.

"Dead. It's all dead." Dess pressed buttons frantically.

"What about the emergency system?" the other guy asked.

"Dead. Get ready to eject."

"We'll lose the—"

"Ready, I said." Dess let go of his seat belt and got up. "We have just a few seconds." He was then opening Saytera's restraints. "You'll eject with me, but if you don't want it, you're welcome to be squashed on the sea."

Saytera saw her pack with bow and arrows on the corner and reached for it.

Dess stared. "Do you happen to have a parachute in it?"

"No." Reaching for it had been a reflex. What would she do with it in the ocean? Or dead?

Sun shone again on them as they left the storm cloud. There was green below them. Maybe they were above Mainland. Right. That would be even worse, as they'd be shot without warning.

"I'm gonna eject," the co-pilot said.

"Wait. Not yet." He then closed his eyes as his colleague's seat was no longer on the ship. Wind came through the opening on top.

Dess sat down again, tied his seatbelt, then pulled Saytera. If she weren't falling to her death she'd notice that she was sitting on a guy's lap. Well, actually, she noticed it, even though she could be about to die, and wondered what it said about her. The guy didn't seem to have noticed anything. His arms were tight holding her, and he murmured something, ending in what sounded like "Stars above, stars within." Maybe she was the one thinking that. And hoping this fall didn't lead to her death.

16

ENEMIES

Saytera was up in the air, being held only by an enemy's arms, probably a Teren, to make matters even worse. Or momentarily better, if he could use his power to make sure they survived. He was murmuring something as they were plummeting quite fast towards a rocky shore. Then their speed slowed, as a parachute opened, but she still felt as if she were falling. Falling toward the rocky shore, then, to her relief, the wind took them to a sandy beach. Beside them, the ship crashed on the rocks.

He said, "On three, jump. One, two, three." He let her go.

No longer having his arms around her, Saytera was floating mid-air, until she saw sand coming fast in her direction, but rolled as she reached the ground, to avoid getting hurt. She was up soon, her right hand hurting—from clutching the pouch with her bow and arrows. Perhaps they would be useful. Further ahead, she saw the chair and the dark-haired guy falling. The rest of the ship was a bunch of pieces floating on the ocean around the rocks.

Saytera looked around. Mountains on one side, sea on the

other. Could they be on the continent? Far from Cliffbound, since she didn't recognize this place.

The immediate danger was the fallen enemy in front of her. Saytera approached him. He was lying on the ground, eyes closed. Breathing, though. She aimed an arrow at him.

He opened his eyes. "Really? You thought I was unconscious and you were going to kill me?"

"If you're still breathing, I didn't want to kill you."

"Same here." He sighed. "We're even now. I saved your life."

He had to be kidding. "You *saved* me? I'm the one who saved you, and you should have left me where you found me."

"Shouldn't have sabotaged my ship."

"Still on that?" Saytera kept pointing an arrow at him.

He pulled a pistol from a baldrick and aimed it at her. "Let's kill each other, then. So useful." He put it back and closed his eyes, perhaps to annoy her, show her that he was not afraid.

Well, she wasn't going to shoot him. Not from that distance, so she put back her arrow. His hair was so black it was almost as if it sucked the light from around him. He had eyes closed as if relaxing on the beach. He *was* beautiful. Way better looking than anyone she'd ever seen outside the islands. Perhaps better looking even than people on the islands, like Cayo. His lined eyes made her shiver wondering if he was a Teren.

Saytera walked away from him as she tried to collect her thoughts. There wasn't much he could do against her without his ship other than maybe kill her, but he didn't seem interested in seeing her dead. Considering they were on the planet, if they were found, he was the one who'd be imprisoned. She sighed. If they were found.

"We're on an island!" he yelled, drawing attention back to

him, as if he'd been guessing her thoughts. He was standing up, now, walking in her direction.

That would be terrible. "You can't be sure."

"The instruments told me that. We're far from the continent."

"Weren't all instruments dead? Since, you know, I jinxed them all and stuff?"

"*Before* you jinxed them." He paused, eyes wide. "Is that what you did?"

She rolled her eyes. "Are you seriously accusing me of causing failure on your crappy ship?"

He glared. "It wasn't crappy."

So much drama for a stupid ship. True that it would have been their way out. To the moon, not very helpful to her.

"Listen." He sighed. "We're stranded. Being enemies is pointless now. We'll have more chances of survival if we work together."

It sounded sincere, but Saytera didn't trust him. "You mean *you*'ll have more chances of survival, right?"

He paused, then crossed his arms. "Absolutely. You know the area more than I do."

She wasn't falling for his humble act. "I don't care if you live or die."

"I just don't want to stumble on your dead body," he yelled.

"Then watch your step."

"I will." He turned around and started walking away from her.

Great. Now she was stranded on an island forever. Suddenly all the anger she'd been managing for so long bubbled up. And if he was really a Teren, then he and his kind, whatever it was, were responsible for all the tragedy that had struck her. That had taken her friend. And now again her life was being ruined.

"Hey," Saytera yelled. He turned and she ran to him. "It's not okay. I was fine. I had a life, a goal, friends. You stole it all. You stole it and now my life is doomed. It's over."

"You did it yourself. I wouldn't have hurt you. But no, let's almost die. And kill Marcus. If he dies, it's all your fault."

How dare he talk about killing his friend? As if he weren't going to take her away from her friends? As if he cared for anyone. Saytera kicked sand on his face. As he raised his hands to block it, she punched his stomach and kicked him between the legs. He grunted then pulled her towards him, stepped out of the way, then pushed her face down on the sand. She was about to get up, when she felt his weight over her. She wanted to struggle and throw more sand, punch him, but soon he grabbed both her wrists, held them down with one hand, and held her face with the other, while keeping the rest of her body down with his torso and legs.

Perhaps he was hoping that she'd whimper or ask him to let her go. She wasn't going to do any of that. She asked, "Are you stupid enough to kill me?"

"You're the one who started with the physical aggression, girl, now don't play victim."

"Not a victim. I win either way, since I stopped you from kidnapping and murdering people." She wasn't sure if he'd ever killed anyone, but it was very likely.

"True." He then whispered in her ear, "And yet look who's at whose mercy."

His words sent a shiver down her spine and some weird feeling as if a spark had ignited in her with the awareness of his body over hers. That soon became terror when she understood that there were other ways he could hurt her other than killing her. Saytera tried to gather all her strength to break free, break her wrists free, push him away, but she couldn't. She felt so powerless and weak. She had told herself she wouldn't beg, and yet...

Saytera choked a sob. "Please. I saved your life."

His hold loosened. "What are you talking..." He let her go. "Oh. No. No."

She got up, turned around, and saw all the anger gone from his face. The color had gone too, his pale face shocked.

"I'd never... You can't possibly think—" He sounded horrified.

She looked away. "I wasn't thinking anything."

"You're trembling. Afraid of me."

That was true. "You immobilized and threatened me. What did you expect?"

"You punched and kicked me. I didn't hurt you. And I didn't mean to scare you. You can't possibly think I'd ever..."

Saytera looked away. He did sound like he'd never hurt her, but still... "I don't know you. You're my enemy."

"I'm not. It's just you and me. And my friend, if we reach him. There's no war here."

Saytera felt a little silly. But his whisper was still in her ear.

He continued, "It's true what I said, you know more about the area than I do. And we can watch each other's backs. I'll do my best to protect you, even if I might be the one needing help the most. I'm sorry if I scared you."

He stared at her, his eyes so dark and beseeching. She looked away. "Don't kidnap people."

The guy looked at the mountain, then back at her. "Listen, I think my friend needs help as soon as possible. You could help me a lot. I'm asking."

For a moment she felt for him, since he was so worried

about his friend. But she had to remember they were enemies. "What do I gain with that?'

"Mutual protection. We don't know how long we'll stay here."

Saytera didn't think he meant to harm her, at least not immediately, but she had to gain something with that. She sighed. "Promise me that if people come and rescue you, you won't take me with you."

He was surprised. "You'll want to stay here?"

Was he that dense? "On the planet."

He hesitated, then said, "Sure. If I'm rescued, I'll leave you on the planet. Just help me find Marcus."

She shrugged. "Let's find your friend, then."

Dess had never been so offended in his life. To think that even for a brief second, the girl thought he would do something against her will. The only reason he didn't say what he felt about it was that she was truly afraid. All he'd wanted was to calm her down. Maybe shake off some of her defiance. It had been in self defense, after all. But then, he had kidnapped her. And who knew what lies people spread about Lunars?

It still hurt. She couldn't look at him and possibly think he'd ever need to do something so despicable. Maybe it was just that they were enemies.

He looked at the green mountain in front of them. "We need a path to the mountain."

"If it's an island, depending on the size, we'll do better walking around it."

That made a lot of sense, except Dess didn't really think

Marcus was on the other side. "I think he's up in the mountain. We'll need a trail there."

She nodded. "That can work, too." Her tone was still cold and distant.

Well, at least she wasn't staring at him in fear. She wasn't staring at all, in fact, just walking in front of him. Her uniform was different; it ended in a skirt. Huge long hair flowing, bow and arrows on her back, she looked as if she'd just stepped out from one of the legends he so loved. Yeah, legends. Like legends of people who could interfere with electrical circuits on a spaceship. What an idiot he'd been by bringing her when he'd noticed there was something odd about her.

His thoughts then turned to Marcus. He'd ejected too soon, when they were above that mountain. Maybe it had been a good idea, maybe he'd had enough time to slow his descent, maybe. He tried to reach his friend's comm and got nothing.

Dess had a weird feeling that his friend was in danger, and it tugged his heart. Knowledge without facts, just that inner knowing, feeling… He trusted it, even if that knowledge told her that the girl had caused the electrical failure on his ship and disabled the antigravity, and now that he thought about it, it didn't make that much sense. Yes, in theory, some Terens could affect electrical systems, but that was in theory only, and what were the odds that a Teren would be volunteering in the shore defenses of an isolated planet? And to disable a spaceship like that? Too much power. But then, his logical mind found no explanation either, and the result was just puzzlement.

The day was still ahead of him, but he'd probably have to walk for hours to find Marcus. Then they needed shelter. Some luck that Dess wasn't hurt. That ejection mechanism hadn't been built to support two people ejecting that late, but they'd managed it and had been lucky enough to land on sand. They'd better keep their luck.

The breeze was cool and the weather was cloudy, and the girl had just a sleeveless uniform. Maybe he could try to bring her to his side.

He asked, "Aren't you cold?"

She turned and looked him up and down. "Aren't you hot?"

Ain't I? crossed his mind, but that was obviously not what she meant. He did have a long coat, but it wasn't too warm. "No, but I can lend you my coat."

"I'm fine."

He then noticed that she only had her bow and arrows for weapons. Who knew what they were going to face?

He took the cracker pistol and reached it out to her. "Take it."

She should have been surprised, grateful, or something. After all, it was an enemy handing over his weapon. But no, the girl shuddered and looked at it in horror. "I'm fine. And I don't even have a place to carry it."

Dess shrugged and put the pistol back in its holder. If she didn't want to defend herself, her loss. He'd offered it as a gesture of goodwill, but apparently the girl completely missed its significance.

He was going to remain quiet about her refusal, but then decided not to. "Fine, then, if we're attacked, you'll have to manage with your arrows."

She stopped and turned, looking at him as if sizing him up. "And you think it's a problem?"

He shrugged again. "By all means not at all, if that's what makes you happy."

"You don't use arrows, then," she said more as a realization than anything.

Strange. "Should I?"

She tilted her head. "And you've never seen anyone using arrows." Again she was trying to figure out something.

"Well, I must confess, archery is not really a thing in Sapphirlune." She still stared. He then added, "But I did read stories with it." He remembered a quote that he liked. "When darkness falls, arrows still pierce. Is that what it is?"

She looked startled. "Where does that saying come from?"

"The Tome of Darkness. Do you know that?"

She stepped back. "Tome?"

"Yeah, I have some rare books. Listen, maybe we should introduce ourselves. I'm Dess."

She just stared. "Are you a Teren?"

Weird. She didn't seem to be joking or anything. "You think Terens hang out in backwater planet moons and get involved in their squabbles?"

"Are you?" she insisted.

Dess snorted. "I'm flattered you think so. I'm also flattered you assume

I wouldn't lie if that was the case."

"What were you doing near our base?"

"Tourism. Not sure you realize it, we don't have beaches on our moon."

She frowned. "If you want me to help you find your friend, answer my questions."

"You already agreed you'll help me. Are you going to go back on your word now? And you haven't even told me your name."

"Saytera." She looked at him as if waiting for a reaction.

"Nice to meet you." He extended his hand.

She slapped his hand. "Nice my ass. You kidnapped me. It's your fault we're here."

"You sabotaged my ship!"

She rolled her eyes. "How exactly? Care to explain?"

That was a good question, and yet he knew it had been her, knew it—and then all of a sudden everything fit into place. The arrows, her skirt, her very long hair, something about her energy, even something about her name. He stared at her. "Are *you* a Teren?"

She rolled her eyes. "You have a wild imagination."

That was a non-answer. He was getting to something. "Yeah, I do. Wild things in my mind. But thinking you're a Teren is not one of them."

Saytera stared at him for a moment. "*If* I brought down your ship, I don't regret it."

"No reason to regret, right? This is a lovely island to raise our grandchildren."

She stopped and put her hands on her hips. "Oh, really? I didn't know you guys already had male-to-male reproduction."

It had been just a manner of speaking, meaning that they were doomed to stay there forever, but he wasn't going to apologize, and he definitely hadn't meant to imply... He just shrugged. "What can I do... superior technology."

They were following a stream towards the mountains. That was a huge island, much bigger than the islands where Saytera had grown up. Her heart tightened with the memory. Meanwhile, her mind was whirling. So her captor wasn't a Teren, and probably hadn't been looking for her. She knew it because of the flicker of wonder and awe in his eyes when asking her if she was a Teren. It meant that her biggest worry—that he'd been sent to capture her—wasn't true. He was probably just a

Lunar out to kidnap sentinels or who knows what. Why he looked like a Teren, she had no idea.

But the downside was that there wasn't much she would learn from him. And the other downside was that nobody would come and rescue them. No, maybe they would. If Lunars could come to the planet, maybe someone could reach this place. The issue then would be trying to get back to Cliff-bound. She didn't trust his word and didn't trust him.

Dess now walked in front of her. She let him. If they came across anything dangerous, he would be the one to face it, not her. And she was wondering why she was helping him, now that she knew there wasn't much to learn. Well, maybe she could get some information about the Lunars and how they were getting to the planet. That could be good knowledge—if ever she found her way out of that island. He also intrigued her. He had that sort of energy about him that she'd only seen in people in the islands or maybe with the seer in the conti-nent. She'd have a long time to figure it out.

Dess turned. "Everything fine?"

"Perfect. Stranded on an island. Haven't had a better day."

He ran his hands through his hair. "You could be in a nice comfortable spaceship. Your choice."

She still didn't understand why he had those rings. And why he was showing off his hair. Saytera crossed her arms. "And then in a prison. No, thank you."

Dess shrugged. "It's not like you'd stay there forever..." He turned as if to continue walking.

Saytera pulled his elbow. "So that was where you were taking me? A Lunar prison?"

He stared in her eyes. "Well, I was taking you somewhere. The rest is your guess."

His gaze was somehow unsettling. "Aren't you ashamed? Of kidnapping people?"

He laughed. "Aren't you ashamed? Of shooting incoming ships?"

"Well, just concede that stupid moon that doesn't belong to you, and you can come all you want. Easy."

"Doesn't belong…" He scoffed. "Regardless, you do realize I'm not in the Lunar government, right?"

"As part of its people, you have a say."

Dess shook his head. "Can we keep walking and debate politics later?"

"You're the one who stopped walking."

"I was just checking on you." He looked at her up and down. "Are you sure you don't want my coat?"

Well, it *was* getting chilly. That said, taking his coat would feel weird. Perhaps it was just that she didn't want to be the one accepting help. And she'd already said no. "I'm fine. I told you."

He nodded and turned. As they walked some more, the trees cleared to a valley with dunes. Saytera's heart sped up, dreading whatever was coming,

"Let's turn around," she whispered.

"Too late. Stay back."

His answer was puzzling until she noticed a large form emerging from under the sand and moving towards them. The guy ran towards it, then to the side, parallel to the line of trees. That didn't make sense. It was like telling the thing "I'm here."

It was some kind of lizard, yellow like the sand. It looked like the canteens from the islands, but much bigger. It was also faster, and apparently aggressive, but then the stupid dude's pointless running was what caused it to chase him. Saytera flinched when the thing approached him, but he turned just in time and shot it. Once, twice. It didn't seem to work. The creature slowed down, but kept approaching him.

Saytera was too far for a decent shot, but she ran towards him and aimed an arrow. It hit the thing's back, making it turn. It was now advancing on her. Saytera had better get this shot right or it would be her end.

She took a deep breath and calmed down. There was nothing in the world other than her arrow and her aim. Nothing else. When the target got close enough her arrow flew and hit the creature's eye. It stopped at her feet, fallen. Saytera's crappy shooting skills had saved her.

The creature was indeed immobile. It didn't deserve to die like that, but then, she didn't deserve to die either and had to make a choice. Its other eye was hurt. So the guy *had* managed a decent shot, it was just that zappers did little against those creatures.

He ran towards her.

Saytera smirked. "Turns out I *managed* with my arrows."

He stared at her bow. "I guess."

His thankfulness was touching.

"Two to one. Twice I saved you now."

The dude ignored what she said, looked at the fallen lizard, and whispered, "There might be more. Let's get away from here."

And that was when three lizards emerged from the sand. They were smaller than the previous one and definitely reminded Saytera of the docile creatures she used to play with. "They might not attack us."

The creatures were still, then started to make a rattling noise. More creatures emerged around them. No way she could shoot them all. Then she heard two loud bangs and couldn't see much more, as they were engulfed in smoke.

A hand grabbed hers and pulled her back from where they'd come from.

"Let's stick together," he whispered.

Only when they were back among the trees her vision cleared. Dess took something from under his coat and threw between them and the sandy valley. It had a loud boom and a bright light. He let go of her hand and they ran some more, then walked back to the beach.

Dess turned to her. "You're right. We'll have to go around the island."

"There could be sea creatures. You got any more of those bombs?"

He shook his head.

That wasn't good. Saytera then said, "Your energy pistol, the zapper, it's useless against creatures with thick skin."

"I noticed it. But I thought the eye…"

"You got it, but it didn't go deep enough." She was curious about something. "Why did you run towards it?"

The guy shrugged. "Maybe I got poor training on what to do against weird sand lizards. What are those things?"

"I don't know. I've seen lizards like those, but they weren't hostile."

They were circling the island by walking on the beach and climbing rocky shores. Saytera didn't think the guy's friend had great odds. They weren't going to make it before nightfall, and perhaps it wouldn't be a good idea to try to get there once night set in.

Dess turned to her. "Are you hungry?"

"Is that a question? Thing is, if we stop to fish we might take too long."

He took something from under his coat, then tossed her a square beige thing.

"What's this?"

"Rations for travel. You can have it."

At this point it didn't make sense that it would be poisoned. Saytera bit into it. It tasted like sand and maybe some kind of insect but she tried not to grimace. Food was food. She ate the whole thing quickly, realizing she'd been a lot more starved than she thought. "Thanks."

"No problem."

Saytera then wondered why he wasn't doing the same. "Shouldn't you eat one, too?"

"It was my last one."

She felt guilty, or maybe angry that he was trying to guilt-trip her and win her over. "We should have shared."

He shook his head. "I'm good. You're the one helping me find Marcus instead of fishing, so it's fair."

Saytera glanced at the mountain. "You do realize we might not reach it before sundown, right?"

He took a deep breath, a wistful look on his face.

She then asked, "And how do you know he's there?"

"I just do. Can't explain it. Same way I know you caused the failure on my ship."

Why was he insisting on that? "I never touched anything."

"Some things don't need touching, do they? It's all the same energy."

"I'm serious, Dess. I wouldn't even know how to do such a thing."

Wouldn't she? All the power failures came back to her mind now. What if? But still…

He rolled his eyes. "Sounds convincing." He then frowned and stared at her. "What are you?"

What? Charming. "Excuse-me?"

"What's a Teren doing in Mainland?" he kept staring.

Saytera once had wondered the same thing, but she didn't know why he was asking this about *her*. "I didn't say I was one."

"Some things don't need to be said."

He had his dark eyes locked on her, which made her look away. "If you know me better than I do, why bother asking?"

"But I don't know anything. I mean, what are you doing poorly disguised as a Mainland sentinel? Where are your people? How many of them are alive? Where are they hiding?"

So many questions for which Saytera had no answer, bringing up memories she'd struggled for a long time to keep buried and pain about to consume her. And even more pain, now that she was stuck on that island, maybe never again to find any answer. All her disappointment, her anger, her regret, came out bubbling.

"Listen, you murderer. I owe you no explanation."

He didn't flinch from her gaze. "True." He looked briefly away. "Talking slows us down and we're running out of time."

She wasn't going to let him have the last word. "You started it!"

"By offering you food!"

"What was it? Powdered cockroach?"

"Cricket."

"I didn't want that." She gestured around her. "I didn't want any of this."

He stared at her, his jaw trembling. "I should have let you die from the fall."

"You would be dead by now, especially considering you don't know basic logic when confronting an aggressive creature."

"Basic logic? Cause I ran towards it? I was trying to keep it away from you. Sorry for my presumption. I had no idea your arrows actually worked."

So that was what it had been? It made sense, in a way. She could have escaped while he drove the thing away. But then, it had been based on his feeling of superiority, thinking that she was weak.

"And no idea your stupid pistol was worthless."

He approached her, his face closer than half a palm away. "Let's see how worthless it is when you need it."

That made no sense whatsoever. "You're stupid. I have my arrows."

He laughed. "Have fun with them."

"I will. Alone." Saytera turned around.

"Hey," he yelled. Saytera turned. He had his arms crossed. "We had a deal. You said you'd help me find my friend. Are you going to go back on your word?"

In her anger, she had forgotten it, or maybe wasn't sure how important her word was when dealing with an enemy, but it made no sense to break it now. She narrowed her eyes. "I just turned around for a second. Of course I'm keeping my word."

He stopped for a moment, then looked down and sighed. "I'm sorry. I'm worried about my friend." He looked at her. "I might have snapped."

It was hard to be angry or annoyed at someone who offered such an honest apology. "I'm stressed, too."

"You're helping me. That's what matters." His smile seemed genuine.

For the first time since the previous night, she had a smile, too.

KEEP WALKING

Dess was still trying to figure out the girl. Saytera. She was magnificent like a Teren, regardless if she was one or not. It was as if he could see the power radiating from her, as if she were brilliant. Pure star fire. Like everyone, sure. But in her case, it was visible. Of course, there was the nasty detail that she thought he was capable of doing despicable stuff and probably thought he was dumb and weak, just because her arrows had been more effective against those stupid lizards. But his bombs had gotten them away, too. Not that she thanked him. Well, he'd kidnapped her, so she'd probably despise him forever. Maybe not forever. They would spend a long time on that island. Being eternally stuck there. Not something he wanted to think about.

He thought back about the moment right before she got scared. Maybe she did have a point. For a brief second, he had enjoyed overpowering her. Perhaps it was just his competitive nature. He then wanted to hug her when she stared at him, terror in her eyes, but he didn't because it would only make things worse. He shouldn't be thinking about any of that, though. They had to focus on getting to Marcus.

His stomach was rumbling. He really shouldn't have given her his entire ration. Shouldn't have given any of it, for that matter. And then there was another matter: water. He was getting thirsty. The sky was cloudy, though. Perhaps it would rain soon, then it was just a matter of finding a place to collect the water. Until then, his throat was going to get glued together.

Saytera stopped and pointed. "I think we can go up the mountain from here."

"I agree." She was walking ahead of him, up the mountain. His instinct would be to take the lead, but she was right that she probably knew the land better than he did.

And so they walked in silence among narrow trees. Sometimes she stopped to look or listen. If he didn't fear he would probably spend years in that place, he'd enjoy the walk. He'd never been surrounded by nature for so long. The trees were all different from each other, some narrower, some thicker, some with plants on their trunk. Then there were sounds as if the whole thing were alive. Insects close by and in the distance, maybe some small mammals, and plus the overwhelming ocean with its powerful presence in sound and smell. He'd dreamed so much about spending time in nature, and now he was getting his wish, except that it was the last thing he wanted. Maybe once they found Marcus he'd clear his thoughts, think about a strategy, maybe try to plan their lives for the next days. Or months. Or years. No, he didn't want to think about that.

Saytera's long brown hair flowed with the wind to add to her unreal, magic effect. Eventually he'd learn where she'd come from. That was something he'd wanted for a long time, too: meet someone with magic, with closer contact with Terens, learn the truth about them. And, again, he was getting his wish in the worst possible way. Stuck on an island. His own fault. He'd known there was something different about her. He just couldn't have imagined that she would have caused his ship to crash. Too late, now.

And Marcus… No, there was no point worrying. His friend should be all right. And yet, Dess had that pang on his chest, an odd feeling pushing him forward. He touched the comm on his wrist, wishing it could work, wishing he could get an answer from his friend.

Something jumped on his head. Dess pushed it, pulled out his pistol and aimed at it, then felt a hand pushing his down.

"It's harmless," she said.

Dess looked and saw a brown, furry, small creature, now running away. "I wasn't going to shoot it."

She let go of his hand. "Didn't look like it."

It annoyed him that she was acting as if he'd been scared of the small animal. It was just common sense and self defense. "First I aim, then I check. The other way around doesn't really work, right?"

The girl just shrugged. It was then that a small red-and-black shape jumped on her face. To her credit, she didn't scream. Before Dess even registered that it was a spider, and probably a poisonous one, he was shooting it with a zapper at full force. The spider fell dead on the ground.

Saytera stepped back and looked at him, livid. "Are you crazy? You could have killed me."

"I have good aim. And it's poisonous. Probably."

"You shot my face."

"That thing could have killed you. It looks like one of the four types of killer spiders on this planet."

She crossed her arms. "But you're not sure."

Dess exhaled, getting exasperated. "Wanted me to wait and see if it killed you first?"

"Just don't shoot my face."

"Well, aren't you glad I don't use arrows? And the *crappy pistol* just saved your life."

"I saved yours more times."

Dess laughed. "So you guys don't learn how to count, huh?"

"And how do you even know about spiders?"

"I studied a bit of survival techniques."

She scoffed. "Already planning for the day you'll come and conquer the planet?"

"Sure." He started walking up the mountain again, and she was beside him. "Our plan is to come and live in precarious conditions in inhabited places. No, we study it as a precaution." They hadn't studied that much, though, except maybe for Dess, fascinated with nature.

"And if you know about our wildlife, you are confessing you don't need me to help you." She narrowed her eyes. "What's up, then?"

Dess shrugged. "What you learn in theory is never the same as reality. You probably know a lot more about the reality here."

She shook her head. "Not here. It's not the same."

"I'm sure you know how to swim, for example. It's helpful."

She stared at him. "Wait. You don't know how to…" She was scoffing now. "Swim?"

It annoyed him, but he tried not to show it. "You think we have swimming pools on our moon? Or beaches?"

She paused for a second, then said, "I don't know. Never stopped to think about what life is like out there."

"It's fake. Just a bubble on an inhabitable rock. The view is great, though."

"Cause you can look at the planet and plan ways to kill us?"

Dess sighed and rolled his eyes. "Exactly. That's what mostly occupies my thoughts. How I can best kill you Mainlanders."

"More like kidnap us. What do you even do with us? Torture us for information?"

He shook his head and focused on walking. "I wouldn't torture anyone."

"Do you think we have some kind of important intel at the shore bases? That they send our best there? Have you noticed our ages?"

Dess stopped. "It's not as if I'm twice your age, you know? It's young people fighting on our side, too."

Saytera shrugged and kept walking. "I'm just saying that kidnapping and killing us is a stupid waste of time and resources."

That made no sense. If the Lunars could disable enough shore bases, they could penetrate the continent through land. As much as Citarella had an impressive anti-aerial defense, it wasn't as well protected by land. She probably knew that. But then, she was likely upset she had been taken. It didn't help, but Dess also regretted having kidnapped her, but then, she'd seen too much.

She looked at him. "Lost your words?"

"I'm just anxious to find my friend." That was also true.

"And why do you think you can find him?"

Dess decided to be honest, and pointed to his heart. "When two people are close, it's like if there was an invisible line between them."

She frowned in confusion, then let out a breath. "Oh. So you two…"

"He's my best friend. The only family I have."

She paused. "We'll find him," she said as if encouraging him, as if it suddenly mattered for her as well.

As they were rounding the hill, Dess yelled, "Marcus, Marcus!"

No reply. Dess thought his friend should be around that area, maybe because of when he ejected, maybe because they were indeed connected. The girl also looked. After a while, behind a rock, he saw his friend's boot and ran to it.

Marcus lay down, eyes staring at the sky, his skin pale. It couldn't be.

The girl hurried and took Marcus's hand. "There's a pulse."

He didn't look alive, though. Thunder roared in the sky. A list of ailments and symptoms passed through Dess's mind.

"It's poison," the girl said.

Right. That made sense. And she was obviously a lot more clear-headed than Dess was. He nodded.

She got up and looked around. "Rain is going to pour down soon. We need to find shelter."

Dess was trembling. Shelter. Shelter. What did that even mean? His best friend was dying in front of him.

She pointed somewhere. "Can you carry him there?"

There was a rock protrusion where she pointed. Shelter from rain. Of course. Dess hesitated. Depending on his friend's injuries, it wouldn't be a good idea to move him like that. But then, he didn't seem physically hurt, just poisoned. Dess carried him to the small cave the girl had pointed.

As soon as they got there, thick drops of rain started to pour outside, and the wind howled. Mouth foaming, fingers turning blue… Perhaps spider venom. It meant that depending on when he'd been bitten, he'd have from a few hours to just a few more minutes alive. Dess should have planned this whole thing better, they should have had some antivenom. This had been so stupid. It wasn't only that. Marcus should never have risked his life coming to the planet. All Dess's fault. Now the only remaining person in his life was about to go leave him. Forever. Tears formed in his eyes, turning into black drops falling over Marcus's jacket.

Everything was silent and strange. It was as if the wind outside or the roaring sea didn't exist. Just emptiness at losing his only friend. The only person who had always treated him well, from the beginning of Dess's days in the academy, the days when people gave sideways glances at him for being the kitchen boy, when Dess so many times almost considered telling everyone that he was a lot more than them, that if his parents were alive he could buy the whole moon.

Marcus saved Dess from exposing himself, from breaking a promise made to his mother. "One friend is all you need", was also something his mother used to say. And with one friend, the pain of his dead family, the hurt of being shunned by his colleagues, was much easier to bear. He didn't know what he would do now.

Slowly Dess started noticing his environment again. His friend was still breathing. Dess looked around. Where was the girl? Had she taken a chance to escape? In the storm? Suddenly the thought of losing the one other person with him on that island, the thought of being completely alone was too much to cope.

Dess got up and went to the edge of the cave and yelled her name. "Saytera! Saytera!"

～

The wind sounded as if it were calling her name. Saytera looked at the edge of rocks and underneath trees for herbs or mushrooms, careful to avoid places with spiderwebs. The storm raged outside her, as if it were all the tears she'd held back for so long. Tears for Cayo, for Nowla, for Yansin, for her islands, for Kerely, for Vivian, even for herself. So much sadness stuffed deep inside, like those storm clouds Vivian once pointed to her. And only now she saw it, in an enemy, letting his sadness flow without restraint, and with such power and beauty, wearing his heart out for everyone to see, something Saytera never had done.

Her own tears mingled with the raindrops. This was more water than even the showers in the academy, cold like in her first night, freezing her skin, her muscles, her bones. Cold like she'd let her heart be once, thinking that strength was in restraint, was in keeping it all down, contained. And now, once sadness was laid bare to her, she realized what it could be.

But sadness sometimes had answers. Having seen herself and her own tears falling from those black eyes, she had to fix it, she had to find a solution. Years and years with Kerely, hunting for rare herbs, would not go to waste. She would find something. Nature was death—but also life. Death and life. And then she found it. Grayish leaves growing on a tree trunk. She picked some leaves and ran back to the cave.

Before she reached it, Dess was running to her, eyes wide as if desperate. "Where were you?"

Saytera raised her hand with the plant, for a moment fearing the worst had already happened and her search had been in vain. "Antidote."

He had a half smile and looked at her as if incredulous. "Thank you."

She almost told him not to thank her yet, but then decided

it was better not to squash his hope. They entered the cave and reached Dess's friend.

Saytera knelt beside him and turned to Dess. "Ideally we should make some tea, but… I'll try my best."

She crushed some leaves between her fingers and put it in the young man's mouth.

Dess knelt beside her. "What is it?"

"Alpanea."

"The one Terens use to see the invisible?"

That was weird. "No. It's just medicine."

He gave her an odd look. "How long do you think until it takes effect?"

Saytera wasn't sure, but she tried a guess. "He'll sleep. Then it will be a few hours, maybe a day."

He nodded.

The wind was still strong and as night was falling it was getting cool. Saytera sat in a corner shivering, suddenly afraid for herself. She'd been cold before, but it didn't last that long. She wasn't sure if she'd be able to stand the whole night like that. Dess had taken off his coat, now drenched, but his clothes underneath it were dry. He had a long black tight-fit shirt over black pants. Drenched, Saytera would probably be the one who died from hypothermia first.

Dess sat in front of her and showed his hands. "Can I?"

Saytera frowned. "What?"

"You're shivering. I can warm your arms."

She wasn't sure she was following. Dess rubbed his hands together then rubbed on her arms. Saytera tensed and looked away.

He stopped and sat back. "It bothers you."

"No."

He sighed. "And it won't solve your problem. Can you make fire?"

Make fire. Make fire. The one thing she should know and she didn't. And now her life depended on it, and yet... All he could do was quench fire, which wouldn't help her now. She shook her head.

Dess got up and started looking around. Faces appeared in front of Saytera; Yansin, Kerely, Nowla, Kilmara, Cayo, Vivian, Kiki, Larissa, Kay, Dess... They faded from view and then came back. Her life could fade as well, just like the lamps she quenched, the lights she faded.

Marcus was asleep and his breathing was regular. He still had blue extremities. Hopefully he'd make it. But there was something more urgent Dess had to take care of. If they didn't make a fire, they wouldn't survive the cooling night. Saytera was shivering and still wet. It would be unfair if her walk in the storm to save Marcus's life took hers instead. There would be no dry wood outside. In the cave, there were just a few twigs, all still humid. The worst was that even if he got the wood and something flammable, there was nothing to ignite it. So much for being a spark...

Still, he put all the twigs he could together, and shot them with his zapper, hoping that its heat would dry them. Yes, his ammunition would be gone, but that was a problem for tomorrow. All he had to do now was make sure that there would be a tomorrow for them. Dess was feeling cold himself, and he didn't think it would help Marcus, even if he still kept his coat. The twigs got dry. Dess then ripped part of his jacket and added it to the pile. How much fire could he make out of it? He had to find a way, knowing he had two lives to save. Maybe even three. If only the stories about people conjuring fire were real. Maybe they were. Still, he had no idea how to do it. He had a pile of dry wood. All he needed was to ignite it. Ignite. He ran to Marcus's and looked at the supplies in his belt. An impact bomb. Except he didn't want it to explode.

Slowly he opened its outer part and dropped the fuel around his improvised fire. This was the only bomb left, and it had to work. Stars in the universe, stars within. He focused all the fire, all the energy in that little bomb. It had to work. Dess threw it on the pile of twigs and held his breath. After a while, some of the twigs started getting red, and he fanned them, hoping it would make them catch more fire. It did. Small, weak, but it was catching.

Saytera rested her back on the stone and had her eyes closed. Her arms were so cold. "Come here," he whispered.

"Where?"

He helped her up and made her sit by the fire. He then pulled Marcus closer to it. The coldest person there was Saytera. He sat behind her and rubbed his hands on her arms. Perhaps she'd call him a pervert tomorrow, but he'd prefer that than not ever seeing her again. If his friend woke up, he'd owe his life to her. It was only the three of them now, and he wouldn't let her die.

Eventually she fell asleep, her back rested against him. Slowly he put her on the ground and got up. The rain stopped outside. Dess got more wood, which he put near the fire to dry, then tossed it in it. He used a bit of his energy pistol, too, until its ammo was gone.

Marcus still had a pulse and was breathing normally. Dess fed the fire, knowing that it would also keep creatures away from them. He let his jacket dry in the smoke, then put it over

Saytera. He'd lay down beside her to warm her, but he still remembered her terrified look and didn't want to scare her or confirm her poor opinion of him. The warm light of the fire illuminated her face and reflected in her shiny brown hair. She was beautiful, the girl who hadn't hesitated to brave a storm to save his friend—her enemy. The girl who knew about Terens and more magic than she was letting him know. Dess sighed. The girl who thought he was repulsive. If only he really had girl-magnet snapping fingers. Nonsense. It probably wouldn't work on her. He'd better lie down, too. His thoughts were going into scary, uncharted territory.

"Dess, Dess, Dess," someone moaned.

Saytera was wondering what that meant when she opened her eyes and found herself lying in the arms of the person being called. She sat up quickly. Awkward. She didn't remember how she'd fallen asleep, but didn't doubt that she'd moved in the night to get closer to the dude to get warm. She turned to the direction of the voice. Dess's friend. Of course. Marcus. He was shivering. Had she made a mistake? Saytera tried to think back and remembered that it should cause sleep and maybe fever. She touched his forehead and indeed it was warm. He still called his friend.

Dess was beside her in a minute. "What's wrong?"

"Just a fever. He should get delirious now."

Marcus extended his hand and took Dess's. "You're here."

Dess squeezed his friend's hand. "I am. Of course."

"Dess, Dess. Sylvia. You love her, she loves you. Take care of her."

Dess stared at Saytera with an apologetic look, then whispered to his friend, "You're confusing me with you. You're the one she loves."

"Take care of her. Promise," Marcus insisted.

"You will take care of her. You're not dying."

"Just promise."

Dess sighed. "Yes."

"You own the moon, you own the moon. Why didn't you tell me you own the moon?"

Dess had wide eyes as if terrified.

"He's delirious," Saytera whispered.

Marcus shook his head. "I'm not. I'm not. Who are you, magic girl?"

She decided to answer. "Saytera. You and your friend kidnapped me."

"Queen of darkness. You saved me. I'm thankful."

"You're welcome."

"It's you. It's you. It's not Sylvia, it's you."

Saytera turned to Dess. "Who's Sylvia?"

"His girlfriend."

Well, that was awkward.

Marcus mumbled, "She's not, she's not. She's not. It was never me. Never me. Never me."

He kept saying more and more incoherent stuff, a lot to do with this Sylvia. Saytera then remembered something Dess had said the previous night. "Do you still think it helps with seeing the invisible?"

He was silent for a couple seconds, then said, "I don't know. It's just something I read. Wrong, I guess." He stared at her. "You obviously know a ton lot more about Terens than I do."

"I've never read the Tome of Darkness, for example."

His eyes sparkled with interest. "I can tell you about it. And you can tell me things I don't know."

Being under his gaze was… She wasn't sure what she felt and got up. "I'll go get something for us to eat."

Dess held her arm. "It's dangerous out there."

"Better than certain death by starvation."

"I'm coming with you."

She gestured towards Marcus. "And leave your friend unattended?"

Dess was silent.

Saytera continued, "I'll find something around here. And I'll watch for spiders. Don't worry."

She walked outside in search of the edible mushrooms and plants she'd ignored the previous night. Dess's tears had moved her so much that she'd forgotten about her hunger—and theirs, especially. The two guys hadn't eaten anything. Perhaps she shouldn't worry, since it had been their fault, but after those stupid tears that could have been hers, she couldn't see them as enemies anymore. The same heart, same soul, same ability to love and hurt and fear. Weren't they all made from the same starfire?

18

IN SEARCH OF A WAY OUT

opefully Marcus would get quiet before Saytera returned. He was now going on and on about how Dess wanted to kiss the "magic girl". At least she thought he was just delirious. Dess wasn't so sure. As much as he denied it, he once had been in love with Sylvia, and it was weird to see the truth spat out by his friend, except that Marcus thought it was still true—and it wasn't. As for Saytera, who in his right mind would *not* want to kiss her?

It didn't mean she had to know about it. At least his friend was keeping it clean talking about kisses only. And hoped he would keep it this way. Some private thoughts should be sacred.

Dess went to the edge of the cave and saw Saytera coming with something in her hands.

She shrugged. "Mushrooms."

Dess took one. "Can I eat it raw?"

She grimaced. "It's not great, but it won't kill you. Shouldn't we go inside?"

"I think we'll disturb his sleep. He keeps trying to talk to us." Dess took a bite of a mushroom. It didn't have any taste. Not the worst thing he'd ever eaten, for sure.

"Maybe. We need to fish, but that's on the beach, and we can't leave him alone."

"And there's no shelter by the beach."

She shook her head. "We need to go there and back. Can you make more fire tonight?"

Dess wasn't sure and he'd need to find a solution soon. "Maybe, but eventually bombs and ammo will be gone."

There was a hint of fear in her eyes. "If we don't find a way out we're in trouble, then."

For sure. Dess tried to think. "Do you know how to make a raft?"

"No." She had a grimace.

Right. As if knowing how to make a raft were in any way weirder than disabling a spaceship.

She then asked, "Any chance your people will come and rescue you?"

Dess remembered Sophie and Tara. Well, he would have tried to rescue them. Perhaps it wasn't impossible. He also remembered the chip on his neck. "Maybe. But we can't count on it."

Saytera sighed. "I'm sorry. Truly. I don't think I caused the failure on your ship, but if it was, please know it was an accident."

Dess shook his head. "It was my fault and you know it. Don't apologize for fighting for your freedom."

She looked away, paused for a moment, then asked, "So you grew up in Sapphirlune?"

"Born and raised there."

She tilted her head. "How come you know so much about Terens?"

He could ask her the same thing, but he'd better start by answering. "I have many rare books."

"Including the Tome of Darkness. What is it about?"

Dess tried to remember it. "There isn't much. It's short. It's a story about when all the lights and all the fire go down. Then they fight with swords and arrows. I always thought it was about trusting yourself, not external things. Trust the real fire, the inner fire. Then they defeat the Master of Darkness and light comes back. It sounds boring, I know, but it's different when you read it. Words get organized in a way that makes sense."

"So you thought I was a Teren because of my bow and arrows?"

Dess decided to be honest. "No. It was something about you."

She straightened and had eager eyes. "So you've seen Terens before."

Dess looked down. "No. I had never seen one." He was going to add "before you", but decided to leave it, and asked, "And how come *you* know about Terens?"

She paused for a moment, as if considering it. "Similar to you. We talked about their traditions in the village where I grew up."

"So you also had books."

She ran her hands through her hair. "A few. People also told the stories orally and in songs. I never saw books about Terens outside my village."

Dess shrugged. "Perhaps people want to hide them."

"Or they're the ones who want to hide."

"And leave us in this mess, fighting each other, starving, dying."

She rolled her eyes. "Kidnapping. Easy to blame others." She stared at him. "I have a question for you."

"What?"

"How many people do what you're doing?"

"That's confidential."

She nodded. "Let me rephrase it. Do you know anything about Somersault?"

Her tone had been accusatory, and he felt anxious, but he had no idea what she was talking about. "We don't know your base names."

"Have you ever killed anyone?"

Dess hesitated, then said, "It's a war, even if you pretend it isn't, with the stupid truce. You wouldn't have hesitated in blowing me out of the air, and you know it."

"The truce was meant for you to leave us alone!"

He snorted. "Without water? Kind of hard."

"Oh." She paused. "Still, why take people?"

"I can't say any more."

"I'll explain. There was a base where everyone was killed. Was it you?"

Dess was surprised. "Everyone? No. No, no. We never—"

"So it must have been one of your colleagues."

"No, we were the only ones…" He stopped, realizing he was saying too much, but then decided it didn't matter. "We were the only ones getting that close to the bases. And it would make no sense whatsoever for us to kill everyone."

"So what happened, then?"

"I don't know. It wasn't us. It wasn't any Lunar." He tried to think. Could it be that there was another team doing it? He couldn't see Sophie and Tara killing anyone, and he knew that the military port wasn't sending ships to the planet. It just didn't make any sense. "We're not interested in killing anyone, we just want access to the planet, and to the Tahari moon. That's all. It's not unreasonable."

"Concede defeat and you get it all."

Dess snorted. "Yeah. Then we'll have to pay your planet more than we even produce just to access your resources."

"Oh, yeah, that would be awful. Coming down, stealing, murdering, and kidnapping is so much better."

"I'm not your enemy, Saytera. It's this war. We'd be friends had we been on the same side."

"Except we aren't." She then entered the cave.

Dess rested his head on his hand.

Hunger was getting to Saytera. Going down to the beach could be an answer if she found something easy to kill and catch, like a crab, for example. Hopefully not a giant one. Here, on this hill, she was getting sick of mushrooms. Marcus slept in silence now. Instead of looking at his friend, Dess watched her in silence, his eyes no longer lined in black, all the painting gone with the tears from the night before.

She decided to ask, "What are you looking at?"

He blinked. "You."

Saytera shivered. It was odd. He wasn't staring at her the way Kay did, it was different, and unsettling for different reasons. She decided to change the subject and got up. "Listen, I'm starving and I'm going to the beach."

He was in front of her. "Wait. I think he'll wake up soon. If he's at least conscious, we can leave him."

Thunder rolled outside. "I'm not gonna wait for the storm."

Dess held her wrist. "Too late. If you go out now you'll come back drenched again."

He was right. So many dark clouds in the sky. It was annoying. She shook her arm free, got back inside, and sat down on a corner. Dess sat by her. "Listen, I'm sorry. I can't change what I've done. But we need to stick together to survive."

"We've been sticking, haven't we?" She glanced at Marcus. "And he's going to make it."

Dess nodded and smiled. "Tell me about the Terens. Tell me what you know."

"I don't really know much. I think you know more than I do. Who are they? Where are they from? What do they want?"

"What I know is that they've been around as long as humanity has, but tend to isolate themselves and focus on magic."

Saytera almost corrected his mention of magic. But if she accepted it as just another name for matterweaving it started to make sense. What were words, anyway? "What about you? What do you do with the people you kidnap?"

"I don't do anything. I just hand them over to the council."

"What about the killings?" she asked.

"You said it was an entire base, right? That I can say with ninety-nine percent certainty that it has nothing to do with Lunars."

"So who, then?"

He was thoughtful. "Internal enemies, maybe?"

"I don't know."

He looked away and shook his head. "See, we're both losing. Is anyone winning anything in this war? There's only pain and loss."

Pain and loss. So much pain and loss, and yet, some of Saytera's didn't really relate to that specific war, but to something else. "Is everyone in your moon that knowledgeable about Terens?"

"Not that I know of. I know about them because I had the books and my parents told me about them. I don't know anyone else who really, truly believes we're capable of a greater power."

"Doesn't that make you the odd one out?"

"I'm an orphan. That makes me stand out enough already."

"But you said your parents…"

"When I was a child. They died when I was eleven."

"I'm sorry." That didn't help, she knew, but she didn't know what else to say.

He shook his head. "It's this war."

"Shouldn't more people be orphans, though?"

"They go to the orphanage, not the academy."

"Hum. I guess we have more orphans then. Everyone I met in the academy didn't have living parents."

"There are lots of orphans in Sapphirlune, they're just not part of its elite."

"How fair."

"So your parents are also dead?"

When asked about her parents, Saytera thought about Yansin and Kerely, and she didn't think they had died. They'd just—abandoned her. Saytera held back a sob.

"Sorry," Dess said. "You don't have to talk about it."

"No. My family died when I was a baby. I don't know who they are." That was true, too, even if it wasn't something her mind went back to often.

He had a curious face. "And nobody knows who they are?"

Saytera just shook her head.

"No records, nothing?"

"Their ship crashed in the ocean."

"How did you survive?"

Saytera had heard this story a long time before. "My seat was ejectable and I ended up on the beach."

"But you don't remember it."

"No. I don't remember anything."

"Have you ever considered that maybe someone knows who you are?"

"Why wouldn't they tell me?"

He shrugged. "To protect you."

All that destiny talk came back to Saytera. She remembered Vivian telling Yansin "you knew who she was." Could it be? It was possible. But she didn't want to think about that right then. She sighed. "I guess I'll die not knowing, if we stay stuck on this island."

He stared at her. "If it helps, I also don't tell people who my parents were."

"Why not?"

"My mother asked me not to. Before she died. They were killed. Whoever killed them could maybe come after me, too."

"Why?"

He had a half smile. "You want me to tell you too much."

"But nobody notices your name?"

"I got a fake name. I'm Dess Starspark."

Saytera snorted. "And nobody notices it's fake?"

"That it comes from the mind of an eleven-year-old? No." He nodded towards Marcus. "Not even he knows."

Saytera was puzzled. "Why are you telling me that?"

"Either we'll die in this place and it won't matter, or we'll go separate ways and it won't matter. Plus I haven't told you my real name. And I also know your secret."

A hint of fear flashed through her. "What secret?"

"You can disable electric systems."

Saytera exhaled. She wasn't sure what secret she was

expecting him to know, but it wasn't that. She waved a hand. "I told you I have no idea how that works."

"But you don't think it's impossible, do you?"

All the pistols failing, lights turning off, even the blackouts in the academy, maybe… Maybe. Maybe he did know a secret about her. "Not impossible. Just unlikely."

Dess smiled and shook his head, his dark hair bouncing. "I won't tell anyone. I've always wanted to meet someone like you."

Saytera froze. "Like what?"

"Who has real magic."

Oh. That. "I can't even conjure fire."

Dess laughed. "You say it as if it were a normal thing to do."

"For Terens it is."

"In my books it says it's a rare skill, but I'll trust you on that. What else do you know?"

"Nothing."

They then heard Marcus's voice, "Dess."

Saytera turned.

The young man was sitting up, alert, his face a healthy color again. "What's happening?"

Dess filled him in on the accident, his spider bite, and where they were. Marcus ate some mushrooms. When the rain fell, he got some water from the edge of the cave to drink.

He looked at them. "Tomorrow, if there's no storm, we have to go to the beach."

"There's no shelter there," Dess replied.

"But they can't land here. You know they're coming for you. Nadia will send someone for you, Dess, you know it."

"It's hard to fly here."

"The weather needs to clear, for sure. But they're coming."

Saytera felt a knot in her stomach fearing they'd take her as a hostage, to be sent who knew where.

"Maybe," Dess answered, voice dry. He then turned to Saytera. "Whatever happens, I'll keep my word."

"Thanks," her voice was thin.

It wasn't that she doubted him, but that there would be more people, more Lunars, and she wasn't sure how much he would be able to do.

A good thing that Marcus was conscious, but she wished she'd had more time with Dess, to talk about Terens and what he called magic. She realized that he was probably right that she had caused his ship to crash, and was stunned to realize that someone saw her power more clearly than even she did. An enemy. A lunar. And yet… Perhaps if there hadn't been a war they could have been friends. No. They wouldn't even have met each other. What was she even thinking?

Dess stared at her. "You don't trust me?"

Saytera laughed. "Since when are we allies and trust each other?"

"A day at least."

"Proof how things can change quickly."

He shook his head. "You can't put spilled water back in a bottle, though. Certain things cannot go back to the way they were. Maybe there is a reason we are here. I've always thought we had to win, but is it victory we need? Or is it peace?"

"I guess it depends. Aren't we just cogs in a bigger machine? The question is what the machine needs."

"But we need to question it. We don't need to be cogs."

"Oh, we can be castaways on an island," she joked.

"That's a possibility, too. But if we're rescued, we won't be the same. We can do things differently."

"I guess."

Saytera didn't want to mention that she had zero chance of making any difference for Mainland. Maybe Dess, among the elite academy whatever, could do something. Saytera was just a nobody in a base nowhere, set up just for the appearance of security or for cannon fodder.

The night came and Dess and Marcus managed to set up a fire. They also caught some sort of rodent and were roasting it, filling the cave with a putrid smell. Saytera wasn't sure if she was going to be able to eat it, but was glad for the warmth in that damp, cool night, when she had no coat or jacket.

They passed the time talking about their childhoods. Marcus had grown up in a rich family. Dess said he had grown up in a mansion, raised by his grandfather, who was the gardener. Saytera knew he was lying, but didn't say anything. When it was her turn, she mentioned her childhood in her "village". Both Dess and Marcus had wide eyes when she told them about swimming in the ocean, catching crabs, shrimp, or fish. Neither of them had grown up near nature like that. When they started talking, she thought Marcus had been privileged, now she wasn't sure. And growing up with Yansin, learning everything she did, had been a privilege. Of course she didn't tell them about that, but still, it was in her thoughts, coloring her memories with sadness and yearning for a time long gone.

Saytera lay down with a half-empty belly. The floor was hard, but this time she at least had Dess's jacket for cover. The crackling sound of the fire and the howling wind outside should lull her to sleep. But her mind was busy wondering if there would be any fire tomorrow or if some kind of rescue team would try to kidnap her for good. She wondered if she'd rather hide and stay on that island, but the thought of eternal loneliness somehow was even worse than the fear for her life.

19

BACK TO THE BEACH

Someone shook Dess's shoulders. Marcus. He sat up and glanced at the fire. Oh, no. It was out. He should have kept it going, but sleep had taken him over. Hopefully they'd find a way to ignite it again tonight.

"We'd better move," his friend said. "So we get to the beach and back before the storm."

Dess sat up. "Quite insightful for someone who's been out for two days. How do you even know when it rains?"

"Our conversation, silly." He then lowered his voice and glanced at Saytera, who still slept, enveloped in his coat. "What do you want to do with her?"

"She saved your life," Dess whispered. Then added, "And mine, too."

"It's just a question, Dess."

"Well, if we keep living in this place, we keep helping each other, right?"

Marcos exhaled. "You know what I'm talking about."

Dess chuckled. "Your commitment to hope is commendable. If we're rescued, we'll see."

"No, you need to plan. And let me know what you're planning."

Perhaps Marcus had a good point. Well, yes, of course he did. It was just that Dess's brain was still half asleep. Then there was the fact that he had no idea who would come for them—if anyone came—and that could change a lot of factors.

A sound came from Saytera's corner. She was sitting, long messy hair, and smiled at him. "Hey."

There was something so casual, intimate about seeing her wake up, and she looked so natural, just… he couldn't quite explain it. Dess wanted to see her wake up many more times. Well, he probably would. Somehow, the idea wasn't depressing.

"Good morning," Marcus said, snapping Dess out of his speechless trance. He continued, "We'd better get going."

Saytera turned to Dess's friend. "I see you healed well."

Marcus shrugged. "I think I got enough sleep for a couple weeks."

Saytera got up. "Let's go. We can get something to eat there."

She then handed Dess his coat. "Thank you."

Her thanks was sweet, sincere, unlike her sharp takes from the first day.

He handed it back. "Keep it. It's windy." She just stared. He added, "It's survival. I don't want you… getting sick. I have long sleeves. I'm hot."

She paused, then smiled and took it back. "Thanks."

Looking into her eyes, Dess wanted to bask in that moment, pull her closer, kiss her. Yes, he wanted to kiss her. Like he'd never wanted to kiss anyone before. He'd scold himself for the audacity of the thought, for his presumption in thinking she could ever be his, except that it seemed as if she wanted it, too. The thought was overwhelming. Here was someone who was more than he'd ever dreamed, with real magic, a real Teren—and despite her denials, he was sure of that. And her eyes were locked in his, beautiful and powerful. All for him.

"Yo, lovebirds," Marcus's voice. It was as if it broke an enchantment. She looked away. He continued, "Make out on the beach."

Dess wanted to reply, but calling him an asshole, telling him he should have left him for dead, or denying anything sounded wrong. Maybe he was still speechless. Dess just glared at his friend. For the first time in his life, he wanted to punch Marcus on the face. Or maybe somewhere lower.

The walk down the hill had been so awkward that Saytera didn't even register the time passing until they came upon the ocean with its roaring waves. Lovebirds. Yeah, she'd been gawking at Dess. Yeah, she wouldn't mind making out with him. And she hated herself for that. That line of thought had only brought her pain, and falling for an enemy couldn't be good. No, no. She wasn't falling for him. It was just that the guy was good looking. More like outrageously good looking, and it was a normal reaction.

But the way he looked at her… Her stupid mind. The same mind that had made her hope about Cayo, even Kay. She'd never been in love with Kay, but she'd been under the illusion that maybe… But it was nothing to the way she was feeling now. Or maybe not feeling, perhaps it was just an impression. She couldn't be so stupid. So stupid.

He walked in front of her, in silence. Now that he no longer wore a coat, she could see more of his shape. Just the way he walked sent shivers down her spine. Oh, dear. This was bad. Meanwhile, she was still wearing his coat, his smell inebriating. She should have returned it, but perhaps it was true that getting sick wouldn't help them. Surviving was more important than making a point. And now she kind of hated that stupid friend of his, who had mocked her without remorse or thankfulness, forgetting she'd gone out in the storm, risking her own life, to try to find a cure for him.

Well, it had never been for Marcus, but for Dess. For his tears. The tears she'd always held back. The tears he let go without any shame or fear. In retrospect, that was exactly when her mind had been gone. When she'd fallen in love. Ugh. No, no. Not love. It was just compassion, something. Empathy. Yeah, empathy. She couldn't be so stupid. And arguing with her mind wasn't helping.

Dess approached her without really looking in her eyes. "So, how do we get food here?"

Impressive. The last thing on Saytera's mind right now was food. She tried to get her thoughts straight. "We'll need to see if there are crabs or sand creatures. Or go to the rocks and get shells."

He smiled. "If it doesn't work, you know where we can find lizards."

Saytera didn't really like that idea. "Last resort, but we'll need a plan so we're not ambushed like last time."

Dess chuckled. "I was joking."

"Uh-hum." Saytera looked down before his obnoxious friend made any comment.

Marcus was actually looking up. "The weather's clear."

Dess sighed. "I know what you're thinking, but I think it's pointless hope, Marcus."

Saytera looked up and touched her back pouch with her bow and arrows. "There are birds. Do you guys know how to defeather one?"

"I guess I could," Dess said. "The issue is how to cook it. I'm not sure we can still make fire."

"Can't we try with rocks or sticks?" Marcus asked. "Or use our energy pistols?"

Dess shook his head. "Ammo's gone."

Marcus just stared. "That's very comforting, in case we're attacked."

"I have my arrows." Saytera patted her back pouch.

Marcus squinted against the sun. "And you can shoot a flying bird out of the sky with that?"

What question was that? "Well, yeah. They are pretty close, and their trajectory is slow and predictable. Anyone can do that. Can't you?"

Marcus shook his head and chuckled.

Annoying. Saytera snapped. "Hey, I could prove it, but I'm not going to shoot one if we aren't eating it."

Marcus showed the palms of his hands, in a defensive position. "I'm not doubting it."

"He's never seen arrows before, Saytera."

Dess was defending his stupid friend, but instead of annoyed, Saytera was stunned by the softness with which he'd said her name. She'd better snap out of it.

Pointing to the edge of the beach, she said, "We'll find shells at those rocks."

The sun shone on the waves crashing on the sand, the water beyond brilliant, multiplying its lights in millions of little suns on its surface. Saytera walked without looking back, but footsteps behind her confirmed that she had company.

Shells wasn't a great meal, especially considering how

hungry she was, but it was something. Perhaps being "rescued" and then captured would indeed be better than remaining here without fire. Fire. She'd always wanted to know how to produce it, and yet, she'd never been in such dire need of it. It made sense that even kids would learn how to do it so early, considering how much of a difference it could make. Well, not Saytera. All she could make was darkness, which wouldn't help her situation here.

Laughter behind her made her turn around. Dess was laughing. He'd rolled up his pants and was putting his feet on the cold water, small waves washing his ankles back and forth. She was going to remind him to focus, help her, but the glee in his and his friend's eyes made her change her mind.

She approached Dess. "Haven't you been on beaches before?"

Marcus was farther away, also looking at the ocean. Dess smiled. "Never in a situation where I didn't fear someone would shoot me."

"Hum. I bet that kills the mood."

"A little." He bent and touched the water with the tips of his fingers. "This is… magical. You have no idea how lucky you are."

"Glad you like it. In case, you know, we spend the rest of our lives here."

He raised an eyebrow. "There are worse things, you know?"

"Starving, for example. Speaking of which, are you and your friend going to help me get some shells or not?"

"Of course."

They walked towards the rocks. Dess then said, "You know, we should try to find shelter closer to here. It would make our life easier."

"Guys, guys," Marcus's voice was eager and scared and made them turn around.

Saytera had her bow ready but there was nothing at the beach. She looked at the sky instead. A black shape approached the island. Perhaps Marcus didn't know what it was, but she knew it: Lunars. And now she'd have mere seconds to decide if she would hide and stay or try to go with them and negotiate a release or become a hostage. She should have asked details about what they did with their hostages before.

Dess squinted at the bright sky. "That's a C-31."

"You think they're Lunars?" Marcus asked, his voice now much more eager and relaxed.

"They are," Saytera said.

Marcus stared at her. "Sure?"

She sighed and nodded. "Positive." How did she even know it? Was it the certainty that Mainlanders didn't have many spaceships? Maybe it was just knowing that nobody from the continent would possibly rescue them, and that ship coming at them was too precise in its trajectory to be someone just surveying the area. They had to know something—or someone —was here, and Dess's chip on the neck was the only explanation.

Dess seemed thoughtful. "I agree."

Marcus started screaming and jumping on the sand. Meanwhile, Saytera's insides were turning to ice as her eyes were fixated on the black shape approaching them. A hand on her shoulder caught her attention. Dess.

"Hey, don't worry. I told you I'd take you to the continent, I will."

Saytera's body was so rigid she could barely manage a nod.

He looked at her. "You don't trust me?"

The weird thing is that she did. But it wasn't him that she

worried about. "There are other people there. Will they listen to you?"

"If I were them, I would."

Saytera forced a smile, unsure if he was joking or not. So much fear and dread, and yet at the same time she didn't want to risk running away and staying stranded on that island. The spacecraft came closer and closer to them, a large, black shape unlike any of the ships she'd ever seen.

Marcus ran in its direction. Saytera didn't blame his relief. At the same time, she knew that once they returned, the two of them would go back to whatever horrible things they'd been doing before. Kidnapping. And more. Dess stood silent.

There was something Saytera had to know. "So the killings. The ones in an entire base. It wasn't Lunars?"

"It wasn't me. I'm pretty sure it wasn't Lunars, but…"

"What?"

He pointed to the sky. "See that ship approaching? They're military. If they can come here, maybe… But then, it just doesn't make sense, you know? It seems way too clumsy, especially for an official operation. It just doesn't make sense."

"Lots of things don't make sense."

Dess was thoughtful, then said, "True. I'll check it. Not sure I'll have a way to let you know my findings, but I'll check it."

"You know where I live."

He raised an eyebrow. "Is that an invitation to visit?"

Was he… flirting? But she had other things in mind. "Knowing they can blow you up? No."

"So you care?"

Saytera tensed. "I know you. Personally. I wouldn't want to learn you were shot and killed."

He looked away, thoughtful. "I guess it's a compliment, then. Even if it means I won't see you for a long time."

She'd been thinking she'd never see him again and now that the thought was clear she realized it almost made her nauseous while all her insides tightened in a horrible feeling. She tried to be playful about it. "It's not like we're neighbors."

"We are. Compared to the vastness of the universe, we're in the same world. The divide is just this war, and it won't last forever."

"Maybe."

There was a spark in his eyes. "No. Truly. You see what I see? We're stupid. We've been chasing victory for so long, waiting for a chance, an opening to strike, because let's not be silly, that's what those truces are, when the solution is much simpler."

"Really?"

"Of course. What we both need is peace. That's what I'm going to fight for."

Saytera considered her time in the academy, even Dess's military training, how they were raising young people to fight, kill, win, how they were told the Lunars were to blame for everything wrong in their planet. "It's tough to oppose people's beliefs."

"I don't think it's opposing, but making them see the easiest way to achieve what they truly desire."

She nodded. "Fair enough. I'll remember that and try something, with all my super influence over Mainland."

He shook his head. "You don't have to. You guys are bigger and things seem a lot more complex. I can do my part, though." He stared at the ship approaching the beach. "Let's go. Stay close to me."

That ship was very large and landed on the beach. A side door opened down to a ramp, reaching the ground. The sand softened its thud, but it still rocked Saytera, not because of the sound, but just the immense dread of being captured, of facing real enemies.

Dess was quite intrigued to learn who had been sent for them, especially considering this wasn't any of the ships from the civil port.

Sam stepped out of the door. "Here I am. To pick up the trash."

Why did it have to be Sam? Dess stepped in front of Saytera to shield her from Sam, then said, "I'm glad they got an expert."

Saw narrowed his eyes. "Trying to hide something, Dess? Is that a hostage?"

Dess was out of ammo. Not a positive prospect. "It's none of your business."

Sam then pulled out a pistol and aimed toward Dess. "Step away and let me stun her, then. I'm not having enemies on my ship."

Dess stepped forward. "Scared?"

Sam shrugged. "Fine, then. Your choice."

It had been a quick reaction started at the moment Sam had a smug smile. Dess kicked the weapon from his opponent. He then saw Amil approaching from inside the ship, ready to fire, and jumped on him, holding down his pistol arm. A foot kicked Dess's ribs. Sam's. Dess then rolled away before the same foot came to his face. He heard a gun firing and saw that Marcus had stunned Amil. Soon after, Sam was stunned, too. It had all been too fast. He looked back. Saytera had her bow ready and was lowering it.

Marcus threw the pistol on the floor. "Great. Now they'll probably imprison us."

"You didn't have to help me."

Marcus puffed. "Right. I should just watch them beating you."

"I can hold my own."

He rolled his eyes. "I noticed it."

Dess ignored his friend and turned to Saytera. "Are you all right?"

"I am." She looked puzzled, though.

Dess felt he had to give an explanation, but then the main reason he'd jumped on Sam was because he feared they'd want to take Saytera back to Sapphirlune. He feared being stunned and not being able to do anything. But he didn't want to say as much. Dess shrugged. "I never liked them."

She chuckled.

"Question is," Marcus said. "How are we getting back home?"

Weird question. "You do realize this is geared for space travel, right?"

His friend crossed his arms. "Are you planning on taking it?"

"Of course not. Just doing them a favor. They can rest while we pilot."

Marcus sighed. "I'm sure they're going to be thrilled."

"I don't care." He turned to Saytera. "We're taking you home."

She looked him in the eye. "Thanks." Her eyes said much more, as if she understood the significance of what he'd just done and understood it had been for her. Or maybe he was projecting it. Either way, her look made it all worth it.

They strapped Sam and Amil on the back seats.

Marcus approached him and whispered. "I don't think it's wise to go to the continent."

"I disagree."

"They'll see it on the flight route."

"Not if it's broken."

"But…"

Dess shot the part of the panel where the flight recorder was. "There. Broken."

Marcus sighed. "We're going to be in so much trouble."

"We won't. Trust me."

"I always do," his friend said. "And maybe I should reconsider it."

Dess shrugged. He turned to Saytera, who was sitting right behind him. "Ready?"

"Yes." She was rigid on the seat, eyes wide.

He stared at the radar in search of clouds and was stunned. "Some luck. The weather is completely clear today."

Marcus frowned. "We could wait."

They could, but then, he wasn't sure how long Sam and Amil would be out and didn't trust them at all.

"Dess."

He turned to Saytera.

She asked, "You use clouds to disguise your flight, right?"

"Maybe."

She rolled her eyes. "Yeah. Anyway, you said you're a good pilot, right?"

"I like to think so."

"There's a way to approach the continent, then."

Dess widened his eyes, curious about what she was going to suggest.

"If you approach the peninsula by the east, it has tons of small islands and many rocks. They don't look for boats there."

He stared at her. "And if I fly low enough nobody will be looking for a spaceship there either."

"Exactly."

This was a lot more like a hard exercise in the simulator, dodging obstacles as the ship almost touched the water and he dodged rocks and islands. He had to be very careful because a C-31 wasn't supposed to be submerged. In fact, it was a big, clumsy ship, and only two idiots could have come to Mainland in it. In truth, it didn't make what he was doing any easier, but at the same time, he'd practiced this so much... Perhaps there was something to be learned in the simulator. Marcus was silent and so was Saytera, probably too scared to break his concentration.

They stopped at a small beach. According to the map and to Saytera it wasn't too far from her base.

He stared at her. This was it. This was goodbye. They stepped outside and he was glad to have a moment with her away from his friend.

She stood in front of him. "Thank you. It means a lot."

"It's nothing. I made a promise."

He wanted to say something else but none of the words circling his mind seemed to fit. Maybe he didn't even know what to say.

She broke the silence. "I guess... goodbye, then."

He reached out and took her hand. "Wait." And then he had the craziest idea. "Come with me. We can fight for peace together. We can work together. I'll hide you. I'll protect you. We'll find a way."

Together, together, together. The word rang. It was the gist of what he wanted to say.

She stared at him in silence for a moment, then said, "Dess..." Her tone was apologetic.

"Fine." He didn't want to hear the rest. He was angry, but he shouldn't be angry. His idea was stupid. She'd probably be imprisoned if she were to go to Sapphirlune with him. Maybe not, maybe he'd find a way. Truth was that this was all too soon and he wasn't thinking straight. "I mean… I get it. Sorry."

"You don't have to apologize."

She stood staring at him, all magic and power, and he was losing her and it tore his heart apart. And yet they were standing so close. He didn't remember that they were this close. It was just a matter of reaching out and kissing her. And if he did it he'd probably decide to become a fisherman, kidnap her, disappear from the world, and forget all about the war. Forget about who he was, everything he'd always fought for.

He took off the ring from his pinkie finger and extended it to her. "Here. So you don't forget me."

She took it and stared at it.

He added, "You don't have to wear it."

She put it on her ring finger. "Are you sure you won't miss it?"

"Not more than I'll miss you."

Her lips parted, surprised. "I wish I had something…"

"I'm not going to forget you. I don't need a reminder."

"Me neither."

Dess smiled. "We'll meet again, when we're at peace. And then we won't have to be enemies anymore."

"What if there's no peace?"

"There will be. I'm as certain of it as I'm certain I'll find you. It's knowing without knowing."

"Perhaps you're right." She smiled.

He realized his hands were running through her hair. And this, this was the moment. He should kiss her. Instead, he closed his eyes and stepped back. "It was nice meeting you."

She was startled. He pointed to the ring. "A part of me will always be with you."

He stared at her. Perhaps he could get someone to remove his chip, maybe find a place for him in the Mainland military, then tell them his moon's secrets. Or maybe both of them could run somewhere. Hide. They could even live on an island, as long as they had enough fuel and supplies. But then, something would always be missing. And he didn't even know what she felt for him. No. There was something there. There was. Despite the short time they'd been with each other, he felt she understood him better than anyone. And perhaps he understood her as well. Which only made it even more painful. He felt tears forming in his eyes. "Goodbye."

Turning around and getting to the ship was one of the hardest things he'd ever done in his life. He took off without looking back. After they braved that rocky ocean and were up in the atmosphere, Marcus said, "You don't look well."

"I'm not."

20

____

NEW RESOLUTIONS

The ship got smaller and smaller against the now graying sky. A gust of wind chilled Saytera, and she set off to the base, wondering if there was still a place for her there, if they'd accept her, and what she'd tell them. The truth? None of it had been her fault, she hadn't betrayed the mainlanders... And yet... There was something off about it. She touched the ring on her hand, thinking perhaps she should hide it. Just a ring. Unlikely anyone would notice it.

Dess's image remained in her mind, staring at her, tears forming in his eyes. Those tears. Always those tears. But then he turned around. There was no point letting his image haunt her. With a world between them, all she had was the ring and the memory. And maybe the vague idea that perhaps they'd meet again. Knowing without knowing. It only cast doubts.

Waves crashed onto the shore and her heart pounded as she reached the top of the cliff. On a clear day like that, it was odd that she hadn't seen anyone on the beach. She gathered her courage—and knocked on the door.

Seconds and seconds passed while she wondered if there

had been any change, if they were still there. It was insane. How long had she been gone? Three days? It felt like forever. An eternity between moments.

To her relief, it was Larissa who opened the door. Her eyes widened, then she hugged Saytera.

"You're alive." She stepped back and check Saytera up and down. "Are you alright?"

"I am. I'm back."

"I see that. What happened?"

Saytera felt a chill in her stomach and hesitated. "I..." Then she felt something else in her stomach, more like emptiness. "I'm starving. Do you have something to eat?"

"Come. Let's get you something."

Leftover crab and rice had never tasted so delicious.

Larissa watched her in silence. "How are you?"

"Better."

"So. What happened?"

Well, she had to tell her story and perhaps it was better to start with Larissa. "I was kidnapped. By two Lunars."

"So they took you?"

"Yes. But we never left the planet. Uh..." The mere idea that she'd taken down that ship caused her chills. But this wasn't something she'd ever tell anyone. "There was a failure and we crashed. On an island. We... survived with some mushrooms."

Larissa thought for a moment. "We. So you worked together?"

Saytera sighed. "We had to. One of them got hurt, there were dangerous creatures, we had to find food, shelter..."

"What are they like?" Her tone was curious.

"They are people. Like us. They were both young, too."

Larissa nodded. "And how did you get back?"

"They were rescued. And they dropped me off here."

Her friend had a confused frown. "Dropped you off?"

"Well, it was an agreement we made because I helped them survive. They kept their word."

"How did they even get here? Do you mean to say that they've been coming in and out? Under our noses? Under our anti-aerial defenses? Not that I'm upset you're back, I'm just…"

"I…" Weird. She'd been looking forward to telling her colleagues about Lunar ships hiding in storm clouds. Now she imagined her information getting Dess killed, and wasn't as sure. "I have no idea how they come in and out."

Larissa clenched her fist. "Damn Lunars."

"He says there are very few people doing this, and it's mostly for food and water."

"And for killing some of us."

"They say they only kidnapped very few of us, they didn't kill anyone."

Larissa rolled her eyes. "Oh, yeah, that's so much better. Take us somewhere to be tortured in search of information we don't even have."

"I don't know. They didn't seem mean. What about us? We just shoot them."

"Well, they're not supposed to come here. When they come, they kill, kidnap, and put our lives in danger." She stared at Saytera up and down. "So you got along well."

"Uh… more like uncomfortable allies."

"And an uncomfortable ally gave you his coat."

Crap. Only then Saytera noticed she was still wearing it. "I… it was cold." What was the point in lying? "Yeah. We got along."

"And you got a ring."

Saytera hid her hand. She was going to say she already had it, but she was realizing Larissa was too good an observer to fall for that. "Yeah. As a reminder. As a symbol for us to hope to reach peace."

"You do know what a guy giving a girl a ring means, right?"

Saytera didn't. "We don't wear jewelry in… the village where I'm from."

"You're wearing it on the wrong finger, but it's a love declaration."

Dess's eyes came to her mind. If only. Maybe. But he was too far away now, and she'd refused his invitation. "No, not in his case. He had a lot of rings, so it was what he could give me."

Larissa narrowed her eyes. "What did you give him? Your ring?"

"I don't wear that stuff. I didn't give him anything."

"That was just a stupid joke. I'm sorry, Saytera. I'm glad you're back in one piece."

Saytera nodded. "I've been thinking about something. They said they had nothing to do with Somersault."

"Some other Lunars, then."

Saytera shook her head. "No. He was pretty sure. He said his was the only team that actually came in contact with us."

"Why do you think it's important?"

"There's something going on. I feel it."

Larissa stared at her for a moment, then said, "He might have said it so you wouldn't be upset at him."

"No. He was surprised. There's something weird happening, Larissa. I know it. I feel it."

"Maybe." Larissa was thoughtful. "We can't do anything other than keeping a better watch and trying to figure out how they're reaching us. And you'll have to fix your story."

"Why?"

"You don't want them asking too many questions. Just say you were unconscious this whole time."

Saytera laughed. "Wow, what a recovery, then!"

"Kay, Nara, and Saulo won't know you came feeling so well."

"I guess that works."

Larissa got up. "You might want to rest now."

Saytera's mind was whirling. "No. Maybe. I mean… I know you don't believe it, but there's something odd happening. Here. In Mainland." She felt it was something she had to go after. "We need to figure out what it is."

"That's a huge task. Do you really think it's important?"

"I… feel it is." Knowing without knowing.

Larissa stared at her for a while. "I'll trust you on that, then. We could go to Citarella and access the files."

"Really? It's something we can do?"

"Yes. We check what's happening, then we see what to do. When do you think you can go?"

Go? Like that? Saytera hadn't imagined she'd get a yes, much less plan to go so quickly. But it sounded exciting. "Tomorrow. As soon as we can."

"Give it a couple days. For your recovery. I'll prepare everything. And remember, you were unconscious."

"Won't they want to test me or something?"

Larissa shook her head. "I'll convince them not to tell anyone."

Saytera realized that she had a good friend and smiled. "Thanks." For so much, but she didn't know how to say it.

"Thank me once we are back from Citarella."

Saytera smiled, excited with the prospect of actually getting up and doing something, or at least trying to. She took a warm shower and changed into her sleeping outfit, even though it was still day. When she got out of the bathroom, Lara, Saulo, and Kay were outside. Kay lifted her and spun her around.

"You're alive. Alive."

She felt a bit uncomfortable with him touching her, but he just seemed genuinely happy, so she just laughed. "I guess it's a great day when we can celebrate the simple fact of being alive."

Even Nara hugged her. "We were so worried."

Kay then took her hand, but she pulled it. He said, "I'm so sorry. You have no idea how I felt. I tried to save you and I failed, and I just wish it had been me instead."

"It wasn't your fault."

He sighed. "I also want to say, me and Cynthia, it was nothing."

"Kay, it's fine. I don't mind."

"I do, though. It's you that I want, not her."

Nara and Saulo walked away and Saytera just wanted to leave, too. "I'm tired."

"No. Listen. I'm sorry. For you, I'd wait a billion years."

"So you can wait for me to rest, right?"

He sighed. "True. You had some tough days."

Saytera went to her bedroom and closed the door. She had no clue what she'd ever seen in Kay, and felt extremely annoyed at herself and what had happened between them. Now she'd have to face him for a long time to come. Perhaps Larissa was wrong. Kay was not a heartbreaker, just a jerk. She understood why a girl would want to be transferred to another base.

But there were more important things. Saytera now had plans and dreams, and the hope that maybe she could find at least a little of the truth about this war. She didn't know how much she would be able to do with the information, if she ever found anything, but at least this was a step.

They had traveled a third of the way to Sapphirlune, and Dess watched Sam and Amil.

Marcus was in the front seat. "You think they'll wake up soon?"

"I think so. Their breath isn't as steady."

"Got a plan?"

At the moment it had been the most obvious idea. Now even Dess was doubtful that assaulting two commander trainees had been a brilliant decision. No. If he hadn't done that there was no way he would have been able to release Saytera and he wasn't going to go back on his word. But now it was time to find a solution. "They're proud."

Marcus raised an eyebrow. "No kidding. That means they'll want revenge."

"True. I'm still wondering why they came…"

"Somebody sent them."

Dess was thoughtful. "And that's key. Whoever sent them wants us back."

"Maybe they just don't want us deserting."

"Or perhaps we're more important than we think."

Marcus snorted. "Wishful thinking."

Dess didn't really agree with his friend, but he didn't want to press his point. "Fine. We'll have to face it. Small lie. We can say we had two hostages. They came out of nowhere, shot them, and were left on the island. If Sam and Amil accuse us of assaulting them, we'll say they're confused."

"So, their word against ours. Nah. Don't tell me you can't see how that's not going to count to our favor."

"They need us, Marcus. Remember that. I don't think they'll want a fuss. And we have to trust that they won't want people to know they were disarmed and rendered unconscious by us. Pride."

Marcus laughed and shook his head. "We're so screwed."

"I'm sorry. If we do face repercussions, I'll claim the blame."

His friend waved a hand. "They're assholes anyway."

"Now that's the spirit."

Sam flinched on his seat. Dess exchanged a look with Marcus, then proceeded to release the guy's restraints. A few seconds later, Sam's blue eyes greeted him.

Dess had a neutral face. "Hey, you're all right." He handed him his pistols. "Here."

Sam was thoughtful or maybe confused, then looked furious. "No thanks to you." He got up and pushed Dess against a wall. "You little piece of shit."

Dess was this close to pushing the guy back when he saw Marcus. He couldn't screw this up. "I'm really happy you picked us up."

Sam looked around and stepped back, perhaps realizing his partner was still unconscious and he was outnumbered. "You'll pay for what you've done."

"No doubt. Now I think you'd like to pilot, right? Get us back to Sapphirlune. Your friend will wake up soon."

Sam stared at Dess as if planning murder, and it made Dess realize that being humble and hoping he wouldn't want to tell anyone wouldn't work.

Dess smirked. "Can't wait for everyone to learn you two were defeated by us. It's going to be lovely."

"Lovely will be to see you in prison."

Dess sighed. "What can I do… everything has a price."

Amil woke up shortly after and the rest of the trip was in an uncomfortable silence. Marcus bit his nails. Dess was trying to think what would happen to them. They were obviously somewhat valuable, otherwise they wouldn't have had an official rescue party. They could maybe be demoted from their task? It didn't make sense, considering how few people could do it. No. Nothing would happen. Perhaps a couple days locked up at most. It had been worth it.

Dess had kept his word, Saytera was safe—hopefully, as he didn't know much about Mainlanders' procedures and if she'd also have trouble explaining how she'd gotten back. He still remembered her standing on that beach, looking at him. A detail jumped up at him now; his coat. She still had it. He was actually glad that something more than his ring was with her, as if he could envelop her in his warmth. He touched his finger with the missing ring. He'd left her with a promise of peace, but now that he was back, and seeing Sam, he realized it would be much harder than he'd thought at first. But not impossible. Never impossible. Weren't they all the same matter? The same energy? There had to be a way to find common ground and growth.

To his surprise, they didn't go to the civil port, but to the military port. It was the first time he saw a ship entering it other than in the simulation exercises. Once inside, its silver tunnel looked a lot bigger than he'd ever imagined. Kind of silly when he thought about it; a huge target saying "shoot me", and he used to think the red shore bases were bad. Well, to be fair, his city was a huge, fragile target, and their only luck was that Mainland didn't have enough power to come at them. This war was insane. The idea of "victory" was naive at best, malicious and destructive at worst. And the insanity of it was that only now his eyes had been open. He had to find a way to fix it all.

A loud thud startled him. So this was it, they had landed. As the door opened, he noticed that there were some people waiting for them. He wondered if somehow they were in trouble, or if they were curious about what had happened. When he stepped out, someone ran in his direction. Nadia. His stomach chilled. He wasn't in the mood to talk to her just then. But it got worse. She embraced him, and before he knew, her lips were against his. Now, pushing her in front of her friends and perhaps even her mother, the leader of the military council, wouldn't be a nice thing to do. He stepped away once he thought it wouldn't seem weird.

She smiled. "You're back!"

"I am."

She then ran to Sam, who was glaring at them. Perhaps she was thanking him. Dess's head was buzzing. So that was how they'd been rescued. Nadia had used her mother's influence to get someone to go there. Or perhaps her own influence. He didn't want to hurt her and he had no clue what to do. Nadia was back by his side. "What happened?"

"We crashed."

"You could have…" She then got serious. "You need to stop this. You should train people. And stay here."

Dess sighed. "Right now I just really need to eat and rest."

"For sure. We'll get you home. Interrogation can happen tomorrow."

He stared at her. "Interrogation?"

"Dess, you know the procedures better than I do, don't you?"

He closed his eyes. Of course. Anyone who spent time in enemy custody required examination and interrogation. Technically, he hadn't been in custody, though, but the logic made sense.

Someone approached them. Leader Aziz. She had a thin

smile. "Actually, you need to come now. We want our doctors to make sure you're healthy. You can see him later, daughter."

Nadia widened her eyes and looked at Dess and her mother as Dess followed the woman.

He was put in a bedroom in their hospital. At least they gave him a plate of food, or rather, poorly seasoned cricket patties. Yikes. He should perhaps tell someone how to calibrate the kitchen droids. It wasn't funny when he had to eat it, even being as hungry as he was. Fresh mushrooms had been better than that. Fresh, alive, from a nature that had been denied from them. Or perhaps a nature they had turned their backs to.

Of course leader Aziz would call them right away. The idea was to question them separately, before they had time to agree on a story. Time to face consequences. Thankfully, he'd already spoken to Marcus, and the fact that neither he nor his friend had any ammo should be evidence that they couldn't have disarmed Sam and Amil. Hopefully it would stick.

It felt odd to be leaving in the middle of the night. This time at least Saytera had had time to plan and gather her things, except that she didn't own anything. Even her clothes were borrowed, a long black skirt and a white shirt, since Larissa said Saytera's own gray clothes looked too bad.

Saytera had feared that someone could find her, recognize her in Citarella, but more and more her vision from the training house came back to her. Saytera's funeral. It had been true—in a way. Not that she'd died, but that they probably had to pretend she was dead. If Terens were looking for her, they'd lost her trace a long time ago. Perhaps she'd been given up as dead when she'd jumped from that boat. From the water came a rebirth—and a chance for a new life. And if she wanted to use it, she had to stop regretting the past, enjoy the chance she'd been given, and try to do something worthwhile with her time.

Last time she'd left a place in secret, she'd been searching for the truth about her, a destiny. Perhaps she should have listened to Yansin. Of course no destiny would be given to her. If she wanted anything, she had to go and get it.

As she and Larissa reached the ground floor, a sound came from upstairs.

Kay was there. "What's happening? Are you..." He frowned. "Deserting?"

21

TRIP

Perhaps trying to leave like that hadn't been a good idea.

Before Saytera could come up with an explanation, Larissa replied, "No. Of course not. We're just going to visit Citarella. And we left a note explaining."

He glared. "Usually we let each other know about our plans before we do them."

Larissa shrugged. "If I thought I wouldn't have any problem, it would be easier. I want to visit an aunt there. She's sick."

He pointed to Saytera. "Why is she going with you? Why not ask for a leave of absence?"

This wasn't going anywhere. Saytera decided to tell the truth. "Kay, it's not that. There's something wrong in Mainland. We want to know what's happening. We'll be back."

He shook his head, as if confused. "What do you mean, something's wrong?"

"Somersault. Those killings. It wasn't Lunars. I feel… they're hiding something from us."

Kay rolled his eyes. "Something? More like a ton of things. What do you expect to accomplish?"

"First we learn the truth, then we decide what to do with it."

He shrugged. "Sounds great. I mean, maybe we can tell the nearby bases. What then?"

"That's a start, Kay. What if it's huge and we can get this information to spread?"

"Exactly," Larissa added. "I'm tired of being here and doing nothing, watching the time pass by while we can't even dream about traveling to other systems or importing anything."

"Why didn't you tell me?" Kay asked.

Larissa sighed. "We thought it would be easier to explain everything once we were back."

"Right," he laughed. "How far would you go with a warrant for deserting?"

That was exaggerated. "We are not deserting. We will be back," Saytera said.

He nodded. "Fine. I'm coming with you, then."

Larissa threw her hands up. "But that will leave this base with Nara and Saulo only!"

"Who cares? There are no killings, right?"

Saytera shook her head. "The killings are real enough. The only thing we don't know is who is responsible for them."

"Kay, think," Larissa pleaded. "You want a promotion, don't you? You have a good relationship with Commander Stone. Use this to your advantage. Be here. Be the point of contact. Help us. Plus, there's a new recruit coming. Someone needs to be here."

He snorted. "Now you want my help? Remind me how kindly you asked for it."

Saytera saw the eyes of someone who also wanted his chance to play hero and do something meaningful. Was it fair to deny him? But then, staying was more important than going, and it wasn't as if they were on the way to end the war. The most important part wasn't getting the information, but what they'd do with it after.

Saytera pleaded, "You have to stay because you're the most important of us. Because we trust you. We'll be back in two days." She tried to give him a meaningful look. "We'll talk, then." Yikes, she didn't want to ever be alone with him again, but she had to convince him.

"You'll help a lot more if you stay," Larissa added. If we need anything, you'll be our point of contact."

He crossed his arms. "Three days. I give you three days. Next time talk to me first. We're a team, here."

Larissa patted his shoulder. "We're sorry. I'll trust you more from now on. But we're counting on you here."

Kay had a half smile. "Good luck."

It would be an hour walking to the nearest village, but they'd have a colorful sunrise to cheer them up. Still, there was something bugging Saytera, like a bit of a chill in her stomach. It was always better to recognize her emotions. "I'm a bit, hum, apprehensive."

"That's normal. You've never been to Citarella before."

"Have you?"

Larissa bit her lip. "Nope. So I get what you're feeling. No worries, though. We'll go to the archive central, get the information, and come out. Super simple."

"But if it's simple, how come nobody has taken it before?"

She smiled. "Maybe because they didn't look for it." She pulled a metal stick from her pocket. "The right way."

~

Dess got up as someone passed him a tray through the small opening in his cell door. Cricket patties. It was still pretty much the same stuff given to the military and the people at school. Whoever took care of punishing military trainees had no idea that guaranteed food and shelter was more than many in Sapphirelune had, who had to venture into dangerous mines. This was a prison for the privileged few who belonged to the elite.

Dess had been admitted back into the military, but couldn't really fight back Sam and Amil's words that he had assaulted them or at least ruined their tracker on purpose. At least he'd negotiated Marcus's freedom. And in fact, Dess didn't mind four days in custody. Once he'd been at a point where he didn't know what he'd have to eat the next day, and now he had it given to him on a tray. Definitely far from the worst punishment a person could get.

Marcus hadn't come by. It wasn't like him. They had probably forbidden him from visiting. Hopefully he'd be all right.

There were no windows in this cell, and the white walls, ceiling, and floor gave the space an even more artificial feel. In the fakeness of his moon, even with the metal structure of the dome cutting the view of the sky, it was still good to see the sun. Not that five days without natural light would kill him. He could still enjoy the silence. The solitude. He could gather his thoughts and rethink who he was.

He touched the finger with the missing ring. It ached. Not the ring, but meeting someone like that and having to let her go, perhaps forever. She had been right that she couldn't have come with him. He'd been so dumb. Perhaps he should have deserted and stayed down there, near real nature. No, there was too much that had to be fixed, and he had to do his part.

Steps resonated in the empty hallway leading to his cell. A bit early for them to be collecting his half-eaten lunch, but then, it wasn't the same guard. The steps were soft. It was a woman or girl.

A blond head appeared in the door opening. Nadia stared at him with concern. "How are you?"

"Not bad. Really."

She sighed. "Marcus asked about you. He's fine. You're both back in the army and you'll train the next water catchers."

Dess leaned back in his chair. "I'm doing a lot of training right now."

She looked down and shook her head. "I tried. I did. I mean… I know you don't like Sam, but there's no way you'd assault him for no reason. Their story is bullshit. Still, somehow putting you here seems to calm everyone down. And you wanted to spare your friend…"

"I did. Thank you." It was sincere.

Dess knew she'd been trying to help him, and knew she'd made some effort to keep Marcus out of it. And it was fair, since it had all been his fault. Other than that, he felt that awkwardness around her. He wasn't sure how to breach the subject or even if he should breach it. What did he have to say? That they weren't together? Maybe she knew it. He'd need to ask what her very public kiss had been about, but then… breaching the subject.

"Dess."

He didn't like her careful tone. "Yes?"

"There are things… in my life. You wouldn't understand. I just want you to know that I'm your friend."

"I'm happy being your friend."

And it was true. Not that they'd ever been that friendly before, but still… She looked down and then back at him, as if unsure how to say something. All Dess wanted to tell her was that he'd be fine with being her friend and nothing else, but that sounded awfully offensive, especially if she knew that already. He wasn't sure if he had to apologize, explain himself…

She finally looked at him with a thin smile. "Friends, then."

He exhaled. That was all he wanted to hear. He got up and approached the bars. "You didn't need to intercede in my favor."

"It was fair. Should you be left down there to die? To be captured? Perhaps tortured?"

"So it was strategic."

She had a small laugh. "That's what I told them. And why you're here. This has to change, you know? It's too risky."

"Somebody has to do it. Unless we find a way to do it legally."

"The truce. We'll renegotiate it in fifteen days."

Dess was pretty sure he hadn't spent a month on that island. The date was wrong. "Already?"

She nodded. "It's been advanced." Her eyes were wide.

"What's happening?"

A noise came from the end of the hall. She stiffened. "I love you." Then she walked away.

What had that been about? A door opened, and her voice and a man's came from beyond it. Dess couldn't quite hear them other than the fact they sounded as if they were arguing.

He was glad she was trying to help him, but at the same time wary about it. Regret was pointless, but he wished they had never been involved. There. He was regretting. No. He had to figure out a way for their past not to upset their present.

Perhaps there was nothing to worry about. But then, there had been that kiss and all the intervening for him. He hoped it wouldn't come with a price.

The trip was a lot longer than Saytera had imagined. They first walked for hours until the nearest village, then took a boat to another village, from where they took a train in the early evening. Its movements weren't smooth, but shaky, almost worse than the truck where she'd traveled until her academy. This time, they would travel for more than a day.

Saytera sat on the floor on the corner of the small container she occupied with Larissa. It was just a small empty box with slits for ventilation through which cold wind hit them. The discomfort reminded her of the two nights on that island with Dess, except that then there was the fire he lit, his voice talking about stories and her own power, a memory remaining in the coat and ring she still wore. His smell was fading away from it, even if the warmth remained.

Later they would sleep on the mats they had brought. This was a cargo train, and traveling in an empty container was what Larissa could afford. That was a lot more than Saytera could afford. As sentinels for the Mainland army, they received a wage, but it was so low that it could barely allow them to travel. The theory was that at least they were provided for in the bases, but considering they got most of their own food, it wasn't a lot. Certainly not enough for anyone to risk their lives, but then, up until recently, nobody really thought there was any risk. Until everything changed. Some of it was Dess, and her stomach knotted with the knowledge, and then, some of it was something else.

Larissa smiled. "Yeah, it's a long trip."

Saytera looked at the slits in the wall. "I wish we had a better view."

Her friend shrugged. "We'll get under the mountain soon. Most of the way is underground, so there isn't much to see."

Saytera stared at the girl she was now considering a friend. "Thanks for doing this. I mean, for believing me, and..."

Larissa waved a hand. "Perhaps I also wanted an excuse to go venturing out there, to get to know Citarella. Maybe I also want to do something that matters."

"We can't know. I could be wrong."

"We'll have tried. Perhaps what matters is following the calling. A bigger reason. Something to remember that life isn't all about catching our next meal and the next and the next."

Saytera sighed. "The calling. But isn't that what might make people shoot Lunars? What might make people get in this war? The idea that they are doing something grand, important, meaningful?"

Larissa leaned back. "Maybe. We all need some meaning, right? And either way, what should we do? Let them have the Tahari Moon?"

"What are we even gaining from preventing them from having it?"

Larissa looked up, thinking. "That's... an interesting question."

"Have you thought about it?"

"Obviously not as much as you. Tell me, Saytera, what happened?"

She flinched. "What do you mean?"

"During the time you spent with the Lunars. I was going to wait for you to tell me, but maybe you won't unless I encourage you, so I'm encouraging you now."

Saytera felt caught. But then, Larissa was there with her, trusting her, perhaps she deserved her own trust too. She wasn't even sure from where to start. "Well, there were two guys. One of them was hurt. Me and the other one, Dess, we had to walk to reach him. He was unconscious, but he healed."

Larissa nodded. "How were they?"

"Normal. That's what was so shocking. I mean, they were a bit more overwhelmed and starry-eyed about nature and the ocean than your regular shore base dweller."

They chuckled.

Saytera continued, "But they were young like us, trying to do the right thing, hoping one day there would be peace, hoping they could make a difference for better. They had hopes, dreams…"

"Dreams of killing us?"

"Dreams of freedom. You know they can't travel to other systems and it's very dangerous to come to the planet."

They were quiet for a while, then Larissa smirked. "And Dess is the one who gave you a coat and ring."

The question caught Saytera by surprise. "How do you know?"

"Do you want to know the truth?"

That was a weird question. "Yes."

"Your tone of voice changes when you talk about him."

Saytera froze for a second, then tried to act natural. "We were just friendly."

Her friend raised the palms of her hands. "I didn't imply otherwise."

True. It was better to leave it. "So yeah. I mean, I guess that's the point. He's someone who'd be my friend had things been different, and that's weird. It's hard to hate the Lunars when there's someone there that I… care about. So maybe that's why I'm changed."

Larissa nodded slowly. "I understand. But it could affect your perception, you know, if he lied to you—"

"He didn't lie. He could be mistaken, though. Either way, we get pieces and bits of information, we're told to do our part and trust our government, and things never seem to change. I guess I want to know more."

Larissa shrugged. "Well, I'm with you. Let's see what's going on."

"I appreciate it. I really do. You're my first real friend in so long."

"I thought the dude was your friend."

Saytera smiled. "You came first."

"Oooh. I'm flattered." Her friend chuckled and shook her head. "What are your plans? Wait until the war is over and try to meet? Or is he going to come to visit you?"

"No plans, Larissa. We'll probably never see each other again." It hurt but it was the truth.

Her friend paused for a moment. "That makes sense. But be careful with your heart."

"I'm not in love. What's the point? It all ends in heartbreak."

Larissa shrugged. "We'll all die. It doesn't mean life isn't worth living."

"I thought you were all against love and stuff."

"Why?"

"Well, the warnings about Kay…"

Larissa frowned. "Being careful is different from avoiding something, especially something you can't avoid. And just because I think one person is not someone you should trust, it doesn't mean you should never love anyone. Kay got two sentinels transferred, he's on and off with Cynthia, a serial flirt. I mean…"

"Yeah, I get it." More than ever Saytera got it, but she wasn't going to explain how much. She then realized she'd never asked anything about her friend's love life. "What about you? Any heartbreaks?"

"Broken, empty, not sure what's worse. I guess I'm waiting. Not for the perfect person. Just… someone… for me."

"It's hard when you're stuck in the middle of nowhere."

"We can try to get a transfer, maybe interact with the sentinels nearby, but it's true. It is hard."

"How did you end up there?"

Larissa snorted. "Some romantic idea about freedom and paradise. Which, in a way, is correct. On the other hand, like you noticed, it's hard for me to find someone. I mean, it's not that I'm looking, but then, can you really forget it? Ignore it?"

"I guess we can try to. But then it catches us unaware."

Larissa sighed.

Yikes. Saytera was wondering if she was really in love. No, she couldn't be that dumb, could she? Regardless, there were more pressing matters. "Before anything, we need to solve this war."

"I don't know, I fear we'll find more questions than answers, Saytera. We'll find complications, not solutions."

"And yet here you are on this uncomfortable train, looking to make your life more complicated."

Larissa stretched her mat and leaned down. "There's nothing simpler than blind obedience. Perhaps I'm getting tired of that."

2 2

THE CITY

Saytera woke up with sun rays coming from the slit in her container. Her back ached from her hard, improvised, shaky bed. She wondered if her friend would be upset if this trip turned out to be for no reason. But then, she had a feeling that Larissa was also out there for adventure and discovery, curiosity. Saytera shivered remembering how these same feelings had led her away from the life she once loved. Nowla came to her mind, with a pang in her chest.

It turned out that unlike what her friend believed, it wasn't as easy to make a difference and to help win that war. Saytera had traced that path and was just a number, maybe not even that. Her previous ideas about a great destiny almost made her laugh, if it wasn't for the memory of Nowla, and what chasing that stupid destiny had caused.

There was no set destiny, there was no set path for anyone; she had to walk her own. More than ever she was sure of that. But then, what about those people who had wanted to kill her? The memory sometimes almost faded, but sometimes it came back, rich as if it had been yesterday.

How would Saytera ever know? Perhaps it was something indeed about some stupid prophecy. More than ever she knew prophecies were stupid—and dangerous. No wonder Yansin forbade them. More than ever Saytera wished she could see her master again, absorb some of her immense knowledge, her power. So much that she had taken for granted.

All that she had were memories and her inability to use firearms. Unless she could also interrupt electricity and other weapons. Maybe. That thought came with the memory of Dess. Beautiful dark eyes so certain, so sure, telling Saytera she was a Teren—like Yansin. That past long gone.

"Hey." Larissa's voice snapped Saytera out of her thoughts. The girl was sitting up and stretching.

Saytera smiled. "We should be getting there, right?"

Larissa got up and stared at one of the slits. "Come, look."

Saytera pressed her face against the opening. There were no visible forests or nature, only buildings, so many buildings, some as tall as mountains. It was hard to see from such a small opening, but she got the sense that they'd arrived at their capital. In fact, even the air smelled different. On their way here, the smell had changed from salty ocean to a more woody, fresh scent, and now it smelled more like… stones and metal, a hint of smoke, and something artificial.

So this was it. They were really getting to Citarella. Going to find whatever secret there was to find—if there was any. The train reduced its speed until it came to a stop. There was no lock on the door, so the girls slid it open and jumped out. This was a trading station, where the train came to deposit fish from many sea villages.

Around it, just buildings farther than the eye could see.

Saytera looked at her friend. "Do you know where to go?"

Larissa looked around. "I'm not sure. We need to find the central government building. It's a pyramid."

Of course. Saytera had studied it in her time in the academy, and assumed her friend had done the same. There was a section there for public consultation. Since Mainland no longer sent data through wireless means, and didn't have cables all the way to the shore bases, information was either passed hand-to-hand, or consulted in person. That's why there was a room full of terminals for public access. The issue now was getting there.

"There are cars we can use, right? Taxis."

Larissa sighed. "I'd rather save."

True. Same reason they had to travel in an empty box. It was annoying that Saytera had so little to contribute to their trip and that she hadn't given thought to money until then. But in a place where there was no food to be caught, everything probably revolved around money. She couldn't fathom what life there would be like.

Saytera looked around, but had no sense of direction. "Maybe we could ask where to go?"

Larissa cocked her head. "Fair enough." She walked away for a bit, approached someone pushing a cart, then returned. "I think it's about an hour walking. You don't mind, do you?"

Saytera smiled. "It will be fun to get to know the city."

The area around the station had houses all stuck together, painted in white, with small square windows. People walked on the sides of the street, leaving the middle for fast cars on wheels. The cars had different colors and were mostly small, with room for two people, but carrying just one.

The triangular tip of a building showed up far away after the girls had walked for a while.

There was a question that had been unsaid all this time. "Do you really think you'll be able to hack a public terminal?"

Larissa pressed a finger over her lips. "I'd rather not talk about this in the open. But yeah, I think so."

"You're so talented. Have you ever thought you could do more?"

"That's what I'm trying right now. To do more." She then laughed. "It's not like I ever told my academy superiors that I was the one messing with their info. But I can see now that it's a useful skill. That maybe it could be useful. Who knows where life will take us after this?"

Saytera snorted. "Back to Cliffbound?"

"Well, it *is* a magnificently beautiful place. I won't complain."

The weather was cool and cloudy, which was good for walking, but after a while Saytera started feeling hot and took off her coat. Or Dess's coat. Her friend's clothes still felt weird on her.

Silence and anticipation replaced the earlier chit-chat, especially considering that Larissa was so worried that they'd be overheard. Her worry made more sense the closer they got to the pyramid, as there were more people on the sidewalks; an anonymous multitude surrounding them.

As they approached the center of the city, there were large displays with images. Some of them said, "Enough is enough", others said, "No more truce."

Saytera turned to her friend. "Do you know what this is about?"

She shook her head. "Something that still hasn't reached us. We're so isolated."

"It's as if… they don't want the truce anymore?"

"Sounds like it. We'll check." She winked. "Get to the root of it."

Saytera almost wanted to ask someone about it, but it was true that it was better to get the information straight from the source.

They reached the pyramid a lot sooner than Saytera had expected, perhaps because she'd been so entranced by her surroundings, seeing a city for the first time, perhaps because her mind had been whirling, wondering what that stuff about the truce meant. The building had a large hall with glass walls. They followed signs and then waited in a line to cross a metal door.

Saytera could hear her heart pounding in her ears, and she wasn't sure if it was fear of what they would find—or fear of what they wouldn't. Maybe it was the fear that the whole trip had been for nothing. Disappointment was much easier when not shared. If there was disappointment. There could be something scarier out there.

The door opened and Saytera and Larissa walked to a very long room with booths on its side and went to the one where a green light blinked. It had a large display connected to a terminal. There wasn't a lot of privacy for talking, since the booths on both sides were also occupied. Without windows anywhere, the place vaguely reminded her of the dark area in Academy Seven, only illuminated with artificial lights.

"What do you want to check first?" Larissa whispered.

A crazy idea came to Saytera. "Terens. Are there any records?"

Larissa rolled her eyes. "You can find this stuff in the entertainment library. You can ask Cynthia and Zack to bring more, if you're into it."

That was surprising. "Oh. Academy 7 didn't have anything about it."

"Huh. Worse than the one I went to. Now, we didn't come here to research stories, did we?"

Saytera had been thinking that maybe there could be something hidden about Terens, but she should have explained it earlier. She shook her head. "No." Then she whispered as low as she could. "Let's check Somersault."

Larissa nodded and entered that name. Photos popped up, and it was horrific. They didn't make any effort in hiding the bodies with bullet holes and blood. A lot more holes than necessary to kill them. It had been a massacre. Saytera felt revulsion in her stomach. At the same time, if it was true that Lunars flew in pairs, it couldn't have been their work, and it couldn't have been Dess. He hadn't been lying. And yet, there it was, proof that something horrific was happening in the bases.

"I guess they were killed all right," her friend whispered.

Saytera nodded while looking away. As much as she should be tougher, she just couldn't keep looking.

"I know," Larissa added. "Seeing it…" She sighed. "And this is public. Let's find out more."

She inserted her master key in the slot for the info stick. Whatever she was doing seemed complicated, as some numbers appeared on the screen, and the screen changed to a black background, demanding a password. Seconds and seconds passed while a light blinked on top, until the screen opened again with a red border around it. Top security. But there were only the same images with the caption: Classified - Project Zeta. Larissa frowned, then tapped her nail on the machine and bit her lip. "It's like we stumbled on a wall."

"A wall hiding something."

Larissa nodded and tapped Project Zeta. Again, it said *classified*. "I don't know if I can…"

The fact that something about Somersault was hidden proved that it was important and that there had been more to learn about it. Her gut feeling had been right. But at the same time, checking this information directly and quickly didn't seem like it would be easy even for Larissa. "Let's check the truce. We'll come back if we have time."

The girl grimaced, probably disappointed she couldn't get through a security protocol, and then typed "truce renewal". Somersault pictures popped up, together with a strong headline: "Enough is enough".

Suspicious. Saytera and Larissa exchanged a glance. So her friend had a similar opinion. The text urged citizens to vote for a breach of the truce, claiming there were newfound allies and supplies who would help Mainland win this war for good.

"Allies?" The thought had come aloud, louder than she expected.

Larissa frowned, and her voice came in a whisper. "And *voting?*"

Saytera read the text. There would be voting in eight days. She looked at her friend. "Neat that they don't even inform us at the bases."

Larissa shrugged. "Maybe they will."

She then turned to Saytera and put a finger over her lips. Her expression was tense.

The screen with the red frame opened again, then other numbers popped up. Saytera wanted to ask her friend what she was trying to do, but it would be hard to discuss it when they had people in the booths next to them. She typed words like "Zeta project", "Zeta agreement", then "Weapons supply". Nothing was showing up. She went to a screen that had "Government information." And then something that seemed interesting. "Tahari Moon Agreement."

The text was long and Saytera scanned it for the important information. There it was: a shieldbreaker ship in exchange for 200,000 kg of Ilanium, or gravity stones. It meant that Mainland would be able to win the war, for a high price. And destroying shields? Shields like the one protecting Shapphirlune city? If that was the case, it would be a massacre. Larissa seemed to have guessed Saytera's thoughts, as she searched "shield destroyers", but nothing happened. The screen was frozen. Then a deafening sound, as if seagulls were being tortured, startled Saytera. Fast steps came in their direction.

Larissa pulled her stick and stared at Saytera, her face ashen. They had seconds before someone came in. If they saw their frozen terminal, they'd know it had been hacked. Perhaps the girls could run. Before they could decide anything, a guard had a zapper pointed at them.

"Security protocol," he said.

He didn't examine the terminal. There was probably someone else who was coming to check. More steps around them revealed that they probably didn't know where the breach was coming from, and were probably keeping everyone in place and then checking terminal by terminal. This would buy them time. Not much. More steps were coming in their direction.

But this place had no natural light—like Academy 7. Perhaps Dess had been right that Saytera could tamper with electricity. Eyes closed, she focused on darkness, just like sometimes she did it to flicker a lamp in the academy.

Another man came in front of them. "Step away, I just need to check the terminal."

The lights were still on. Damn it.

But as Saytera looked back, the terminal's screen was dark.

The man looked behind it, to check cables. "When did it turn off?"

Saytera didn't think she had to disguise her fear. "I thought the alarm… What's happening?"

"Nothing to worry about. You'll just have to follow me."

Perhaps they were detaining everyone in the public archives, perhaps they suspected them. Saytera wasn't sure what was going to happen and was about to panic, when all the lights went off. They were immersed in darkness. This was their chance. Perhaps it was reckless, perhaps, unnecessary, but she couldn't shake the thought that staying would be dangerous. "Run!" Saytera yelled.

She passed the two men and dashed toward the backdoor. Larissa was running, too. For a moment Saytera had feared her friend would stay behind, perhaps thinking this idea was too outrageous. But there was no way to stay back and wait for whatever consequences they would face. Her fast-beating heart pushed her forward, even if steps behind them told her they were being followed. Without electricity, the back door was unlocked, of course. They opened it and came to a dark place. Stairs.

"Lean on the wall," Saytera whispered.

Soon the door was opened, and in the darkness, some pursuers went up and others went down, without seeing them. "Let's go back, now."

They opened the door and got back to the terminal place, still shrouded in darkness. They stepped slowly towards the main entrance, but bumped someone on the way.

"Hey!" a woman screamed.

Saytera got back to running. They got to the front door,

opened it, then before anyone noticed them, dashed to a side door, leading to stairs. They got out at a side street.

Saytera was about to run, when Larissa said, "Let's walk slowly, mingle with the crowd."

This was a back alley and there was no crowd, but perhaps her friend had a point. Archive guards were probably still looking for them in those dark stairs.

Then she heard the sound of a zapper and a cracker hitting the pole in front of them.

"Halt or I'll shoot you!" A woman's voice.

Saytera turned and saw someone on a roof, a gun in each hand. A gun in each hand? With that freaking insane aim? Could it be?

"Kiki?" Saytera's voice was incredulous.

"The name's Christina." Then she jumped down and faced them.

FINDING OUT MORE

It was indeed the short girl from Academy 7, the girl Saytera had once thought was her friend. "What are you doing here?"

"You know each other?" Larissa asked.

"Not sure," Kiki replied.

"Please," Saytera pleaded. "We need to hide."

Kiki stared at her for a few long seconds, then finally put down her weapons. "Follow me."

"To hide or to be detained?" Larissa asked.

"It depends."

They followed her to a car. Larissa sat in the front and Saytera crouched in a small place on the back. Kiki took off.

Saytera had never been in a car, other than that refrigerated truck, and the twists and turns almost made her nauseous. Relief washed her when they opened the door. They were in another back alley. Kiki led them to a metal door leading to decrepit stairs. After another door, they were in an apartment, with a table, kitchen equipment, and a bed all in one room.

"I'll listen," Kiki said. "And you'd better have an insanely good story." She stared at Saytera. "You can't imagine how happy I'll be when I take you to prison."

She then pulled both pistols and pointed at them, as if to prove that she wasn't kidding, or not to give them any ideas.

Saytera stared at the girl. "We once were colleagues, Kiki."

The girl frowned. "Christina! And you were the one who didn't want to train with me."

That had to be a joke. "You pretended you didn't know me."

"I told you it wouldn't be like that forever. But no, let's just ignore everyone."

"You can't be upset, Kiki."

"Christina!"

Saytera exhaled. "Christina, then."

"So you guys are friends?" Larissa asked.

"No," they both said at the same time.

Larissa nodded, then turned to Christina. "Right. So… are you a guard in the archives?"

"City police. Why?"

"You know about the voting, right?"

Christina rolled her eyes. "Who doesn't?"

"We come from a shore base and we didn't."

"Well, information travels slowly. Now get to the explanation. Were you involved in the breach in the public archives?"

"No," Larissa said. "But we were scared, so we ran. We don't know the procedures in Citarella."

Christina raised an eyebrow. "Likely story."

Larissa shrugged. "We're shore sentinels, you think we can hack a terminal?"

The girl was lowering her pistols. "True."

Saytera wasn't sure if lying was the greatest idea. Either way, she wanted more information. "What do you know about the truce?"

"They want to end it. Apparently, there will be a way to defeat the Lunars. Someone will send us weapons."

"Do you know what kind of weapons?" Saytera asked.

"I think they'll reveal it closer to the voting, right? I mean, if we get a strong fleet, the Lunars won't stand a chance. They are not that many. If we can win this war, it's good, right?"

Saytera was careful. "Have they mentioned the price for this support?"

Christina shrugged. "If we get back the Tahari moon, I don't think price's a problem."

Saytera took a deep breath, and made a wacky decision. "The price is two hundred tons of Ilanium. We read it."

The girl looked at both Saytera and Larissa. "How do you…" Then she aimed the pistols again. "Great, so you thought you could fool me."

"Not me, I'm not fooling you," Saytera said quickly. "Larissa doesn't know you. We found out that someone will give Mainland a shieldbreaker. Do you know what it does?"

"Probably allows us to shoot shielded ships."

That made sense. A lot of sense, and was much less nefarious than Saytera's first thought that they wanted to destroy Sapphirlune city.

But then Larissa voiced her concern, "Or else destroy the Lunar city's shield."

Christina frowned. "No. That would be… And what did you say the price was?"

"Two hundred thousand kilos of Ilanium," Saytera repeated.

Christina shook her head. "That's impossible."

Saytera didn't understand. "Why?"

Christina laughed. "*Why?* Are you kidding me?"

That was annoying. "No."

"Well, don't you know how rare Ilanium is?"

Where was she going with this? "It's only available in a few places, one of them the Tahari Moon. So?"

Christina grimaced. "Yeah. But how much? You would have known if you'd followed classes with us."

"The Tahari moon has a deposit of almost fifty tons of it." Larissa's voice came softly.

Saytera blinked. "That's… not a lot."

"Right?" Christina asked. "So there's no way they'd promise four times that to the company."

"But that's what we read," Larissa insisted.

Christina narrowed her eyes. "In the information you hacked."

Saytera was trying to think. "Well, an alarm sounded, right? So we did access classified information."

Christina shook her head. "True. But it doesn't make sense."

Larissa was thoughtful. "Well, we don't know. Maybe the deposit is bigger than they first thought, maybe… who knows?"

Maybe. Something else bugged Saytera. "And you don't have any information about what a shieldbreaker is?"

Christina shrugged. "Never heard of that." She looked at both girls. "So *that's* what you accessed? Information about the truce?"

Larissa nodded. "Yeah, we found that."

"And you risked getting caught for that?" Christina's voice was incredulous.

Saytera shrugged. "Well, we found something."

"Maybe not. Maybe we'll learn about all that stuff in a couple days. Maybe they're just waiting for the right opportunity to announce it."

"See?" Larissa shrugged. "One reason we shouldn't get detained."

"Well, that was completely reckless. Why didn't you just try to check the information available to the army?"

Saytera and Larissa looked at each other. "What information?" Larissa asked.

"In the Citarella army facility," Christina said it as if it was the most obvious thing in the world. "Look. Did you bring your identification?"

They both nodded.

"Great. Let's go there, then, and see what's been officially announced, stuff that hasn't had the time to reach your base. It's close by. From there we might understand what's going on."

Saytera was startled. "You want to help us."

Christina rolled her eyes. "It's my duty, that's all. And you two are obviously just trying to do your job. The wrong way, but still."

Larissa exhaled. "Thanks."

Christina raised a warning hand. "This time, no hacking. Or they'll figure it out before you even have a chance to blink."

The girls followed Christina as she led them down a corridor. Saytera could feel her heart slamming in her chest as they drew closer to their destination. It was probably just the memory of their slim escape from the public archives. Here, they'd have no chance to do the same if they were caught. No hacking, though, so no worries. They'd just find out stuff that was not available to the general public. Maybe it would clarify some of what they'd found. Probably not, but it didn't hurt to try. It was nice that Christina was helping them, but Saytera wasn't sure how she felt about the girl. Some of her anger had ended a long time before, but at the same time she felt uneasy.

This facility was actually quite near Christina's apartment, but they still took the car, having had to circle training grounds and a huge hangar. This was likely one of the few places with still functioning spaceships on Mainland.

The information center was next to the building housing the main Citarella army, and this was basically a resource room for personnel working elsewhere, like in the shore bases or city guard. Not that Saytera had ever known they could come in person and consult it. At least she felt less watched than in the public archives, which had the line to get in and people on every booth. This also had booths with terminals, but the room was empty.

As they researched the information, though, it was pretty much the same as in the public archives. Nothing about Somersault, project Zeta, and certainly nothing about details on shieldbreakers or any agreement to get one of those. That wasn't surprising.

Christina stared at the screen, eyes down, then turned to Larissa. "Are you sure you read 200 tons?"

"Well, yes, but I guess we'll never understand why. I mean, perhaps one day."

Saytera was turning around to leave, when Christina said, "Wait." As she noticed they were staring at her in curiosity she repeated, "Wait." She took a deep breath. "I believe you."

That was odd. Saytera was sure that her former academy colleague had bought their story a long time ago. Why was she saying it now?

"And…" she continued, "I agree with you that this might be important."

Larissa shrugged. "Sure. What's your idea?"

She looked at both her and Saytera. "This… is not as closely watched." She pulled a stick from her pocket, then whispered,

"If we just copy the information then leave, it can be really fast."

A frown formed in Larissa's face. "Are you suggesting…"

Christina nodded fast. "If it's true they're asking for…" She lowered her voice even more and looked down. "More Ilanium then we can give. And… I don't know…" She looked at them. "I want to do something, too."

Larissa had a thin smile and took the girl's stick. She inserted it and went back to her weird number-punching thing.

Saytera swallowed. Perhaps this wasn't the best time to wonder if she was really interested in being arrested for illegal access of classified information.

Five seconds passed, and still only numbers, no red-framed screen. If this were like the public records, anything longer than fifteen seconds would get them caught. But that time they'd spend precious time reading. It would be different now. Except that chances were this would be a lot more secure than the public records.

Larissa still struggled to access anything. It had been what? About ten seconds now. Saytera took a deep breath, wondering if she should convince her friend to call its quits. Christina for her part watched her friend closely, eyes wide, probably about to regret many of her recent decisions.

Was this even worth it? They had no idea what they'd do with the information they'd found. Other than satiating their curiosity, what else would it mean? Saytera was almost about to tell her friend to stop it, when she finally got to the screen they'd seen in the public archives. But it seemed to be the same thing.

Christina voiced Saytera's fear. "We'd better go."

Larissa shook her head. "Just a bit."

Saytera and her former academy colleague exchanged a worried glance.

Screens passed by, too fast for Saytera to understand what was being shown. Then more numbers. Fifteen seconds had already passed, and they were going on longer. At any moment now, a siren could blare, and then who knew what would happen to them.

Not if they left before they were caught. "Leave it."

Larissa didn't stop or look in her direction. "Shh. Almost there."

Saytera could feel her pulse accelerating. There was no backdoor escape. Perhaps she and Christina could pull the stick and pull Larissa away from the terminal, but it would be worse, since neither of them would be able to get out of whatever her friend was doing. It was all on Larissa now, and she was apparently intent on getting to the bottom of things, ignoring what it could mean for them. How had her friend turned so reckless?

Finally, Larissa closed the screen and pulled the stick. "There. Nobody died. Thanks for not disturbing me."

"Let's go." Saytera wasn't sure they'd gotten through the worst of it.

If only they could run out of that place. But that would obviously draw eyes to them and get them in trouble. Instead, getting back through the corridor and passing through security in the front was an eternity. Saytera felt as if all eyes were on her, as if at any time someone would stop them.

They got in Christina's car without a word.

After a while, Larissa broke the silence. "Guys, it wasn't that bad, right?"

"We were lucky," Christina said in a small voice.

Maybe. Saytera had a question. "Where are you taking us?"

"You think I'd risk my skin for that info and wouldn't want to see it? I'm taking you back to my apartment."

"Thanks. For everything."

Christina kept looking ahead. "Yeah, I mean, I still wish you hadn't hacked that."

Larissa shrugged. "Nothing happened. We're here. Sometimes we have to take risks, you know?"

"Maybe."

The stairs to Christina's place didn't seem as decrepit as before, perhaps because this time Saytera knew where she was going, and knew it was a friend's house. Friend? Perhaps. That was an interesting thought.

The girl wasted no time, and right away took a handheld terminal where she plugged the stick.

The bluish glow illuminated her surprised face.

Larissa pulled the terminal. "Let me see." She then frowned.

Saytera approached.

On the screen, ZETA PROJECT.

It was a paragraph, but Saytera scanned it quickly to see phrases like *annihilate Sapphirlune city, technology to destroy their city shield, two hundred tons of Ilanium from Tahari moon as payment.*

There was a chair near her, which was good, otherwise she might have fallen. She felt a tug in her heart thinking about Dess, about his city, about the horrific thing the Mainlanders were about to do. And why Zeta project? What did it have to do with the killings in Somersault? Her head started to buzz.

Larissa turned from the terminal. "Are you okay?"

Barely able to breathe, Saytera just shook her head.

Christina sat by her. "It looks bad, right? Do you think it's real?"

Larissa shrugged. "You think they'd falsify information accessible only to a few people in the government?"

Getting worked up about it wasn't helping. "Right. So you guys read it. They're really planning on attacking the Sapphirlune city?"

Her shore base colleague sighed. "Looks like it."

Right. "And for more Ilanium than the Tahari moon has."

Larissa shrugged. "Unless they found more. I don't know."

Christina kept looking at the display, her face pale. "You know what the problem is? Let's assume they just threaten the moon with that shieldbreaker, let's assume the best. The issue is that we'd take years mining Ilanium for this company. I mean… When we were studying the Tahari moon, they said it could produce up to a ton a year. This would mean 200 years of mining and giving them the compound if we were to sell it at maximum capacity, which is hard to believe. It is going to be more expensive and laborious than just letting them have the moon. What was the point of this anyway?"

Saytera shrugged. "There is no point, Christina. If you think about all the losses, all the restrictions, there's no advantage in fighting for that floating rock. There has never been."

"It was about being fair!" Christina protested. "I mean… but this is ridiculous."

Larissa gestured for them to calm down. "Fine. Let's check the rest." She took the terminal.

"What rest?" Saytera dreaded the idea of finding anything even worse than that.

"Zeta Project," her friend replied. She stared at the screen. "Somersault, not much more. It's as if project Zeta is a response to the killings there. Well, there could be more, but you guys were hurrying me."

There was a soft *click, click*. Saytera looked around. "Do you have an alarm or something?"

"No," Christina seemed confused.

Saytera got up. "Silence." She could hear it, something getting ready, fire contained into something, ready to... "Explode."

"What?" Larissa seemed puzzled.

There was no time to explain anything. "Do you have a backdoor? We have to run. NOW."

Christina didn't move. "Yes, but...".

Saytera pushed the girl and pulled Larissa, who still held tight to the small terminal.

They came to a balcony leading to a ladder. Saytera said, "It's a bomb. We have to jump."

The girls didn't seem much convinced. Right then a bang came from the inside, together with broken glass in their direction. Saytera hung herself from the balcony, then jumped. Christina and Larissa followed.

"Let's get to my car!" Christina yelled.

Larissa grimaced. "You think it's a good idea?"

Christina sighed, then looked up. "No snipers at least."

Larissa was limping. "If we're lucky they'll think we're dead."

"Isn't this my lucky day?" Christina sounded bitter as she stared back at what had once been her home.

Saytera tried to think, tried to come up with an escape plan.

They would be surrounded, without any chance to reach the train station, to escape that place, unless...

"Let's go back to the military grounds," Saytera suggested.

"Are you nuts?" Christina asked.

Just then, a zapper ray passed them. Two people were running in their direction, shooting.

Christina turned and shot them. Saytera was about to stop her friend when she fired the first shot—and hit one of the people's legs. Another shot, and she hit a hand or the weapon.

No time to check. They ran, climbed a fence, and were in the military port.

This was a desperate, reckless decision, but she found no other way. Saytera scanned the facility and found her answer in a black L2. "The one by the fuel station." It wouldn't make sense to put fuel in a non-functioning ship.

Christina stopped. "They'll shoot us down!"

"They are already shooting us. And they won't get us if we fly low enough." Assuming Saytera could do it, of course. "Let's go."

Christina didn't move. "I don't agree with this."

"Well, stay, then." Larissa snapped.

Saytera pulled Christina's hand. "They already tried to kill us. I don't see another way."

They came to the black ship. Saytera closed the fuel compartment. Larissa thankfully was able to get the main door open.

Some ten people entered the grounds, weapons in hand.

Saytera tried to recall everything she'd read about that type of ship and how it worked. Words and illustrations had to make sense and become something real. Larissa was trying to open its system. They were facing the door to the hangar and saw it burst open while six or eight people came running and shooting. This was a space-compatible model, so the windshield was strong, otherwise they'd be dead by now. Larissa unblocked the system, and Saytera took her best guess and pushed the launch button. They were accelerating upward.

Saytera sat and took a deep breath. They'd escaped getting shot on land. Would they be shot out of the air?

WHAT NOW?

On the pilot seat, Saytera tried to change the ship's direction, but somehow couldn't do it. They accelerated upward as the city got smaller beneath them.

Larissa stared. "Why is it going up?"

Saytera's stomach formed a knot. It couldn't be real. "It's… It's launch mode. As in launching into outer space."

"That's it. We're dead." Christina rested her forehead on her hand.

Larissa bit her lip. "The anti-aerial system is set for incoming ships. If we're fast enough…"

That made sense. "Let's hope we leave their range soon enough, then."

Christina looked down and shook her head. "We're so dead."

Larissa shrugged. "Look at the bright side. At least it will be fast."

The other girl glared. "I'm not ready to die."

Neither was Saytera. It felt odd to be on the receiving possibility of being shot from the air, without any chance of defense. The worst was that for now the mechanism was locked, meaning that there was absolutely nothing she could do other than hope that the people in the city's defenses took long to notice their escape.

Yes, they'd gotten the information. Yes, it was important. And yet, what would be the point, if it got blasted with them? She sighed.

It was better to focus on the future, even if it didn't come to pass. "We'll have to reenter the atmosphere. Larissa, do you think you could reach Kay?"

She frowned. "For what?"

"To disable our canon. Then we land near our base. Otherwise, from where are we going to enter our atmosphere?" Saytera didn't have any illusion that she could face a storm the way Dess did.

The girl nodded. "I think so. That works."

Christina looked at them. "But won't it be obvious that it's where you're going?"

Yes, but… It was obvious. "The tracker! They'll know where we're going regardless! Larissa, can you disable it?"

"I thought you were the ship expert."

Saytera tried to think about that type of model. She'd never been in one. The memory that came to her was a different one: Dess breaking the tracker in the Lunar ship. She looked at the corner of the dashboard. There, a light blinked.

She looked to the others, for some reason unsure. "We should disable it, right?"

Larissa rolled her eyes. "Is that even a question?"

The model of that type of ship came to her mind, what was beneath it. She turned to Christina. "Can you shoot here?"

"Are you sure?"

For some reason, she wasn't, there was a cold dread coming

to her, but it was probably because of the situation they were in. "It won't damage the ship, just the tracker."

The girl took her cracker and shot that part of the panel. Beneath the top, a metal ball was broken.

Christina looked at them. "There's no point in doing this if you guys go to your base."

"I think there is," Larissa said. "They won't be sure. They'll think we'd want to avoid going back there."

"They can send someone," the girl insisted.

Larissa waved a hand. "Someone. One, two people. We'll deal with them. It's our safest bet to land in one piece."

If they left the atmosphere in one piece. Saytera's heart was pounding. They could die at any moment. The three of them. She felt a bitter taste in her mind thinking that her two friends were there because of her.

Saytera looked at her friends. "I'm sorry, guys." It didn't help, but there wasn't much she could do right then.

Larissa waved a hand. "Not your fault."

Christina just looked away.

Saytera was out of words as she stared down at the city and the mountains around it, wondering if they were still in the range of the anti-aerial system. She checked the display. They were reaching 14 kilometers of altitude, out of the range of inner planet ships, but still in danger of being shot. Anti gravity was on, acceleration was maximum, and the numbers kept climbing, 25, 26, 27... 30 kilometers was their own base's range, but she wasn't certain about the limit in Citarella.

She looked at Christina. "Do you know if we're clear?"

The girl bit her lip, seeming unsure.

Larissa looked at the display. "We should be fine at 50."

When they reached 70 kilometers of altitude, Saytera exhaled in relief, then disengaged the launch system. They still kept going up because of the anti-gravity. They'd escaped Citarella. The issue now would be getting back on the planet safely. It wasn't as if she'd studied piloting or ever used a simulator. Her friends weren't pilots either.

She opened the map on the display to find the general direction of the base. Home. It was funny to realize that she thought about it like that. A small consolation.

She then looked at a light on the display and her heart sank. It couldn't be. She tried to engage thrusters and change the direction. Her insides were turning cold. How would she tell her friends?

Larissa beat her to it. "What's wrong?"

Saytera swallowed. "I'm… so… sorry."

"What? You're freaking me out." Christina snapped.

So stupid. Why? Why had she been so stupid? But she had to face her friends. "We're… out of fuel."

Their faces paled.

"No," Larissa shook her head. "Wasn't this by the fuel station?" She sucked in a breath. "You didn't check…"

Saytera sighed. "No."

Christina looked at them both. "So what happens now?"

"I'm trying to think."

"Hang on." Larissa gestured as if to calm them down. "What if… we turn off the anti-gravity. Won't we go back down?"

Saytera tried to recall what she'd read. "We're still under Mainland's gravity. Unless we get in orbit, which we won't, we'll fall. We'll crash."

"No, no," her friend said. "We turn it back on."

"We'd need the thrusters to slow down the fall. Even without being pulled by the planet, if we're accelerating towards it, just turning the anti-gravity won't make us stop."

Larissa bit her lip.

"Plus we're near Citarella," Christina added. "I'm sure you'll guess what will happen if we try to reach it."

Saytera had a sick feeling in her stomach. No. There had to be a solution. It came to her in a flash. "Lunars."

Her friends seemed puzzled.

"We need to try to contact them. We have information they'll want. It's our only shot."

Larissa looked away, as if thinking. "If they hear our contact. If they believe us. If they have a way to take us there." She then stared at Saytera. "But I think you're right."

"Hang on." Christina frowned. "We're gonna become… traitors?"

"Do you have a better suggestion?" Saytera was asking in earnest.

"Dying. How's that? Do you know what will happen if they come across this information? What kind of retaliation they might plan? They've already been inflicting carnage on us. Somersault, hello?"

"There's no proof it was the Lunars," Saytera said.

Her former academy colleague rolled her eyes. "Well, who was it, then? The *fire people*?"

Her friend's superstition was surprising.

Larissa then spoke. "Remember it's related to this Zeta Project. We really don't know who did it and for what."

Saytera then added, "And, about the information… Remember that ending the truce is just a proposal. To be voted. Maybe they'll help us find a way to let people in Mainland know about it. It's in their interest."

"They might just kill us. We have no idea what these people are like."

Saytera stared at her. "I do, Christina."

Her friend seemed puzzled.

Saytera continued, "There are a few things that happened. In the last few days."

She then proceeded to tell her about Dess and Marcus, and their days on the island, including their insistence on why they didn't think Lunars had anything to do with Somersault. Christina listened. Larissa also listened with attention, as if it weren't the second time she was hearing it.

Christina was thoughtful. "Just because two of them can be nice, it doesn't mean they won't kill us once they get the information, or even attack the planet."

Larissa shook her head. "If they were capable of attacking the planet and winning, why would they keep dragging this truce?"

Christina stared in silence. After a while, she sighed. "Try to contact them. Not sure they'll listen."

Saytera hoped someone did. She had to find a solution for her friends. Maybe, maybe they could reenter the atmosphere. "If nothing happens, and if we see we're almost out of oxygen, I can turn off the anti-gravity just for a short while."

Larissa frowned. "You said we'd crash."

"We probably will. I mean it as a last resort. Once we're almost dying."

Saytera didn't want to think about that possibility, but now that her friends agreed in contacting Sapphirlune, she realized that their odds there were quite slim. They were far from the moon, didn't know the right channels or frequencies, and didn't know if anyone would believe them, let alone do anything.

Would apologizing ever make up for what she'd done? It had been her idea to go searching for this information, then her idea to get on this cursed ship. Now the three of them were doomed.

They stared at each other. Fear was visible on their faces.

Larissa bent over the control panel. "I'll try to get a communication channel going."

"Wait." Christina held back her hand. "What if Mainland hears it? I think… we've been left alone because they know we wouldn't have gone anywhere. But if they see we're trying to contact the Lunars…"

Larissa sighed. "I can try a neutral call for help."

"Why would they answer that?" Christina asked. "From the goodness of their hearts?"

"Starspark." The word came out even before the thought had been fully formed.

Her friends were puzzled.

"The guy I met. I know his full name." Fake last name, but it didn't matter, apparently it was official enough. "Dess Starspark. We could use that."

Larissa seemed uncertain. "You think it will reach him?"

"If it reaches Sapphirlune, I guess it will reach someone. They would at least be curious, right?"

Larissa nodded and sighed. "Yeah, if it reaches them. I'll try sending 'Help, star spark' in all the ways I can find. It's innocent enough that I don't think Mainland will come after us, if they intercept it."

"We're getting away from the planet," Saytera added. "I don't think they'll risk a space confrontation to shoot down a doomed ship."

"Let's hope." Christina's voice was barely audible.

Hope was all that was left. And it got fainter and fainter as the hours passed by. What were the odds they could reach Sapphirlune? That anyone would pay attention to it? But then, all wireless communication on the planet had been shut down. In theory, the Lunars spied on their communication all the time. Wouldn't they notice communication from a ship? Wouldn't they notice that the planet had launched a spaceship? These questions circled Saytera's mind.

They had no water and her throat was getting super dry. Would they die first from poisoning from their own CO2? Dehydration? There were no air or urine filters on this ship, which had probably been built for short commutes to the moon. Eventually they'd just try to crash land, but the odds of survival there were close to none. This ship didn't have ejectable seats. Some luck.

Larissa turned to them. "The call is being sent. What now?"

Saytera shrugged. "We wait."

They stared at each other in silence.

"I have a story," Christina said. "Perhaps not a story. It's a secret, I guess. Not that I think we'll die. Well, actually, I sort of do, but that's not the reason…"

Larissa leaned over. "Just say it."

Christina sighed. "My parents are fishermen. I'm from a fishing station. They saved a lot to send me to the academy."

"That's why…" Saytera was almost going to say *you were teased*, but caught herself in time. "You were so dedicated."

Her friend looked down. "Yes. That's why I was saving money. To send to them. And why I don't want to die."

Saytera felt even worse than she'd been feeling before. "I'm so sorry."

Christina shrugged. "I made my choices, too, you know. Of course I could have turned you in. Of course I didn't need to bring you to the military archives. I should have known that either it was nothing, or, if we found secrets, there would be a price to be paid."

"Sapphirlune might still reply." Saytera tried to be cheerful.

"It's been hours," Larissa said. "Eventually we might just

have to say 'yo, we have some top-secret Mainland information. Want to get it?'"

Christina laughed. "That would get a spaceship after us soon. From *Mainland.*"

"That's why we'd better keep talking," Larissa said. "To avoid making stupid decisions." She looked at her companions. "I'll tell you how I ended up in Cliffbound. It was love. Or the impression that it was love. Something like it."

"For who?" Larissa wondered if her friend had also been interested in Kay.

She shook her head. "You don't know her. She was in the academy with me."

Her. So Larissa… Right. Saytera had never noticed it.

Her friend continued, "We had promised to love each other forever. I thought she was my other half, the one for me. She was sent to Water Edge, a base also in the Northeast shore. A few months later, I took the opportunity and went to Cliffbound because it was close to it."

Christina was perked up. "Did you meet her again?"

"Yes." Larissa snorted. "She had someone else. She practically *was* someone else. I'm not sure if I imagined what we had, if I imagined our promises. I don't know."

Saytera wasn't sure what to say.

Christina extended a hand towards her friend. "I'm not sure it helps, but at least you knew love. I never liked anyone who liked me back. The emptiness hurts, too."

"Does it? More than the betrayal and the loss?" Larissa asked.

Saytera was thoughtful. "We just can't know. I guess nobody knows what it's like to be someone else."

Larissa looked down. "No." She then stared at Saytera. "What about you? Any love in your past?"

Dess. Dess, Dess, Dess, there was only Dess, and the realization surprised her. She had to remember that reaching him now was about survival, not whatever feelings that might be illusions.

"Ha!" Larissa laughed. "You look guilty. Spit it."

"In my village." Saytera decided to talk about the past. "There was this guy, we grew up together. And… I thought I loved him. But then he moved to, uh, another village. At first we corresponded." She looked down. "Then he stopped." Odd that it still hurt a little, even if she didn't think he was anything remotely close to Dess. "Eventually he came to visit—with another girlfriend." Saytera snorted. "I guess there was only friendship where I saw something more."

They were quiet.

"So… you guys never kissed?" Larissa asked.

"You don't need to be in love to kiss a guy. Or a girl, in your case," Christina said.

"Yeah. I've done my non-loving kissing, too." Not that she was going to confess she'd kissed Kay.

Larissa shrugged. "That's neat. I guess I'm a hopeless romantic."

"Romantic and hopeless shouldn't be used together," said Saytera.

"Sure." Larissa glared at her. "Tell that to your past self when she had a heartbreak."

"I mean in general. With a specific person, we might get mistaken, but in general… It's a hopeful thought."

"Maybe."

They filled the following hours with talk until sleep came to them, even on those uncomfortable seats. Saytera woke up a few times, with an insatiable thirst and the agony of feeling death looming over them.

"Help, Starspark." The call was being sent.

Perhaps they were doing it all wrong. She'd been trusting their communication system. What about one great ocean? One great universe? Stars above, stars within? Connecting to the inner fire within all living beings, all stars, she sent her own call, "Help me, Dess."

CALLING INTO NOTHINGNESS

Even with the blinds shut, Dess had trouble falling asleep when they were in the day cycles on the moon. Their hours made no sense, attached to a planet with a real cycle, but pointless to them. So many pointless things. He got up with a start, chest feeling tight. Saytera. Of course his chest would be tight thinking about her. There was that possibility that he'd never see her again. As much as he'd never believed in the idea of soulmates, he doubted he would ever meet anyone like her again.

It had crossed his mind once to just go there and find her, but what for? She wouldn't come with him. In fact, she couldn't. Still, he kept thinking about her. It was as if he could rescue her from something. As if he had to rescue her, answer her call.

Dess sat up, wondering if there was something truly wrong with her. Knowing without knowing. There was more to the way people communicated than humanity could understand. He took a deep breath. It could also be an excuse his mind was making to take a ship and go to Mainland to find her. His chest was so tight, though, he couldn't even breathe.

Dess closed his eyes. They'd been training the new recruits in the last few days, but trips to the planet had been suspended. Until when? This inertia was upsetting, as if they were waiting for something. Something he had no idea what it was. Eventually his moon would need water. At least this time they wouldn't send unprepared teams down there. He took a deep breath. It was dangerous even for prepared teams, especially if Mainlanders already knew how they hid in storms. If Saytera had told them. Would she tell them? This was a stupid question. Would she risk her colleagues, her planet, to protect Dess?

So much anxiety bubbling up, he felt he might burst. He felt like the answer was to go to the civil port, take a spaceship, and just fly there, find her. Perhaps he was going insane. Perhaps it was just that he missed her.

Saytera dozed on and off sleep. It had been a tiring day, after a poorly slept night. The spaceship still kept the antigravity and its heater. She wondered if the battery could fail. Better not wonder about electricity outages and cause one by accident. True that once she'd realized she was capable of causing electricity outages, she'd never done it by mistake again. It was as if the understanding of how she'd caused blackouts allowed her to control when to do it.

Still, perhaps her mind was trying to find out what could kill them first. Or rather, what would force them to go on a deathly plunge. Still, she didn't let her thoughts reach that place in her mind from where darkness spread. She now knew where it was.

And Dess. Could he hear her? One great ocean. One fire. One light. Through it all, she should be able to reach him. But then, it was like radio waves. It wouldn't help much if he didn't check that frequency.

The hours passed slowly. Too slowly. An eternity in a night. Or night cycle. Dess got up, even though in theory they were far from the earliest hours in the morning. He stopped by Marcus's room and hesitated. If he woke up his friend, this would become real. A real decision. Not that he had properly decided anything.

His knuckles were hitting the door before he had completely accepted that this was a good idea.

After a long while and more and more urgent banging Marcus came to the door, eyes half closed. "What?"

"I couldn't sleep."

His friend's eyes got even more closed. "And… you want company in misery?"

"A bit worse than that. I want to go to Mainland. You don't have to come with me if you don't want to, but I thought I should ask."

Marcus stared at him for a moment. "Why?"

Dess sighed. "It's… hard to explain. But I'm thinking…" Was he thinking? He'd better do it alone. "I'll get in trouble. Just help me leave."

"We don't have a ship anymore, you know that."

"I'll just take one."

Marcus looked awake now. "Trouble for sure."

"Just help me. Open the gate. Monitor things for me."

His friend was quiet for a long time, then said, "I'll get dressed. But you'd better explain it on the way."

"I will."

What was Dess even going to explain? He was almost regretting having woken up his friend. He shouldn't get involved in that. But someone had to monitor the entry gate in the civil port and make sure he would be allowed back in. Maybe he could do it on his own. Perhaps Dess was going insane. Except… What was sanity?

There was nobody on the streets despite the daylight, when they walked to the civil port.

Marcus stared at him. "So… basically you're saying that if you don't go to Mainland you'll have a *heart attack?*"

His friend made it sound quite silly, but it wasn't. "That's what it feels like."

"And you're sure you shouldn't head to the hospital instead?"

"I'm not sure of anything, Marcus. Everything is dark and strange and suffocating."

"We're facing the sun," Marcus said. "You shouldn't say it's dark."

Dess had a small laugh.

Marcus then asked, "So you're considering illegal, unauthorized takeoff. We could have issues with the military port, though."

"You think they'll shoot me or something?"

"Who knows?" Marcus stopped. "We could talk to Sylvia. See if with her contacts…"

"You do it," Dess interrupted. "After I'm gone. I've wasted too much time."

"Nobody's dying! We just need to make sure they authorize your departure."

Dess snorted. "That could take a day, two. I don't have that time."

Marcus raised an eyebrow. "Because of your impending heart attack."

"Precisely."

"How long do you think we have?" Christina wasn't annoyed, angry, or anything anymore, just asking a question that had become normal to them. They'd passed the point of blaming each other or trying to find new solutions. The biggest issue now was how thirsty they were.

Saytera checked the display. "Air quality is still at acceptable levels. Everything else is working…"

"It's going to be dehydration, then." Christina closed her eyes.

"Still a day or two for *that* to kick in," Larissa said.

"It's just," Christina said, "we need to plan for when we'll take the plunge. I mean… I don't even think the Lunars are getting our transmissions."

Saytera understood her friend's apprehension. She sometimes thought the same thing, but there was only one thing they could do. "We wait. Tomorrow evening, if nothing happens, we land."

Larissa laughed. "*Land.* Love your optimism."

"At least we can still laugh." Saytera shrugged.

But they were silent and quiet after that. Being so thirsty, talking wasn't comfortable. This was definitely a ship for short distances, without air filtration or pee filtration. It should have a small water tank, but unfortunately, it was empty. No food supplies either. Saytera's stomach had growled in the beginning. Now the feral beast inside her had gone tired and quiet, lying down and waiting. At least she and her friends were keeping their cool. A situation like this could cause everyone to go on each other's throats. But it would only make things worse. Saytera focused on Dess. That wasn't hard at all. She hoped that he could hear her through the dust of space. It would be a pity to die without kissing him. Assuming he wanted to kiss her. Saytera chose to assume it, and have at least one good thought lighting up the hope in her heart.

It had taken longer than Dess would have liked. The model he picked, a T-3 was quite small, but very maneuverable, which could be helpful if he had to dodge some anti-air cannons. The tricky thing had been inspecting it, replenishing fuel and supplies, and making sure all its parts were functioning well.

Then he had the communications from the central tower, forbidding him to leave, to which he just said he'd been authorized by commander Serra. By the time they woke her up and realized he'd lied, he'd be long gone.

Now he was on a strange ship, going to Mainland, without a clear goal, based on a very, very loose hunch about something going wrong. He couldn't even imagine what it could be, or even what he was going to do. Perhaps the best plans were the simplest ones.

He decided to land near her base, go there, and knock on the door. Knock. How come they had never considered it? Nothing identified him as a Lunar, and he could hide his pistols. If it was just about a question, he didn't think they'd refuse to answer. And he knew what he wanted to ask. "Where's Saytera?"

It was all he needed an answer for. And maybe he'd be proven insane if she showed up to greet him. Dess would like that. Insanity was better than learning that his vague fears were right.

He was going to approach Mainland by its east side, hoping to catch a storm. The planet was now turning away from the moon, which would increase the distance. Being alone wasn't good. Dess sighed. Everything about what he was doing was illogical and brash. He'd never considered himself any of that. He was rather thoughtful, calm, and yet…

There he was, ready to descend. He scanned the clouds near the continent. Not many. The feeling now was physical pain, as if someone were tying a knot around his heart. It just felt wrong. Nothing was making sense. Dess leaned back and tried to think, if ever he was still able to do that. He was still far from the planet, and then decided to scan the skies above the continent. There were a few artificial satellites, most deactivated since the war. And then there was something else, deemed unknown by his system. A ship, maybe.

Mainland hadn't been in space in years. There wasn't much point. The lunars also had their defenses and would shoot any approaching ship. The system gate had been shut, so there was no way to escape their solar system. Who would do something so dangerous? And why? But then, they were close enough to the planet that they wouldn't face the Lunars' forces. Some recognition mission? It didn't make much sense.

Perhaps Dess should just ignore that ship. He had come all the way here because of his unease about Saytera, and there was no way she was there. But then, who knew? Perhaps his decision to come hadn't been about her. The ship was very close to Citarella or even right above it. Could it be some form of bait?

It was reckless and stupid, but he just wanted to check. It looked like a civil model. It wouldn't shoot him. He didn't think the ground cannons could reach that height. It could cause a diplomatic incident. No. Again, too high. If Mainland were to complain about Lunars ships, they would have complained a long time ago.

Dess turned into that direction and approached. It was indeed a very small transporter, an L2. Why would it be just left there, above the planet, going nowhere?

When he was close enough, he opened the communications channel.

"Dess Starspark, from Sapphirlune," he almost said Sapphirlune defense, when he remembered that he should present himself as being unrelated to any military activity. "Are you in need of help?"

No answer.

He tried another frequency. "Contacting the Mainland L2 vehicle. Anybody hear me?"

That was very odd. Anyone on that ship should be wondering at someone coming that close to them. Unless… They could be dead. He maneuvered his ship to face it, see if he could catch anything through its front viewer.

Dess caught his breath. Was he hallucinating? That didn't make any sense. Saytera was there, beside a girl with dark hair. They both had eyes closed as if asleep—or unconscious.

That was her. What was she doing there?

He tried to connect again. "Dess here. Can you hear me?"

No answer. So odd. Were they unconscious? He again felt that knot on his chest. There was no EVA suit on this ship. He wouldn't be able to come near them. But then, she opened her eyes. Surprise, disbelief, then a smile. Dess smiled, too. The knot untied on his chest as their eyes locked. He'd found her.

She shook the other girl then pressed a button and said something. He pointed to his ears and shook his head, trying to tell her that the communication was not working. These girls were stranded there. He knew it. How it had happened was a mystery, but they needed help. There wasn't much he could do with the small ship he was in and he couldn't come knocking on their door. One alternative would be to go back and seek help, returning with a large ship, except that they could refuse him. They'd probably refuse.

If he had a cable, and if he could throw it in such a way that it would attach to the L2, he could tow them. Back to the moon. No way he could face a storm with another ship so close to him. He looked at Saytera. She gesticulated something, but he couldn't understand and shrugged. She shrugged, too. If he took them to Sapphirlune... what could happen? They'd be detained. He could try to make sure they were not harmed.

Another girl popped up her head and looked. They looked tired and had faint smiles. If the ship had really been stranded, they could be without food. Perhaps even without water. Going to Sapphirlune was a better option than remaining there.

A crazy idea hit him. He could perhaps push the ship. He maneuvered behind it, then, very slowly, touched it. It moved. Dess would need to be careful not to cause a major impact. It was moving.

Going around the planet took a couple of hours, but once he could path a straight line to the moon, they moved fast enough that they reached the outskirts of the dome in about four hours. This would be the tricky part. No, not so tricky. He could push the ship through the tunnel and the gate. Once inside, the ship could be left floating with the antigravity on, then they could perhaps fix it or use other means to help it land. He hoped that it made sense.

There was another hard part; getting authorization to land.

He contacted the civil port. "Dess speaking. Authorization to enter?"

"Starspark." The voice was icy. Commander Serra. "Your entry is required at the military port. And what is it you have with you?"

"Mainland prisoners. They can't communicate." He hated saying that, but it was the only way they'd allow them to enter.

"On a spaceship. We are absolutely not allowed to seize a Mainland spaceship."

"They were stranded," Dess said. "There was no way for me to provide them help."

"Abandon the ship, lest we face diplomatic consequences."

"And let them die?" Dess was furious. "How is that more acceptable?"

There was a brief murmur over the radio. "Just a moment, Starspark."

The radio was silenced. Dess waited agonizing minutes, until it went back on. "Authorization to enter the port. How is the Mainlander spaceship going to land?"

"I was pushing it. I can push it to the port."

Silence. After many seconds, she said, "Proceed."

His fears were released in a great exhale. This was getting complicated. Pushing the ship through the tunnel was complicated, too. Eventually, the last gate was opened and he was floating on the Military port.

There were people at the observatory. He wasn't sure what was going to happen, so he maneuvered to match his door with the L2's. It opened. Saytera was there and Dess jumped on their ship.

Seeing her, but in these circumstances, was agony and elation. He touched her face. "How are you?"

Saytera had a small smile. "Very thirsty."

Dess nodded, then noticed her two friends and pulled back his hand. "We'll get you what you need."

She looked at him with her beautiful eyes. "How come you couldn't hear us?"

"I think your communications are off."

"But then…" Saytera bit her lip. "You heard our call."

He wasn't sure how to explain it. Maybe, if he had time, alone with Saytera, he'd tell her what happened. Dess shrugged. "Coincidence, I think. Do you think you can jump on my ship? To land?"

She nodded. "Yes. Listen, we have important information. Secrets about the Mainland government. It will interest your people."

Dess was taken aback. "That's why you were trying to come here?"

"We were just on the run."

He was running his hand through her hair. "What happened?"

Saytera closed her eyes.

"Not complicated," the tall girl with the bushy black approached them. "They found out we found out their secrets."

Dess pulled back his hand and nodded. "Fine. I guess you need medical attention now. You can share what you know once you're all feeling better. Shall we jump?"

He went first, then stood a step away from the door to extend his hand if necessary, but it wasn't. Saytera and her two friends jumped well. He then landed.

As he stepped out, and before he even noticed who was in the port, had a pair of arms around him. Nadia's. He didn't want to hurt her, but this was not the time.

She whispered, "Don't ruin this. I'm saving your ass."

"Whatever."

"So thankful."

He didn't completely push her, just looked back to see what was happening. Three soldiers had guns pointed at the girls. Commander Serra and Leader Aziz were there. Dess said, "They need medical attention. They also came to share confidential information from Mainland. They're our allies."

"This is just precaution," commander Serra said. "We'll get them to the infirmary, then we'll discuss the information they have."

"I'm going with them," Dess said.

Marcus approached Dess "Stay with Nadia. I'll try to check on them."

Nadia was then pulling him away from the port.

Dess stopped. "Nadia, I need to—"

She had a firm grip on his arm. "Come with me."

"Mr. Starspark," a deep voice called him.

Dess looked.

It was Mr. Tarell, Nadia's father and owner of Staralloy. He continued, "I need a minute with you."

"Now?"

"Right now." His voice was ice.

This was a terrible time, but there wasn't much he could do. "Of course."

Dess was taken to an office in the port building itself. The man sat behind an empty desk and gestured for Dess to take a chair. Dess couldn't help but hate him, hate the fact that he was so powerful, hate that he was in the place his father and mother should have been, hate to feel so powerless and small, and now hate him even more for making him abandon Saytera.

The man had a hard stare.

Dess kept his face calm. "How can I help you?"

Tarel smiled. "How? How indeed." He leaned over on his desk. "Do not humiliate my daughter."

"I don't mean to do so."

The man leaned back and laughed. "Is that so? Funny, I thought you were pushing her away. Now let me be very clear. Dess, you're a vermin who does not deserve to enter my family. That said, it's not up to you to reject a Tarel. Is that understood?"

"Very clearly."

The man scoffed. "Indeed. I'll make it slightly clearer, in case you get, uh… let's say… confused. We have three hostages from Mainland here."

Dess clenched his fist under the desk. "They came to help us. They have information about their planet."

"Very well. That's great. I see you're concerned about their well being."

Dess had a queasy feeling in his stomach and hoped he was perhaps misunderstanding the man. "We're Lunars. We treat our enemies decently. We treat our allies even more decently."

"Absolutely. Absolutely. Never meant to deny that. It's just that…" He got up and walked behind Dess, putting his hand on his shoulder. "We're not perfect. Accidents sometimes happen."

Dess turned. "Accidents? Are you threatening murder?"

The man frowned. "What a fascinating assumption. Of course not. I'm just saying that I don't want to see my daughter humiliated. I'm also saying it would be sad if an accident happened to our visitors. You're the one implying any connection."

"I'm not dumb, Mr. Tarel. I know very well what you're saying."

He shrugged. "That is your point of view, and I'm not on a mission to change it, Starspark."

Dess scoffed. "Of course. You're mentioning two unrelated events for no reason."

"Careful, boy. Accidents happen to our recruits, too. Not sure why you're laughing. But of course the events are completely unrelated. We wouldn't want to think there was any relation between you dismissing my daughter and any of those girls, right? We wouldn't want anyone to think that, either, right?"

Dess was almost shaking. "You think your daughter would like that? You think she wants anyone pretending to like her? You think it's not humiliating?"

"Oh, no, I would hate for her to learn about this. That's the stuff that can cause accidents, you know? As long as she doesn't know, and as long as nobody sees her being scorned, I frankly don't care. I hope we're understood here. Not a word to anyone. Accidents don't always cause death. People… can get hurt, right? I'm not implying it will happen and we'll assure nothing like this happens, of course. So will you, right?"

There were so many words Dess wanted to scream right now. He kept his face steady. "Of course."

Tarel had a smile that didn't reach his eyes. "Good to hear it, boy."

Dess walked out of that room trying to process what had just happened. They'd just threatened Saytera and her friends. How could that be? How could he know? Could he gleam so much just from the way Dess looked at her? Not unlikely.

"Dess!" The second voice he most hated in the world.

He turned to face Nadia. "What?"

She approached him, concern written on her face. "What was that about?"

Or was that fake concern? "Your father. Can't you guess?"

"I… don't know. Is everything alright with you?"

He stared at her wondering if she was really as oblivious as she looked. He had no idea. "I'm just feeling really tired and need to rest. We can talk later." Dess noticed her father at the end of the room, looking at them.

Dess kissed her cheek fast. She stepped back, startled, then turned to check what he was looking at, and Dess took the opportunity to turn around and hurry home. Perhaps she should ask her father what that had been about. Assuming she didn't know what it was, of course. Dess felt almost sick. Sick with worry, too, now that he knew that Saytera could be in danger.

ENEMIES AND ALLIES

Saytera started to feel and think only after drinking water, eating a thick soup, and receiving an intravenous fluid. She and her friends were in some kind of hospital room with four beds. Christina unfortunately had to relinquish her weapons, and her face was almost pained as she did so. A female soldier sat at a chair, watching them.

Here they were, in the custody of the enemy. That said, they had received medical attention and care. Combined with the fact they would give them precious information, there was probably little reason to worry. She still wished she could have talked to Dess a little more. She could almost still feel his fingers on her hair, the way he looked at her. He managed to be even more beautiful than she remembered. Just looking at him caused what felt like physical pain.

But then he disappeared. Marcus had walked all the way to the door but left as well. It was scary to be in Sapphirlune without any acquaintance. Without any clue as to what was going to happen to them, or someone to guide them on what exactly to do with their information.

Larissa took a sip from her juice. "We survived."

Saytera smiled at her friend. "Sounds like you were doubting it."

The girl raised an eyebrow. "You think?"

Christina put a finger and thumb together. "It was this close." She also had a relieved smile, though.

Larissa glanced at the female soldier sitting in the room. "So, what's your name?"

The girl was young, perhaps a little older than they were, and had brown hair and blue eyes. She seemed not to have noticed the question.

"Yo, you. Lunar," Larissa insisted. "Do you have a name?"

The girl was startled. "I, I'm not supposed to talk to you." She shrugged. "Sorry."

Larissa turned to her friends. "Should we just pretend she's not here?"

"Not sure we have a choice," Christina said.

"So rude." Larissa grimaced.

Saytera laughed. "I guess we need to wait for them to want to talk to us."

"And make sure they keep us alive," Christina added.

Saytera didn't think they should worry that much. "They're not monsters."

Larissa rolled her eyes. "You have your… *bias*. But the issue is that once we tell them what we know, we have nothing left to negotiate." She then whispered, "And Mainland doesn't want us. It's not like they can't hurt us from fear of repercussions."

She had a point, but at the same time… "People don't kill for the kick of it. What do they have to gain by killing us?"

"What do they have to lose?" Larissa scoffed.

Saytera tried to think. It would be so much easier if Dess was there, if they could talk to him, get some guidance. But now… "We can ask them to give their word they won't harm us."

Larissa shook her head. "Yes. We could do a contract. Then who's going to go after them if they break it?"

"Dess," Saytera mouthed. They had at least one ally there.

Christina was quiet and thoughtful. Larissa looked uncertain, but didn't have time to say anything, as the door was opened.

A stern-looking woman accompanied by two guards entered. She might have been in the port when they came in, Saytera had been so out of it.

"How are you feeling?" she asked.

"Much better," Saytera replied.

The woman looked at them and nodded. "I'm Commander Serra and I'm going to set up your deposition. You said you have important information for us, and I think you're feeling well enough. Is that correct?"

Saytera felt a chill in her stomach. One thing was to imagine coming into Sapphirlune and giving them their information, another was to actually do it.

Larissa raised her hand. "Yes, but… we would like the pilot who brought us here to be there, too. Because… he saved us."

The woman stared at Larissa as if examining her, then said, "That's a fair request. We'll arrange it. Anything else you need?"

"We want our safety," Saytera said.

She arched an eyebrow. "Well, obviously. You'll depose in front of a formal board and you'll be important war witnesses. We need you alive. No question about it."

Her words put Saytera more at ease.

. . .

About half an hour later, Saytera and her friends were being taken through even more corridors. In one of them, there was a glass wall through which she could see a city in daylight. It had tall buildings with glass and steel. Saytera looked up to try to see the frame around their shield, but it was too sunny. The Mainland planet was huge in the horizon, blue and grey, with its wild ocean. The view was great.

The room they entered had chairs around a large circle, empty in the middle. Saytera's heart was pounding as she sat. The woman was waiting for them, together with three more people. A woman and two men. One of the men was wearing a dark suit that wasn't from their army. No sign of Dess. It had been a good thing that Larissa asked for him. It would make her much more at ease. And yet, the fact that he had turned around and disappeared didn't sit right. Either he was ignoring her or he was being told to stay away. Then maybe he didn't want anyone to know that they knew each other.

After some time, he came in, together with a petite blonde girl. She might have been in the dock when they arrived. Maybe… Could she be the one who was hugging him? Saytera felt something cold inside her. Dess sat without ever even glancing at Saytera and her friends. He was still impossibly good looking. Painful to look at, even more painful when she realized that she meant nothing to him. She felt as if she'd swallowed a ball of lead.

Everything was blurry. He proceeded to explain how he'd rescued them. He claimed he intercepted a call for help and saw an opportunity to get more hostages.

One of the women stared at him. "Their shuttle was examined. Their radio wasn't working."

He looked unfazed. "True. After a while it stopped working."

The woman looked at Saytera and her friends. "Do you confirm that?"

"Yes," Larissa said. "I mean, I was likely half passed out."

A good thing that Larissa was doing the talking.

The woman nodded. "And you have important information for us?"

"We do," Larissa said. "But we'd like a promise that we'll be kept safe until we can return to our planet, or else be given refugee status here."

"You will be safe. As to granting refugee status, it will depend on a lot of factors. We still don't know who you are, your intentions, and if what you are going to tell us is true."

The blonde girl slammed a hand on the table. "You can't be serious. They want to help us."

Dess glared at the girl then looked away, as if uninterested in what she said.

The woman scowled. "Ms. Tarel, you can talk when it's your turn." She turned to Saytera and her friends. "We are being honest, and I hope you appreciate our honesty. We have a mandate to protect our fragile city, and we need to be sure this isn't a plan by Mainland."

"Of course," Saytera mumbled.

It wasn't as if they could just decide to withhold what they knew and then stay there waiting for the day a Mainland shieldbreaker came and toasted the city with them in it.

She had to say it, and she was going to ignore the rude black-haired guy sitting there. Saytera got up. The guards pointed pistols at her. She raised her hands.

"The Mainland government, they are planning on bringing a shieldbreaker." The old people listening to her didn't seem impressed. "It can break the shield protecting this city. The idea is to annihilate Sapphirlune."

The man in the suit frowned. "That's impossible."

"Well, it's the plan. It's in the documents we found. It's from Mainland, but it's not something our people are being told. It's for whoever is sending this warship. They are the ones who are going to get the Tahari Moon, they are the ones who are going to profit, while we bring death and devastation to innocent people. For no reason. It's time we stop bickering. This war has only harmed everyone in this city, everyone on our planet. We gained nothing from it. There's nothing to be gained with it. We need an agreement. We need your help in guiding the people on Mainland to refusing this nonsense. Together, we can be one system again."

Saytera sat down, wondering if she had said too much or if her words had been stupid. And she felt stupid noticing Dess was looking elsewhere while the girl by his side was staring at her in curiosity.

The woman had a hard stare. "Can you prove your allegations?"

Larissa had her information stick. Was it a good idea to give it to them? The girl was the one who replied, "We can't. We just read it. Our only proof that we're saying the truth is that our government tried to kill us. You can imagine there was a good reason for that."

Saytera doubted they were going to believe them. Still, she pleaded, "We have to do something. Mainland is a democracy. If people don't vote for this, it won't happen. Instead of a truce, we need a peace agreement. Help us convince our people."

The woman had a smile that didn't reach her eyes. "We will investigate your allegations and do our very best to reach an agreement with the planet. Peace is what we most want. We'll forever be thankful for your help."

Her words should be calming, but they weren't. They

sounded empty. Saytera felt hollow. Maybe there were things she and her friends didn't know, maybe the Lunars would just try to outbid whoever was selling the shieldbreaker. So many horrible possibilities.

They were escorted back to that hospital room, but this time they were left alone. The door was barred, though.

Christina sat on a bed. "I'm not sure it worked."

Larissa laughed. "I guess we'll find out in a few days. In case a shieldbreaker looms above us and kills us, we'll know what happened." She looked around. "Right? People hearing us."

"You think they are listening?" Saytera asked.

Larissa rolled her eyes. "Think? More like sure. What would you do if you were them?"

"Listen to us when we depose and tell them what we know?"

Larissa shrugged. "Maybe they think we'll spill some juicy secrets."

Christina was thoughtful. "They are scared. It's normal to be cautious."

Saytera sighed. "It's just… What was the point of getting this information? If it's not going to make any difference?"

Larissa was quiet for a moment, then said, "Maybe they already knew it? Maybe it's like they said: they'll do their own investigation?"

There was something Saytera didn't understand, but she couldn't ask knowing that they might be heard. She tried, "If only we had some piece of evidence!"

"It would be the same," Larissa said. "They could then use it to attack the planet. Or, let's say if we had more information about this shieldbreaker, they could just find a way to counter attack them or something. And *if* we had this information, it would still not mean it was true. I mean, they could claim we faked it."

"It would have been more convincing."

Larissa smirked. "Pity we don't have anything, then."

Saytera stared at her friend, wondering what she had done with it, but she wasn't going to ask.

"Right. Pity." Saytera sighed. "This information shouldn't have come here. It was meant for Mainlanders."

"There." Christina cocked her head. "What I said."

By that she meant treason.

Larissa scoffed. "No kidding, right? But it's not like they gave us much choice."

"They didn't shoot us down." Suddenly that sounded weirder than ever.

Christina was thoughtful. "Maybe they couldn't."

Larissa cocked her head. "Maybe they wouldn't dare. Imagine them having to explain shooting one of their own?"

"They could just blame it on Lunars," Saytera said.

Larissa was frowning, thoughtful. "Our tracker was down. So they lost us. And they didn't hear our radio signal for help."

"But…" Saytera was going to say "neither did Dess", but caught herself. "Yeah, that explains it."

Christina gave her a questioning look.

Dess's story that their radio was working only at the beginning wasn't totally convincing. But then, the other explanation was that he'd heard Saytera's call, and more than ever she doubted it, seeing the way he acted among his people.

Christina took a deep breath. "Again, we're alive. I guess. That counts, right?"

"I hope we're interesting as hostages," Saytera said.

"Of course we are." Larissa smiled, then yelled, "Yo, we're super great hostages. And allies."

They laughed. At least her friends were there for some levity. The truth was that they were imprisoned, even if in a very nice cell, that they'd given confidential information to their enemy, and that none of it was going the way Saytera had thought it would. Instead of peace, it was possible that they were only bringing more war, more conflict. Unless there wasn't anything they could do, in which case, it was just a matter of waiting for the shield destroyer to blast them all. Including Dess. Maybe not, maybe he would be among the few people saved, if he were in one of his planet incursions.

Saytera was upset, and it wasn't just because Dess had been one of her most prominent thoughts in the last few days. He should have understood that they were in an unknown place, scared, trying to help. A friendly smile could do wonders. The only friendly smile they got was from that woman, and it reeked of fakeness. That, and Dess's blond friend. Saytera's stomach turned thinking that she was more than just a friend. Why did these things keep happening? Perhaps it was Saytera's own fault, imagining things that weren't true, letting her heart project feelings that were hers only. But they had bigger issues. And no way to deal with them.

After Saytera and her friends left, Tarel stared at Dess. "Let's make sure these words don't leave this room."

"I don't think they were lying," Nadia protested.

Why couldn't she shut up? It could just make matters worse with her father.

"That's quite possible," her mother said. "But remember that they might have been manipulated into a complex hoax. There's no evidence that this technology exists or that anyone would provide it to Mainland. The girls are either accomplices or victims."

Nadia was about to say something, but Dess whispered, "Leave it."

He feared the girl would only make things worse. Tarel watched him closely as he left the conference room. So much to take in. So little time.

"We have to do something," Nadia said as they left the building.

"For what? Your dear parents are already investigating it, in case you didn't notice."

"You're angry at them. I understand. I am, too."

She had no clue, but he nodded.

She continued, "Perhaps we could investigate."

Dess stopped. "Absolutely not. No."

"You want them to blow up our city?"

"I trust your parents to act on their own self interest. I'm pretty sure they don't want this city to blow up any more than we do. I would just leave it if I were you."

"Leave it?" Nadia looked horrified. "When we just learned that there's someone behind this war?"

"They'll deal with it." Dess was shaking, trying to come up with a solution, with a plan, while at the same time having this pointless conversation with a girl he now hated. "I'm tired, if you don't mind. Can we talk tomorrow?"

"Tomorrow? You're going to act as if nothing happened."

"A lot happened. Maybe you should ask your father. Or did you ask your father?"

Nadia stepped back. "What are you talking about?"

"Nothing. It was a tough trip. I am tired."

She touched his arm. "You acted like a hero, Dess. I'm so proud of you."

"Heroes deserve rest, right?"

She looked down and bit her lip. "Yes, it's just… I already wanted to talk to you. I had to beg my mother to let you back in…"

"Effort noted. Thank you."

"No, no. It was my duty. Now, it's our duty to see this matter resolved."

Dess closed his eyes. "If this story leaks, who do you think will pay for it?"

Nadia seemed confused. "What do you mean?"

Dess looked away and back. "The Mainlanders are hostages. You know that, right?"

"And you're afraid…" Nadia was thoughtful.

"I rescued them. I feel responsible."

Nadia looked at him. "Did you… know any of those girls?"

"I don't socialize on Mainland, in case you haven't noticed."

She cocked her head. "You did. On that island."

"And?"

Her eyes were wide. "Is it… some kind of plan?"

Dess glared. "Just listen to you and think about your words. You'll find your answer."

"You're afraid, Dess. You're afraid they'll harm them. Is that it? What's happening? What is it you aren't telling me?"

Dess crossed his arms. "I told you everything I know."

"I'm your friend, Dess, I want to help you. I need you to trust me."

That was it. He couldn't take it anymore. "Friend? All the time you and your friends made fun of me at the Academy?"

"I never… You can't blame me for what a couple of dumbasses did."

"I'm not blaming anyone. I'm just saying. We were never

friends. And I'm not sure you want to call me a *friend* now, do you?"

She frowned. "You aren't making sense."

He pointed at himself. "The kitchen boy here is tired."

Dess then turned around and walked away.

"Dess," she called.

He turned. "What?"

She frowned. "You think people weren't friendly to you because you worked in the kitchen?"

"You have an alternate theory? I'm curious."

She stepped close enough to him that she had to look up.

"If anyone was *mean* to you," she had a mocking tone. "It might have been because you were a self-absorbed asshole who thought you were better than everyone."

Dess was taken aback. He hadn't expected that. "Nobody's begging you to give attention to any asshole."

"I thought you changed. Or that my impression had been wrong. It wasn't."

It was Nadia who turned away.

Dess called her, "Nadia!"

She turned.

Dess smiled. "I *was* better than everyone."

She rolled her eyes. "Congratulations."

Dess walked back to his apartment hoping maybe she'd give up on him. He would never know if she had anything to do with her father's request and how much she knew about Saytera, but he hoped he hadn't given anything away. Dess felt as if he were in a room with walls closing in. The only thing he could do was help Saytera and her friends to escape. But how could they leave the moon without alerting anyone and without

Sylvia or Nadia's help? There was also the threat on Sapphirlune, and the horrific realization that the leaders of his city didn't seem to care. But he was only one person. Just saving Saytera would be almost impossible. How many impossible things could one person do?

27

THROUGH THE GATES

Being locked in that room without any idea about what was going on had Saytera on edge.

Larissa leaned on the wall. "Do you think if we had gotten caught in Citarella our life would be any different?"

Saytera glanced at her other friend. "We wouldn't have dragged Christina."

"I dragged myself into it." Christina sounded resigned.

"Do you regret it?" Saytera was curious.

She thought for a moment. "Parts of it. I wish we had planned a better escape, I wish I had known the military archives would be so closely watched."

"Wishing about the past is a pointless thought," Larissa said.

Saytera shrugged. "You started it."

"I was hoping one of you would remind me that we'd probably be dead."

"Right. Let's cheer each other up by thinking about dreadful alternate realities." Saytera laughed, but she could hear her heart beating. The uncertainty of their situation and their powerlessness were getting on her.

"It is cheerful, in a way," Christina said. "I think I learned to appreciate the value of food and water. Before this, I would feel horrible by being locked in a room. Now I'm like; well, at least there's water."

Larissa put her hands behind her head. "I feel it's pointless to lock us here. I mean, it's not like we can grab a spaceship and escape this satellite."

"We did that in Mainland," Christina said quietly.

"Well, they don't have an artificial bubble, and controlled gates and tunnels."

Saytera was thoughtful. "If they fear we're spies or something, it kind of makes sense to lock us up. I wish they wouldn't think that."

"You—you hear that," Larissa looked up and yelled. "Creepy hearing people, we are nice and not spies."

Saytera chuckled. "That's definitely going to convince them."

Christina was looking down. "I truly wish we had allies here."

She probably meant Dess. Saytera thought the same and felt as if she'd betrayed her friends by misplacing her trust in him. But then, it wasn't as if she had come to the moon on purpose. They had just been desperate, on the run, and forced into these circumstances. He had saved them. It still hurt that he was ignoring them now.

Another thought came to her. "I wonder what they're going to do about it."

Larissa wiggled her eyebrows. "About us not being spies?"

"About a threat of somebody destroying their shield and annihilating their city." Then it hit Saytera. "Weren't they... too calm?

"If they truly think we're lying, it makes sense, right?" Larissa said.

"It means they won't do anything." Christina grimaced.

Saytera was still thoughtful. "And what if, what if what we found out isn't true? What if it's just a plan, for a distant future, or a way to enact an empty threat?" She wasn't sure she was making sense.

"Anything is possible, right?" Larissa said. "That said, you need to consider that they want to end the truce. Why would they do that for empty promises?"

Saytera exhaled, annoyed. "So why aren't these Lunars more worried?"

"Maybe they know something we don't," Christina said softly.

Larissa snorted. "Imagine if they have an even worse super-weapon." She then stopped laughing.

The three friends looked at each other.

Thoughts kept circulating in Dess's head without getting anywhere. He'd need to find out where Saytera and her friends were, render some guards unconscious, rush to the civil port, and hope that there wasn't much security there or around the gates. He'd need help to leave, and yet felt torn at the idea of ruining Marcus's life. But how could he do it alone? At least his friend wasn't there, and Dess was free to ruminate his thoughts in solitude.

That was until somebody knocked on the door. Dess knew who it was, and when he opened the door, his suspicions were confirmed: Nadia. Perhaps it wasn't her fault that her father was threatening Saytera, but then, perhaps it was, and that small possibility was enough for him to feel almost nauseous at seeing her. But he'd better not show any of that.

"Hey, Dess!"

Her tone was cheerful. Lovely to see someone happy and ignoring all that was happening.

"Hello." He managed not to sound angry or annoyed.

She then put a finger over her mouth, pointed up, and made a circle with her hands, then pointed to both ears.

He was wondering if she was feeling well, when he realized what she meant. Well, duh. It was obvious, and yet, he hadn't considered it. Somebody was watching him and had microphones in his apartment. Dess was stunned, and yet, he shouldn't be.

For once, he wanted to hear what the girl had to say, and asked, "Do you want to go for a walk?"

She shook her head and pointed to the apartment, then said, "I'm a little tired. Do you mind if I come in?"

This was not good. He wanted to know whatever she had to say and how she'd found out about them hearing him. "Are you sure? It would be nice to go for a walk."

"I'd rather not, Dess." Nadia grimaced and pointed inside, then to him and to her ears, as if saying, "it's you they are watching". It didn't really explain why they couldn't go out, but he didn't want to argue. Well, he couldn't argue, not without dragging her outside.

"Do you want something to drink?" he offered.

"Sure. Some water."

Water. He had no idea she was capable of drinking anything without alcohol.

She sat down and asked, "So what do you think about the Mainlanders' talk?"

"I… don't know what to think." Indeed he had no idea what to say in those circumstances. "I mean, it's possible it's a setup."

Nadia took a sip. "I agree. I mean, no way they would have access to a kind of weapon we didn't even know existed. But who knows, we might learn more about whatever Mainland is planning. It was a good thing you brought them here."

Dess sat at the table. "Glad to serve Sapphirlune."

Nadia pointed to him and to her neck. She meant the chip on his neck. Wild. The government could control each of his movements. Then she pointed inside the apartment. "I'm tired. Do you want to lie down?"

Was she for real? "Sure."

Nadia got up, but to his relief, she didn't go to his bedroom. Instead, she headed for the door in silent steps. She put her hand over her lip and asked him to open it. Open silently. Dess didn't like it.

He whispered in her ear, "What are you going to do?"

"Stay here with you." Her whisper in his ear was barely audible.

He stared at her.

Nadia then whispered, "Don't worry."

Dess shrugged and watched her go, partly wanting to run after her and demand the truth, partly glad she was leaving, but most of all, curious and worried at whatever she was going to do. Regardless, as soon as Marcus got home, they'd go for a walk. Dess wasn't going to stay home and wait for things to get sorted out by themselves, regardless of what Nadia thought.

It was hard to sleep in that place, despite how tired Saytera was. The lights had been shut down and there was no switch in the room. The Lunars wanted to keep them in the dark—literally. Saytera was lying down, trying to come up with a solution to end their predicament. Nothing came to her mind other than waiting and hoping that the Lunars weren't murderers and didn't use torture methods for interrogation. One more thing they hadn't counted on. Somehow, Saytera thought that Dess there would be enough to keep them relatively safe. Unfortunately, she had been wrong.

The door opened suddenly while she was about to doze off.

The blond girl who had been at their testimony pointed a pistol at them.

"Get up, get up."

A dark-haired girl was with her, also pointing at them.

"What's happening?" Saytera asked.

"You're being transferred," the blond girl replied.

Strangely, the girl's hand was shaking. Saytera glanced at her friends. This would be a perfect opportunity to overpower them and get their weapons. Saytera closed her eyes. There were probably more guards in the corridor and they wouldn't go far anyway. Both Larissa and Christina got up and also seemed confused.

"C'mon. Quick," the girl said.

They followed her as they passed two guards in the hallway and a safe door, which the girl opened with a code. As they were outside, the other girl took three pistols from a bag and handed them to Saytera and her friends. That was surprising and probably meant that they weren't just transferring them.

"They are set to stun," the dark-haired girl said. "Use them only as a last resort."

"How do you know we're not gonna stun you?" Larissa whispered.

"We're assuming you're not stupid," the blond girl said. "C'mon, let's move."

Saytera felt weird holding a pistol and handed it to Christina. "More useful with you."

"Are you sure?" Christina whispered.

"Positive."

Her friend shrugged and took it while they walked in fast steps through a corridor surrounded on one side by glass walls from where they could look outside. It was still day. No. Stupid idea. Of course it was still day. Lunars didn't have night-day cycles like Mainland. A strange place for a person to live on.

They were on a balcony overlooking the port from where they had come in. Their Mainland ship was at a corner, battered and bent from being pushed. The way they'd been brought was completely insane. Saytera's heart tugged, thinking of what Dess had done for them, and how he'd found them. It was just that it didn't make sense and it made her even more confused.

There were some six guards around the place. The dark-haired girl called them. She pointed at each guard and at one of them. Of course, they should split and get them by surprise. So many things could go wrong, though.

Christina turned to Saytera and mouthed, "I got it."

The one assigned to her, she meant.

The dark-haired Lunar girl pointed to the two stairs, made a gesture to split the group, then raised three fingers, then two, then one. When she closed her fist they ran to the stairs. Saytera ran but found cover, until she realized it wasn't necessary. Christina had jumped and already taken four guards. The two others were easily overpowered. The blond girl went to a control booth while they followed the dark-haired girl to a spaceship. This was a military model, with a powerful cannon and a shield. Inside, it had seats on the sides, and an open area with handlebars, so that it could transport people standing. Saytera, Larissa, and Christina sat on the sides. The dark-haired girl went to the front.

"What's going on?" Saytera managed to ask.

"Exactly what you're thinking," the girl in the front said.

The blond girl came running in, they closed the door, the ship took off and sped up through the tunnel.

The passage opened for them and soon they were in outer space, the moon getting smaller behind them.

"Who are you guys?" Larissa asked.

"I'm Sylvia," the brunette girl replied.

The blond girl was shaking, and started sobbing.

Her friend, Silvia, touched her back. "It's fine, it's fine. Do you want to go back?"

"No," the girl said between sobs. "I just… I can't believe… I can't believe it worked." She turned back to face Saytera and her friends. "I'm Nadia."

"Are you taking us back to Mainland?" Saytera asked.

The girl shook her head. "No. No. We need to figure this out." She turned to Saytera. "Like you said, work together." Her voice was cracking. "But it's much scarier in reality than when we planned this."

"Where are we going, then?'

"Tahari Moon." Her voice was still weak.

"Can anyone land there?" Larissa asked.

Nadia was still sobbing. "Probably. Maybe. According to my plan, yes. But… we'll only really know when we get there."

It didn't take any effort to notice that the girl was absolutely terrified.

∽

Marcus was taking so long to get back that for once, Dess started fearing for his friend. When he arrived, he was not alone. A middle-aged man with dark skin and grey hair and beard, carrying a case, accompanied him. Before Dess asked anything, Marcus put a finger on his lips. Right. It sounded as if they were all in some joke Dess didn't understand. The man put a finger on the back of his neck and pointed to Dess.

The idea of removing his chip was amazing, even if it was what had saved him from being stranded on an island. At the same time, he feared what would happen if they made a mistake.

But then, Dess trusted Marcus. The man he brought was unlikely to be some clumsy noob. And it could be a ticket to freedom. If it didn't get Dess killed.

Saytera was still stunned and somehow suspicious that these girls had taken them out of Sapphirlune.

When they were far away, and certainly not yet followed, Saytera asked, "Do you guys have a plan or something?"

"It's what you said," Nadia turned back to face them. "We need to work together."

"How is going to Tahari Moon going to help?"

The girl sounded uncertain. "I'm… not so sure. You need to tell your people about what you found out. We need a safe space to stop and think."

"Thank you for rescuing us," Larissa said.

Nadia frowned. "We're the ones who should be thanking you. I mean, it's my city that's being threatened, and you're trying to stop it. You should have been treated as special guests."

Larissa was thoughtful. "Any idea why we weren't?"

The blond girl shrugged. "My parents. I don't know, I guess they think they know everything, they think they're mighty and invulnerable, or they don't want to create panic. I'm not sure."

"Who are your parents?" Saytera asked.

"Leader Aziz and Mr. Tarel, they were both in your testimony."

That woman who interrogated them. "I see."

"I think they're stubborn," Nadia said. "Maybe they didn't believe you."

"Why do *you* believe us?" That was genuine curiosity.

"Nobody almost dies for some kind of sham. And your ship had no food and no oxygen. I saw the reports. If it hadn't been for Dess, you'd have died. It would be a pretty flawed plan to count on such luck."

Larissa cocked her head. "Wouldn't it be easier to stay in Saphirlune and convince your parents we were telling the truth?"

Nadia sighed. "They wouldn't hear it."

Larissa scratched her head. "And they'll… hear it better from the other moon?"

"*Mainlanders* can hear it better from the Tahari Moon. And Lunars."

Of course, it made total sense. "There's a communication station there," Saytera said.

"So we can send a message to the planet," Larissa added.

The blond girl smiled. "Exactly."

Saytera sighed. "Let's hope they hear it."

"Hum," Sylvia had a grimace. "First we have to land there."

Nadia waved a hand. "You know I got it. Don't worry." She

looked back at Saytera and her friends and got serious. "Also, I don't think you were safe in Sapphirlune."

Probably. But there was something Saytera had to ask. "Weren't you worried about the other Mainlanders who were taken to your Moon?"

Nadia looked away. "No, because I was sure they were being treated well and just imprisoned."

"So they are fine?"

Nadia's face was blank. "They were killed."

"Oh." Saytera leaned back, trying to register the shock, counter the revulsion she felt. Then she thought that someone else would be even more shocked. "Does Dess know that?"

Nadia was teary-eyed. "No. No, no. It's better if he doesn't know anything. For some reason my parents stopped trusting him after he was rescued from the planet."

"Well." Sylvia shrugged. "He did assault a superior and purposefully deactivated the tracking system."

Nadia stared at her. "It was probably some silly dispute with Sam and Amil. Dess hates them. He hates everybody."

"How come they let him bring us in, then?" Larissa asked.

Nadia laughed and rolled her eyes. "Me. I was all 'but mom, I love him, he loves me.' They were so eager for me to get a boyfriend that it was easy."

Why was the girl making fun of it?

Larissa raised an eyebrow. "So you don't love him."

Right. That made sense.

Nadia sighed. And showed the palms of her hands. "Look, I tried, I really did. He's not my type." She looked down. "I thought I could change… my type. I can't. But it was nice to make my parents happy for a while."

Strange to hear that a girl could not be interested in Dess, and horrible to know that Dess was probably interested in a girl who didn't like him. Not in Saytera. Better not think about it.

Sylvia shot her friend an annoyed look. "It must be so cool to know you can pick and choose anyone you want."

Nadia scoffed. "It's not like that. He didn't like me either, but I assume for completely different reasons."

Saytera felt lighter, and hoped they didn't notice her relief sigh.

The blond girl shrugged, then looked at Saytera. "Hang on, how do you know Dess?"

Oh, no. Saytera had said too much. But she tried to pretend she hadn't. "He brought us to the moon, remember?"

"Yes, but how come you asked if he knows about the Main-landers? And you even knew there were some here."

"We knew people disappeared. If he was out, near Main-land... I mean... it was sort of obvious, right?"

The girl looked at her for a while, then said, "I guess."

Saytera looked down. She wondered if Dess knew where she was and if he was safe, but didn't want to ask. It wasn't that she didn't trust these girls, it was just that she wanted to be cautious. Larissa stared at Saytera with worry, which likely meant she felt the same. Christina, as usual, watched them quietly.

After a while, Larissa asked, "Isn't it forbidden to go to the Tahari moon?"

"I think I can make it," Nadia said.

Sylvia stared at her friend in disbelief. "You think? I thought you had it all figured out."

Nadia shrugged. "I do, and that's why I think we'll make it."

Sylvia facepalmed.

Larissa leaned forward. "There's a cannon there. Basically

anyone who approaches will be shot down, right? Did you manage to disable it remotely?"

Nadia shook her head. "Only the Peace Alliance can do it remotely. They locked it when our war started, hoping it would make us reach an agreement." She scoffed. "Right."

Saytera had a queasy feeling in her stomach.

Larissa glanced at her friends then turned to Nadia. "So… what's your solution for landing there?"

Nadia shook her hands in front of her. "Listen, I know what I'm doing. If I tell you, you'll start doubting me, and I'll start doubting it, and it won't work. Some trust, please."

It sort of made sense. So far she had rescued them, and it was true that having people doubting you could make things harder. "I'll trust you."

Larissa snorted. "I guess."

Sylvia puffed. "Nadia, I swear, if you're wrong you'll hear so much from me."

"No." Christina broke her silence. "If she's wrong, none of us will ever hear anything again."

28

NEW MOON

Drip, drip, drip. Blood fell on the basin beneath Dess. He bit on a cloth, wondering if it had been a good idea to do this with only a light analgesic pill and in an apartment where he couldn't scream. Or complain. Or anything, really.

Despite all the pain he was already feeling, when the chip came out, the sharp pain brought him a feeling of relief. The chip was immediately put inside a strange, small spongy ball. The man was now patching up Dess's skin.

Freedom. Freedom to do so much. Once he was out of his apartment. The man took a display and wrote on it: "The small ball is a heater. The chip must always be at body temperature, or an alarm will be raised. You can recharge the heater on the black disk. The battery can last up to three days. Rest and clean the wound often."

Dess took it and wrote: "Thank you. Who are you?"

The man wrote: "Don't you worry about that. Take care." He then opened the door slowly and left.

Dess called Marcus and decided to write to him: "Who was he? Why did you decide to do this now?"

"It was me, Sylvia, and Nadia. When you were away. We were worried about you."

"Nadia? What about her parents?"

"It's fine. We can talk about it tomorrow. You'd better rest now."

"Thanks for being my friend."

"You saved my life, Dess. I had to save yours."

Dess stared at the chip in its warming circle, fake life surrounding it. Like his city. He wanted to go out and do something, but was still in pain, and the analgesic made him drowsy. If he were to do anything, he had to be alert, so he had no choice but to rest.

"We're approaching it." Sylvia's voice trembled.

The Tahari moon was smaller than Sapphirlune, its surface darker. It was odd to hear so much about something, then get to see it for real. This was the reason Saytera's planet was at war, the reason Sapphirlune didn't get enough food or water, the reason some people died. Yet it was just a ball in space. A ball with something very valuable in it. The truth was that they were just fighting for money. As if the common Mainlander citizen would even see any of that.

But now what Saytera wondered was how exactly they would bypass the moon's defenses. As much as she wanted to trust the girl, she would only really relax once they indeed landed in one piece.

"Nadia," Sylvia's voice was tense. "They're preparing to shoot."

"I know. Silence."

Saytera leaned over to see an orange light becoming brighter. She then fell to her side, as the ship jerked sideways quickly. A few seconds later, an orange ball passed them. Nadia exhaled.

"That's your plan?" Sylvia sounded furious and terrified.

Nadia kept looking ahead. "Quiet."

The ship jerked down, now. That had been so close. The closer they got to the moon, the harder it would be to evade those shots. Saytera closed her eyes, aware that there was nothing she could do other than hope they didn't get hit. After some ten sudden movements and a low crash, when it hit their shield, the ship started flying freely.

"We're out of its range!" Nadia yelled.

They all sighed.

Saytera looked out the window. "But… we're not getting into the city."

"We'll have to land outside, then find a way in." Nadia turned. "There are suits on the back."

Saytera was stunned. "So we're walking in."

"Yeah." Nadia nodded.

Their ship landed on a rocky surface, right beside a domed city, sort of like Sapphirlune, but apparently smaller. Such a lifeless, desolate landscape.

They went to the back and pulled the extravehicular suits.

Larissa looked at them. "We don't all need to go at once." She turned to the Lunar girls. "Do you have a plan on how to open the entry door?"

Nadia took a deep breath and looked down. "We'll… have to figure out a way."

Larissa pointed at herself. "Fear not. You got an expert here. If it's a digitally secured door, I should be able to open it." She turned to Nadia. "The two of us can go, then we signal for the others."

Nadia nodded fast. The girl was so terrified that it was hard to believe she'd gotten them this far.

The two of them went to the airlock after suiting up. Saytera watched the side window to see when they would show up, but instead the airlock opened again and they returned.

"What's wrong?"

Larissa removed her helmet. "There are automatic pistols. They were shooting us."

They all looked at each other.

Christina said, "I could, maybe, try to shoot these pistols, but it depends on how many they are. If we have a shield, something to take cover…"

Nadia shook her head. "Too many and too fast."

Sylvia was thoughtful. "What if… we placed our airlock right in front of the door? So there would be no space between us and the door?"

Larissa shook her head. "The shots are coming from the door. We'd stand no chance."

"Do you think it's only the entrance that's protected?" Saytera asked.

Nadia sighed. "They have thick walls, we wouldn't be able to—"

"No. I mean…" Saytera was having an idea, but not sure if it made sense. "If I find an electricity panel, I know how to cause a blackout. It would shut off the automatic pistols."

Larissa was thoughtful. "Would they leave a panel unprotected?"

Christina was staring at Saytera with eyes narrowed. Sure. The word *blackout* certainly reminded her of something. It was a try. Saytera wasn't sure it would work, and technically she didn't need any panel, but there was no way she could explain it.

Saytera shrugged. "Trying to find a panel won't kill us."

"Oh, I'm sure it will," Larissa said. "If we go out there—"

"I mean we fly there."

Nadia shrugged while she removed the thick jumper. "We can try. But I won't go outside this time. I need to get us back to the door."

"Let me go alone." Saytera hoped they'd agree.

And that was how Saytera was left by herself around the outer wall of the city, to "look for an electricity panel". Did anyone even believe that? It didn't make any sense even for Saytera. She'd only gotten there because Christina and Larissa somehow trusted her, Christina with more knowledge than the others.

Saytera had trouble moving. Instead of steps, she jumped. She felt a weird fear that she wouldn't go back down and instead would float into space. It wasn't logical, of course, but her body was not used to walking in so little gravity and thus played tricks on her mind.

Saytera approached the wall. This was when things would get real. She remembered all the blackouts in the academy, and yet had trouble reconciling these outside events to her own mind, her own power.

The ship was now away from her field of vision, having gone back to the door. They would need to go out and open it or at least shoot and disable the pistols during the time the electricity was out. Saytera waited. This was lonely as she'd had never felt before, on a land without life, only black sky above her. So many stars as she'd never seen before. A shimmery universe reminding her how much more power there was out there. Stars in the universe, stars within. And yet they were so many more than she had even imagined she could see with her own eyes.

But her job now was not to connect with the stars, but with the darkness between them. Her darkness. Solitude. Quietness. Peace. As if things could stop burning and changing and atoms would stop moving and reacting. Just quietness. In the silence on that moon, it was easy to find that. There wasn't that much breathable air in her tank, but she took a deep breath as she focused on darkness. No, not focus; relax. As if she were in the training house and the city were the lamps. That wouldn't work. The door was the one lamp she had to quench. And whatever security system was there.

Saytera suddenly remembered being in that house, hoping to do her exercise well, hoping that Yansin would appreciate her. Why did it seem that Saytera had always yearned for Yansin's approval, when it was something that she always had? It was like a person swimming in the ocean, yearning for water. The moment in that morning came back to her mind. She remembered then how much she anticipated meeting Cayo again. That was a thought long gone, too. Now she wasn't even sure if young Saytera had ever truly felt anything for him. Hard to know when he was the only guy around. As if her life now were any more different.

And yet none of it mattered, only darkness. And then she remembered the vision at the house, the funeral ceremony. And then darkness was not only outside, but within as well. Saytera collapsed.

Despite being tired, Dess didn't sleep much. He sat in the

kitchen, eating his morning porridge while Marcus still slept. The city still slept. He had no idea what was happening to Saytera and if she was safe. He kept the chip close to him. Would anyone be able to track his movements inside his own apartment? Would anyone be watching? Dess didn't know, but didn't want to take a chance.

What he had to do today was go out and get some answers, out of this apartment where he was watched. He had no doubt it had something to do with Nadia's parents, and his only question was whether they wanted to make sure he wouldn't break his precious daughter's heart or if they somehow mistrusted Dess. Well, they probably did.

Loud knocks startled him. Dess put his chip in his pocket. More knocks before he even made it to the door. Who could be that desperate at that time in the morning? The door was pushed open before he got to it. Five people were coming in, pistols in hand.

"You're under arrest," one of them said.

Dess raised his hands, trying to come up with a solution, a way out of this.

"Get his friend," the man then shouted.

"Leave him out of this," Dess protested.

As a reply, he got punched in the jaw. Sam was one of the people invading his apartment. Predictable. Dess swallowed his instinct to strike him back.

Someone was about to handcuff him, when he raised his hands again. "I'm unarmed, outnumbered, and have all the reasons in the world to want to cooperate." He stared at Sam. "You can't be that scared of me."

Sam laughed. "Still slime and will be treated as one." He turned to the other man. "Get him locked."

Dess extended his hands, wrists up, as if submitting to the

handcuffing. Only a fraction of a second to think. So little time. Little time was what he had, and if he didn't do anything, they could do something to Saytera. He had to get her out of this moon, and he wouldn't be able to do it while imprisoned. In a quick movement, Dess stole the guy's weapon, shot him, hoping it was set to stun, then turned and shot Sam and the other guy. He heard steps from the hallway and shot the two soldiers bringing Marcus. Dess tossed his friend a pistol and signaled for him to follow him. Dess and Marcus were silent in the elevator, then walked outside. The official transport was in front of their building. Dess got into it.

"What are you doing?" Marcus asked.

"Gaining time. They were probably going to take us to headquarters. So that's where we'll go." Dess took his chip and waved to his friend. "I need to get Saytera out."

"They're already out."

Dess's stomach sank. "What?"

Marcus looked away. "I couldn't tell you. Sylvia made me promise. They took her to the Tahari moon."

So many questions in Dess's mind. "How were they able to leave Sapphirlune? How are they going to land there? It's impossible."

"Nadia found a way."

Dess covered his face with his hands. This was terrible. "Why?"

"To stop the destruction of our city, how's that? They believed in Saytera and her friends."

"Is that why you got my chip out?"

"I thought there could be consequences."

"You could have told me."

"I didn't know they'd come here before morning to arrest us. Us. As if I'd done anything wrong."

Plan, plan, plan. Dess had to plan something. "We're going to the academy."

"What?"

"Kitchen. There shouldn't be anybody there. Yet."

Dess's passcode still worked. He approached the grabber droid, which had been his favorite one. "Sorry, little buddy."

After opening the droid's control panel, Dess put his chip inside it, then undid some of the grabber's programming.

Marcus watched him in curiosity. "Are you going to poison people?"

"Why are you giving me this idea only now? It's brilliant." Dess laughed. "No. But this little droid will move around enough to give them a chase. I hope." Then he shrugged. "And we don't have any narcotic. We barely have food." Dess got up. "Let's go."

"Where? The civil port is the most obvious place they'll look for us. The military port will also be impossible to reach."

"I know a place where they won't expect us."

Saytera woke up and noticed her head was on someone's lap; Larissa's. She sat up surprised, sitting in a strange room with controls in one wall and some sofas on the corners.

"What happened?" her friend asked.

Nadia sat by them.

Saytera was confused. "I don't know. I'm the one who missed the last few minutes."

Nadia shrugged. "You did it. You turned off the security system. But when we went to pick you up, you had fainted.

Christina and Sylvia went to try to find the medical center to see if they could get you anything. I'll get them back." She walked away, to the door.

Looking down, Saytera noticed she was still wearing the outer suit, and took it off, then looked around. "Everything is working, then? Temperature, breathable air…"

Larissa laughed. "Imagine if it weren't. We'd be so screwed."

"I had some extra air in the ship," Nadia said as she re-entered the room. "But not much."

Saytera looked at the terminals again. "This is the communication center."

"Yep," Larissa nodded.

"Is it working?"

"We're testing it. We might need to break it through."

That shouldn't be too hard for Larissa, so Saytera was quite hopeful that they were going to accomplish their goal.

Right then, Sylvia and Christina entered the room. Christina sat by Saytera. "Feeling well?"

"Yes." It was even strange to imagine that she had passed out or anything like that. Stranger was to realize she'd actually disabled the security system.

Christina nodded. "Nice." She turned to Nadia and Larissa. "We'll try to see if we find supplies, then."

Saytera got up. "I'm coming with you."

Her friend bit her lip. "Sure? You'll need a zapper. I mean, there were some security droids."

Christina was among the few people who knew how little Saytera and weapons got along.

Still, Saytera wanted to go out and explore, and didn't think she'd be much help cracking a communication system. "I'm coming."

"Let's go, then," Christina said.

There she was, about to explore a human construction on a moon, a moon that until then had not seemed real to Saytera, a place she would never imagine she would set foot on. And there she was, going with someone she would have considered an enemy until recently, and someone she… Well, she would never have guessed they could be friends again. If they were getting along, anything was possible.

Victory was not in war, but in understanding. Hopefully people on Mainland and Sapphirlune would see that, too. Or else they would all be done for.

29

DEAD GARDEN

Dess found the familiar gap beneath the fence leading to his old house.

"Are you sure?" Marcus asked.

Of course he wasn't. Dess looked at his friend. "Stay. Your father will protect you."

Marcus scoffed. "And miss all the action? No way."

Dess put a hand on his shoulder. "This is no joke. We don't know what's going to happen, but it's possible that after this… we might have to hide. Who knows?"

"And you expect me to stay here while Sylvia's there?"

Dess sighed. Of course there was no convincing his friend. "Let's go."

"How do you know there's a hidden gate here?"

Those memories still hurt. How many times Dess had relived the scene, hadn't gone back for the doll, and their family had escaped. The thing is, they were on an interplanetary ship, so they weren't going to the port. There was an exit there, within these grounds, and hopefully a functioning spaceship as well. Knowing how much of a coward Tarel was, Dess had no doubt.

"I know this house. And I don't think anyone will look for us here."

They walked over the now dried ground. Odd to bring someone else to what used to be his sanctuary, his memory of his lost past, lost family, lost everything. Almost everything. At least Azael had been with him for some time. Now gone, too. In a way, Marcus was the family Dess had left, so it made sense that he should be there. His heart tugged thinking about Saytera, too, but he didn't know what she was to him yet.

He knew how to deal with the security in the garden, but wasn't sure what would happen if he tried to steal a spaceship and open the gate. If there even was a spaceship there. This was a huge gamble. The docking station for ships was on the other side of the house. Dess took a deep breath. This had to work.

In seven years, nobody had bothered to change the security system in the garden. Perhaps they hadn't changed any of the security systems. Dess could dodge the scanners as easily as he could fly a ship in a simulator. They reached the walls of the mansion. Tum, tum, tum. His heartbeat. It had been so long that he'd touched those walls.

There was a window open. The right thing would be to go straight around and try to get to the presumed spaceship parked there. And yet, it was as if the window called him.

Dess turned to his friend. "Stay here. I'll go up there and back here again. If I don't show up in five minutes, you can either go around the house and see if you find a ship, or get back through the same gap and then hide.

Marcus pulled his arm. "Where are you going?"

"I'll be right back." Dess moved away from his friend and

climbed the wall. The window led to a living room. The place used to be warm and lively in Dess's time. Now it had white furniture which just gave him a feeling of coldness and dread. It didn't take long for him to find what had certainly brought him here. Tarel's office. Or at least an office.

There were two terminals, a desk, and some notes. More than that, there was an information stick. Dess pocketed it and crouched as he heard steps coming in his direction. Some luck. Tarel himself.

He spoke on a comm. "She can't have gone to the Tahari Moon. Its defenses are up."

The man paused, as if hearing something, then sighed. "Find the Starspark boy and we'll get our answers. He's responsible for that." He paused again, then said, "Right. I'm waiting, then."

And would keep waiting. Provided Dess could control his sudden urge to come out of hiding and punch him. Now he was the concerned father—blaming Dess, who had absolutely no say in what his daughter had done.

Tarel stepped out of the office. Dess would need to climb down this window. It was a steep descent. It would have to do. After looking around, to check if nobody was getting back, he went to the window—and then Tarel entered again.

Dess shot him with his zapper before any of them could say anything. Hopefully it wouldn't kill him, for Nadia's sake at least. Then Dess crossed back to the other window and climbed down, trying to forget the odd feeling of walking in that house when it was the same and yet completely different.

"What was that about?" Marcus asked.

Dess shook his head. "Getting in trouble." Then he smiled and pulled a stick. "And some information."

"I'm sure the girls have it all."

Dess shrugged. "Never know." He gestured to his friend. "Come."

They walked around the house, pausing when the scanner moved, and came to the side. There was a spaceship there, by an auto-opening station. This was made for a quick escape for the moon. Something that could be quite useful in case they learned that the city would be under attack. Interesting. This was not exactly where his family had died, but another station, connected to the same gate out of the city.

"We'll never open this," Marcus said.

Maybe not. Then, maybe, it was worth a try, in case the override security still existed. He remembered his mother taking his hand and explaining to him how he could hop on a ship and escape. Strange that they thought perhaps Dess would need to do it on his own. But he would never be able to do it, not alone, not so young. And yet, if the security system hadn't changed, he could do it now. Dess pressed his hand on the panel—and it lit.

"Let's go. There should be a 20-second countdown."

The ship also opened to his hand. Idiots. They thought they had killed Dess's entire family, including him.

"How are you doing this?" Marcus asked.

"Luck." In a way, it was true.

When security guards came shooting, they were already escaping the circle protecting Sapphirlune city and in open space.

Marcus leaned back and sighed. "You think they'll send anyone after us?"

"No. I think they want to know where we're going."

"Then they'll find Sylvia."

Dess shook his head. "They would find her regardless, Marcus. I doubt they went there to hide."

They were in a large building, which was probably meant to be the center of operations in the Tahari moon. Saytera, Christina, and Sylvia came to a huge deposit with heavy mining machinery.

"It's weird, isn't it?" Sylvia asked. "To see this all empty."

Not so much. In a way it reminded Saytera of the hangar in the Academy. "A little. We have abandoned spaceships on Mainland, too." Then she wondered if she was giving the enemy too much information, which was ridiculous, since she wasn't sure who her enemy was anymore.

"In Sapphirlune, too, they're on standby," Sylvia said, thoughtful.

Christina looked around. "It's all here waiting until it's useful for someone outside our system. We've all been duped, that's what I think."

"That's the truth." Saytera sighed. "Let's go. There should be a residential area somewhere. We'd better find it."

Sylvia took a moment, looking back at the machinery. "Do you think… we'll make a difference?"

Saytera shrugged. "No way to know other than to keep trying."

Then, Sylvia's comm beeped. The girl opened the audio for them all to hear. It was Larissa. "Do you think you can disable the main cannon?"

"But it keeps us safe, doesn't it?" Saytera asked.

"They're friends."

Saytera wasn't sure if she could be that precise. "If the cannon's controlled remotely, the only way would be to deactivate it. But then…"

"Leave it," Nadia replied. "You're right that it keeps us safe. They should be able to land just like we did."

"It's Dess?" Saytera asked. Then she realized she should have stayed quiet.

"I think so. I'll get back to you." The comm was turned off.

Sylvia looked at Saytera. "You know him."

"I know he's a good pilot."

The girl shook her head. "No. I mean. You *know* him. Was it you with him when he crashed in Mainland? Are you planning something?"

Saytera stepped back. "We aren't planning anything."

"You didn't answer the first question."

The question sounded accusatory and Saytera didn't like it. She looked at the girls' eyes. "Yes. I crashed with him in Mainland. But him rescuing us was a coincidence. Why?"

Sylvia looked away and shrugged. "It sounded... convenient."

"It sure was."

The girl looked down and away. "You could have told us."

"I didn't know you or trust you." Saytera paused. "Let's go to the communication room, see if they need help."

Sylvia sighed and was the first to head to the door. Christina glanced at Saytera, as if surprised, then did the same.

They entered the communication room.

"Where are they?" Saytera asked.

Larissa glanced at her. "The equipment here is toast, but they contacted us."

Saytera was anxious, worried about Dess, even if he hadn't been the nicest to her last time she'd seen him. "Contacted. In the past. What about now?"

"They're too busy to talk," Nadia said.

Meaning avoiding the canon. "If I know where it is, we can

stop the current going to it," Saytera said. "I don't want them risking their lives."

Nadia leaned back. "I got us here. Dess should have no problem, since, you know, he's soooo much better than I am." She chuckled.

"That's not funny."

"I'm serious, Saytera," Nadia replied. "That guy would sleep in the simulator if given the chance. He'll make it."

"True." Sylvia rolled her eyes. "I'd say flying simulator is his sexual orientation."

Larissa turned to Saytera. "They'll land inside, though. We got the gate."

Saytera was still barely able to breathe.

Nadia got up and approached Saytera. "Hey. Chill. Look at Sylvia. Her boyfriend's there, and she's calm."

The girl looked down. "He's not my boyfriend."

Nadia rolled her eyes. "Right."

"What about you?" The dark-haired girl shot back. "Also quite calm when your *lover*'s there."

"Not lover. Just… a failed experiment." Nadia shrugged.

Larissa chuckled. "Why? You thought he could make you straight?"

"Sort of."

That conversation was uncomfortable. What Saytera really wanted was to see Dess and Marcus landing and safe. "Where are they landing?"

"The inside port, so that's much better than us. But we're not sure how to get there," Larissa said.

Saytera looked around and remembered the little she saw of the structure from space and from when she was walking outside it.

"I think I know where to go."

She ran towards a door and pressed to open it. And got no result.

Larissa was beside her. "We're figuring out the doors. But I need to control the gate first."

Saytera sighed and sat down, watching as her friend focused on the controls. There wasn't much she could do right now, and that was agonizing. She wished she could help Dess the way he'd helped her when they had been adrift in space. Sitting and waiting was dreadful.

Larissa turned to Saytera and smiled. "Landed."

Saytera closed her eyes. So much relief.

Her friend was in front of her. "Let's find them."

Saytera was rather thinking of the way he'd ignored her in Sapphirlune. "You go. I'm fine here."

Larissa knelt in front of her and whispered, "You're dying to see him."

Saytera didn't understand why her friend was insisting, after everything. "Yeah. He was so nice to us…"

"Give him a chance to tell his side of the story," Larissa said.

"I don't need to go to the landing pad for that." Saytera wasn't even sure how he'd act in front of her, and wasn't looking forward to it.

"Stubborn." Larissa shook her head.

Only Larissa and Sylvia went to meet Dess and Marcus.

Nadia, Christina, and Saytera were quiet for some time.

"You know," Nadia said. "They were supposed to stay in Sapphirlune."

"Wouldn't they be in danger, though?" Saytera asked.

Nadia sighed. "That makes sense."

Saytera had a curiosity. "And why has nobody else come after us?"

"I hide my trail well." Nadia laughed.

"They found us."

"Nah. Sylvia told Marcus. She pretends she doesn't but she's crazy about him."

Saytera smiled, remembering him saying her name on the island. "He loves her, too."

Nadia narrowed her eyes. "How do you know?"

It was better to admit it. "It was me. On the island with them."

"Oh."

"But the fact that we ended up in space, that was a coincidence. I never planned on leaving Mainland. I just wanted to know what was happening and then tell my people. It was just a desperate escape."

"You knew you would find allies in Sapphirlune, though, so maybe you meeting them, in a way, helped you decide to risk going into space."

"That makes sense," Saytera conceded.

"Thank you for coming to us," Nadia said. "We'll make it right. We'll end this war."

"Why are you so cheerful?" Christina asked.

"It's already hard to do what we're doing. If I start to doubt us, then we'll just be paralyzed."

Saytera took a deep breath. "But there's so much that doesn't depend on us."

Nadia smiled. "Why we must nail our part."

Saytera smiled back. "We will."

The door opened and Dess stepped in. Saytera got up, stunned. He was outrageously good looking and it was hard to ignore it. With his eyes locked on hers, he ran to her and held her face in his hands.

"How are you? Are you hurt?" His voice had the ability to speed up her heart.

"I'm fine," she managed to reply.

He took her hand. "Can you come with me? I need to talk to you."

"Sure."

Saytera followed him, without any idea where she was going, surprised that the doors were working.

They were in a deposit with empty shelves.

Dess stared at her.

"What is it?" she asked.

He was silent. Saytera looked down, then felt his hands pulling her face gently towards him.

Then she didn't see anything more. He was kissing her. There was no darkness outside or inside, no stars. Just them and their fire becoming one. One universe, one ocean, two in one. One breath. One heart divided in two, setting the same rhythm.

And then they were apart again, his eyes on hers.

Dess smiled. "I wanted to do that from the moment I met you."

"When you were pointing a pistol at me?"

"You had a bow and arrow. That causes a reaction."

Saytera had a light laugh, but then decided to get to what had been bothering him. "Dess, in our testimony—"

He caressed her face. "I know. I'm sorry. That Tarel guy, he threatened to kill you. I thought..." He looked down, then back at her. "If he thought I didn't care, I thought you would be safer."

"Oh. Can we trust his daughter, though?"

Dess shook his head. "I don't know. Sylvia I kind of trust, but Nadia..."

Saytera remembered the girl's words, and how hopeful she

sounded. She remembered her fear when bringing them to the moon. "I think she's fine."

"Let's hope so." He then looked at Saytera. "You called me, didn't you? When you were adrift."

"We sent a signal."

"That's not what I'm talking about. I heard *you*. I had to steal a ship and come to your rescue."

She knew it made sense and knew she'd tried to somehow reach him through the great ocean in the universe. "I'm glad you did."

He looked at her. "What do you want to do now?"

"Stop a war? And stop the destruction of your city?"

Dess nodded. "Let's try it, then." He took her hand. "Together."

They walked back to the control room.

Sylvia and Marcus weren't there, which was a relief, somehow. Saytera didn't want the girl's judgemental look on her. Still, Saytera let go of Dess's hand.

He glanced at her then turned to Nadia. "So, any clue on what your father was doing?"

Instead of answering, the girl asked another question. "How did you leave Sapphirlune?"

"I stole your father's escape shuttle."

Her eyes were wide. "You what?"

Dess walked to the edge of the counter and leaned on it. "Did you ask them to arrest me?"

Nadia got up. "Dess! No. You should be safe."

He rolled his eyes. "Should, right? It wasn't as if Marcus and I wouldn't be the first people they would look for after you escaped. They think I'm guilty."

"Well, you wouldn't talk to me or trust me. I had to do

something. I doubt you would be able to get the Mainlanders out of the city with everyone watching you. I did it."

Dess stared at her. "And you didn't ask your father for any favors?"

She frowned. "No idea what you're talking about."

Dess pointed to Saytera and Christina. "Your father threatened to kill them."

"Why?"

Larissa stepped between them and extended her arms. "Guy, guys, no arguing. There was clearly a misunderstanding. Now everyone's here and we're all safe for now. Great, right? We need to get the systems up and running."

Dess pushed her hand and pointed to Nadia. "I need to know if I can trust her."

"You got no choice," Larissa replied.

Saytera walked to her friend. "I don't understand. You're so fast at breaking into systems. You've been working here for hours… You still haven't figured it out?"

She shook her head. "No. And it's not only that. We need to get the residential area working, and see where to get resources. It's a strange system with a master control. I'm hitting dead ends."

Saytera tried to encourage her friend. "It's fine if it takes a while. I'm sure you'll figure it out."

Dess was beside her. "What kind of master control?"

"A lot of it seems bio-based. You'd need the right fingerprints or blood."

"From whom?" Dess asked.

"The creators of this place and I guess a handful of authorized personnel," Larissa replied.

Nadia sighed. "Probably all dead by now. My house had some of these bio-security systems, too."

"There should be a master security room," he said. "I'll find it with Saytera."

He reached out his hand. Saytera took it. They turned around and left in time to see a grin on Larissa's face and a look of surprise in Nadia's and Christina's.

Dess led Saytera to a corridor, and wasn't surprised anymore that the doors opened at his contact. Memories came back to him, his mother, showing the plans for a building, his father, putting Dess's hand on a mold. Their excitement about planning something.

Dess walked to a round room with a small circular column in the middle. He put his hand on it and it lit up. Saytera's strange, beautiful eyes were locked into him.

"Can you guess why I can access the master lock system?" he asked.

"You're authorized."

Dess nodded.

She thought for a moment. "Your family. Were they involved in building this?"

He took a deep breath. "I think so. I didn't know it. Or didn't remember. They had so many plans."

She looked away, thinking. "Your name… it's the family that discovered this moon. Tahari. You're Dess Tahari."

"Kades." It was strange to say and hear this name after so long. He looked down. "My little sister called me Dess." He felt his eyes getting misty from emotion in remembering little Anise and relief in telling someone this secret. "You can still call me Dess."

She held his hand tight. "I'm sorry for your family."

Dess pulled her closer and hugged her. Perhaps this was what he needed to confront his past, someone to hang on to.

"All this time, I've been hiding who I am, lying about who I am, knowing very well I wasn't hiding from the Mainlanders, I was hiding from Lunars." Dess looked down. "And yet, somehow I still manage to be surprised when I see corruption and stupidity."

"Do you know who you're hiding from?"

Dess ran his hand through his hair. "I told myself it could be a Mainlander spy. I told myself that if I ended this war I could maybe tell the world who I was. In a way, I'd never have my family back. I couldn't undo what had already been done. But deep down I know that whoever killed my family is in my city, or at least works close together with someone there. And now they'll figure out I'm alive."

"You can hide if it comes to it."

"Maybe I'm tired of hiding." He looked at the panel again. The lights lit, and he unlocked all systems. "There. They'll have an easy time now."

Saytera smiled. "I'm glad you're here."

"Cause I'm Kades Tahari? Or because I'm Dess Starspark?"

"Aren't you both?"

"I am. But the only reason I came here was because of you. I was worried. I wasn't thinking of... reclaiming this, confronting any of this."

"I went to Citarella wanting to know more about Somer-sault and the killings. I never thought I'd visit Sapphirlune, Tahari moon. And yet... "

"Sometimes destiny comes to us."

Saytera looked away. "I don't believe in destiny."

"I thought Terens..."

"I never said I was one."

"Are you going to tell me now? Tell me who you are? Not that you have to, but…" Perhaps all he wanted to know was whether she saw him the same way he saw her.

She took a deep breath. "I guess I owe you the truth. I was raised on an island. Down in the middle of the ocean, where nobody can go, due to the storms. But there were people there. We studied matterweaving, which I guess you could call magic." She looked at him. "You ask me if I'm a Teren, I had never heard this word when I lived there. We were… the islanders. We didn't talk much about us versus the rest of the world, even if I studied Human politics, especially about Ringon and stuff. I didn't learn much about Mainland, though. It was as if we weren't part of it. In a way, we weren't."

"And how did you get into their army, then?"

"I came to the continent once, to visit. I was supposed to go back." She hesitated, as if afraid of saying something, then closed her eyes, looked at him, and continued. "I never made it back. The woman who brought me was killed. There were Terens trying to kill me. I hid and never heard from my people again."

Dess was shocked. "There are Terens in Mainland wanting to kill you?"

She shook her head. "They came from another planet. They have… other ways to travel. I don't know exactly how. There are many things I don't know. The people who lived on those islands left the planet, too. So I was left alone in this system."

It didn't make sense. "Why were they trying to kill you?"

There was a hint of pain in her eyes. "I don't know. Something about destiny, who I am. But Yansin, uh, the woman who brought me up, she doesn't believe in that. The Islanders don't believe in that. But I have nobody to give me answers." She looked down. "They're all gone."

"Maybe one day you'll see them again."

Saytera shrugged. "I sometimes wonder if hope is good or bad."

"You take the Mainlander-Lunar war pretty seriously for someone who has no stake in it."

"It's the destiny I found. I don't want to hear about some distant planet, some abstract notion of what one day I could do. I want to do what I can do. I want to make the difference that I can. I'm trying."

"We're trying."

Dess pulled her for a hug again. He still felt somewhat surprised that he had a girl that could have stepped right from his dreams in his arms. He kissed her chin, then moved slowly to her lips, pulling her even closer, delighting in the moment, the feel of her. Two flames burning as one. He ran his hands through her magnificent hair, moving down to her hips. There was nothing else in the universe but him and her. That moment. How much he truly wanted them to become one.

30

REVELATIONS

Dess smiled at those eyes as he pulled back from the kiss.

Saytera was breathless. "We'd better go help the others."

Dess knew she was right, but at the same time it was hard to let go. He took a deep breath and nodded.

They were back in the control room.

"You did it." Saytera's tall friend, Larissa, smiled at him. "What did you do?"

There wasn't much point in hiding anything anymore. "I can control the master system. This place was designed by my parents. My fingerprints will work on everything here."

Nadia cocked her head. "Your parents?"

"The Taharis." There. The truth was out.

Her eyes were wide. "What?"

"I never told anyone for fear of being killed and because I promised my mother."

Nadia looked at him. "You're Kades Tahari, then."

Dess nodded.

"Why did you hide it?" She asked. "You know you would have inherited a fortune, right?"

"A fortune and a target on my back. Do you think whoever killed my parents wanted me hanging around?"

Nadia frowned. "We don't know who killed them. It was an accident, wasn't it?"

"That's a valid theory, for sure. Can you come up with other theories? Now just think for a moment on the implications of that."

The girl was thoughtful. "My father worked for your parents. He would have done anything to help you, Dess."

"Sure. Maybe. In fact, I brought something from your father's office." Dess turned to Saytera and her friends. "He owns Staralloy, the mining company in Sapphirlune. The company that used to belong to my parents." Dess took the stick from his pocket. "And I think we should check his information."

Nadia crossed her arms. "What do my father's matters have to do with anything?"

"He was in their testimony. Too calm. Wanting to arrest me. I'm almost sure my suspicions are wrong, but I'd rather be a hundred percent sure."

Nadia snatched the stick from his hand. "Fine. Let's check it, then. Let's invade my family's privacy, just because he happened to act like a concerned father."

Dess glared at her. "Concerned? Threatening people's lives?"

"I mean arresting you or whatever he was going to do."

For a second Dess feared she would break the stick, hide it, or do something else with it, but she inserted it on the terminal. "Ready to fall asleep with business stuff?"

Project Zeta popped on the screen.

"Wait," Saytera said. "We saw this in Citarella, too. This project was somehow related to the shieldbreaker."

Nadia moved to the next screen, and there it was, a diagram of the weaponized ship, showing its ability to destroy Sapphirlune. It was very long with a bulge on its bottom, probably from where it shot whatever it did to break a city shield. It also seemed to have a dock for some fighter ships, probably to defend it.

"That's what we saw," Saytera confirmed. "Not that there were that many details."

Dess scoffed. "It explains why they weren't surprised."

Nadia shrugged. "So they knew it already. I guess we'll see what they're planning, then."

The next page was entitled *New Sapphircity*, depicting a modern city, not on a moon, but on a planet, likely Mainland.

For some reason the sight gave Dess chills. There was something horrific about it, and yet, he couldn't quite put it into words.

Nadia tilted her head, as if there were a different angle to see it. "It's as if… they're planning an alternative… in case our city gets destroyed."

That made some sense, and yet, the fact that they had known it and told nobody, apparently had taken no action…

Saytera's short friend, Christina, who was normally quiet, approached the screen. "Hum. It doesn't sound as if they have any issue with Mainland's plan. If anything, it's almost as if…" She paused. "They're working together."

Nadia rolled her eyes. "Nonsense. It's clearly just a prediction for a worst-case-scenario."

Dess dreaded whatever came next. "Let's check what else is there."

A document popped up on the screen.

Nadia exhaled, as if relieved. "It's the peace treaty, from the Peace Alliance in Ringon." She then read, "Unmotivated aggression against civilians results in severe penalties for the systems who commit it."

She pivoted in her chair and faced Dess, Saytera, and her friends. "You know what this means, right? They know the plan and they'll find a way to negotiate, to prevent Mainland from going ahead with it. Because if they go ahead with it, they'll suffer even more than they're suffering. The Peace Alliance in Ringon will have the power to intervene. So I think they'll use this argument to convince Mainland not to strike."

That was one theory, for sure… But then, there were other possibilities that made Dess shiver. And it sounded somehow off, perhaps naive even. Or Nadia was the naive one.

"Is there more?" Saytera asked.

Another document.

"Staralloy and Heliumforge… merge? It must be something related to business." Nadia sounded uncertain.

There was just the title, without more explanation. A plan to merge the companies. They were silent for a moment.

Dess was thoughtful. "Heliumforge is a mining company. They explore Sumeria. They also manufacture weapons. Can you go back to the shieldbreaker?"

Nadia begrudgingly went back. There is was, Heliumforge's symbol.

Dess said, "It seems that Heliumforge is providing the shieldbreaker. They are the ones Mainland is dealing with."

Saytera said, "Well, it is about business, right? Heliumforge is providing the shield destroyer. If they are planning on merging… "

The unsaid words rang heavy in the room.

"Is there more?" Dess asked.

Nadia shook her head.

Larissa approached. "There should be encrypted details there somewhere. I can try to break them." She pulled a stick from her pocket. "I also have the information from Mainland."

Nadia's eyes widened. "You had it with you?"

"Aren't we glad we didn't give them to the nice people on your moon?" Larissa said. She then turned to everyone. "Can you give me some time? All of you. I want to check this stuff but I need peace of mind. I'll have an answer in an hour or so. Go." Her eyes were beseeching. "All of you. I need to focus."

Dess, Saytera, and her other friend were leaving the room. The girl turned to Nadia. "You, too."

She got up and followed them. Once they were out in the hallway, Dess said, "I'll try to see if I can get a kitchen working and maybe find supplies." She turned to Nadia and the other girl. "You two, can—"

"Dess, you're not giving orders," Nadia said. "You just got here."

"Wow, sorry. Didn't know I was disrupting an already established hierarchy."

Saytera turned to him. "We could all go together to the kitchen and try to find something comforting."

The architecture in that place was similar to Sapphirlune, with hallways with glass walls. The kitchen was similar to the one in the academy. Dess smiled. "I could get this up and running." He opened the storage. "There are some supplies."

"Are they still good?" Saytera asked.

"I'll check. Anything with less than 7 years expiration will get thrown, of course. Did you guys bring anything?"

Nadia bit her lip. "Not anything to make new food, just meal bars for a couple days."

"I think there were supplies in your father's ship," Dess said. "I'll try to bring them here."

Saytera turned to Nadia. "Has your father ever said anything about escaping or something?"

"We had a ship ready—which Dess took. But it's normal, right? I mean, if things get bad, we're obvious targets."

"True." Saytera nodded.

Perhaps she was getting into something. Dess tried to insist. "But did you think he'd been considering leaving Sapphirlune? Building another city?"

Nadia sighed. "He's always wanted to leave. I always thought that he would like the war to end, then move to Mainland. We all do, in a way. Nothing out of the ordinary." She then got serious. "Guys, really. I get that my father was hiding something, but he's a good person. You're acting as if he had some kind of cunning, evil plan or something."

"No," Saytera said. "We're just trying to understand what's happening in Sapphirlune, and what they're planning. And since you're close to people who make decisions there, you could know something."

Nadia crossed her arms. "Well, I don't know anything."

Dess looked at the shelves and found something. "Hey, this is powdered juice. We can mix it with water—" He stopped. "I need to check the water deposit. The main one." He checked the kitchen deposit. "We have enough for juice, at least. Who wants one?"

Christina frowned. "Seven-year-old *powdered* juice?"

"Life on a moon. We learn to appreciate sugar and flavoring." Nadia said. "I'll have one."

Saytera bit her lip. "Later, maybe."

Dess poured two cups.

"What are we going to do?" Saytera asked. "Once we figure out what's going on?"

Nadia took a sip, then said, "Larissa said you wanted to send a transmission to Mainland. Maybe try to convince the people there to vote against breaching the truce."

Saytera was thoughtful. "So we record something telling them what's going on."

"We do it all together," Dess said. "And send it to Sapphirlune, too. We need to stop this nonsense, once and for all."

Nadia shrugged and pointed to the floor. "Planet and moon have to agree on what to do with this piece of rock, though."

Sylvia and Marcus came in. "So that's where you are," he said. "Hey, what are you drinking?"

"Powdered juice," Dess replied.

"Can I have some?" Sylvia asked.

"Me too," Marcus added.

Saytera and her friend Christina exchanged baffled looks. Or maybe disgusted. Easy for them to think that, who had grown up with real food—and real fruit—available.

Marcus leaned on the counter. "So, what's happening?"

Dess pointed to Saytera. "Her friend is trying to decode some information. Then we'll see what we'll do."

Nadia got up. "I get the feeling she's stalling." She turned to Saytera. "Do you think she's stalling?"

"We're running out of time here. Why would she do that?"

Dess looked down. He had a feeling that whatever they were going to hear would be unpleasant, and could maybe guess that the girl wanted to find a nicer way to break the news, or else be sure of what she was saying before letting all of them know about Tarel's plans.

Nadia looked away. "No idea."

They were silent.

Christina then said, "Well, she was freakingly fast when we were accessing a military facility in Citarella."

"She knows what she's doing," Saytera said.

Marcus turned to her. "You know, it's proof of our trust. We're letting a Mainlander alone with a bunch of confidential information."

Saytera narrowed her eyes. "What do you think she'll do with it? Take it back to the planet and get herself killed?"

Dess sighed. "Depending on what we're uncovering, all our lives will be in danger. Or almost all."

Marcus laughed. "Hey, maybe we'll have to stay here forever and make sure the defense system never stops working."

"By forever you mean until we starve, right?" Saytera asked.

Marcus waved a hand. "Nah. There's a lot of powdered juice. We'd last a while."

Dess laughed. He glanced at Saytera, who laughed, too. He wanted to hold her hand, and yet wasn't sure what she thought about it. If they started acting all couply, the Lunars would have some questions. Maybe not. Marcus wasn't that oblivious, and perhaps he'd said something to Sylvia.

So the issue was just making sure that their kisses meant something more for Saytera, too. There was one way to know. Dess reached out his hand to hers and laced his fingers over hers. She shuddered, but smiled, and didn't pull her hand away. Nobody said anything.

The door opened and Larissa entered. "I'll show you what I got." She sounded resigned, then noticed Sylvia and Marcus. "And everyone's here. Wonderful."

They entered the control room. Nadia was glaring at

Saytera's friend. "Everything, Larissa. I don't need to be protected like some fragile creature."

That didn't sound good. They stood around the monitor. He pulled Saytera towards him and hugged her from behind. Perhaps he was the one who needed comfort the most.

Larissa turned to them all. "All right, then. What we have from Tarel and Staralloy Industries is that they'd been in touch with Heliumforge for a while. Remember, Staralloy is Sapphirlune's company, Heliumforge is bigger and operates in many systems. This contract is old, like some six months old."

"What does it say?" Saytera asked.

Larissa glanced at Nadia, sighed, then said, "It is a transfer of ownership. After the attack, Heliumforge will belong to Staralloy."

"But why..." Marcus said. "Why would a powerful company, headquartered on Ringon, be willing to give itself away to a company in a tiny system?"

Larissa took a deep breath. "There's only one way it makes sense. Hear me out. I don't see anything here about avoiding an attack." She looked carefully at Dess and the other Lunars. "In this case, Mainland would suffer sanctions, but Heliumforge, too. It's illegal to sell this type of weapon, at least according to the rules laid down by the Peace Alliance, the government of the Human Systems. So, to avoid these sanctions, they become Staralloy."

"And then they can explore this moon to their heart's content," Saytera added.

Dess was thinking. Something didn't make sense. "Why would anyone on Sapphirlune support this, no matter how corrupt they are?"

"Well, the Lunars get New Sapphircity on Mainland, get all our natural resources, and get all the money from the sale of

Ilanium. The Mainlanders would be their slaves. Since Mainland will be the bad guy, the Peace Alliance will just look the other way. They might support Sapphircity for all we know."

Saytera stepped out of Dess's embrace. "The Lunars get everything, then. They get this moon and they get a new city in a place with real food and real air. Why is *our* government supporting it?"

Larissa gulped. "Some of them would get a new identity, large benefits, and passage to Sumeria. They'd be gone before anyone could touch them."

Saytera snorted. "Great."

Dess crossed his arms. "There's one thing I don't get. You're talking about New Sapphircity. How can they evacuate thousands of people from our moon?" He was pretty sure they didn't have that many transports.

Larissa shook her head. "Who said they'd evacuate thousands of people?"

Dess felt nauseous. "So… this would benefit… just a few. And that way they can use the tragedy to pose as victims and do whatever they want with the planet."

Sylvia shook her head. "It doesn't make sense. I doubt they'd do something like that."

Saytera stepped forward. "I don't think we need to worry about the aftermath of a Sapphirlune City destruction just yet. Let's focus on preventing it."

"Yes," Larissa said. "It's all we have. Let the people on the planet know that the government isn't acting on their best interests. That destroying Sapphirlune isn't in their best interests."

"Wait," Christina said. "We need a name."

Saytera asked, "For what?"

"For us. What we stand for. Something about peace, alliance… Ugh, that sounds terrible."

Larissa stroked her chin. "Yeah, Peace Alliance sounds catchy. Pity it's been taken."

"Peace Warriors?" Marcus suggested.

Sylvia grimaced. "That's horrible."

"I like it," Dess said. In truth he thought the name was stupid, but he wanted to support his friend. And the idea was what mattered most.

Sylvia rolled her eyes. "Dudes."

Larissa shrugged. "It sucks. But I don't have a better idea."

Nadia was incredulous. "So we'll sign as the *peace warriors?*"

"If everyone agrees," Dess said.

Saytera also had a grimace. "It's… not the end of the world."

Larissa looked at them. "Anything else? Other ideas?" Everyone was silent. "Peace warriors it is." She smiled. "It got the most votes."

Marcus laughed. "Isn't democracy amazing?"

They all laughed, except Nadia. "Let's hope they listen to our message."

31

MESSAGE

Saytera tried to put all her hope in the message being broadcast to Mainland and Sapphirlune. They'd spent a long time planning it. In the end, they showed the evidence they had and urged people to demand a peaceful solution. They also warned against the horror of killing thousands of innocents, hoping that the message would reach Sapphirlune as well. Finally, they all appeared on the message, saying that if they could work together, Mainland and Sapphirlune could work together, too.

It had been done. Now all they had to do was wait. Odd that for so long she'd wanted to learn matterweaving, get stronger, when in fact this time, what it took was not weaving skills or even fighting skills, just a willingness to learn the truth and cooperation between former enemies. In a strange way, Saytera would hopefully help make a difference.

They had all split to try to make the base habitable, after all, they were tired and needed food and sleep. Saytera was with Dess in the kitchen. She couldn't complain about that arrangement.

He was opening cupboards and checking supplies. Funny to see him busy with something so mundane, and at the same time extraordinary, considering where they were. Either way, he looked extraordinary.

Saytera observed him. "Are you sure we can eat seven-year-old food?"

He turned to her. "It's better than nothing. Nadia and Sylvia didn't bother bringing supplies, and there was very little on Tarel's ship."

She ran her hand over an orange container. "It's so odd to see it all... Abandoned. And yet, it was ready to receive workers."

Dess ripped open the seal on a package. "Funny, right? Once we got ready to explore the moon, my family was killed and the war started."

"I bet you miss them."

"I do. And yet, it's bigger than me or my family." He didn't seem to want to continue the conversation and poured a powder on a circular container.

Saytera was curious about the powder. "What is that?"

Dess looked at her. "You don't want to know."

"I hope it's edible."

He smiled. "You'll have to trust me on that. We'll have a warm, fresh dinner."

Saytera laughed. "Fresh?"

He raised an eyebrow. "Fresh is all a matter of perspective." He took the container and poured some water on it. "And what an interesting perspective. I never thought my skills as a kitchen assistant would one day be just as useful, or even more, than all the stuff I studied in the academy."

"I'm also not using any of what... I thought I'd need. It's all so different."

"I guess…" He was thoughtful. "We were trained to support their plans, not contradict them. I mean, me. You are something else."

Saytera chuckled. "I have no clue what they were preparing me for, or even if there was a point to any of that. Before I left."

Dess's eyes were on her. "You also miss them."

"Yes, but it's different because it's my fault. If I had stayed, obeyed, listened…" She shook her head, wishing that pain would go away.

Dess stopped what he was doing and took her hands. "I don't know the whole story, but you said people were trying to kill you. I mean, you couldn't have known."

"I just shouldn't have left the island."

He looked in her eyes, and it was almost unsettling to be seen by such dark, penetrating eyes. "Then you wouldn't be here right now."

Saytera paused. That was true. Being there, holding his hands, was exhilarating in a way she couldn't quite describe. And still… "Sometimes there are different paths to the same destination."

"You can't be at two places at once, so if you hadn't left… you know the answer."

Maybe. Why regret, then? Well, it was obvious. "I just wish people didn't have to die. I didn't have to be away from the people I grew up with. But it would be sad not to meet you."

He still held her hands, but now tilted his head as if examining her. "And what happens after this?"

Saytera could feel her heart beating. "You mean if we survive."

"Worse comes to worst, I could land us on Mainland and we could try to hide there." He smiled. "We'll bring supplies this time."

He was very close now, staring at her.

Saytera caught her breath. "That's a decent plan. Why then you're asking what happens?"

He kissed her cheek then brushed his lips on her face, sending shivers through her body. "I mean, are you going to run away, try to find your people? Is this some past time for you? Or am I in your plans somehow? I asked you to come with me once," he whispered in her ear as he put his hands on her waist then slid them to her hips.

Saytera closed her eyes. It was hard to talk. "You think it would have been a good idea?"

"The idea was terrible." He kissed her lips, then.

They were so close together, and it felt so good to feel his body against hers. Everything else faded but the physical sensation.

They had things to do, though. She parted, breathless. "You're giving me terrible ideas right now."

He chuckled. "Why terrible?"

"Everything has a time and place. You know I'd been imprisoned if I had come with you."

"Maybe." He brushed a finger on her face. "But what's your current idea?"

He was going to ask her about that? "Guess."

"And you're going to tell me it's the wrong time and place."

"I need to tell you?"

He took a deep breath. "I'm not good at that stuff either, you know? I spent my life training, I don't know anything about relationships and stuff and all that stuff."

Saytera remembered what Sylvia had said and couldn't suppress a laugh.

"What?" he asked.

"One of your friends said flying simulator was your sexual orientation."

"Ouch. It's so accurate it hurts."

"But…" Saytera hated thinking about that. "I mean, I know you and Nadia…"

His hands were still on her waist, but they tensed. "What did she say?"

"That you had something."

He bit his lip. "I frankly don't remember what happened. It's embarrassing. Not whatever happened, but not remembering. I think it was just a couple kisses, though." He stepped away. "We'd better finish dinner."

Saytera felt bad that he was distant, and perhaps regretted having said that. "Sorry for mentioning it."

"It's good." Dess looked down, stirring the powder and water. "In fact it makes things a lot less awkward, knowing you guys are buddies and she even got to tell you all that." He looked at her. "Hang on. What *did* she say?"

It would be a great opportunity to prank him, but the truth was that she still didn't know him that well. "She didn't say anything other than that she thought you'd make her straight."

His eyes widened. "Straight? As in… she's not. Wow. First prize for effort."

"So you do remember."

He nodded. "Getting… intimate. Is sacred. At least as I believe, you're melding your energy, your fire with the other person."

That was pretty obvious. "Well, yes."

"So you agree. Right. I can never know what's really a Teren thing or something I picked up somewhere else."

"A Teren thing? As in… there are people who think otherwise?"

He raised an eyebrow. "Yes. I mean, lots of people, lots of different beliefs, right? But for me it should be something special. But it wasn't at all a big deal. It was just… I don't even know what I was doing. I'm not going to say I regret it because it's not fair to her, and it takes two to… you know. But, yeah." He looked at her. "And I hadn't met you."

"That would have made a difference?"

"What do you think? I guess that was what I was getting at. That… I don't want… anyone else. Just you… I wanted to know what you think."

Saytera smiled. Strange how when it was her turn it felt uncomfortable to talk about her feelings. "I don't want anyone else either. And yes, whatever happens, after this is done, it would be nice…" How could she word it? "Not to be apart anymore."

Dess smiled and nodded. "Yes. That was my point."

"As long as it's not a terrible idea." Saytera laughed.

"Don't say that. I liked to hear you were getting terrible ideas."

"Maybe I'm reconsidering whether they were really terrible." She looked down, feeling her face hot. "Before that, I hope your dinner's not terrible."

"Dare me. I'm good at this, just so you know."

"Transforming very old powder into food. Is that matter-weaving?"

"Ma… what?"

Saytera just then remembered he didn't know it as such. "Magic."

He raised his eyebrows. "You'll see."

～

Dess hoped he indeed had magic, as they sat for dinner for very old cricket patties and powdered puree. At least he'd found some seasoning, so hopefully they'd all be able to swallow that junk. In a way, it was neat to have them all sitting at a table together and get a feeling of normalcy. Neat and symbolic.

Still, the atmosphere was tense. Larissa had a wireless comm with her, connected to the main terminal. Everyone glanced at it from time to time, waiting for the moment it would give them a reply. Seconds, minutes, and hours were running by, and that silence was unnerving. They all knew that there was a possibility that communications were blocked and that their message wouldn't be received. He was thinking that if by tomorrow morning they got no reply, they'd need to plan something different—and a lot more dangerous.

Saytera was drinking water, still uneasy about the juice. Well, she had a point. Water. There was enough water for them to last a couple weeks, using it mostly for food and drinking, but it was enough. As long as the Mainlanders learned to wash like Lunars. Dess figured they must have learned it in their night spent on Sapphirlune.

Saytera took a bite, turned to him, and mouthed, "Magic."

Dess smiled.

Marcus raised his glass. "I think we all owe a huge thanks to Dess and Saytera, who made this absolutely amazing dinner."

Saytera was going to say something, but Dess raised his glass. "Thank Saytera." He looked directly at her, hoping she understood what she meant. Perhaps all she'd done for that dinner was stand by him, sometimes even interrupt him, and yet, that was what made it all special, what made it worth it.

Saytera had an almost imperceptible shudder. "*You're the kitchen expert!*"

Dess chuckled. "Expert. I've been promoted." From kitchen boy. But the Mainlanders knew nothing about it, and even the Lunars who were there hadn't really mocked him, except Nadia a little. It wasn't worth insisting on the point.

"Now seriously," Marcus said. "They should train us about that in the academy. I mean, if it wasn't for you, we'd be out of food by tomorrow."

Right. His friend also noticed that the skill Dess had been mocked for turned out to be pretty useful. "Funny how things people despise can become important."

"Cause people are stupid and they distort things," Nadia said.

Weird to hear her addressing him, weird to have her and Saytera at the same table, but at the same time, he was glad she'd helped them and rescued the Mainlanders. They wouldn't be there without her.

"Aren't we glad we're all past our period of stupidity?" Dess asked.

"Oooooh, we're so wise!" Marcus laughed.

They all laughed as well. Still, Dess sometimes wondered whether they'd chosen the right path, if this was the right way to fight the horrible destruction planned for his city.

After some silence, the comm beeped. Dess had that odd panic of anticipation, not knowing if he'd feel dread or relief.

They all stared at each other.

"I'll get the transmission here." Larissa pushed a button. "Larissa speaking from the Tahari moon, we're listening."

"This is a message for Nadia Tarel and Nadia Tarel alone." It was her father.

"I'm here," Nadia said.

"I don't want anyone else hearing this," he said.

"Do you want me to lie and say it's only me?" she asked.

"You have no way to know. But you can talk to all of us. We're eager to hear what you have to say."

"That's treason! Is that how you treat your father? How dare you spread unfounded rumors, lies? How dare you?"

"We..." She seemed to be scrambling for words. "Might have been... mistaken. If you can clarify any of the information we have, we'll be happy to hear it."

"Clarify? Clarify what? What you had was our plan to prevent us from getting attacked. Now that this information is out, our enemies will get us. Thanks to you and that traitor Starspark. He brainwashed you. Come back and we'll fix this. Get out of there. You don't belong with that scum."

"Dad, if you have an explanation, work with us. Help us. We can fix this. We want to save our city, find peace. If we misunderstood something, explain." Her voice was beseeching.

Dess wondered if a part of her actually believed that this had been some horrible misunderstanding. Well, it was her father, she'd probably want to hang on to a slight hope that he wasn't planning on killing thousands of people. Poor girl.

"I'll explain it all when you're back," Tarel replied.

"If you have an explanation, please, send it to us. If all you want to do is ask me to come back, don't bother wasting your time." Her voice was tight.

"Conspiracy and nonsense. Nonsense. We wanted to prevent the attack on Sapphirlune. Isn't that obvious?"

Pain was visible on Nadia's face. "Isn't it obvious that what we're doing will also prevent the attack? Isn't it obvious that if we get a deal with Mainland we can also stop the war? We didn't even spread all the information we had about your plans or your involvement with Heliumforge. But again, if there's something we're missing, we'd love to know."

"Come back. Come back, or I'll have to send a squad to bring you by force." Tarel's voice was thunder.

"Try it." She sounded sad, more than anything.

"He brainwashed you. Starspark, do you hear me? You think you can steal my daughter, then take my company? Foolish, foolish, ignorant, unimportant kitchen boy, you'll never achieve anything. You've just ruined your future."

"Yeah, my future would have been wonderful with a destroyed Sapphirlune city," he said.

"You'll die, and die in a lot of pain."

Larissa then cut the transmission.

"What did you stop him for?" Nadia asked.

"It was going nowhere." She then typed something on the device. "I'm telling him that whatever he wants to send needs to be in writing or documents. That will get him to think twice before threatening us." She then looked at Nadia. "I'm so sorry."

The girl shook her head. "I... should have seen it earlier." She sighed, then looked at Dess. "Thanks, the food was wonderful. I'll get to the bedrooms." After getting up, she left.

Larissa got up, too. "I'll check on her. I'll leave this with you, guys. Maybe we'll get better transmissions."

Saytera took the portable comm. She wasn't as good with it as her friend, but she knew enough at least to handle it.

The conversation had left her anxious. She looked at Dess, Marcus, and Silvia. "You think he can... I don't know. Do something?"

"He'll try, but I think we're safe here," Dess said. "We also have a shield, just like Sapphirlune, plus we have the main cannon and more manual anti-aerial defenses. Unless they get a shieldbreaker, we're relatively safe."

Marcus took a sip of his juice. "Technically then we could live here, as long as someone fetched water and some supplies. Hang on." He looked at Dess. "Aren't we the experts at it?"

"We'd need a ship with a tank, for starters," Dess said.

"Who knows? Everything here has been so well prepared. I wouldn't doubt there's one lying around somewhere."

"Except we're sitting on a fortune," Sylvia said. "Not sure how long they'll leave us alone."

She had a point. But they obviously didn't need to spend that long on the Tahari moon. "We need just enough to get Mainland to change their minds. Even if nothing much changes, just avoiding the destruction of Sapphirlune city is a great start. I mean, it's the most important, right?"

The comm beeped. It was written communication. "We received something. I can go check."

"Suggestion here," Dess said. "Five minutes won't make much difference. Let's finish eating, then we check. I can't guarantee you'll be able to swallow this once it's cold."

Marcus stretched his hand and pinched Dess's cheek. "Oh, no. Don't worry, we aren't going to snub your impressive dinner."

Dess slapped his friend's hand. "I just don't want us to starve."

They finished eating and headed to the communication room. Saytera opened the message. It was again from Taro. It said:

Dear friends. Please return to Sapphirlune. The brave Mainlanders are welcome as well. Let me explain the extent of your misunderstanding in person. I'm sure we can all come to a positive agreement. I'll promise you all some of the Staralloy's profits. There's always something to be gained. I hope you consider your future.

Dess glared at the screen. "How dare he? How dare he promise something that's not his? Try to bribe us?"

Sylvia put her hand on Dess's elbow. Saytera felt as if someone had punched her in the gut. The girl said, "Technically, Staralloy is yours. Maybe you should offer him some profit in exchange for the rest of the information."

Dess snorted and shook his head. "We'd just get deeper into trouble."

Sylvia still had her hand on him. "Do you have plans for the company?"

Thankfully, he stepped away. "No!" he said. "For now I just want to survive and save our system."

Marcus pulled Sylvia's hand. "Let him be. I bet things are stressful enough as they are."

There was a slight edge in his voice. So Saytera hadn't imagined that the girl and Dess… But no. Maybe they were both overreacting. But then, she remembered something Marcus had said on the island while hallucinating. Saytera's stomach sank. No, it was too early to start with petty jealousy. Dess had been very clear to Saytera that he wanted them to be together. Dess then approached Saytera, put his hand around her waist, and kissed her cheek. This was the first time he was doing it in front of everyone else. Nobody batted an eyelash, though. Saytera turned and hugged Dess. He closed his eyes and leaned his forehead on hers.

Christina, who had been sitting, got up. "I think we'd better get to bed. It's past midnight on Mainland."

"True," Dess said. "Odds are slim we'll get anything else tonight, and we need rest."

Christina led them to the hall. "Come, I'll show you the bedrooms we prepared."

They followed her. Only after entering the bedroom assigned to her did the reality of it dawned on Saytera. She was with Dess.

NIGHT

The room had two bunks and a door to a small lavatory. Saytera could feel her heart pumping blood to her body.

Dess pointed to the beds. "Which one do you want?"

She pointed to the one on the right. "That one."

"Okay. I'll go wash. Or do you want to go first?"

"You can go."

Dess took some clothes and disappeared in the lavatory.

They didn't take showers, but rather washed with a very small amount of water. It made sense, but it was odd for Saytera. And even odder was being here, about to sleep in the same room as Dess. She'd dreamed so much of seeing him again, and this was like a dream, but perhaps it was going so fast that she was startled or maybe even scared. He came out and then it was Saytera's turn to wash. How she missed taking a shower or a bath, she missed walking in the ocean and feeling the water around her.

Dess was asleep, lying on top of the covers, when she came

out of the lavatory. He had been tired. Saytera decided to fix the covers over him, but then he woke up and sat up. "Sorry."

"It's fine. We are tired."

"You know what I'm thinking?"

Saytera had no idea.

He continued, "I wish I had my reader with me. I'd love to… I don't know… tell you some stories or maybe compare them with what you know."

She held his hand. "After this is over, maybe."

"If my reader is still there. I don't even know if they haven't ransacked my apartment. If I have anything left."

Saytera laughed. "If we end up having to hide on an island on Mainland, we might not need anything."

He raised his eyebrows. "Except a lot of fuel for fires."

His eyes were so pretty, and his hair was magnificent. "How do you wash your hair with so little water?"

"Well, we… ration, I guess." He ran his hand through her hair. "I can see how in your case it would still be a challenge."

Saytera looked down. "I don't want to cut it."

"No. I'll check the deposit. We might have some hair products there. And I could help you." He then grimaced as if catching himself. "I mean, you could lean your hair back on a chair, you don't have to—"

"Thanks." Saytera kissed his cheek. She knew his offer had been made with the best intentions, and it was actually really sweet. She decided to change the subject. "Your parents built this, right?"

"Didn't exactly build, but planned it. Imagine how hard it must have been for the first people here."

"They had to live on their ships, right?"

Dess nodded.

"It's just…" Saytera was thinking. "We have a war based on

something that doesn't belong to either the moon or the planet. And it's related to your family."

He closed his eyes for a moment. "I know. But then you have to wonder if the idea wasn't just to stop us from exploring it."

Saytera ran her hand through his beautiful hair. "Being here must be so painful for you."

"No. It's healing. Things make more sense now. And you're here. It can't be painful."

Saytera almost wanted to ask "Really?", wondering if it was true that she could help ease his pain and longing, but the truth was that he helped with her own pain and longing for her past.

She just smiled. "I hope we fix this mess."

He was staring at her.

"What?" she asked.

"Your eyes… are mesmerizing."

Saytera looked down. "I think they're odd."

Dess chuckled. "Definitely not even."

There was sunlight coming from the window. So strange to spend time in that place where days and nights meshed together.

Saytera got up. "I'll shut the blinds so we can sleep."

As she closed the thick layers blocking the sun, she realized this was another way to create darkness. She stared at the remaining slit, reminiscing older times. "Funny. This reminds me of my bedroom in the Academy. But we didn't have windows."

Dess was behind her. "You lived in the academy? Sounds nice. One reason I had to work in the kitchen was to pay the rent."

"I guess tonight we were all glad you had to pay it, then."

"Glad to be useful." Saytera felt his arms around her, his

body behind her, his face over her shoulder. He asked, "Missing your planet?'

"Missing more water and fresh food. I bet you've always missed those things, haven't you?" It was amazing to be in his arms.

"Even if I hadn't experienced them? I guess. In theory we shouldn't miss things we don't know, but the reality is that there are things we'll always crave no matter what. Nature is one of them."

Saytera took a look at the planet and how they were facing its stormy, unknown side, then closed the blinds a bit more, while still leaving an open slit through which light penetrated the room.

She felt his lips on her ear. "I missed you before knowing you."

Saytera closed her eyes and shivered. She remembered the moment on the island when he had his body against her, whispering in her ear, and what had been terror then was very different now. She could feel him behind her hips, and she leaned in that feeling.

Something shifted in their energy then. Dess was now kissing her neck, pulling her even closer to him. After a fraction of a second of hesitation and fear, she decided to enjoy the moment, enjoy the feeling, and guided his hands up, to caress her chest, the firm grip of his hands igniting something in her.

Saytera couldn't stop thinking about his body behind her and turned suddenly. Their eyes met, but it wasn't just the eyes, but their entire beings. His eyes had love and yearning, but also a certain hesitation, a question.

He looked down. "It is… early, I guess."

It was actually late. No. He'd meant… early… for them. Definitely. Still, Saytera wasn't even sure what they were doing, but she didn't want it to stop. "We don't have to go all the way."

His breathing was heavy. "How far do you want to go?"

"We'll see."

She pulled him to his bed and they kissed. It was almost as if voicing her desires had toned them down a notch, or at least toned down the desperation in being with him, the crazy yearning. They spent a long time just kissing. Saytera basked in his closeness, his warmth, the feel of his arms.

And more and more she wanted to be close to him, feel his touch, his skin. As she relaxed in that feeling, her layers came off, his clothes came off, and so did hers. Saytera didn't feel ashamed or afraid, but free. Kissing him while feeling the touch of his chest against hers was one of the most amazing feelings she'd ever had.

Dess was strong but also fragile. A sad boy craving for love and she wanted to embrace him. Embrace all of him. See, feel, and taste all of him. Dess was insanely beautiful. Under his dark gaze she felt safe, more than safe, she felt a different kind of fire in her, a flame growing bigger than anything, one she didn't want to quench.

And she understood why what they were doing was so sacred, as she let the flames meld together, as she let herself be open and vulnerable and welcome his flame into her.

Dess felt something tickling him and realized it was Saytera's hair covering his body. They had slept in the same bed. There was something magical in her, magical in her caresses, and something absolutely wondrous in being welcomed into her and feeling like one. Her power, he wasn't sure what it was, but somehow he could feel it, like the thunder and lightning lying in a quiet storm cloud. His magic girl.

He took a deep breath, realizing he was no longer the same person that had entered this room the previous night. Neither was she. Neither were they.

Someone knocked on the door.

"Coming!" he replied.

Then he felt the surprised gaze of odd brown and green eyes on him. Dess kissed Saytera's forehead, then hugged her, feeling her face on his chest while he ran his hand through her hair. They remained like this for a moment, hugging. If he could, Dess would want to spend the day, the week, the month like that.

But Saytera sat up. "We'd better get moving."

Dess should be getting dressed, too, except that as she opened the blinds and let in more sunlight, all her majestic, natural beauty was revealed to him. He couldn't forget his hands on her, his lips kissing her, as she watched her pick up her clothes and put them back on.

Something hit him in the face. It was his shirt she'd thrown.

"Get dressed," she said. "Stop staring at me as if you'd never seen…"

"Well, technically…"

Another impact. His pants had been thrown at him and he put them on quickly. He got up, pulled her for a kiss, then put on his shirt, and opened the door.

There was nobody in the hallway, so they rushed to the communication room. Everyone else was already there.

"They're sending a fleet," Marcus said.

"From where?" Dess asked.

"Sapphirlune."

That didn't make sense. "And what do they expect to

accomplish? We haven't turned off the main cannon, and it's not like they can break our shield. This is the same technology as Sapphirlune city."

Marcus shook his head. "It's insanity. But we're trying to contact them."

Indeed Nadia and Larissa were hard at work testing frequencies. After some time, a voice came through the speakers.

"This is Alpha leader Sam Sahoi. Who's speaking?"

Of course it had to be Sam. Always Sam.

Nadia took the comm. "Sam, did you by any chance see the information we sent?"

A pause. "What information?"

"You didn't get anything? What were you told we were doing here?"

A pause. "This is confidential."

"Confidential my ass," she said. "This base has a powerful cannon defending it. You won't all make it. You won't be able to get to us. What are you trying to do?"

"We're following orders."

"You're not mindless robots."

Larissa then spoke in the comm. "Does your ship take encoded transmissions?"

"That's confidential," he replied.

Dess stepped forward and addressed the girls. "It does. You can send him everything we have, and he'll be able to send it to his teammates. If he wants to."

Nadia nodded, then spoke in the comm. "I'm sending you what we found. We need you to convince people to demand our government to work with Mainland to find a peaceful solution. We're also trying to convince Mainland not to go into a deal with Heliumforge."

"Sent," Larissa said.

There was silence for a long period, then Sam said, "Do you have any proof that it's true?"

Nadia spoke, "The only proof we have is that the Mainlander girls warned us that their planet wanted to destroy our shield and my parents ignored it and didn't tell anyone. Please. I beseech you. Go back and tell more people about it."

"We'd be disobeying direct orders. If you were to come with us, then it would be easier. We can all talk once we're back in Sapphirlune."

"We're safe here and in neutral space. Once we go to a government-controlled place, they can threaten us and even kill some of us."

Dess decided to approach the comm. "Sam, this is Dess. I know we don't get along. But I also know you always wanted to be the best." The exact reason why they had never gotten along. "And I know that you wanted to be the best to protect our city, our people, our moon. You had ideals. Our government, or at least a part of it, is not representing what we've always wanted to fight for. You can make a difference."

"Shut up, you," Sam replied.

That didn't come out as expected.

"Sam, I trust you," Nadia said. "Dess is right. You've always been the best of us. We need you. I need you," she beseeched.

If Dess didn't know better, he'd think she was flirting with him. Then, maybe she was.

There was a long silence, then he said. "We'll go back, and we'll try it. But remember it's for you."

"I won't forget it," she replied.

Nadia's voice sounded as if she were alone with Sam, about to get intimate. The image triggered some awful memories. The communication was then interrupted.

Larissa seemed surprised. "Are you and him…"

"He's a guy!" Nadia protested.

"She likes to play with guys," Sylvia rolled her eyes. She then laughed. "Nadia, that's evil. *I need you,*" she mimicked her friend.

Nadia shrugged. "What was I supposed to do? If I can give him some motivation, why not? He'll thank me once he's a hero and Sapphirlune is saved."

"Do you think they'll help us?" Saytera asked.

"Yeah," Nadia nodded, sounding certain. "They're good people. I wasn't kidding when I said I trusted him." She turned to Dess and Marcus. "I know you guys don't like him, but it was some petty dispute in the academy. It's time for all that to be over."

Dess crossed his arms. "Trying to be the best at that academy was the stupidest waste of time in my life."

Nadia pointed a finger at him. "You're a good pilot, though. Quite handy."

He shrugged. "I guess."

Saytera then turned to Larissa. "Anything from Mainland?"

Her friend sighed.

"What if," Saytera said. "Maybe… Do you think we could reach our former base? Get Kay?"

"Yes." Larissa smiled. "Brilliant. I'm on it." She then laughed. "I know how you got the idea!"

"Who's Kay?" Dess asked Saytera, a slight pang of pointless jealousy in his chest.

She shuddered but so softly Dess doubted anyone else could have noticed. "A guy who was in our base. There was also another guy and a girl but they were pretty much…" She hesitated.

"Useless," Larissa said. "But Kay's all right."

∼

Saytera had never imagined that she'd be doing something important while doing pretty much nothing, as most of what they did was wait, and what she had to do now was wait for her friend to get to Kay or someone else to contact them. They ate those lunar bars for breakfast. The taste was still horrible, but she started to understand how people could eat them.

The previous night and its memories then came to her. Saytera had done something absolutely not related to saving her system. It wasn't the way she'd expected it to be, and it happened much sooner than she expected, but still, it had been easy, natural, as if it had always been meant to be. Perhaps they had always been meant to be. It did make her wonder about destiny when she considered how they had been brought together. And it felt good to be together. Dess was so incredibly beautiful, and yet, what was most beautiful was his good heart.

Later in the day, Larissa found Kay. They had received the message. All the bases had seen it. There was a movement to depose the government and try to reach a deal. The communication off-planet was being cut, though. That was the reason they hadn't received any response. Still, knowing that their plan had worked took a weight from Saytera's chest. Now all they had to do was hope for its conclusion. Perhaps they could even go back to the planet, but being on this moon was strategic. Later they heard from the Lunar guy, Sam. There was something similar going on in Sapphirlune City. Perhaps they'd reach victory, and that was without any bloodshed.

Dess prepared dinner again and somehow transformed that

powder in a stew. They all sat happy and relaxed, a huge difference from the previous night. After dinner, while others were cleaning, Dess called Saytera to a small office. He was serious and focused, so it was probably to talk about something.

"This was my father's. I was looking at it. You know what his plan was?"

Saytera shook her head.

"To share. This wasn't going to be a city, like Sapphirlune. His plan was to have more transports. Workers here would spend two weeks on land, then two weeks here, so that nobody would need to live away from nature. It makes sense, right?"

"For sure." Then something came to her mind. "But then… He was looking into having workers in Mainland. So this was for the planet, too, in a way."

Dess nodded. "Indeed. And the war started when my family was killed. Maybe because of it. This moon was never meant to create discord, war. His plan had been to unite our system. Ironic, right?"

"I'm sorry."

He sat on a chair. "Did you notice we're ignoring the black hole in the middle of the galaxy?"

Saytera wasn't sure she understood.

Dess shook his head and chucked. "It's a manner of saying. We're ignoring the most important thing in all this stuff. We want to stop a war, right? And we're sitting on the very reason for this war."

"This moon."

"Exactly. It sounds neat to tell Lunars and Mainlanders to reach an agreement, and yet, we aren't proposing anything."

"They need to find a solution."

He got up and put his hands on his waist. "Do people come to solutions easily? Do people agree easily?"

Of course not. "No, but all we need them to do is not buy that stupid shieldbreaker."

"True. And then what?"

Saytera didn't know and she understood what he meant by ignoring the black hole, as in ignoring the center of it all. But he was too certain to be just talking generalities. "What's your suggestion?"

"We need to draft a plan for peace. If the plan is in place, all they have to do is agree. Or maybe adapt it, offer suggestions. But it's at least a starting point. It's much simpler. We need to draft a solution to this war."

That made a lot of sense, but there was one thing that didn't make sense. "Why are you telling me this? I mean, just me, not the others?"

"Because of this." He pointed to the floor. "This is the key to everything, and do you know who owns it?"

"Nobody, at the moment."

He shook his head. "It's Staralloy. This base is Staralloy. The war is about the right to explore this moon, not about this particular unit. And it's all equipped. Ready to go."

There was something heavy in those words. "Tell me what you're thinking."

Dess sighed and sat down. "Claiming Staralloy and this base. It's mine by right. But... you have to agree. It's not going to be easy."

"I'm in this with you. I want this system to find peace."

"If I start this... I don't know if I'll be able to drop everything and go live with you on an island, Saytera."

She laughed. "That was a worst-case scenario. We didn't really plan what we were going to do."

"Exactly. I'm sure you can see the flaw in our lack of planning. I want to do something about this moon, this base, that company, but you have to agree."

That made no sense. "Why wouldn't I agree? And what would you do, then?"

He shrugged. "I could see if someone else could take the company. But we need a plan and a proposal."

Saytera reached out and stroked his hair. "What do *you* want?"

33

DECISIONS

"I want to make a difference," Dess said. "My family was killed so that this war could start. I want to make it right for them." He looked determined.

"So you have your answer."

He stared at her. "Yes. But what's *your* answer?"

"I support you in whatever you choose."

"Really?" He laughed. "What if I decided to destroy a city just to get more money?"

"That wouldn't be you."

"It's about choosing our future. We need to think this through."

Our future. That warmed her heart, but it wasn't the most important thing then. "The moment we decided to fight, we decided to leave our own choices behind, right? It's not about what I want for myself, but what's right for our system. If we'd go so far as living as outcasts," she laughed, "I don't see why I would have a problem if you take Staralloy."

"And that's the difference. Being willing to run and hide is not as brave as stepping up and taking the responsibility for leading this."

She understood his question, then. It would be a lot more work than just sitting in this base until Sapphirlune and Mainland reached an agreement. But it was also about doing their best, and if it was important for him, of course she'd supported it. "Step up, Dess. I trust you."

"We'll both have to step up."

Saytera smiled. "I'll be right there with you."

Dess kissed her cheek then laughed. "We'll get in so much trouble…"

"Kades Tahari." Nadia was staring at Dess. "I'm glad you're done playing Dess Starspark.

They were all looking at him, but Nadia's reaction was the one Dess had been dreading, as she'd be the one to lose the most. "Listen, I don't want to ruin your life or take anything away from you. This is—"

"It's fine." Nadia waved a hand. "I don't really want any of that. And we need support. Convince people quickly. The lost son of the family killed to start this war is a lot more interesting than a rebellious daughter."

Christina broke her normal silence. "I like *rebellious daughter*."

Nadia laughed. "The rebellious daughter is here, too. We're a group, right?"

Dess nodded. "Exactly. We're together in this. The idea is just to claim ownership of Staralloy and draft a deal where both Mainland and Sapphirlune profit from the exploration of this moon."

Marcus stood up. "I guess that means we'll record another message."

"We'd better." Larissa nodded. "Then we can send it tonight."

Dess held Saytera's hand. Perhaps he was the one who was terrified. For so long he'd been hiding, blaming the world for the injustice he'd been living, or worse, blaming Mainland. Now that he had to come out and tell everyone who he really was, it was about fixing things, not blaming anyone, not feeling like a victim. No longer he'd follow orders, he'd try to win favors and appreciation, he'd try to follow a path that was not his. This time it was up to him to carve his future, to choose his path. There was freedom but also responsibility. And if he failed, there would be nobody to blame. That thought was terrifying.

When they were all in the communication room except for Marcus and Sylvia, waiting for them to prepare the message, Nadia opened a written communication and froze, a shocked look on her face.

"What is it?" Larissa asked.

"It's Sam. They found out… my parents. They left the system." There was so much fear and dread in her voice that one would think she was reporting the destruction of Sapphirlune.

Larissa frowned. "Isn't everyone blocked from reaching the gate?"

Nadia shrugged and shook her head, looking as if she was trying not to cry. Dess knew what it was to lose his family, but this was very different.

He said, "Hey, they are probably afraid of what might

happen to them. They probably bought their way out. I'm sure they'll be all right."

Dess didn't really like the idea of Tarel escaping all this without consequences, but then, if they fixed everything, it wasn't worthwhile to be focusing on revenge.

Nadia stared at them all, tears in her eyes. "Why are you all calm?"

Saytera approached her. "Were they the only ones who left?"

She shook her head. "No. More people from the government."She glanced at Marcus. "Counselor Okonjo is still on Sapphirlune, though."

Dess didn't see the issue with people running away. "It just makes it easier for us to step in. Take control. Do it differently."

Nadia frowned. "That's what you think?"

Saytera looked at her. "So you think… they wouldn't give up that easily?" She sighed and put her hand on her heart.

Dess closed his eyes. Of course. They could be planning something. Or maybe not. "Perhaps they're just saving their own skins. Some people do that when they're scared."

Larissa leaned back and looked at her friend. "Do you know what they could be planning?"

Nadia sighed. "I don't know. Maybe I am overreacting."

Hopefully. And still. "Are people monitoring the gate? As long as nobody enters the system nothing can happen."

"They are monitoring." Nadia nodded.

"Do you guys still want to send the message tonight? Or do you want to wait?" Larissa asked.

Dess didn't like the idea of waiting. "We can use this to our advantage. In a way, we won. Now all the Lunars need is to agree on new leadership. Mainlanders need to know they won't be dealing with the same people. It makes a difference."

Nadia sighed. "Let's do it, then." She got up. "I'll go get our lazy late friends."

Saytera was looking down, thoughtful, and perhaps worried.

Dess approached her. "What is it?"

"Don't know. Funny feeling. It might be nothing."

Dess kissed her cheek. "It's been some stressful days. And things are changing fast. I'm sure there will be new challenges. Still, not destroying Sapphirlune city is an amazing start, right?"

Saytera smiled. "True. I know. And you… tons of responsibility. That must be it."

The temperature in the base was reasonably comfortable but Saytera felt a chill in her bones. Perhaps it was just that they were heading for a conclusion, and maybe, like Dess had said, stepping up was harder than hiding. And would they have to step up! The message had been sent. Maybe this was what was bothering her: what would happen, what kind of response or reaction they would get.

Saytera washed but decided to go back to the communication room.

"I just want to check it," she told Dess.

"I'll come with you."

Larissa and Nadia were there, too.

"Do you guys sleep here?" Dess asked.

Nadia kept looking at the terminal. "I couldn't sleep."

Saytera approached it. It didn't look like they'd gotten

anything new. "So no news?"

Nadia's eyes didn't move. "It always takes a while."

Larissa looked at them. "If we get anything, it's going to be tomorrow. I think we'd better sleep." She shook the small transmitter. "I'll keep this with me and wake you all up if something unusual and important happens."

"Like now?" Nadia asked. "It's voice. Sam." She pressed a button. "We're hearing you."

"There's something coming through the gate. We're trying to contact them."

Saytera felt a chill all over her body.

"Any idea who they are?" Nadia asked.

"Not yet, but we'll keep you informed."

They all looked at each other.

Larissa frowned. "Weird, right? For years those gates were sealed, now people just come and go..." She sighed. "Anyway, what do you think it is?"

Saytera had a sinking feeling.

Dess sat at another terminal. "We can check in our equipment. If we get their size and numbers, we'll know. Sapphirlune will block most of our vision, but still."

"What if..." Should Saytera voice her fear? It seemed almost stupid. Then maybe not. "What if they're delivering what Mainland ordered?"

Dess shook his head. "Without the agreement? That would be stupid. If they're mistaken we can clear that up." He blinked while looking at his terminal. "That's... a huge ship. Military class or transport, like for large machinery or something. We'll need to contact it."

Saytera then felt even colder and dreaded that her hunch had been right.

Larissa checked her terminal. "On it. No way to know their

frequency, so I guess I'll just throw a request for communication out there. Sapphirlune should have better luck than us, since they're closer." She bit her lip, then was thoughtful. "It could also be... someone coming to attack us. Here. I mean, we're the ones here stirring trouble."

Dess crossed his arms. "Maybe. But this is a pretty expensive facility, and not a lot of people know how to get a living complex up and running on an inhospitable moon."

Saytera disagreed. "They don't need to destroy everything and shoot us from space, just get close, get in, and fight us." She then had another thought. "But then we still have our canon."

Dess was thoughtful. "A large spaceship wouldn't be able to approach, but if they are a fighter-carrier, they could send a large fleet to overwhelm us. That's possible. If it is any kind of military ship, we'd better leave."

Nadia looked down. "I think we're safe here." She turned to Larissa. "You know that garbled communication we got earlier?"

Larissa nodded.

Nadia sighed. "It was my mother. She was asking me to stay where I am."

"So that's why you were worried." Saytera then realized she might have sounded harsher than she'd meant.

The girl looked down. "Maybe."

"We have no reason to assume those visitors have anything to do with your parents, though," Larissa said.

Saytera felt her heart pounding and a feeling like a cloud surrounding her.

The communicator beeped. Nadia flipped it. "Yes?"

"Hey." At this point Saytera recognized Sam's voice. Weird to think he'd been the one sent to rescue Dess. Weird to think about that time. He continued, "Abby and Carmon went for a visual."

Dess approached the mic. "Call them back. Right now. Don't send fighters without communication."

"Spare your words," Sam said on the comm. His words were heavy. He continued, "They were at a safe distance. They were contacting them and had the universal peace signal on. It was meant to be safe. They went. They went." His voice became frantic. "I didn't send them. It was meant to be safe."

Nadia shot an annoyed look at Dess and then took the mic. "Sam. We trust you. Whatever happened, we know it wasn't your fault."

Sam's tone didn't change. "I could have stopped them. Called them back. I thought it was safe. I swear I did!"

"We know. We all do," Nadia said. "What happened?"

"They… didn't come back." He sounded as if he was crying. "But they sent an image. I'm sending it to you. Tell me what you think."

Nadia took a deep breath. "They were heroes, Sam. They died as heroes. It's all a soldier can ask for. It's what we were trained for."

"Look at the image and then call me back." His voice was dry.

When the communicator was turned off, Nadia broke into sobbing, her body shaking. They must have been people she knew. Larissa rubbed her back and tried to calm her down. Dess was serious and troubled.

Nadia looked at them. "Abby, we were best friends. We drifted apart, but we used to be best friends. I never got to say goodbye. I never got to say I was sorry."

Saytera didn't know what to say or what to do. Even her,

who had never even heard of Abby until then, couldn't help from feeling sad.

"Let's check the image she gave her life for," Larissa said.

It was a blurry blob. A long blurry blob with a large bulge underneath it. Very much like the diagrams of the shield destroyer.

Nadia wiped her eyes. "I guess Mainland never changed their plans."

"No," Larissa said. "The truce is still up. This has never been voted. It's illegal. Mainlanders would never approve of that."

A horrible realization hit Saytera. "But it doesn't matter. All they need is the destruction of Sapphirlune to blame Mainland. That's all they need."

"No!" Larissa protested. "We can prove we never wanted this! We can prove it!"

Her friend's hope was commendable, but there was no point. "How are we going to prove it? To whom? If they close our gates and make decisions outside their systems, will they send anyone to hear our story?"

Dess turned the communicator on. "Sam."

"Yes."

"Whoever decided to send them for a visual might have saved thousands of lives. This will give us time. It's a shield-breaker. Get all the fighters you can. We need to stop it from reaching Sapphirlune."

There was silence for a moment. "Are you sure they are going to attack?"

"They already attacked, right? But we can try to communicate with them. Maybe they'll go away."

"I'll keep trying to reach them," Larissa said.

"I'm also coming," Dess said.

"Me too," Nadia added. "Get everything organized.

Larissa pressed a button and a siren blared in the room. She cringed. She pressed it again and it stopped. "To wake up the others."

Nadia was up. "I'll get on a fighter and I'll blast them. I'll blast them."

Saytera understood the girl's anger and need for revenge, but she wasn't sure it was the best way to solve the issue. "It's heavily armored. You guys will be like flies on a whale."

"Mosquitos," Nadia said. "Mean mosquitos with ugly bites."

Dess turned to Saytera. "I know what you're saying, but we can't just stand and do nothing. I am the best pilot in Sapphirlune. Nadia is probably the second best. We trained for this. If there's one chance in a thousand, we have to do it."

Saytera tried to come up with another solution. "We could maybe evacuate them. Get them to Mainland."

Nadia shook her head. "No transports and no time."

Marcus and Sylvia came to the room. "What's happening?"

"Somebody is sending a shieldbreaker to Sapphirlune," Dess said. "We think they are going to attack. The Lunars are going to take all the fighters they can and try to bring it down."

He looked confused. "Isn't it like… humongous?"

Dess shrugged. "We need to try to do something. We have just a couple hours. You guys can stay here. Try to contact people, communicate. Marcus, if the worst happens, you take our transport and take them to Mainland."

"I want to help."

"Help me then. Live a long life. Be happy. Take Saytera to safety."

It was then that she realized Dess was walking away from her. Walking straight into death.

Marcus was silent.

Dess approached Saytera and took her hands. He had tears

in his eyes. "I'm so sorry our time was so short." He took a deep breath. "There are... so many words I wish I could say, so many stories I wanted to hear, wanted to tell."

She looked in his eyes. "Stop. That's foolish. There's nothing glorious in dying in vain."

Dess shook his head. "I'm not going to die in vain. I'm going to save the lives of the people on that moon."

"You need a decent plan, then," Saytera pleaded.

"We don't have time."

And if Saytera didn't come up with a better idea in mere seconds he'd walk away from her forever. She closed her eyes, trying to find her answer, feeling darkness settling in her. Darkness. "Dess, take me. If I can get into that ship, I could disable it."

"No, Saytera. I won't have *you* risking your life."

"Right? Cause it would suck to see me die. And yet you want me to do the same for you. You want me to see you dying, and yet you know damn well the pain of seeing someone you care for dying. Or the fear of that. That's not fair, Dess."

He sighed. "You want to die with me?"

"I want to *live* with you. And make sure that thing doesn't shoot a helpless city. But I want to do it right, not just for a blaze of glory."

He was thoughtful. "Very well. I'll get you on that ship." He then turned to the others. "Change of plans. I'll try to get into the shieldbreaker with Saytera. We'll disable it from the inside. We'll just need cover. I'll take Tarel's ship. Those of you who want to join the Sapphirlune defenses, come with me. We need to leave the other ship for whoever remains in case they need to go back to Mainland."

"I'll stay," Marcus said. "I'll be here making sure this facility is safe for you, my friend. And if they come and try to take it, I won't let them."

Dess shook his head. "I'd rather you just ran, but at this point, I don't even know."

Larissa said, "I'll be here trying to contact everyone I can. If this is a terrible misunderstanding, we'll get someone from Mainland to contact them."

Christina sat beside her. "I'll help."

It was in a daze that Saytera embarked on Dess's ship, actually, Tarel's ship, on their way to Sapphirlune, without even a proper goodbye to her friends. Friends she had no idea she'd ever see again. Perhaps her life was all about leaving without saying goodbye.

There was something bothering Saytera. "If they can shoot a ship when it's way out of range, how are we going to reach it?"

Dess sighed. "I think they sent a fighter. We'll be in large numbers. Hopefully they won't be able to reach all of us at once."

"We could fly around them and get them from all directions," Nadia added.

Saytera looked down. That still meant some of them would die. Die for a small shot of defeating that monster. They could instead try to fly to Mainland and save themselves. And then leave everyone in Sapphirlune to die. No, that wouldn't work.

When they landed on the military port in Sapphirlune, Saytera remained on the ship, trying to calm down, find that strength within her, or perhaps just tell herself that this would be possible. Dess had chosen to go on Tarel's ship due to its powerful shield and because it fit two. Fighter ships were meant for only one. Dess would be weaponless, though.

They took off not long after, together with so many other ships, then split in two directions.

Dess stared straight ahead and asked, "Do you… need to be inside a place to… turn off its energy?"

"I don't know. I think I need to be close enough. I don't know how it works or if I'll succeed."

He took her hand. "We'll die together, then. It's not the way I would have chosen it, but I…" He sighed. "Understand."

Saytera nodded, getting lost in her thoughts. Strange to be facing death looming so close, with only uncertainty, a poorly-formed plan, and the fear that their failure could cause dreadful destruction and pain.

Strange to think that they'd been pawns for a plan that had nothing to do with freedom, that they'd been involved in a war that was just make-belief to support greater interests, and that they'd bought into all that. Saytera got into it late, but still, she'd bought it. Attacking and winning had never been a path for victory.

34

DEATH

Time had no meaning. Had it been minutes, seconds, hours? The shield destroyer loomed before then, far away. On the way, though, small black fighters, some twenty. Their group had only ten ships. Saytera hoped they would be enough.

"Hold tight," Dess said.

She didn't need to, strapped as she was to the seat in all directions, even if artificial gravity should keep her seated.

A fighter was straight ahead of them. Dess dove just before they were shot and then flew up to be right beside the fighter. It turned, but too slowly, and got hit. Dess flew above it to escape the debris. Whatever instructions he was getting were coming to his headset. She could feel it in his face, his demeanor, the feel of death. Some of their companions must have been shot, and maybe the fleet on the other side wasn't faring as well as they were.

Dess's strategy was to dodge. Funny how he could do it just at the right moment, sometimes causing the enemy's shot to hit another enemy. It was like a strange dance of death.

After a while, the fighters retreated. Dess exhaled, seeming relieved. "They quit."

Saytera just nodded, more on edge than before. Their enemies disappeared in the distance.

Dess then spoke on the mic, "I'm ready to advance, just give me cover."

The huge destroyer was turning and facing them now. Saytera had an ominous feeling. "Dess, they're gonna shoot."

"No worries, I'll dodge."

But the energy coming from the destroyer wasn't a ray or a projectile, it was like a circular wave of yellow energy. Fire was life. And fire was death. A circle of death advancing on them too quickly for them to escape. Saytera then realized the futility of their endeavor, perhaps the futility of her idea. Dess would never even have the chance to get anywhere remotely close to that monster.

The same power that could destroy a city's strong shield could also destroy an entire fleet. Perhaps they were mosquitoes, but they'd never get a chance to bite. Not even a fair chance to fight.

Milliseconds can sometimes stretch in an eternity. Saytera accepted death. The end of this physical life. The quenching of her fire. It wasn't the end, but freedom, transformation. No need to mourn. Except that it wasn't the right time. She glanced at Dess, not scared or angry, but in silent acknowledgement. They would still be together. What hurt was the pain they'd leave behind. Everything had been useless.

Perhaps everything was useless. Even the brightest star would someday fade. It didn't mean it didn't exist. They just existed in a precise moment in time. The four dimensions of existence, of matter.

Saytera embraced darkness. No, she was darkness. She

could create darkness. In that moment in time, nothing existed but darkness—and death. One and the same, finishing the cycle of that horrible ray, that horrible destroyer.

Saytera opened her eyes, trembling. The ray coming to them was gone. The lights on their display had faded. Even the artificial gravity on the ship was gone, Saytera still sitting just because she'd been too well strapped in.

"That was you," Dess whispered.

"Kind of." Saytera wasn't sure how to explain it. It wasn't exactly her, but something greater she had connected to. The great ocean of life. It's just that darkness and death were also part of it.

He unstrapped himself and hugged her. "I'm sorry I ever considered leaving you behind."

Saytera stared at the shieldbreaker, dark for now, but surely not forever. "We haven't won yet."

Dess laughed. "We haven't died yet, so I'll take it as a win."

After a few seconds, the instruments were back on. Dess took the mic. "There's a power failure on the destroyer. We don't know how long it will last. All our forces need to approach it and hit their weapons. Break that cannon. If we can, we shall board it and take the crew hostage."

"I thought you weren't leading this," Saytera said.

"They don't know there's a power outage, right?" He smiled. "You're brilliant."

"More like dark."

Dess shook his head.

There was something about what she'd just done giving her a nauseous feeling. Perhaps it was the realization of the extent of her power. Perhaps it was a lingering feeling of connecting with darkness and death. Then, maybe it was just that she'd felt death staring at her, touching her, and for a moment, had been ready to let it take her, until she realized she could be death, too.

They stood behind while the fleet shot the cannon. Saytera wasn't sure if the damage would do much. But then, she had another, odd feeling, that they had nothing more to fear from that shieldbreaker, as if its light had gone out.

The fleet proceeded to the ship's dock and Dess followed them. Its entrance was an opening right above its lower bulge. When they were almost getting there, he heard something, got serious, then turned to Saytera. "Maybe we don't need to go."

"Tell me what's happening."

Dess sighed. "Some things don't matter, Saytera. We won. We saved a city. That's what matters."

"So you're just going to hide it from me?"

"It's not hiding. It's just… Why worry?"

"Dess, I want to know what's happening, or it will be hard to trust you. Don't make me crazy wondering what I did."

He closed his eyes. "There are some… dead people. In the docks. In their fighters. I mean, we don't know what caused it. It could be dangerous going there."

The information was chilling. Death. So she'd really connected with it. She stared at Dess. "You know what killed them. You know there's no danger."

"We can't really tell them, can we? They'll think there might be some sort of radiation, or maybe a malfunctioning of that energy blast. That's actually good. People will probably stop manufacturing those shieldbreakers."

"We need to finish destroying that thing from the inside, remember? To leave just scrap metal and make sure they won't try shooting at Sapphirlune city again. Also," she looked down, "I want to see it."

It wasn't a morbid curiosity. Maybe it was.

Dess clicked on the comm and spoke on it. "I'm still coming in. I want to make sure thor weapons are no longer functioning."

"It could be dangerous," a girl's voice came from the system.

"Our suits will protect us," Dess replied.

"Dess, there are pilots there," the girl's voice continued. "On their fighters. Wearing suits. They're all dead. We don't know what happened there."

"Their energy ray hit them back, of course." He looked at Saytera and winked. His levity was a little unnerving, but he probably wanted to make sure nobody suspected what had really happened. He continued, "We're not going to use it. I'll go in and destroy what needs to be destroyed. Everyone else's obviously free to do otherwise."

"Suit yourself," the voice replied.

Dess clicked off the comm and looked at Saytera. "You don't have to do this."

"But I want to."

He stretched a hand and caressed her hair. "Fine. You know it's not your fault, right? You had no choice."

"If you could blast that thing, wouldn't you? Wouldn't you do it knowing it would kill all of them?"

"Yes…"

"I guess it's the same," Saytera said. "I'm not gonna feel bad about it. I didn't spend that long in the academy, but it was what they were preparing us to do; kill if necessary. Wasn't that what *you* trained for?"

He paused, then said, "Yes."

"So don't make it seem like this was any different. You're just making it worse."

Dess looked away, then back at her. "All right. Let's dock,

search for survivors, and inspect the damage, then." He held her hand and squeezed it, as if to reassure her, then let it go.

They landed soon after, proceeded to their airlock, then were on the dock, wearing their helmets connected to their small air reservoirs. There were fighters from Heliumforge parked. Through the windshields she could see that the pilots had open, lifeless, glassy eyes. Two other Lunar fighters were there. Nadia and Sam came out of it. She pointed up. The entry for the ship was through ladders leading to airlocks, which then led to its interior. Saytera climbed it, removing her helmet once they were safely inside. It was all dark and she lit the light on her wrist. There was a dead person lying there. A young man. She knelt and checked his pulse. Dead indeed. No signs of any physical damage.

"It's better not to touch them," Nadia said.

"I was just checking."

They proceeded to the bridge. It wasn't where the control of the cannon was. A man and a woman were dead on their seats. Dess shot the controls.

He looked at Saytera. "Scrap metal."

"We need to find where the core power is," Nadia said.

Perhaps Saytera's learning would be useful after all. Ships had a certain logic. "I think I know where it is."

Saytera led them through dark hallways illuminated only by the dim light of their flashlights.

"You think Heliumforge will come and pick this up?" Sam asked.

"They should, right? At least to bury their dead," Nadia said.

"If they leave it here, this could be the next ghost ship," Dess said.

"That's a legend, isn't it?" Nadia asked.

"It isn't," Dess replied. "It's an Alien spaceship. Blue technology. Floating abandoned on the Samitri system."

"Why then haven't we studied it?" the girl insisted.

Dess sighted. "Cause nobody comes out of it alive."

Nadia pointed her light straight ahead. "I hope we get out of here alive, then."

"We will. It was obviously their own energy ray that killed them." Dess would probably keep insisting on that story.

"Weird," Sam said. "There is no burning or anything."

Of course. They weren't hurt, just had their fire quenched. Not something anyone would understand.

"Should we take a body and study?" Nadia suggested.

"I'm not taking back a body," Dess said. "Let Heliumforge deal with this."

Their talk was making Saytera anxious. She didn't think anyone could guess what had happened, and yet... Those deaths were unexplained. She'd just shut down their light. Like that. She wondered if she could do it with people in other situations. Probably yes. Indeed, the thought was chilling. She understood why Dess hadn't wanted her to see this. But she had to. And now she was helping them find the core of the ship.

Once they got to the core, the three Lunars shot strategic parts. They couldn't leave such a dangerous weapon operational in their system.

Dess and Saytera were silent for some time on the way back.

He then said, "You know, I wish they knew you saved us all. I wish you'd get the hero reception you deserve."

"It would scare people..."

He took a deep breath. "I know. I'll never let anyone know anything about it."

"You think Sam and Nadia bought it?"

Dess shrugged. "They have no clue what happened, but they don't have the slightest idea that you had any role in it, so it's fine. Let's leave it a mystery."

They landed on the military port. A few people greeted Dess. There was relief but also pain on their faces. They had lost friends. And perhaps they had no idea how their actions had helped save their city. They would never know.

For a second Saytera felt dizzy. She held Dess's arm.

"Tired?" he asked.

They hadn't slept for a long time. "And hungry."

"I'll take you home."

Home. An odd word. Was it her island, the base on Cliff-bound, or even the base on the Tahari Moon? No. He meant *his* home. In a way, if it was with him, it was home. After such a long time longing for her home, Saytera had found it.

Dess's kitchen was rather empty. He realized that was a terrible first impression but hoped his performance in the Tahari Moon kitchen would have made up for that. At least the apartment wasn't dirty. He gave Saytera porridge. She ate it slowly, her eyes almost closing. Who knew how exhausting it was to use that much power? Dess gave her a shirt and put her in his bed, but had to kiss her goodbye.

"It's all a confusion now. Power vacuum. I need to make sure I'm there."

Saytera just mumbled something. She looked so little and so fragile there, even if she wasn't short. Nobody would ever guess what she was capable of. Perhaps anyone but him would be terrified. Dess had always felt she was unusual. Maybe she was a bit more powerful than he'd suspected at first, but that was in line with what he thought of her. And now she slept peacefully, hopefully leaving behind all thoughts of death and darkness.

Meanwhile, Dess was going to claim Staralloy, tell Helium-forge to come pick up their mistaken delivery, and make sure the new Sapphirlune leadership had the people's interests in mind. Tons of things. His head hurt just to think about it. A few months before, all he wanted was to be a good pilot and do his part for his moon. Now he understood that doing his part in a system that was rotten would never change anything.

A week had passed since the Lunar victory. Might as well have been an eternity. Saytera never felt guilty for what she'd done. Like Dess had said, if they had the choice to blow up the Shieldbreaker, they would have done it without blinking or considering the lives there. Perhaps it was just that she had seen so many deaths that something in her had been numbed. Perhaps she'd always been cold-hearted. Another question she had was whether her power had anything to do with the Terens who had chased her. Would she ever know?

They were back in Citarella to sign a new agreement and elect new representatives. Larissa had been "the voice of peace", working incessantly to connect everyone, inform everyone, and to bridge Moon and Mainland.

As the voice of peace, she ended up elected for Mainland's highest representative. On the Lunar side, it had been Nadia. It couldn't have been any better. Nadia's connection to Staralloy, to the top military, and her involvement in the Peace Warriors movement had been important. Her father was still alive and hadn't been arrested. He'd sent a message shortly after their victory, congratulating them, saying he was happy Kades Tahari was alive, and willing to assure a smooth transition and cooperate with interstellar deals. Saytera didn't trust Tarel, but then, neither did Dess. So far, Tarel's new position had only benefited them.

Dess was going to implement his parents' plans for that moon, so that it would benefit everyone equally. He and Saytera were going to live near Cliffbound, going back and forth to Tahari Moon as necessary. Saytera would be back near the ocean, ready to try to connect with her magic even more.

Tonight they were going to celebrate the new Agreement. Lunars would be able to visit Mainland, even live on Mainland. In a way, things were going back to the way they'd been before Sapphirlune's independence. But then, it was one system.

Saytera had tied her hair in a complex braid so that it looked shorter than it actually was. The party was at the Military headquarters. Dess and Saytera were in a hotel near it. Before leaving, somebody knocked on the door.

Dess got up. "Weird, they should have announced them."

Saytera shrugged.

He stood beside the door and asked, "Who is it?"

"I want to see Saytera."

Saytera's knees gave away. It was a voice she thought she'd never hear again. A memory from her past walking back in her life. Kerely.

35

MEETING

"**I** know her." Saytera went to the door and opened it.

Kerely wore a grey cloak with a long hoo, covering her face and stepped inside. She turned to Dess. "I need to talk with her alone."

He crossed his arms. "Won't do."

"Dess, please. It's all right," Saytera said.

He sighed. "I'll be outside, down the hall."

Once he'd left, Kerely lowered her hood and hugged Saytera. It was weird because she had dyed her hair blond, and maybe it was weird to get that hug since Saytera thought Kerely would still be angry at her. Tears came out of Saytera's eyes and she wasn't sure if it was relief, surprise, sadness.

Kerely stepped back and put her hands on Saytera's face. "How are you?"

"I'm fine—Now. How come…" The words got caught in her throat. Saytera wanted to understand how they hadn't found her earlier but at the same time how she'd finally found her. So many emotions at the same time.

"They're watching Yansin closely."

"Who?"

Kerely sighted. "Other Terens. Some of them know people in our group. They think she'd come looking for you."

Saytera snorted. "How wrong they are." There was unexpected bitterness in her voice.

"It's for your safety. Don't think for a second she hasn't thought about you every day since you left."

Saytera looked down. "I know it was my fault."

"Of course not! We should have told you the truth earlier, that's all. It's just… You see, you grew up so fast. You were just a kid the other day." She pointed to a chair. "Come. Sit."

Saytera sat down.

Kerely continued. "The last person who had contact with you was Carla, right?"

That memory was so old… Almost buried. The woman who had led Saytera to a truck—and, in a certain way, to safety. "Yes."

"Did she tell you that you had to hide?"

"She did."

Kerely thought for a moment. "Right. You're at the center of a revolution that's being talked about all over the human universe, so I'm not sure this is a great hiding strategy."

Saytera stared at her. "It's not as if I chose to do all this. It happened."

Kerely nodded. "I see. Well, you need to be careful."

"Are you going to tell me why?"

"Yes. It's time for you to learn the truth. You've studied the fall of the Ringon monarchy, right?"

Saytera groaned in frustration. "Why do you guys always bring up that stuff… It has nothing to do with anything that matters to me."

"Well, no. Indeed, no. But… You know that there was a king and queen."

"Who were killed, yada, yada. Yes. I know that. And?"

"They had a child. Who everyone thinks was killed, too. There were Terens involved in that revolution, Saytera. In the beginning. And they killed the little prince. Or that's the story everyone tells."

"And what do I have to do with any of that?"

Kerely narrowed her eyes briefly. "You never suspected." She sounded surprised. "Never connected the dots, did you? Never even tried to peer into it. Always hated the subject, avoided the topic, right?"

Because it was pointless and boring. Saytera took a deep breath. "Can you skip to the part that matters?"

Kerely observed her, as if waiting for a reaction. "What if I told you it was never a prince, but a princess. And they never killed her?"

"The girl is still around, then."

"Yes, Saytera, she's still around. But, thanks to Vivian, some people found out she had survived. Some wanted to kill—"

That couldn't be. "You're talking about me?" Saytera didn't know what she felt. Disgust, shock, surprise? It didn't make any sense.

"Yes, we're talking about you. You're the daughter of the Human Alliance monarchy."

Saytera got up, a nauseous feeling in her stomach. "So you've always known who my parents were."

Kerely nodded. "Yes, but it had to remain a secret. There are some Terens who believe they should control the human universe."

Saytera remembered that. "Maxterens."

Kerely rolled her eyes. "They call themselves that. If they

could, they would love to use you to claim the government of the Human Universe."

Saytera frowned. "Those were the people who wanted to kidnap me."

Kerely nodded.

"And what about the ones who wanted to kill me?"

She shook her head. "They think they mean well. They're misguided by a stupid prophecy."

"What prophecy?"

"Nonsense. You know what Yansin says…"

"I do. I'm just curious. What's the prophecy?"

Kerely took a moment, then said, "That the child of this queen and king would bring darkness to our world."

Saytera swallowed as she felt her heart race. That couldn't be a coincidence. Could it?

"Don't stress about it," Kerely added. "I know what you did. I know how you defeated the Shieldbreaker."

Saytera was surprised. "You do?"

"Well, there's talk about a secret weapon and things that don't make sense. Any Teren would know what happened."

Saytera felt a chill down her spine. "Can't they believe that their ray malfunctioned?"

She shook her head. "It would have damaged the ship."

Saytera shrugged. "So, as you can see, I can unleash darkness."

Kerely laughed. "You can't *unleash* it. It would be like unleashing cold. It has no existence in itself."

"What do I do, then?"

"You quench fire, that's all."

As if it were so simple. "Maybe you could give that explanation to the really nice people who want me dead."

Kerely's face was somber. "They wouldn't care. Still, I bet

nobody has yet connected the dots that it was you who disabled the shieldbreaker. Some people think Yansin was here. She's the only other person who can do that, but even her… I mean… So yes, that's something else that might bring attention to you. People will come. They'll want to know who was fighting that Shieldbreaker. But… as to the people who want the princess dead, they just heard a prophecy and they want to prevent it. They are blind and don't want to see how they might be misinterpreting it."

"But…" Saytera stared at Kerely. "It has some point, doesn't it? Or else it's an insane coincidence."

Kerely sighed. "Maybe it has a point and they are misinterpreting it. Someone who can quench flames can be quite useful when your house is on fire. What you did was good. You can use it for good, Saytera. But please be careful. People would kill to grab their hands on someone with that much power. They are thinking that this system has a weapon. What if they realize *you* are the weapon?"

Saytera didn' like the thought. She looked down, thinking. "So that was why I was kept with Yansin? Why she raised me. And why would she teach me to quench flames knowing…"

"She took you to protect you. She taught you I think because she saw your talent, or because you took after her. You're like a daughter to her. No, you *are* a daughter to her, Saytera, and it's no wonder you can do something that, until then, only she could."

"Don't people want to kill her?"

Kerely chuckled. "Tons do, but it isn't that easy. For different reasons. Nobody made any prophecy about her."

"When can I see her?"

"Soon. She'll send you recorded messages. That's the safest thing we can do."

"So you didn't come here to take me home." Saytera didn't know if she felt relieved or disappointed.

"It seems that you found a new home, haven't you?"

"Which, according to you, is problematic, since we're being at the center of this whole system and now people are all curious about us."

Kerely nodded. "That's true. Your challenges are far from over. The Peace Alliance and people connected to Heliumforge would love to come here and crush you all."

"What are they waiting for?"

"Figuring out the weapon you guys used. I'm pretty sure nobody is sending any military ship here any time soon."

"That's a relief."

"Yes." She paused. "Work together. More than ever, the planet and moon need to be united. The enemy is not here."

"I know. But am I supposed to hide or help?"

"Help. But be careful." She took a small box from her purse. "This is for you."

Saytera opened and saw a small golden circle in water. "What is it?"

"It's for your eye. It will turn it brown. That should help. But stay away from cameras, meetings, anything where someone might identify you. The messages you sent had poor image quality and I think it will be fine."

Kerely took her to the bathroom and showed her how to use the small lens. It felt odd when she put it, but after a while it was comfortable. Saytera looked at herself in the mirror and saw two matching brown eyes.

There was a loud knock on the room's door.

"Saytera!" Dess was calling.

"I'm fine. Just a minute." She turned to Kerelly. "Anything else to tell me?"

"That was all for now. Keep it a secret. Even if you trust someone, don't tell them."

It would be hard to hide that from her friends, but she would try. "Other than that, I suppose the idea is for me just to ignore it."

"Unless you want to go to Ringon and lay your claim. "

Saytera snorted. "I would last how long? Five minutes?"

"More like one or two." Kerely looked at her. "You're happy here, aren't you?"

"I am. Finally. No ideas about going anywhere. I will want to learn more about my parents, though."

Kerely nodded.

Saytera added, "And I need to learn better matterweaving. Desperately. I don't regret what I did, but…" She looked down. "Had I been better, I wouldn't have… killed."

"You can't know that. You already did something almost impossible. I can't imagine you could—"

"I want to learn more."

"You were training alone, right? Keep doing the same exercises. Once I can bring transmissions I'll have Yansin prepare more for you. Read our Tomes." She frowned, thinking. "I think I can maybe get you some…"

"Dess has them."

Kerely looked surprised.

"He's fascinated about Terens," Saytera added.

Kerely chuckled. "I can see that. Well, some people have the upbringing but not the practice. That might be his case. I'll let you celebrate. I'll be at the party. Watching. You'll hear from me from time to time."

Saytera still had a question. "Why then… couldn't you come earlier?"

"Not to draw attention. Now that the gate has been opened, it's a lot easier."

"But you left the system before."

"Those are Blue gates. We use them under secrecy. But every Teren knows about them."

"You know Blue technology. Do you have contact with them?"

Kerely shook her head. "Not right now. I swear. You'll learn those secrets, too. But learn the tomes first. And continue your training."

"I guess I'll never complain you're teaching something useless."

She smiled. "No."

There was something else she wanted to say. Saytera hesitated, then decided to open up. "I always thought… I was weak. Because everyone could make fire and I couldn't. I couldn't even get a pistol to fire. Why—"

"Yansin focused on teaching you how to quench fire. Considering what you just did, I'd say her methods are pretty good, aren't they?"

"So I'll never be able to make fire?"

Kerely shrugged. "Can't you use a lighter?"

"Yes, but…"

"I don't know, Saytera. When you talk to Yansin, you'll need to ask her."

"Yansin can make fire." Saytera remembered that.

"Yansin can't turn off a military-class ship from a distance. I don't think she can even turn off the electricity of any place. Appreciate the uniqueness of who you are."

"So… I'm not bad at matterweaving?"

Kerely snorted and started laughing. "Sweety. You are one of the most powerful Terens in existence."

Saytera felt another chill down her spine but at the same time a small pang of pain that Yansin had never told her that. "That never seemed to be the case."

"Yansin is a tough teacher. She'll push you to your best and if she were to see you now she'd tell you where you're slacking off."

"I wish…" Saytera had no words. What did she want? Compliments? Validation.

"She loves you, but perhaps she kept her master hat for too long. She'll send you a message as soon as she can. I promise. I'll leave you now because you have a party, after all."

Kerely opened the door and left.

Dess came in right away. "Are you alright?" He took a moment looking at her. "What's wrong with your eyes?"

"I…" How could she say it? "Can't have people recognizing me. That was Kerelly. She raised me."

"And you're upset."

"Not upset, just surprised." And shocked and still partly in denial. And so many things more.

"Do you want to tell me what's going on?"

Saytera took a while thinking. She didn't want to carry that burden by herself. She looked at him. "I do."

Dess knew he'd have a target on his back the moment he decided to take over Staralloy. Now he just learned the reason Saytera had an even bigger target on hers.

He took her hands. "I'll make sure you're always safe."

She smiled. It was probably a lot to take. He hugged her.

After a while, she said, "We'd better get to the party."

. . .

Dess was glad to see his friends, and some of his new friends, the Peace Warriors. It was a historical moment, when they celebrated the union between Mainland and Sapphirlune. Even Marcus' father had come for the celebration, although he had chosen to keep living in Sapphirlune city. He had been among the few people in its government who had been honest—and now he was proud of his son. For so long Dess thought he was leading his friend astray, and yet, together they had found the answer. Even Sylvia had stopped with the nonsense about not being seen with him in public—but her parents had disappeared, like so many people from Sapphirlune. At least she and his friend seemed to be truly in love.

The Peace Warriors were going to record another united message, even if Saytera would stay out of them from now on. As they were ready to record, someone approached; Tarel.

He went straight towards Dess—and hugged him. "My boy. You have no idea how happy to see you're alive."

Tarel had to be joking. No, not joking, performing for the cameras.

The man continued, "I'm doing everything to ease the transfer of Staralloy for you and connect you with importers from other systems."

Dess smiled and patted his back. "Glad to count on you."

Perhaps it was good to keep his enemies close. The enemy who had probably ordered the killing of his family, who was willing to destroy a city. At the same time, it was Nadia's father, and also the enemy who could make things much, much smoother for Staralloy, for the Mainland system. Tarel knew that well. He could fight Dess in court, use his influence to shut him out. Instead, he cooperated with him. And this cooperation was very good for the people, so Dess tolerated him.

~

Saytera stared at the fire while listening to the powerful waves crashing down in the cliff. *This* was their real celebration, the Peace Warriors celebration.

They had chosen Cliffbound because the place was so remote. This was where Dess and Saytera had decided to live and build their house. Larissa, Nadia, Marcus, and Sylvia were also going to live in the area. Christina was going to live in Citarella, where she was reworking the military training. Ideally they should focus on peace now, but there was always the possibility that their system could be attacked again, so they couldn't slack off. But she had come for their party.

Larissa, Saytera, and Nara prepared the crab. Dess was amazing at an industrial kitchen but still learning what to do with real food. Kay was there, and he didn't bother Saytera anymore. Cynthia, Zack, and even people from the nearby bases were there. They had done their part, too, making sure Mainlanders spread the message and rejected breaking the truce. It almost had not mattered, but in the end it did, and helped them change their planet.

Saytera's heart warmed at the sight of Lunars and Mainlanders sitting together, some of them holding hands.

Dess sat by her. "I've always wanted to see a fire by a beach."

"Where did you guys make fires?"

He frowned. "We didn't. We had to be careful with our oxygen."

Saytera laughed. "Tough life. I wonder why some people decided to keep living there, and not move to Mainland."

He raised an eyebrow. "Can't beat the view. No. I guess they were used to it. But I think people who have moved here are happy, too."

"Are you happy?"

"Ha, ha. Is that a question?" He then looked around and sighed. "I wish this could last forever. This harmony, hope, peace."

"Even the brightest star one day fades. This moment is all that exists."

"That's great, then. I don't need to worry about what Tarel will do or if anyone will send a fleet to try to find our *weapon*." He rolled his eyes.

More and more there had been pressure for them to tell how the shieldbreaker had been defeated. But this was not a time to think about any of that. "Exactly. It's time to celebrate what we helped accomplish."

He looked at the people and had tears in his eyes. "This is amazing."

Those tears. Always those tears. At least they were happy tears. Saytera brushed a finger under his eyes, cleaning some smudged eyeliner. She'd consider asking him why he'd always wear it knowing how easily he cried, but maybe he knew well what he was doing and was going for the smudged look.

"What?" he laughed.

"Just… cleaning it."

He took her hand. "Thank you for existing with me at this moment in time."

"Let's pretend it's infinite, then."

Dess nodded at her, then pulled her in for a kiss.

ABOUT THE AUTHOR

I'm originally from Brazil but I've been living in Canada for over 10 years now. I have some influence from Brazilian writers and Brazilian culture, but I also read popular books in English. I watched some Anime as a kid, my favorite being Yamato. I'm a longtime Star Wars fan and I'm active in the fandom podcasting at Lords of the Sith as Denise.

I've always loved to write stories, and I like to always include romance, action and humor in my writing. I think stories can touch us deeply. I live in Montreal, Canada, with my son.

My books include the Ya fantasy series Portals to Whyland, and the sci-fi standalones The Sphere of Infinity and Star Spark. Check out my blog for some news, updates, and nonsensical ramblings.

Don't forget to sign up for free books at dayleitao.com and to keep in touch.

www.ingramcontent.com/pod-product-compliance
Lightning Source LLC
Chambersburg PA
CBHW061344190726
48288CB00005B/1594